MAZEWAY

MAZEWAY

JACK WILLIAMSON

DEL REY A DEL REY BOOK BALLANTINE BOOKS NEW YORK

A Del Rey Book
Published by Ballantine Books

Copyright © 1990 by Jack Williamson

Library of Congress Cataloging-in-Publication Data

Williamson, Jack, 1908–
    Mazeway / Jack Williamson.
        p.   cm.
    "A Del Rey book."
    ISBN 0-345-34032-9
    I. Title.
PS3545.I557M39   1990   89-37936
813'.52—dc20   CIP

Design by Holly Johnson

Manufactured in the United States of America

First Edition: April 1990
10 9 8 7 6 5 4 3 2 1

When the all-cutting blade
Meets the uncuttable stone . . .
Can you guess the consequence?
      —AN ANCIENT RED DELVER RIDDLE

CONTENTS

CONTENTS

MAZEWAY

THE GAME OF BLADE AND STONE

1

Dad, when can we go home?"

"The halo *is* our home, Benn." His father frowned. "We must earn our right to stay here."

They were jogging together in the squirrel cage. That was an odd name for it, Benn thought, because there were no squirrels in the halo. Squirrels from old Earth couldn't live here, because they needed air. The exercise made Benn and his father puff and sweat, but they had to do it every day because they needed the gravity of Earth as well as air to breathe.

"Better forget your dreams." His father looked hard at him. "Learn to like the halo."

Benn shook his head and kept on jogging. The cage was in the gym tank. That was part of the big wheel they lived in, spinning very slowly here at the fringe of Cluster One. The cluster was a city, a little cloud of ice-moons and strange eldren places spinning around the home of the Eldermost, all so far out that the Sun was only one more star. He had never seen Earth at all, but his mother still called it home.

"Let's cool off." They slowed the cage and jumped out into the cold thin stink of old sweat and alien plastics. "You wouldn't like Earth." They sat on a bench. "Not the way it is."

But he loved Earth, the way it was in his mind. The huge home world, so much bigger and stranger than these bare gray snowballs. He wanted to walk on soft green grass under tall green trees and a bright blue sky. He'd always dreamed of towering mountains and stormy oceans and the great human cities hung like diamonds in the skyweb above them. He wanted to feel the strong pull of Earth and the push of the wind and heat of the sun on his bare face, with no eldren lifeskin sealing them away.

"Why?" he whispered. "Why?"

His father took a long time to answer, and his voice seemed tired. "Old Earth was wonderful once, at least for your mother. But we can't go back."

He waited for his father to explain.

"We never told you, Benn." A little muscle bunched on his father's jaw. "But you're six today. I think you're old enough to know what happened."

He waited again, but his father sat staring off at the thick green vines of the walls of the habitat till he had to ask, "What did happen?"

"A thing came out of space and tore the skyweb down."

He knew about the web. Runesong had told him what it had been: the great human city, really a thousand cities hanging in the sky, its houses and factories and space docks strung like shining beads on strong kwanlon wires that spread midway out to the Moon. He'd seen holo pictures of the web and read about it in flimsy old paper books.

"What kind of thing?"

He could hear his mother, softly singing the way she used to sing when she was putting him to sleep. She was out in the garden tank, picking newberries to bake him a birthday pie. His mouth had watered for it, but suddenly his stomach had twisted hard. He stared at his father, wondering. The web had surely been too wide and strong and splendid for anything to tear it down.

"I saw it." His father looked grim. "Nothing I could believe. Half machine, the eldren say, yet half alive. It had wings to fly in air and jets to fly in space. It sliced through the web. The ballast parts flew off into space. Most of it crashed down on Earth."

"Why didn't you tell me?"

"We didn't want to hurt you." His father tried again to smile.

4

"The eldren called the creature the heatseeker queen. It came out of space and made a nest in an iron asteroid. One of the young came down to wreck the web."

"Is it—" He stared at his father. "Is it still—"

"It's dead. It fell in the ocean. The queen must be dead by now."

"Bennie?"

His mother was coming in. Her face and arms were freckled purple with newberry juice, but he thought she was as beautiful as Runesong had been. Almost, anyhow. Her basket was full of the sweet-smelling berries, and he felt suddenly hungry again.

"Tell him, Quin!" She stood looking at his father with an odd little smile. "Tell him what happened to the queen and her brood."

Quin grinned, saying nothing.

"Your father killed them." Smiling proudly through the freckles, she came to stand with her arms around both of them. "He's a hero, Benn!"

"The halo wants no heroes." His father shrugged. "The eldren way has no room for them."

"He's still a hero." His mother's face grew very serious. "Benn, we're here in the halo because of what your father did. He saved the eldren from whatever that creature could have done. It's true that most of them don't like killing, but the Eldermost brought us out here to be speakers for mankind. That's our job, working for permission for human people to stay in the halo and join the Elderhood."

"I see." He nodded slowly, not quite sure he liked what he saw. The Earth would surely have been a better home. He asked, "What happens if they don't let us stay?"

"Nothing good." His mother's voice was slow and small. "They've got to let us stay."

"Your job, Benn, when you grow up." His father's strong arm slid around him. "The eldren never hurry anything, but you must carry on, doing whatever you can to convince them. It won't be easy. Too many of them don't think we're fit for the Elderhood."

"If they don't let us stay—"

His father's head shook and his mother's face looked sad beneath the purple freckles, but neither spoke.

"If that will be my job—" He sat straighter on the bench,

feeling proud for a moment and then suddenly afraid. "How can I begin?"

"Get to know the eldren. Learn the eldren way."

He nodded. "Runesong used to tell me that, but I never quite knew what she meant."

She was eldren, and he had loved her. He had seen a good many other eldren beings flying past the big windows of the habitat. Some of them frightened him. They had come from all across the galaxy, even from beyond it. They were hundreds of different races, all with different shapes and different languages. Their leader was the Eldermost, the great wise being who lived down in the core of a big snowball in the middle of the cluster.

"They're too strange." He shook his head. "They can't even talk."

"They do talk," his father reminded him. "In ways of their own. Not with sound, but with radiations that carry where there is no air. With light. Ultraviolet. Infrared. Radio. We have to use translators."

"I know." But even in translation, most of what they said was hard to understand. Uneasily he looked at his mother. "Are they smarter than we are?"

Her lips drew tighter, but she didn't answer.

"Could be." His father shrugged. "Hard to say. Certainly they know more. They've been learning things and filling up their libraries and museums for half a billion years. They don't think quite the way we do. But most of them mean well enough when you understand them."

He asked for more about the eldren way.

"Remember Sunshine?" His father grinned. "Your trouble with her?"

Sunshine was the cat. The trouble had been long ago, but he rubbed his wrist when he thought about it now. It had happened out in the hydroponic garden, when she was drinking the soya cream his mother poured for her breakfast. He tried to pick her up. She scratched him. His wrist bled and stung. He kicked her.

"Don't do that," his mother had scolded him. "It isn't nice. The eldren wouldn't like it."

She didn't say why. Sunshine was a Terran cat, not eldren at all, but his mother only frowned when he told her that. He had to go to Quin, who picked him up and put a patch over the scratch.

He asked why the eldren would care what he did to the cat.

"You hurt her," his father said. "Hurting anything doesn't fit their lifestyle. They don't fight, though they certainly could. Their high-tech industries could build weapons more terrible than any we used to make on Earth. In half a billion years, they've never fought a war."

Lifestyle had been a new word, and the scratch stung again when he thought about it now. He waited for his father to explain more about Sunshine.

"When you kicked her, you broke a very simple eldren rule. It says you don't hurt people."

"She scratched me first."

"She's still planetic." Quin frowned, thinking how to say it. "We humans used to be planetic. We will be again, unless we're able to learn the eldren mind-set."

He waited again, but Quin had stopped to stare at the climbing vines of tomatoes and squash and melon that provided food and oxygen for the habitat.

"It looks easy when we talk about Sunshine," he finally went on. "But there's more . . ." His voice trailed off, and his gray eyes had sharp lines around them when they came back to Benn. "You'll do it, son. Because you must."

"How can I learn?"

They both looked at him, and he thought he saw the shine of tears in his mother's eyes.

"There's a game," his father said at last. "The Game of Blade and Stone."

"Runesong talked about it."

That was long ago, back while she still lived here. She had been a Newling, different from all the other eldren because she loved him and he could love her. Very different, too, from anybody human, because of her shape and because she liked empty space better than gravity or air. Yet she had never been strange to him, because he had known and loved her since she received him into her shining wings when he was born.

She had been still lovely when she had to go away. Lovely in spite of the long laser scar that made a stiff black ridge across her shining side. Her body had been sleek and soft to touch, tapering neatly to the tail-jet she used to move in space because her nanionic centers had been crippled. Her long thin nose ended in a quick little-fingered hand. Her eyes were a little like Sunshine's, but they shimmered with rainbow colors when she spoke. Her voice was that shimmer, and the flicker of her wings. It had always come to him through speakers, but it was the warm human voice she had learned from his father's mother.

She used to amuse him with poems and stories out of human books she had read. He loved one poem she remembered when he asked her about the Game of Blade and Stone. He memorized it and copied it into a little green-backed notebook when he learned to write, and he could still recite the opening:

In Xanadu did Kubla Khan
A stately pleasure-dome decree:
Where Alph, the sacred river, ran
Through caverns measureless to man
    Down to a sunless sea.

Of course Xanadu was just a dream the old poet had dreamed, but Runesong had told him about Mazeway, which was a double world, its two planets named Blade and Stone. He used to wake with those pleasure-domes shining in his mind.

Stone, she told him, was the underground arena for the game. The old Red Delver warlords had invented the rules, she said, when they got tired of killing one another to choose their ruling primarchs, and the caves were still full of their tricks and traps.

He asked if he could ever play.

"Not very likely." The light dimmed in her wings. "The game was never meant for human people."

Remembering all that, he sat straighter and asked for more about the Game of Blade and Stone.

"It's a sport for the eldren," his father said. "And also a school in the eldren way. When new peoples want to settle in the halo, it is used to teach them the eldren style of life."

"But we—" His voice caught when he thought of Runesong. "We can't play?"

"I've inquired." His father nodded, looking at him very soberly. "I'm always told that the game was never planned for planetics. I suppose some human might be allowed to enter, but he'd be facing terrible handicaps."

"I want to try," he told them. "When I'm grown."

"Perhaps you can." Pride shone in his mother's eyes. "But don't promise too much now." Her hand caught his, and he felt her tremble. "The game isn't really meant for us."

"We'll see," he said. "We'll see."

CHEETAH

2

Roxane Kwan was born on the far-off Earth a year or so after the skyweb fell. During a monsoon season, so her father said, in a hunting camp somewhere on the Serengeti plain. He never pointed out the place, and she never knew the date. She couldn't remember her mother.

"The lions ate her."

That was all he ever told her. The hard truth, or only a bitter joke? She used to wonder. He was a grimly silent man, even with those he commanded, yet he had cared for her as tenderly as their hard lives allowed and she thought he loved her.

She grew up as a sort of mascot for the Kwan Corps. That was his brave name for the handful of hopeless human relics he had gathered from the wrecks and life-pods and ejection gear that had brought them down alive from the falling skyweb. Half naked, half clad in odd rags and scraps of half-tanned hide, half armed with rough-forged knives and swords and the few precious service guns and lasers they had salvaged from the ruins, they followed him back and forth along the belt of desolation where the sky cities had come flaming out of space.

Perhaps because they had no other hope. Exiles from the sky, they lived like hungry predators, hunting with the lions and leopards and hyenas in the old game preserve, digging for useful loot in the shattered ruins of the old Sun Country lodges. Without his cold nerve, few could have stayed alive.

All wore the golden Sunmark, the bright-glinting badge of what they once had been and what he promised to make them again. Though that laser-printed brand was all he required for enlistment, his discipline was strict. He allowed no women among them. Growing older, Roxane sometimes wondered if her mother had left him nursing some secret bitterness against all women.

The year she was six he taught her to shoot a little target rifle he had found in the abandoned ruin of a shooting blind. Lying downwind from a water hole, she got her first game with it, a young waterbuck that had come to drink.

It was too heavy for her to carry, but she gutted it with the long knife one of the men had forged for her and stayed proudly with it, standing off the vultures, until he came to help. He never said she had hunted well, but she saw his pleased grin at the blood that had smeared her when she tried to lift the carcass. The men dressed it out and took it back to roast on the campfire. They gave her the first good-smelling slice, and said she hunted like a cheetah.

Afterward, they called her Cheetah.

All except her father. To him, she was always a Kwan, elected at birth to be a Signer for the Sun Company and next after him to head the House, destined to succeed him to the proud title of Sun Tycoon. When they had made a way back to space. When they had rebuilt the skyweb, restored the Company, reconquered the planets. That was his dream.

He stood proudly straight as she always recalled him, lean and ready as a leopard, hair and beard sun-bleached to the color of his brown-burned skin. His uniform was gone long ago, but he wore his old service pistol in a sturdy leather belt and clung to the tattered wreck of a blue service cap, pinned with a golden sun circled with silver stars.

His right eye was weak and squinted. He commonly covered it with a faded black patch, cut like the patch in pictures of Ivan Kwan, the legendary founder of the House. His nose had the same haughty jut, though a dark scar crossed it. Wearing the patch and the nose and that battered cap like insignia of power, he called himself a general.

General Maximilian Kwan. That may have been his actual name. Growing older, she was never really sure. Some few of his genes may have come down from old Ivan, who had claimed to be an actual Romanoff. Or perhaps the iron Kwan nerve was all he ever needed. No actual proof was possible. The official Sunblood registries had burned, with all the Company records, as they fell out of the sky.

She always longed to know about that wonderful fabric where the cities of the sky had been hung, but her father seldom spoke about it, or the stranger wonders of the Oort halo far on beyond. She had to listen to the men when they sat around the campfires. They all had lived in the web, and they spoke of the splendid times before the fall with a wistful sadness in their voices.

They were tutors. It was Marco Lara who taught her to read the yellowed old paper books they sometimes found in buildings not entirely burned or flattened. He was her father's first lieutenant, a wiry little one-armed man, the right arm off from the elbow down, lost she never knew how. When she could read, she used to carry the books in her backpack till they fell apart, because they carried her back to discover all the wealth and pride and power that had been. In dreams of her own, she ruled with the Sun Tycoons, spun the wonder of the skyweb, voyaged farther on to the planets and the halo.

Bit by bit, she learned what the halo was: a vast swarm of small ice-worlds formed in the outer fringe of the condensing Solar nebula, reaching out nobody knew how far. Strange space beings had come from there, the starbird and the skyfish. The monster, too, the great space creature that had come to tear the skyweb down. In spite of the monster, she kept on begging for more about the halo than anybody knew. When her father's dream came true, she wanted to go on out, to explore the unknown ice-worlds where the starbird and the skyfish had lived.

Most of the men believed in her father and his dream. So did she—at least while she was young. Belief came harder as the years went by and he grew older and she saw no promise of any kind of magic ladder back to space. There were always a few who muttered their doubts, though they seldom dared to challenge him.

One doubter spoke on a lean day in a cruel season when the monsoon nearly failed. They were crossing the Great Rift valley. There was no food except for her, and too little water. Half the hungry men wanted to turn back to look again for game closer to Mt. Kenya. She heard that skeptic whisper that her father was never born a Kwan.

"Listen, mister!" He halted the company there in the desert. One hand near the old projectile gun, he swung to face the challenger. "If you don't believe me, why are you here?"

The skeptic's name was Blixter. A big man, fat in better times, he had no pigments fit for Africa. His hair was yellow straw, his face loose and flabby now where the fat had been, burned red-raw and always peeling. He carried an old laser pistol, useless until he found a new power cell, and an eight-foot spear that he used like a walking cane when he limped.

"Prove it, sir." He blinked at her father, leaning on his cane. "If you can." His pale eyes were rimmed with red. They fell before her father's one-eyed stare, but still he muttered stubbornly, "Show us anything!"

Marco Lara moved to her father's side, hunting gun cradled in his one good arm.

"You can try to kill me." Her father stepped closer to Blixter. "If you've got guts for it."

Blixter shuffled his broken boots on the gravel and shook his head. Like a crippled wildebeest, she thought, dying with a bullet through his belly. She felt sorry for him.

"Or else—"

Her father stopped to glance at her, and she was proud of him. His single eye scanned the other men, who stood squinting against the sun at Blixter and Lara and him.

"Or else—" His thin lips drew into a snarling smile at Blixter, and he rasped the words, loud and slow and savage. "You'll confess yourself a lying coward and tell the corps that I am in fact a space-born Kwan, the true and rightful heir to the Family of the Kwans, sole owner now of every Sun Company share, destined by legal right to become the next Sun Tycoon."

Blixter stood still blinking for half a minute, till Lara leveled the hunting gun. He gulped then, and spat dry foam and said he did believe.

Her father turned that hard dark eye from him to the other men.

"Listen!" he rasped. "One more time, I'll tell you who I am."

They looked at him and looked at each other and looked again at Blixter, who had dropped his spear and sat slumped down on a rock. Finally, sweating in the breathless heat, they squatted in a circle to hear what he said.

"I was born in the High House." He paused to glare again at Blixter, who wilted under his look. "I have my Company microcard to prove it." He slapped the worn leather pouch belted to his hip, but he didn't show the card. "My mother came from the true Kwan line. My father was a Kwan by election. I grew up in the web.

"I was a Sun Fleet commander, out in space the day the seeker struck. Bringing the *Moon Queen* home from the Pallas wire. The attack caught me alone in the control dome, nosing down to dock at Kilimanjaro High."

He stopped and looked away toward the faint white crown of the mountain itself, so far and low in the south that it rippled like a banner in the heat.

"Kilimanjaro!" He spat the word at Blixter, and paused as if he expected one more challenge. Blixter sat still, gasping in the heat, and he went on. "My signal officer had caught some warning from Fleet Command, but nothing he could believe. Made no report to me. The thing caught us by surprise. It flew out of Earth's shadow cone not a dozen kilometers ahead. God knows what, or where, it came from.

"Something shaped more like some weird insect than anything I'd ever thought we'd meet anywhere off Earth. Climbing out of the shadow, shredding the web with a blue-blazing tail-jet. We tried to fight it. Turned the ship to meet it. Fired two nuke torpedoes."

He shrugged and turned to Marco Lara. They nodded together as if in some bleak understanding.

"Spitballs! The nukes went home. Dead on. Blazing through the filters on ignition, hot enough to kill anything we ever put in

14

space. But that damn thing—it never seemed to feel 'em. Just went on wasting the web. The ballast satellites kept sailing out of orbit, dragging docks and labs, minigrav factories, Sun Fleet bases, the High House itself!"

Lean lips shut tight, he turned again to wait for Lara's nod of bitter affirmation. A thin streak of bright red blood had begun to ooze down his gray-stubbled chin from where sun and wind had cracked his lower lip.

"Nightmare! A picture I'll never forget! The shape of the monster and the wreck of the cities. Ships and pressure spheres and the tangled ruin of everything, bright in the sunlight and shining against the dark like broken strings of beads! The whole sky world coming apart and falling up to nowhere.

"The wires themselves could have killed us. Kwanlon cables, too small to see, tough enough to slice our hull. We steered clear of them, but that blue jet caught us, close enough and hot enough to fuse all our external signal and observation gear. We lost air pressure in the crew compartments and the engine room.

"Killed all the crew."

Lara was nodding again, and Roxane wondered how he knew.

"Kwan luck! I was still in the control dome, where the pressure hatches saved me. Alive, but I had to make the rest of it. The hulk was disabled, all power gone. We climbed halfway to the Moon and fell back to graze the atmosphere, climbed and fell again, till I was able to get outside in emergency gear to restore thrust to the steering jets.

"Thrust enough to let me get us down. The hulk crashed and burned at a spot I can show you, out on the Masai-Mara." His restless hand left the gun to gesture again at the dusty shimmer of the hot horizon. "A couple of hundred kilos south, if you ever care to look."

His fleshless hand back near the gun, he glanced once more at Lara, who nodded silently again, dexterously shifting the hunting gun in that lone left arm.

"That's how I got here, mister." He took a quick step toward Blixter. "It's where I mean to go, with whoever wants to follow."

He paused to scan the squatting men with that one good eye, waited for their nods of tired assent, and swung back to the skeptic.

Blixter had reached for the spear, but only to drag himself upright and make a limp salute.

"Sorry, Captain Kwan."

"If you're with me—" Her father spat at the dust and tilted the old cap farther and beckoned the men back to their feet. "On to the stars!"

Limping, straggling, a few still grumbling, they followed him on toward the sinking sun. Blixter hobbled along behind, the last in the line. She still felt sorry for him.

Marching with them as she always had, learning to be a soldier, she lived her father's dream in her own imagination. She never really minded hunger or the sun or the mosquitoes in the swamps, because she knew how to get away. Sometimes to dreams out of those tattered books. Dreams of the wonderland of the skyweb, out between the great round Earth and the mines of the Moon. And more thrilling dreams, when she dared the monstrous thing that had torn the skyweb down, out to the unknown treasures of the far halo.

Listening to the men when they talked of all they had lost, she grew up sharing all their wistful longings. When life seemed hard, when the game had failed and water holes went dry, when rocks had cut through the soles of her rawhide boots and her feet were bleeding, when they had no shelter from a cold monsoon rain, she used to beg the men for all they knew about the halo and Janoort, the lonely snowball where old Fernando Kwan had left a tiny human colony.

Once she asked her father what he knew about the halo creatures.

"Forget 'em." His face was set hard. "We trapped those two. The next we knew, that monster came to ruin the world. Connection? I don't know. All I want is our own space back. Our planets and their moons. I'll let 'em keep their halo."

In spite of that, she used to watch the sky. She learned young to name the planets as they crept among the stars. The Sun Fleet explorers had found most of them cold and harsh and airless, unfit for human settlement. It was the halo that held her imagination, unknown and vast and wonderful, its mysterious promise greater than any danger.

The starbird and the skyfish had been pathetic things, so the men said, helpless in the air and gravity of Earth. Even that monstrous destroyer had finally fallen into the sea. The unknown peoples of the halo became fairy creatures to her, strange but kind, waiting to welcome mankind.

The seasons passed, monsoon floods and parching droughts. Though her father clung to his stubborn vision, the whole corps was never more than thirty trail-worn men, hunting wildebeest and impala that had already been hunted too thin, scouring the wasted world for such rare treasures as a blanket or a sheet of waterproof plastic or a good pair of boots or anything else that might help keep them alive.

She saw him getting slowly older, that jaunty cap worn threadbare, white patches creeping into his hair and his beard, sometimes a limp in his step and a hard twist to his mouth from pain he never spoke about.

Sometimes when they passed some black and crumpled bit of metal fallen from the sky, her eyes filled with tears. The wires of the web had been kwanlon, magical stuff far stronger than steel. She used to look for bits of it, till Marco Lara said it had all burned up in friction with the air.

Who knew how to make it now? Where were any rockets to lift new wires into the sky, even if they could be made? How could anybody hope to get back to space? She never put such questions to her father, but sometimes on those long hungry treks through the thorn bush and desert jungle, she used to wonder.

One clear night when they had camped on the edge of the Serengeti, she lay half asleep in her hard bed watching the creeping constellations. She saw a strange new star. Brighter than Venus, it rose out of the west and climbed so fast she could see it moving. Almost overhead, it suddenly vanished.

Just a shooting star?

It had seemed too bright, and it left no trail. She decided to wake her father. Slow to say what he thought, he sat up in his own bed and turned to face the west. They watched together until it rose again.

"A satellite," he told her at last, and she heard her own troubled wonder echoed in his voice. "A new satellite in low orbit. When it seems to go out, that's because it has come into Earth's cone of shadow."

"Whose satellite?"

"Not ours." He watched in silence until it was gone into the dark. "No friend," he told her then. "After the monster, we'll meet no friends coming out of space."

She heard him sleeping soon, but she lay awake, watching the dark east until she saw its bright white spark burning again, falling toward where the sun would rise.

"I want to know," she whispered to it then. "I want to know who you are and why you came to Earth."

THE PHYSICS OF THE SNARK

3

After the newberry pie, his surprise gift was a black robot. Benn named him Friday, for his birthday and a black man in a story Runesong had told him.

"We know how you miss Runesong," his mother said when they called the robot in. "It will be a new friend for you."

No friend at all, Friday was a hard, lean, ugly thing, not at all like Runesong. Remembering her, he had to blink the tears back. The computer brains of eldren robots could be cased in any shape. Friday's case was halfway human, but naked and bald, with great unblinking lenses for eyes. He was made of slick black plastic, because steel in the halo was as rare as gold on old Earth. He had black spidery claws for hands.

"It has come to be your tutor," his father said. "It can load programs to teach you nearly anything."

"How to play Blade and Stone?"

"Forget the game," his mother said. "There are other things you need to know."

Friday had been designed at the core-star observatory to help care for the human survivors of Captain Bela Zar's *Spica*. His memory cubes held nearly everything. His different programs spoke in many different voices, but all of them came from the shimmer of cold blue fire in a knife-edged crest of something like black glass that ran from the thin plastic ridge that was his hard plastic nose back across his bare black skull and on down to the nape of his plastic neck.

He was useful enough, and he did become a kind of friend. He never got angry. He was quick and strong. He could stay in the habitat, because oxygen didn't burn him. He could answer questions. Yet he had ways that made him hard to love. Quin said some of his control programs must have been installed by a very junior human officer from the *Spica,* working with some eldren technician who took a dim view of Terran intelligence.

"Okay, old chap." At study time, Friday used to greet him with what his mother called a British accent. "Let's see your homework for today."

Trying to forget Runesong, he studied hard. The first lessons were in language and math and the astrographies of the Solar system. The eldren languages were too difficult for him, Friday said, but he studied English and Spanish and Russian. He learned about the star called Sun and the planets down around it and the billions of snowballs in the halo. He worked through calculus and computer math.

Friday never seemed pleased with anything he did, yet never scolded him. When he couldn't answer a question, Friday just seemed amused—or the instructor program made him act that way. He seemed to feel that Benn was only a planetic, anyhow, with no proper place here in the halo.

They came at last to the physics of the snark. Friday said it was something no planetic would ever need, but he wanted Benn to learn. The ideas seemed simple at first. Speaking down to him in that slow, half-mocking drawl, as if he were still too young or dumb to understand, Friday talked about the structure of the universe.

"A new concept for you, Master Benn! A fact that seems to startle you Terrans, but you must expect to be startled when you get off your primitive planet. I suppose you think your desk is something real, really standing here in a real habitat?"

"It looks real to me."

"Because of what you are." The slick black head jerked to make a nod. "I suppose you think your own planetic body exists all the time. True, Master Benn?"

"I guess that's true."

"Wrong, old chap!" Friday couldn't smile or laugh. That hard black face was always the same, and the lenses always had the same cold stare, but the drawling words seemed to keep making fun of him. "Half the time, Master Benn, you don't exist."

He knew he shouldn't be angry. Not at Friday, anyhow. Friday was only a robot, programmed to move and remember and speak. No robot could really feel superior to him, or feel anything at all. Yet he wanted to kick the plastic shins or smash his fist into that stiff plastic face.

"Do you doubt me, Master Benn?"

"I do feel real." He slapped his hand on the desk, so hard his fingers stung. "The desk is real as anything."

"A Terran illusion, Master Benn. Allow me to tell you why. First of all, you must understand that every item in the material universe is composed of smaller items. Can you accept that, Master Benn?"

The notion seemed strange, and he shook his head.

"Look out through the window, Master Benn."

He looked through the window. The sky outside was scattered with tiny silver moons, the mirror shells around the snowballs of the cluster. Beyond them it was black, and bright with blazing stars.

"What do you see, Master Benn?"

"The Milky Way."

"You see our galaxy, Master Benn. It is composed of stars much like your own native Sun, most of them with smaller masses in orbit around them, masses like the planets and the ice-asteroids of the Oort halo. Agree, old chap?"

"I do."

"Now look at your hand, Master Benn."

He looked at his hand. It was grimed from working with his mother in the hydroponic garden, transplanting mutant seedlings, and the thumbnail was broken.

"What do you see, Master Benn?"

"Just my hand."

"With better eyes, old chap, you could see a little deeper. You would perceive that your hand is made of molecules. They are smaller masses than galaxies or stars, or even the planet where you planetics evolved. Looking even deeper, you would perceive still smaller masses, the atoms that make up the molecules. If your vision could extend a little farther down the ladder of size, you would discover that the atoms are made of fermions and bosons. The fermions, if you ever found them, would be made of quarks, which themselves occur in several different colors and several different flavors. Is that progression clear to you, Master Benn?"

"I think so."

"It would be clearer, Master Benn, if you had been an eldren infant. With eldren senses, you might even discover that the quark is not the last rung on the ladder. The next one down we call the snark."

Benn squirmed in his chair. He didn't much like being reminded that the eldren possessed gifts that he didn't. He didn't see how such invisible particles should matter to him, but Friday was hard to interrupt when he had a program going.

"Please attend, Master Benn!" The lazy drawl had a sudden edge, borrowed, he imagined, from a moment of temper in that unknown junior officer. "The snarks, when we get all the way down to them, are formed of still smaller items of energy-mass called nanions. At the nanionic level, things get interesting. If you will listen, Master Benn!"

"I'm trying to."

Friday's lenses were huge and oblong, placed on his narrow black face like human eyes. They were flat and blank and dark. Benn had to remind himself that there was no actual brain behind them, but only a program running, because they were staring at him now in a way he didn't like.

"Down at the nanionic level, Master Benn, we reach an exciting interface. That is the boundary between the false vacuum and what we know as space and energy and matter. Is that a concept your infant Terran brain can grasp?"

The notion of a false vacuum seemed to be nonsense. He wanted to throw his homework in that bright black face and stalk out of the room, but he had tried that once and found that the program had subroutines to cope with anything he did.

"Why get so pink, old chap?" The lenses had seen his hot resentment. "Don't you want to learn?"

"I do." He had to gulp before he said it, but if the lessons could help prepare him for the Game of Blade and Stone, he really did want to learn. "What is this nanionic level?"

"It's a horizon of reality," Friday said. "The nanionic wave-particles flicker back and forth across the interface, out of existence and back again, into the false vacuum and back into our own space-time universe, a trillion times in a trillionth of a Terran second."

He blinked and waited.

"That's the reason, Master Benn, that you aren't always real. I'm not surprised if that surprises you, because you planetics have evolved no nanionic senses. Most of the eldren have. They are able to fly the way they do because they can reach through the interface with their transport vector effectors to synchronize the vibrations and cause the particles to make each return to a slightly different position. A false motion—"

"I've seen the eldren flying past the windows," he objected. "Without wings. Out where there is no air. I've even been on one of their ships with my father. They really do move to wherever they want to go."

"Wrong again, Master Benn. It's true they do change position, but with no motion in our universe. Grasp the paradox, Master Benn?"

"I'm trying."

"False motion, real result." A black claw stabbed at him, the blue crest flashing. "That should be simple enough, even for you. The point is that nanionic flight sidesteps all the ordinary relativistic limits of mass and momentum." The lenses stared sternly at him. "Really, Master Benn, you must apply yourself."

"If I learn about these snarks and nanions—" He peered into the black plastic face. "Can I learn to fly?"

"Please, Master Benn! You're a Terran, even if your birth took place in space. You planetic people have evolved no nanionic sensors or effectors. In a million years, you may. But here and now, Master Benn, there's no way you'll ever fly.

"In fact, old chap, the future of your species in space is subject to question."

DON DIEGO BOLIVAR

4

His mother was born in Ecuador, somewhere under Chimborazo High, to no name she ever knew. She learned early to scrounge for survival in the barrios of the squalid villages beneath the splendor of the skyweb, living on her wits and later on her looks. Peering wistfully through a tall wire fence around a Sun Country estancia, she won her first patron and a way into a Tycoon's mission school, where she learned Sun Country English and Sun Country etiquette. A precocious fourteen, with a forged work permit that added a few more years, she talked her way through a checkpoint into Chimborazo Down.

Those early years were hard, even there, until somebody taught her to dance and sing, at least well enough. Her name by then was Isabella Bolivar. At seventeen, singing in a nightclub, she caught the eye of a Company man named Chandra Bey.

Diego was their natural son, though Bey never made him legal. That wasn't done. Not by the Sunbred, whose laser-tattooed Sun-marks tagged them for the aristocracy of space. A Company official might take an Earthside mistress to ease the tedium of a downside duty tour, but he went home to a Sunbred wife.

At school, he couldn't be Diego Bey, or even Diego Bolivar.

He was Diego Ruiz, though he made the smaller boys call him Don Diego and sometimes tried to start a rumor that his real father had been a Chen, a wealthy heir to the great family that rivaled the Kwans.

Sometimes kind, Diego's father gave him gifts. The best was a shiny new computer with its own holo monitor. When Bey was unkind, they had to live in a cheap downside hotel. The computer was his best friend then. He took lessons from it and learned to write new programs of his own.

He had one thrilling year when Bey sent him to school up in the web. He told his Sunbred friends there that he was kin to the Kwans. There were wonderful trips to the space docks and the gravity power installations, where he could look giddily down to the blue-white blaze of the sunlit Earth.

His friends were waiting to be tested for their own Sunmarks, but his father had never certified his name for the Sunbred Registry. His mother begged Bey for that until they quarreled again, and suddenly there was no money. They had to go back downside. That misfortune saved his life.

His mother was working as an entertainer in Kilimanjaro Down. To keep him out of sight, she had sent him to a camp for boys, out of the city in a Sun Country game preserve. He liked the camp. He could look through electric wires at the sleek, lovely animals that the Tycoon's favorites were allowed to shoot. On clear nights he could see the web, a shining wall of diamond lights that climbed and climbed to the very top of the sky.

He was there in that dreadful night when the seeker came— one of the boys called it Leviathan when they saw it, because he had seen the Revelator's outlaw holocasts, prophesying that a great beast would be released from Hell to humble the Sun Tycoons and punish the Sunbred for all their iniquities and the blood of space demons they carried in their veins.

A yelling counselor roused the camp. Diego scrambled out of his tent in time to see the creature. High up, above Earth's shadow cone, it shone huge and strange in the sunlight. At first he thought it was caught like some huge insect. Then he saw that it was tearing the web apart.

He stood with the boys, watching in the soundless dark. At

first it all seemed unreal. The web had taken a hundred years to spin. It contained everything. The Kwan Tycoons didn't own or rule or tax Earth. Not exactly. They were too clever to invite resistance or rebellion. But the Kwans owned the Sun Company. The Company owned the web, the great ring-world around Earth that fed mankind with gravity power and held the best of civilization. The Sunbred, the Sunmarked people of the web, had all the money, all the power, the brightest brains, the high science.

With horror beginning, he stood with the boys watching the monster rip that whole bright fabric apart. From where he stood, it seemed to happen very slowly. There was no sound, at least not at first. It all seemed like a holodrama, raising goose bumps that ought to go away when it ended. Yet he already knew the terror of it would never go away.

With a terribly intelligent purpose, the creature was cutting the tough kwanlon skywires. The whole top of the web, the docks and the ballast satellites, began drifting off into space. Slowly, so it seemed, the rest of the web crumpled toward Earth. Sector by sector, as power failed, the diamond-bright navigation lights blacked out.

The counselor's holo crashed loud into the silence, with breathless newspeople trying to tell what they saw and silly Company men begging the world not to panic, till something hushed the holo. The lights in the camp went out. He heard boys crying in the dark and the counselor yelling again, telling them to gather their things and stand in line for the transport craft. He already knew there would never be anywhere to go, even if transport came.

Silent fire began to blaze, all across the north. All the lower web was coming down, the cities of the sky, the gravity wires, the labs and factories, the hotels and the palaces, the schools and museums, perhaps even the High House where the Tycoon had lived. All dragged down by the same kwanlon cables that had suspended them, burning when they hit the atmosphere.

The noise came at last, a far thunder rolling out of the north that soon began to shake the ground. A sudden wind rose out of the east, as the air caught the motion of the wreckage. It grew into a hurricane, searing and terrible. As bad as anything could ever be, it got worse and worse. It whipped him with bits of flying stuff and choked him till he couldn't breathe and blew tents and boys and everything away. He lay in a hollow, hanging to a bush, till something knocked him out.

The next he knew, it was over.

The wind had stopped. He heard no sound. The air was still, but filled with bitter dust. His lungs ached. He coughed and spat black gobs. His whole body hurt when he tried to stand up. Most of his clothes stripped off, he was shivering, scratched and battered all over. One hand was numb and dead when he tried to move it.

Day had come, a dreadful dawn. Yellow flames still licked the sullen sky, all across the north. The rising sun made a dull red spot behind the dust. Fires still smoked and smoldered, where anything had not blown away. Where the camp had been, all he found was naked ground. One bare body lay crushed against a knob of rock; another was wrapped around the stump of a broken tree; but nothing was alive.

At first, he didn't want to be. Chandra Bey must have died, somewhere in the sky. His mother in the nightclub must have been too close to the falling web.

He cried when he thought of her, and remembered her face. Not smiling, not even beautiful, it was set hard the way it used to be when she had quarreled with Bey. But then he saw her toss her dark hair back and smile a stiff little smile.

"Never blame *su mala suerte*," she used to say when everything was wrong. "Just find another mark with money and make your own better luck."

He tried to grin the way she grinned, and looked again at the body against the rock. A golden glint caught his eye, the shine of a yellow topaz ground to make the Sunmark on the face of a fine chronograph that showed Terran time and Fleet time and Moon time and Mars time. The owner had been a legal Kwan, but now it was Diego's own first stroke of *la buena suerte*. He took it off the stiffened arm, snapped it on his own wrist, and started limping south.

He never saw his mother again, but his share of her wits and her dark good looks helped him stay alive. He searched through the ruined world for anything to eat. He looked for friends who wouldn't rape him or steal the chronograph. He hid from cannibal gangs. He pushed on south when he could, away from that great belt of fire and death.

Things got better at last, though he never needed Fleet time or Moon time or Mars time. In the far south of Africa, he talked his way into a little colony of Company survivors. Most of them wore the Sunmark. One man had even known Chandra Bey, but Diego kept silent about him. Hunted by the Holyfolk, they had taken refuge in the ruin of the old gravity-power station on Table Mountain.

He lived with them till the Holyfolk starved them into surrender. Most of them were burned alive, to kill the space-born demons in them, but Diego wore no Sunmark. He had listened to the Revelator and learned enough to play the Holyfolk game, letting an imam baptize him with the blood of his Sunbred friends.

Marching with the victors through the next dry season and another monsoon, he drifted north again. When a new star appeared, rising low in the west and crawling low and fast across the north sky, his new companions were afraid something new had been loosed from hell, but Diego wondered.

A spacecraft? From the human colony old Fernando Kwan had planted on the ice-world called Janoort? Returning, perhaps, to bring some better future to Earth? When his companions fled, he pushed on alone, toward that racing star.

The equatorial zone the web had spanned was still a vast desolation. Returning jungle had begun to cover the burned and twisted stuff out of the sky, but people were few. Nobody he found had news from space, but he stayed alive and watched the night sky until he saw a spark that fell from the star toward the far dark loom of Kilimanjaro.

After walking many days toward the mountain, he climbed it at last, across a waste of naked stone where that terrible wind had swept everything away. Above a water hole, he found a great pile of ruin. An old hunting lodge, he thought, where the Tycoon's guests had come down to shoot.

Stumps of walls rose out of new jungle, though doors and windows were gone. He found a wing where part of the roof was left and paused to shout that he came in peace. Nobody answered.

Climbing into musty silence, he found flies buzzing over drying blood in the empty doorway.

He pushed uneasily on into a musty reek of old decay and the stink of new smoke. Something crackled like breaking glass. He glimpsed a fearful head peering through a dim hallway. A thin old voice commanded him to halt. When he had laid his machete on the floor and denied that he knew anything about the Holyfolk, a withered old man shuffled out to meet him.

A time-dried Kikuyu, stooped and frail, a faded Sunmark gleaming faintly on his seamed black cheek. He looked hungry. Diego shared dried meat and fruit out of his pack. They sat outside in the shade of a young tree, where they could watch the slopes for danger.

The old man talked. His name was Jomo Uruhu. His birthplace had been just a few hundred kilometers north, in ancient Kenya. He had reached Janoort as a ship's engineer and met the eldren there. When the orbital observation station was set up, after the skyweb fell, he had come back with the robot crew to bring humankind the news of the halo and the promise of a new way of life in the Elderhood.

That was half a dozen years ago. He had found few to listen, still fewer to believe. He had planned to leave on the ship that came to supply the robots every five Terran years, but nobody was aboard to relieve him. He chose to stay, still stubbornly hoping for more converts. Just a few days ago, the Holyfolk had come. His own former comrades, Diego imagined, but he didn't say so.

"Butchered!" Jomo swayed where he sat, mumbling the words, blaming himself. "We had no weapons ready, because the eldren way allows no weapons. My people showed their empty hands, and the fanatics butchered them."

Yet a few had escaped. Hiding him, they had saved his life. They had fled again, when they saw Diego coming. Jomo was alone.

"One old man. I brought a handful of eldren gadgets, meant to prove what I said." He coughed and spat on the gravel. "Useless junk! All smashed and burned now, because the Holyfolk took them for works of their demons." The catch in his voice was almost a sob. "I never—never had a chance."

"I think your space friends let you down." Diego frowned at the jungle-grown ruins around them and the empty slopes of Kilimanjaro slanting away into misty distance. "If they're so wonderful and great, why don't they show themselves? Show their power? Instead of sending only you?"

"They never sent me." Old Jomo sank into himself, thin-haired head sagging into his lean black hands. "They just let me come."

Waiting, Diego brushed at an ant exploring his knee, and brushed again when it came back.

"To them, it's a sort of test." Jomo caught a raspy breath and raised his gnarly head. "To see if we've evolved far enough to join them. They don't want us till we are. They're patient. They don't care if we take another million years, but I came back because I hoped our time was now."

Tight lips quivering, Jomo blinked his bleary eyes.

THE HYDRAN STYLE

5

Edward Gibbon *Beta* was a big, fat, pink, jolly fellow with a queer sense of what he thought was humor. The translators called his people Hydrans, because their section of the halo was toward the Hydra constellation when you looked from Cluster One. Benn had known him nearly all his life, because he had always been Quin's best eldren friend. He was a historian studying Earth, which he called Terra. An odd profession, Benn thought, because he had never been there.

He had been watching, however, from the core-star observatory, down closer to the Sun, for several human lifetimes. He had known the unlucky Captain Bela Zar and *Spica*'s unlucky crew. He had studied artifacts from the ship and every other relic of Earth that came to his lab.

"And he studies us," Quin said, once when they were fixing up a habitat tank to be his own study. Benn had been excited to see his new computer, but he stopped to stare at Quin.

"Like bugs?" He squirmed away from the notion. "Under a lens?"

"Not exactly. He just wants to know everything about us. And he likes a lot of what he knows. Many of the eldren don't think we're ready for the halo, but he sees promise in us."

"Friday doesn't." Benn had sent the robot up to the shop to assemble his new desk. "He doesn't think they'll ever let us stay here."

"Friday doesn't think." His father frowned. "All he knows is his programs. They were mostly written down at core-star to teach the *Spica* crew."

"He says we'll never fly like the eldren."

"Maybe not." His father shrugged as if that didn't really matter, though to Benn it did. "But we do have those new thrusters for our space gear. Our problem is to learn the eldren way."

"Can we?" He watched his father's face. "Really? Friday says nanionic flight is easy for any eldren infant, and then he says it's impossible for me."

"Forget Friday," his father said. "Gibbon is a better model. Learn the Hydran lifestyle. The Hydrans have been here a long time, in peace among themselves and with everybody else. They seem content. Learn their style."

"Gibbon's?" Benn shook his head. "We'll never be Hydrans."

"They are different." His father nodded soberly. "They do have the Hydran shape and Hydran gifts. They don't marry. They don't die. Instead, a grown-up Hydran can split into two children."

The Hydran style looked as impossible as nanionic flying. He said no more about it, but Gibbon began coming to tutor him. Only now and then at first, because he was so busy. Director of Terran research at the new core-star station, he also taught seminars at the great Hydran university and sometimes advised the Eldermost.

Gibbon had a clone-twin brother, born with him when their parent fissioned. His translator name was Galileo *Beta*. A scientist out at Starsearch Station on the fringe of the halo, he was a sort of ambassador to other stars. He sent laser signals and nanionic signals and listened for messages from anywhere, searching for other civilizations fit to join the Elderhood.

"Are we fit?" Always uneasy about that, Benn frowned uneasily at Gibbon. "Friday says we aren't."

He had to wait a long time for any answer, because the eldren had their own scale of time. Waiting, he studied the Hydran. Big and fat and pink, Gibbon had nearly the shape of a potato out of the hydroponic garden. Moving himself with nanionic forces, he needed no permanent legs or arms or wings.

Most of the time he had no visible limbs or organs at all, but he could grow whatever he wanted out of bumps that looked a little like potato eyes. One of those knobs opened now, into a single brown eye that looked exactly like one of the eyes Benn saw in the mirror. Two human-shape lips sprouted out of another knob, but the actual words came through the translator, spoken with the pink shimmer of his upper body. Gibbon could use any voice he had ever heard. He was suddenly very serious now, the voice he chose solemn and deep.

"A grave dilemma, Honored Schoolboy."

"We aren't like you." Benn felt worried. "We aren't at home in space. We need air. We aren't nanionic. We're adapted for Earth, but my father says we can't go back. Do you know how we can stay?"

"The evolutionary leap is never easy." The little pink lips hardly moved, but that great voice boomed loud out of the speakers. "More races fail than ever complete it. Yet I think you have no choice except to try."

"Can we do it?"

"Some succeed." Gibbon opened another eye to examine him with frowning attention. "Hundreds of our races here in the halo did complete the jump from their own planetic origins, most of them back before your own ancestors came out of the sea. We have made contact with several hundred more, scattered across our own galactic arm. There must be thousands we've never known about."

The big potato body tipped in the air like a quizzical human head. Benn waited until at last that huge voice rumbled again.

"Given time, Able Schoolboy, you yourself may live to write the answer. I am a student of Terra and its beings. Your respected parents are allowing me to work with you as an experimental specimen. For my own part, I shall attempt to educate you as a potential citizen of the Elderhood. For yours, you should devote yourself to learning whatever you can. The fate of your race must be left to the Council and the Eldermost."

"I thank you, sir." Benn nodded, feeling as solemn as Gibbon's voice. "I'll do my best."

"Then let us cement our agreement in your Terran style."

Benn watched, fascinated and somewhat startled, while the

33

curved seam on another potato eye split to sprout a bare human arm. It reached out with a hand that looked like a copy of his own. Gingerly he took it. Cool and strong, it shook his own hand heartily and then slid smoothly back to let the seam close behind it.

Gibbon never offered another handshake, but Benn never forgot that one. Through the passing years, he tried hard to prove himself a really able schoolboy. Gibbon was certainly a better teacher than Friday. Forever changing voices and sprouting new organs, sometimes trying an experimental joke to test the human sense of humor, he was always fat and jolly, always interesting.

His own jokes, though, were never very funny, and he seemed hurt and bewildered once when Benn tried an April Fool joke on him, planting an explosive to go off with a loud bang when Gibbon opened the lab door.

"Poor Schoolboy." He shook his body sadly after he was calm again and Benn was trying to apologize. "The noxious fumes were painful to me, and the demonstration had no useful point that I can understand. I suspect that this behavior you call humor is a relic of your planetic past, ill adapted to the halo."

Yet Gibbon seemed to forgive him. Often away on research trips to core-star or Hydra, often gone to Starsearch to visit his clone-brother there, he kept Friday's memory cubes programmed with fresh lessons. Once, after the little nanionic ship they named *Terra Two* was fitted for life support, he took Benn with him to Heart of Hydra.

A slowly spinning cluster of mirror-shelled ice-moons, that was the central Hydran city. The university was a separate satellite system, in orbit around it. Gibbon was there to chair a symposium on Terra, and he had brought Benn as a live exhibit. Sealed up in a crystal life-shell, Benn floated with him at the center of the auditorium while he spoke.

The place was a huge hollow sphere. Lumpy Hydrans lined it all around him, above him and below, everywhere he looked, all their attention fixed upon him. Some formed eyes to inspect him; most seemed content with their sharper nanionic senses. He wanted to shrink away, but there was nowhere to go.

Even after the lecture, they came flying to cluster outside the cell, examining him at closer range. The translator squealed and rattled and boomed a long time with their questions.

"Do you Terrans really consider yourselves the species of your planet best evolved for space?"

"If you cannot recall the lives of your parents, what is the reason for that defect?"

"Will freezing or dehydration result in permanent injury to your watery body tissues?"

"If your life really depends on the regular ingestion of chemical nutrients, do you not have problems with the accumulation of excess mass?"

"Is it true that you cannot bud or fission without the cooperation of some secondary individual?"

Some of them wanted to come into his cell, maybe to poke and prod him. Gibbon rescued him from that, but he was sweating and trembling before the ordeal was over.

"Thanks!" he muttered when they were alone. "I nearly died!"

"We are scientists, Brave Schoolboy." Gibbon's chosen voice was soft, almost apologetic. "We wish to know everything. Even after half a billion of your Terra years, there are new facts to be pursued. Some of them are useful when we learn them. All are good to know."

"Your world seems awfully strange." He had to shake his head. "It makes me wonder if we ever can belong."

"Ask yourself, Fortunate Schoolboy." Gibbon rocked back and forth in his version of a human shrug. "You are our test specimen. Your question is yours to answer. Perhaps I should remind you that every race in the Elderhood once was young."

Yet Benn remembered that many more had perished than had ever finished their evolutionary leap from planet to space.

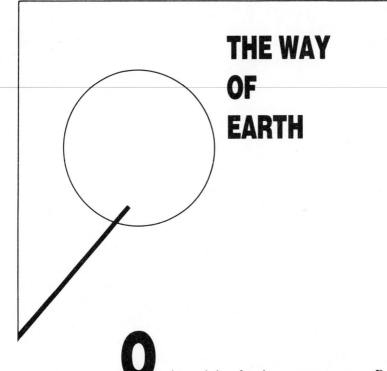

THE WAY
OF
EARTH

6

On clear nights for the next two years, Roxane watched that new star. The brightest in the sky, it rose out of the western dusk, climbed fast, and vanished as it entered the shadow of the Earth. Long after midnight, it swam back to drop toward the dawn. Sometimes her father watched it with her.

"Somebody's satellite," she heard him whisper once. "If it were ours—"

He said no more, but she knew it tantalized him. His hungry dreams of space as far off as ever, he was growing older, always limping at the end of a long day's trek. A thin little man in shapeless leather garments, no longer very straight, yet he still wore his air of proud command. She ached for him when she saw him stumble, or caught that cold scowl of pain that had left lasting creases beneath his bleached and ragged beard.

She herself had become a woman. Often she wished her mother were still alive. Her father never spoke of any change in her that he may have noticed, but sometimes she thought she saw approval on his bleak face. Now and then she caught the men staring, sometimes with a calculation that dropped her hand toward that rough-forged knife in its thin leather sheath against her thigh.

Her father came back from one fruitless hunt followed by a

new recruit, a hard-bitten dwarf of a man named Julio Vargas. He carried no Sunmark, only a livid triangular scar across his warped cheek where he swore he had cut it away to save his life from the Holyfolk. Accepting that, her father said he was a skillful hunter, an expert tracker, and swore him into the corps.

Vargas had been alone, or so he said, wandering the slopes of Kilimanjaro. He brought tales he had heard from the Kikuyu hunters, about a strange old man named Jomo Uruhu. An aged tribesman who claimed that he had been out beyond the Moon on an ice-satellite in what he called the halo. He had returned in a spacecraft to invite mankind to follow the strange new customs he called the eldren way. Vargas laughed at that.

"*Loco, señores!* Here on Earth, we live the way of Earth."

The old man had found few to follow him, Vargas said. Most had heard the gospel of the Revelator, which revealed no kind of paradise in space. The only believers were a few old men and women who said they had known Uruhu here in Africa, back before the falling of the skyweb.

Her father questioned Vargas. No, he had never himself been drenched with human blood in the baptism of the New Revelation. His own Sunmark, where the red scar warped his narrow face, had been earned in Company service. He had never seen Uruhu, or any shuttlecraft descending from space to Kilimanjaro. He shrugged. Perhaps they had never existed.

Roxane didn't like or trust him. He spoke too fast and seemed too fond of the heavy little crossbow he wore strapped to his back, yet the story filled her mind. Life was often hard and cheerless. Escaping the weariness and monotonies of the trail, she used to watch the sky toward Kilimanjaro, trying to believe that survivors of the Sun Fleet might in fact be returning.

For one dry season, her father did lead them toward the mountain, but they found the hunting poor. The Kikuyu they met were no disciples of Jomo Uruhu. A crazy old man, they said, who had never been far from Kilimanjaro. Or maybe not so crazy, if his lies had persuaded his deluded converts to bring him the mealies and yams he was too lazy to plant for himself. Perhaps even to chew food for him if his teeth had rotted out.

Hunger turned them back before the rains came, east and south, across the Serengeti. Even there, the hunting was little better. And time went by. She saw her father grow older, saw the fire of hope dim slowly in that lone good eye. Her own life seemed no better. A ceaseless discontent tormented her.

Could her life ever get better?

The next year was even harder. Again the monsoon failed and most water holes were dry. Lions as hungry as they were had scattered the dwindling game. Julio Vargas muttered that they should push even farther south, to look for kinder country, where the falling web had not burned and poisoned the land.

One long day she had waited for her father in a dry camp on a rocky knob. Their hoarded ammunition running out, she had thrown away the empty target rifle. Her weapon now was the knife against her thigh. She spent most of the day at practice throwing it, because she must learn to aim it well. A merely wounded animal might carry it away forever.

Her father was on a hunt with Vargas. Night came, and they did not return. Next day she waited again, still in camp with a few of those too sick or lame for anything better. Noon had passed before Vargas came back alone, limping under the weight of a gutted impala.

"*Que lastima, señorita!*" He dropped the carcass beside the dead fire and spread his empty hands toward her, grimed with drying blood. "Our brave general! Your own dear father!" His small eyes rolled upward. "Sleeping now in paradise."

She stared at him, shivering.

"*Mal suerte!*" His blood-black shoulders lifted. "Evil luck, which we could not avoid."

"What do you mean?"

"*Por favor.* Listen and allow me to describe the manner of it. Hunting, your father wished to master the crossbow. We exchanged weapons. He gave me his pistol." He touched the worn old weapon, belted around him now. "We lay near the water till the impala came to drink. Your father's first bolt hit the impala. It ran. We followed. He stumbled and fell behind. A long chase, but I overtook the wounded buck. Returning with the carcass, I heard a gunshot. Far ahead, I saw many men.

"Holyfolk, as I believe. *Hijos del diablo!* Too many for him. Too many for me, with only the pistol. Unable to aid him, I concealed myself. He must have taken a bullet, because I saw him stagger and fall. He had lost the crossbow, and he seemed to have no weapon. *Los cabrones!* They overtook him. Many men with spears and guns. The rifle must have hit him. He surrendered. They tied his hands and dragged him away.

"Of a surety, *señorita,* your brave father would never surrender!" He spat on the ground and spread his open hands. "Believe me, I could do nothing. I lay hidden all night in the brush at the bottom of the wadi. When daylight came, they were gone.

"*Que lastima!* I grieve for you, *señorita,* but it was the will of God."

"We're going—" Her voice quivered. "We've got to go after him."

"*Señorita, no!*"

Vargas's dark-stained hands gestured vaguely. The pursuit of the wounded impala had taken them too far across bad country. The Holyfolk had been too many, with too many weapons. The general—solemn-eyed, he shook his wild head at her—the general had worn the Sunmark.

"We're going." She cut his protests off. "Now. You will show the way."

"*Muy lejos! Muy lejos!*"

He shrugged again. It was very far across rough country strange to that wadi and the hills beyond it. He had been exhausted from the hunt and the burden of the impala. Too tired and too hurried to note landmarks. Even if they recovered the general's body, it was not a thing for her to see.

She quit listening.

Marco Lara and three others volunteered for the search. She made Vargas come to guide them. The country in fact was bad. Maybe fertile once, it was eroded to gullied stone where farms must once have been. Hostile desert now. They found no water hole, no wadi, no body. Vargas grew more and more uncertain which way the hunt had taken them.

"*Que lastima, señorita, pero somos perdidos.*"

A pity, but they were lost.

"A hard, hard thing."

Lara was husky-voiced with his own emotion. He had first met the general back before the skyweb fell, when they were both Sun Fleet cadets, but now the troop must come first. Her father would have commanded that. Here among Holyfolk raiders, they must stay together and move on toward water and a better chance of game.

When she wouldn't give up, they went on with her till sunset. She had to let them go back then, but she told them she was pushing on alone.

"*Loco!*"

Vargas called her that. Her food was gone, her canteen nearly empty. The company would have to move again, in search of a range where they could stay alive. She must not be left alone to face the Holyfolk or die from thirst and hunger. For her own sake, he wanted Lara to bring her back to camp by force.

Marco Lara refused. He still had hoarded bullets for his rifle. Leaning on it, he warned Vargas not to touch her. He made them empty the little water left in their canteens into hers, and she went on by moonlight, searching for the wadi where Vargas said he had lain hidden to watch the attack.

She followed rocky slopes toward lower ground, where the wadi should be. The moon reached the zenith. The alien satellite climbed again and yet again to wink out almost overhead. It was midnight when she came to a dark mass of trees grown where water would run when the rains came back.

She slept there on hard ground. Awake at sunrise, she followed the line of trees and brush till she saw vultures wheeling and found the body. Her father had dragged himself into the tangle of logs where hungry elephants had uprooted a clump of acacias to eat the foliage.

She sank down beside him, too numb to move. He had taught her not to cry, but dry sobs shook her. Since she could first remember, he had been her world, watching and shielding and teaching. In his hard and silent way, he had loved her. Without him— she couldn't think of that.

When at last she could touch him, she found the weapon that had killed him, still in his back. No Holyfolk bullet, it was a feathered bolt of old iron from Vargas's crossbow. Sick and trembling, she wrenched it out. The cold weight of it turned the world real again. She heard the flies buzzing and caught the scent of death.

She knew what she must do.

EVIDENCE
OF
EVIL

7

Benn was twenty-one at last, anxious to try his luck on Mazeway.

"Not yet, Bennie!" Both his parents looked suddenly older when he spoke of going, and he saw the quiver of his mother's lip. "You're still too young."

"We're human." He grinned and tried to blunt their concern. "We don't live a thousand years."

His mother refused to smile, but Gibbon had declared the tutoring done. There was no good news from Earth, where Jomo Uruhu had gone to teach the eldren way. None from the Council of the Elderhood, which always had weightier business than the future of Terra.

"Go if you must," his father finally agreed. "You know the odds, but it's true we don't live by eldren time. True, we need some new achievement to prove that we can earn our right here."

"If Dr. Gibbon can sponsor you," his mother said. "You can't go alone."

"Indeed, Ambitious Schoolman," the big Hydran shimmered when they spoke to him, "you cannot enter without a sponsor."

"Will you, sir? Can you sponsor me?"

"If you will wait," Gibbon said. "I must leave at once for Starsearch Station. My brother has called me back because of some urgent problem there. If you want to come along, I'll take you on to Mazeway when I can."

There was no time for the farewell feast his mother wanted to plan. Her cheek was wet when she kissed him. His father gripped his hand, with an oddly wistful smile. They both donned lifeskins and came with him and Friday to see them aboard the *Terra Two*.

Gibbon stayed with the signal gear through the flight, trying to call his brother. Transmission had been interrupted. That much Benn knew, but Gibbon himself had gone bleakly silent. Approaching Starsearch, they were in the signal room together. Hydran emotions were hard to read, but he had watched the pink glow of Gibbon's skin fading to a pale and patchy blue.

"Sir?" Not for the first time, he begged to know more. "Can't you tell me what's wrong at the station?"

Floating over the comm console, flashing impatient calls to the input panel, Gibbon seemed not to hear.

"Sir, please!" Gibbon disliked being prodded, but he tried again. "We're homing on the Starsearch beacon, almost in close approach. Our calls for landing instructions are getting no response. I need information, sir."

Gibbon's big potato body hung pale and gray where it was.

"Excuse me, sir!" He raised his voice. "I left Friday at the controls. Before I replace him, I need to know why we're here."

The air had a strong scent of Hydran frustration, but he caught no other response.

"Sir—"

Gibbon was twisting in the air, lifting from the console. Slowly a more normal pink flowed back across his rugged knobs and bumps. A single eye budded from one of them, to stare at him unwinkingly.

"Faithful Scholar, please forgive my inattention." He had found a hollow funereal voice. "I am trying to reach my brother."

"I know you are." The air had a sudden sharper bite that almost took his breath. "But I need instructions. Shall we proceed to land, with no permission?"

"A grave dilemma, because my brother—"

Gibbon dived abruptly toward the input sensors and hung there for an endless minute, flashing unanswered signals, before he shook himself and lifted slowly back, his skin still a slaty gray.

"Anxious Scholar, I cannot reach my brother." His dismal voice spoke, or seemed to speak, through thin and colorless lips sprouting just above that lone eye. "Therefore I have no information. No basis even for rational speculation."

"When he called you back, he must have been expecting trouble?"

"He had a problem, Benn." Gibbon dropped closer. "A difficult problem. He was not, however, anticipating—" A shadow dimmed that solemn voice. "He was not anticipating evil."

"Now you do have evidence—"

Gibbon recoiled from the word as if from some hard impact, and again Benn had to breathe that bitter reek of Hydran pain.

"Terran Scholar," the pink voice shimmered feebly again, "I beg you to understand my apprehensions. My brother has been cut off from me since before our flight began. I know nothing about his situation now, but I fear—I fear—"

Color and voice were gone.

"Sir, can you say what you fear?"

"Companion Scholar, I have no evidence for anything." Faint color winked and steadied. "However, since we are here together in this difficult situation, I see that I must tell you what I can."

"Please!"

"At Starsearch, my brother—"

Yet another delay, while Gibbon spun in the air to search the monitors again. He turned back heavily, as if dragged down by gravity Benn could not feel.

"At Starsearch, my brother is Inspector of Contact. Using the nanionic facilities there, he has been searching the galaxy for other minds. His duty has been to welcome them when he perceives a probability of mutual benefit through contact, and to reject them when he does not.

"He called me to come because of a dilemma arising from three recent arrivals at the station. He has discovered neither sufficient evidence to support their exclusion nor adequate evidence to justify admission. Other staff officials were urging admission, but he was unconvinced. Delaying any decision, he was holding all three in separate detention cells.

"If you wonder why he wanted me, you know that we are Hydrans. Meeting my kinsman in Heart of Hydra, you must have felt the force of kinship among us. Born of fission, my brother and I are one, neither complete without the other. In this difficult situation, he wanted us to be together.

"But now—" Gibbon quivered and darkened. "Now—"

"Now?" Benn tried to stifle a sneeze. "Did he say why he suspects the aliens?"

"Ambiguity." Gibbon paused as if to master his ammoniac emotion. "Ambiguities surround them. He said all three display high intelligence and technological competence. Qualities required for admission, but also dangerous in beings who may have no equivalent of our eldren way. When my brother called, he had found no logical basis for decision."

"If he's so doubtful, can't he just expel them?"

"They protest that they are unable to leave the halo because they have no means of interstellar transportation."

"Then how did they get here?"

"My brother has inquired." Gibbon's eyes and lips had been withdrawn, as if he had no resources left for human courtesies. "Each tells her own story—it seems that all three call themselves female. My brother believes none of them."

He whirled to inspect the monitors. Benn sneezed again and waited.

"Because of coincidence." He spun back, with a sudden burst of voice and color. "Because of discrepancy. Because they cannot or will not present any believable evidence that they are what they say they are. He says they clearly belong to three vastly different races, all previously unknown. They insist that they reached the station as utter strangers, knowing nothing of one another. Yet they all three appeared within a single cycle of time."

"Without spacecraft?"

"One was rescued from open space, where she was found adrift with no equipment whatever. One was picked up from a small ice-mass, from which she had been calling for rescue. The third simply appeared on the terminal stage, again with no equipment.

"With so little we can find in common, translation algorithms have been difficult to establish. Communication is still fragmentary, but all three claim that they were drawn here by the new nanionic beacon. One says she was forced to abandon her craft in flight because she lacked fuel to brake and land it. Another says she left her craft drifting in some location she will not reveal. The third simply refuses to speak.

"None will disclose the position of her home world. One staff member suggests that they are simply trying to protect their race from possible invasion, but my brother thinks they must be fugitives. From what, he has no idea. All three have now grown silent, responding to nothing."

"Were they armed—"

"Listen up, chaps." The ship's phone had thumped, and Benn heard the robot's unhurried drawl. "Curious business ahead."

"Friday?" Gibbon had faded gray again, leaving Benn to ask, "What's so curious?"

"I have been homing on the Starsearch beacon, as you instructed. I now report an unpredicted datum. The beacon is weakening. I compute total failure within three point six Terran minutes. In event of failure, sir, I lack expert programming competent to locate the station and complete our approach. Have you new instructions, sir?"

"Call the station. Report the malfunction."

"I have called the station, sir. My call was not acknowledged."

"Continue calling. Try the laserphone. Monitor all signal bands."

"I have signaled on all bands, sir, receiving no response on any band."

"Call again—"

"No use, old chap." The easy drawl reflected no emotion, because Friday had no circuits for emotion. "Additional data, just observed. Transmission of the Starsearch nanionic beacon has now ceased. Transmission of radar and lidar beams has now ceased. The station now shows no lights. I detect no nanionic or electromagnetic emissions of any kind."

"Hold our course toward—"

His voice caught, choked by a sudden ammoniac gust. Gibbon

was tipped askew in the air, his whole cragged body drained to a lifeless gray.

"Trusted Schoolboy—" Still he made no eyes or lips; only a faint shimmer of his upper body brought that dismal voice. "Trusted Schoolboy, I despair for my dear brother."

"We don't know—" Retreating from that suffocating cloud, Benn had to wipe his eyes. "Except for this blackout, we have no actual evidence—"

Gibbon's dull body rolled in the air, as if all will to control it had died.

"You must understand, Hopeful Schoolboy, that my brother and I were once a single being. Even since our parent fissioned, we have been one. Even far apart in space, we lived as one, thought as one, felt as one. I was he. He was me. Now something uneldren has cut us apart.

"I do not feel him now."

THE IRON BOLT

8

Roxane wiped her father's blood off the heavy little missile and slid it into her belt. Vargas had left his worn gold ring. She slipped it from his finger and rubbed a thin red smear off the round yellow topaz that had been the Kwan family emblem. She found the old Sun Fleet cap he had worn like a crown, the leather pouch that held flint and steel and tinder, the woven kwanlar wallet he had never let her open. A throb in her throat, she unfolded the wallet.

A thin slip of yellow kwanlar held the queerly real holo image of a handsome, smooth-faced stranger who wore a cap like his own must have been when it was new. Laserprinted to identify a Sun Fleet commander rated for heavy rocketcraft, it was oddly worn and faded along the lower edge, where that tough stuff should never wear or fade. She couldn't make out the commander's name or service number.

Another holo startled her. Almost a mirror, it showed her own face. The same tawny hair. The same bronze glint in the blue-gray eyes. A hint of mischief in the upward quirk of the lips.

Her mother?

Now she would never know. After staring at the picture till

tears burned her eyes, she tucked it back into the wallet and picked up the cap. The threadbare fabric had a smear of new blood, but the golden sun and circling stars still shone bright. Bleakly proud, she put it on her head.

That nerved her to move the body higher among the dead logs. The wallet had set an ache in her throat, but it had held his secrets. She left them with him. There was wood enough. She stacked dead branches over him and lit the pyre with his own flint and steel.

Listening to the crackle and hiss of the blaze, she stood close to it, blinking at tears that misted everything. The sun was too bright. The smoke had a bitter reek, and it stung her lungs. Remembering many moments, she felt too numb to think of words. But then he never wanted words. The heat was suddenly blistering her face. She turned away.

A long day of walking, thinking too much to feel all her weariness and hunger. When she reached that waterless camp, it had been abandoned. Late next day she overtook the troop gathered at a well dug long ago. Watching for Vargas, she slogged into camp with a hand hovering near the hilt of her knife.

The odor of roasting meat knotted her stomach, but she had no time for hunger. Searching the circle of waiting men, she found Vargas beyond the cooking fire. He squatted beside a big man named Hagland, his crony now. Vargas grinned and called a welcome through the smoke.

"*Señorita! Bienvenido!*"

His voice, she thought, had an anxious edge.

"I found my father."

She saw him start and squint at Hagland. Watching her warily, they listened while she told where she had found the body among the uprooted trees and burned it there. They relaxed and grinned at one another when she said nothing of the crossbow bolt.

She kept her voice steady enough, but she saw grief for him and for her in most of the men. Marco Lara laid his rifle aside to come and stand with his arm around her. Vargas and Hagland rose to join the file of men shuffling by with murmured words of sympathy. She made herself take Vargas's offered hand, but she shivered at his touch.

Lara called them together next morning to honor General Kwan. They sat on the rocky slope above the spring. He spoke briefly about their long friendship, beginning when they had been cadets together. His own good luck had tossed them back together in the madness after the skyweb came down. Through the hard years since, the general had led them well. Most of them could remember occasions when his courage and his wisdom had saved all their lives. His goal for them in space had become a thing perhaps impossible in these cruel times, but he had done his utmost. In better days, he might have made a great Tycoon.

Sadly, now, they must elect a new commander.

Roxane raised her hand. Vargas turned to mutter at Hagland when she nominated Captain Marco Lara, but most of the others seemed to listen with respect. Lara had shared her father's drive to lead mankind back to space. Through many years of sharing her father's leadership, he had proved his courage and devotion.

Lara thanked her and bowed to the men who cheered. He would serve them proudly if they wanted him. Vargas and Hagland had risen and, with a few cronies, moved apart from the rest. When her little talk had ended, Vargas interrupted the patter of applause.

"*Señores!*" He cleared his throat. "I respected and admired *el general*. Before we vote for anyone, however, there are issues to be considered. Though I knew General Kwan only through the few years since I joined you, I came to admire him as the true heir to the power and the splendor of the Sun Tycoons. But—and we all join the *señorita* Roxane in her grief—General Kwan is dead.

"With all due respect to our fond memories of him and our great regard for the *señor* Lara, our strategy must be reconsidered. We have all watched this new star that is a space machine. We have heard the Kikuyu tales of an old tribesman who claims that he returned from the ice-asteroid Janoort to be a prophet of what he calls the eldren way. The general and *Señor* Lara used to hope for friends aboard that alien craft who might lift us back to space and help restore the Kwans.

"*Loco!* Madness! Consider, *señores*. The star has been there through many years of our hard marches. If it meant any benefit for us, the benefit would surely have been perceived. Though I am no believer in the Revelator, I do suspect that the masters of that star are more akin to Leviathan, the space monster that came to destroy our world, than to any friends of ours.

"Consider again! We have hunted here too long. Now we find no game. The same Holyfolk who murdered the general will surely be seeking to kill us all. A dozen times—a hundred times the number who killed our honored general." He paused to bow, and Roxane saw his quick little eyes dart a covert glance at her. *"Con permiso, señores—"*

He stopped again to look at Hagland and the handful of men who had quietly drawn together around them.

"Mis amigos—" He nodded at Hagland and those others and waited for their nods. "After all these years of pain, we have come to see that they have been spent in pursuit of a madman's dream. Now, our noble general so sadly dead, we have awakened. We wish to leave this zone of devastation and march into the south, where game may be more abundant and the Holyfolk may not be hunting us."

The whole circle turned expectantly to her and Lara.

"The general is dead." Leaning on his rifle, the old soldier spoke solemnly and slowly. "Out of respect for his memory, I suggest that we should visit Kilimanjaro before we go anywhere. I would like to know if in fact some spacecraft has returned from the Janoort colony. If we should find that true—"

"Tonto!" Vargas's voice was suddenly shrill. "Fool! You ask the Holyfolk to murder us all!"

"We may find Holyfolk in the south as well as here—"

"More of them than on Kilimanjaro." Roxane raised her own quivery voice. "Let me show you what killed my father. No Holyfolk bullet!"

"Perdone, señorita!" Vargas bowed to her, with a dark ironic smile. "I heard the shot and examined your poor dead father—"

"Did you see this?" Hand trembling, she showed the long iron bolt, already rusting with her father's blood.

She saw Vargas jog Hagland's arm. They stepped apart. Vargas's hand was at his hip, near her father's pistol. Hagland carried a long spear. He had been leaning on it, but now she saw him lifting it.

"Puta!" Vargas screamed. "You ask to die?"

His cold stare turned her weak and giddy. Her meager breakfast of boiled mealies became a cold rock in her stomach, and the heavy little bolt fell out of her numb fingers. Lara must have moved to grasp his rifle, because she saw the pistol stab toward him.

"You, too, fool?"

The pistol crashed. She threw the knife and saw it in Vargas's leathery throat. Dark blood spurted. Gurgling, he toppled slowly forward into the dead campfire. Lara swayed and went to his knees, his rifle clattering to the gravel.

Sudden stillness. Her ears pounded. Though the morning was merely cool, sweat chilled her. She needed to sit down, but she heard gravel grating under boots. The men around her were backing away, gaping at her, their own weapons ready.

"Crazy!" somebody rasped. "Stop her!"

"Look at it." She stooped to recover the bolt and offered it with shaking fingers. "From Julio's crossbow. I found it in my father's back."

A man took the bolt, made a wry face at it, passed it on. She stumbled to Lara.

"Thank you, Cheetah." His lone hand clutched his side, blood seeping through his fingers, but he looked at her with an ashen grin. "You saved our lives."

She sat weakly beside him on a rock and watched the circle of men, almost beyond caring what they thought. She saw them frowning at the bolt, shaking their heads perhaps in disbelief at the body in the ashes, till at last the bolt came back to her. Silently one man wiped the blood and ashes off her father's pistol and put it in her lifeless hand.

"We loved the general." Hagland was a heavy, swarthy man with ragged black hair to his shoulders. He spoke up abruptly, with an air of taking charge. "We respect Miss Roxane." An oblique nod to her. "I trusted Julio. I am shocked by this incident. So are we all."

He looked around the circle, and a few men nodded.

"Comrades, in this emergency—" His voice lifted slightly. "We cannot choose a leader now. Not without inquiry and due consideration. Our immediate tasks are to care for Captain Lara and prepare a grave for Julio."

Already the leader, he began assigning men to find tools and chose a site for the grave. Roxane gathered herself to clean and dress Lara's wound. Though a rib had been grazed, the chest had not been penetrated. Barring some severe infection, she thought he should recover fully.

"Miss Kwan—" His faint voice had a diffident tone. "It's time you took your father's place. If you will—"

"I'm still Cheetah," she whispered. "And you're the one to lead us."

If Hagland and his gang will let you. She breathed that uneasy thought, but not to him.

The ground on the knob was hard. Digging the grave took all afternoon. When Vargas lay beside it, wrapped in his bedroll, Hagland called the men into a solemn circle around the pit. They stood silent for a time, with no words spoken, until they lowered the body and replaced the rocky soil.

She slept early that night, exhausted, and woke to the gray, chill dawn. She saw no fire. The camp seemed oddly still. She found Lara lying near her, where she had helped him spread his bed. All the others were gone, with their packs and their weapons. Trying to wake Lara, she found him stiff and cold, his skull caved in.

STARSEARCH

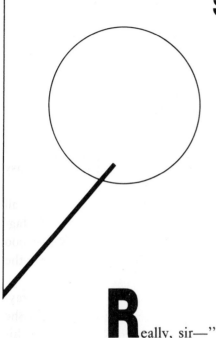

9

Really, sir—"

Benn stepped back into air he could breathe. "We still have no proof—"

"Proof enough!" The sudden blaze of Gibbon's knotty body rattled the speakers. "Respected Schoolman, I feel—"

His voice was cut off, that glow abruptly quenched. Benn sneezed and wiped his eyes, watching the dark body stiffen and go limp as it floated away from the console. Catching it in his arms, he saw a faint blue shimmer and heard a fainter whisper:

"—uneldren. Leave me, Benn. I need time—time—"

Benn belted the lax body into the holdfast seat and shouted into the intercom phone.

"Friday? Give me a status report."

No reply.

"Kind Scholar!" Gibbon's skin flickered again. "I feel—"

His body jerked against the holdfast belt and hung there, limp and dark and shapeless. Benn shouted into the phone again, and again got no response. In the control bubble, he found the black robot sitting rigid, great lenses blindly fixed on the blank nanoscope monitor.

"Friday?" He seized the hard plastic shoulder. "What hap—"

"Out of service." A faint, toneless singsong. "Reporting malfunction. Storage overload. Out of service. Reporting—"

It stopped when he took his hand away.

He turned to the controls. The viewscreens showed the blazing sky he knew, the nearer stars a little shifted from their places when seen from Cluster One. The nanoscope and lidarscope were dead. The chart on the pilot monitor showed two bright points, the blue for the station's known location, the other a red blink for the present position of the ship. The blink meant *Estimation Only*.

The problem that had baffled Friday's navigation programs. At effective velocities beyond the speed of light, nanionic pilotage was possible by dead reckoning only. Approach had to be made at lower effective speeds, with lidar or radar and finally visual observations required for the actual landing.

Where was Starsearch?

Those empty monitors gave him no hint, because all the nanionic facilities were dead. Here in the deep night of space, most of a light-year out from the Sun, his unaided eyes were useless. The charts indicated the station's known location, but the ship's position was no better than a guess. The error might be two light-seconds, ten, a hundred.

"*Terra Two* calling Starsearch Station."

He tried the nanophone, tried the laserphone, tried again. The scopes stayed blank. Assuming that the red-winking estimate on the chart might be more or less correct, he plotted a course toward the station's indicated true location, pushed the ship toward it, and slowed as they reached the computed point.

Nothing.

The monitors stayed dead. Drifting slowly on, he called again, and yet again. No result, until at last a sudden green point flashed in the nanoscope, and flashed again. Crackling speakers translated an automatic recognition signal.

"Service craft *Mindquest*, home port Starsearch Station."

He beamed a nanionic signal at it. "Private craft *Terra Two*, home port Cluster One, calling service craft *Mindquest*."

"Service craft *Mindquest*, home—"

The automatic signal was cut off.

Searching space where it had been, he picked up a green-and-amber wink. Faint and far, but it came again. A feeble laser beacon. He soon had a lidar range that showed it a bare light-second away. He steered toward it, wondering again.

"Benn?" Gibbon's voice on the intercom, so papery and faint it was hard to recognize. "What can you report?"

"I've picked up a beacon, sir. We're approaching the station now. It still looks dead. But—something else, sir. I got a recognition signal from the service craft. Just taking off, I think. The signal was quenched when I responded. There must be trouble, sir. Somebody in flight—"

"Not my brother." He caught Gibbon's whisper. "Not my brother—"

The whisper faded.

"Sir, can I help you?"

"My brother." He barely heard the words. "Help my brother—"

He completed the approach. In the pilot monitor, the blink had vanished. Two bright points merged into one, position and destination. By starlight, he made the station out. A tiny triple system, two moonlets in orbit around the mirror-shielded central snowball. The farther moon was the observatory, a slender framework bristling with spidery telescopes, spidery lidarscopes, spidery nanionic transceivers. The lidar beacon marked the nearer moon, flashing green and amber, green and amber.

He called again. The beacon kept on flashing. He steered toward it. The observatory instruments were remote-controlled, kept vibration-free, never meant to be alive. This moonlet had been the place for life, the work and dwelling place. A shapeless cluster of silvered tanks and crystal shells and open platforms and big machines he didn't know. The power plant, the labs, the computer section and the comm section and the life-support section, the terminal stage itself.

Once alive. But now?

The beacon kept on winking, green and amber, green and amber. Its flashes lit the narrow stage, dazzling, too brief to be revealing, green at one end, amber at the other. Squinting against them, he saw no change, no motion. He found his breathing slow-ing to the rhythm of the flashes. He caught Gibbon's scent when he had to gasp for air, and discovered the Hydran behind him, a sting in the air, a faint blue shimmer.

"The terminal stage." He pointed. "Empty, since the supply craft took off. The station looks abandoned."

"Abandoned?" Gibbon's voice was a faint dry crackle in his ears. "My brother would never abandon Starsearch."

"Perhaps he had to, sir. Things go wrong. Machines fail. Illness strikes. Accidents—"

"Words enough!" A brittle command, but then a softer voice. "Forgive me, Companion Scholar, but our machines do not fail. I perceive no need for such irrational speculation."

Gibbon's cragged body quivered in the air, dark for a moment, before that pale blue shimmer continued.

"My brother was truly eldren. His mission here was to welcome emerging peoples. He hurt no one, made no enemies. No harm should come to him. Yet I fear—fear something irrational—some-thing uneldren—"

He sank into a blue-gray huddle.

Easing them on toward the stage, Benn found no cheer for him. They came down into starlight and amber, starlight and green. He peered out into the dazzle and the dark. The terminal platform was empty. No other signal met them, no machine or creature moved to greet or challenge them. A breathless stillness filled the bubble until his arm brushed the black robot.

"Out of service." A faint singsong, yet it startled him. "Re-porting malfunction. Storage overload. Out of ser—"

"One machine has failed." He tried to grin at Gibbon. "When we know why, I think we'll know what hit the station."

"We must find—find out why." Gibbon stirred, as if with stub-born effort. "Call again. If we get no answer, we'll go out to search."

Nobody answered. Nobody came. Securing the craft, Benn car-ried the rigid black robot back to a locker. Its crest shimmered at his touch, and again that dim singsong came, "Out of service. Re-porting malfunction. Storage overload. Out—"

He stripped and pulled on his lifeskin. One more cunning eld-ren device, designed never to fail. Yet not quite perfect. Sealing it around him, he caught a faint stink of old sweat. He always itched inside it, somewhere he couldn't scratch.

"I fear this place." Gibbon followed him into the lock, and out into the flashing dark. "I fear for my—"

"Translation difficulty, sir." The crisp synthetic voice of the translation program cut in. "Data banks contain no precise equivalent for Hydran term. Possible approximations: *wholeness, sanity, soul.*"

"We are Hydrans." Gibbon's own uneasy voice returned. "We are bred for a rational universe. I sense illogic here, and it disables me. Bold Scholar, I am pleased to have you with me here. Though your primitive nature may cloud your future in the halo, it can serve us now. Will you let me follow you?"

"Okay."

Off the craft, Benn anchored it to the empty pad where the supply craft had been secured and swam ahead through the green-and-amber flicker.

"Which way now?"

"Take the transport tube."

A thin pencil of blue light shone out of Gibbon's knobby body, pointing where to go. Benn followed it to the lip of a dark-walled pit. Gibbon waved him into it with a bare, human-formed arm and flashed his light against a glowing panel.

"This should move us."

They waited. Nothing happened.

"Maybe the power plant went out," Benn suggested. "Perhaps the whole station failed."

"Power plants do not go out." Gibbon's voice grew sharper in his helmet. "The entire station could not fail. Not from any rational cause I am able to perceive."

"Let's find out."

His headlamp lit the pit, and his thruster pushed him down it. At the bottom, they came out upon another open platform, where skeletal towers and tanklike shells loomed against the stars all around them. Gibbon's searching beam darted across it and stopped on a motionless robot.

Few eldren robots were human-form. This one's body was a flattened globe, glinting blue in that thin blue beam. Two of its thin limbs coiled around a railing. Three more held burdens: a boxlike object and three lumpy bags.

"Lyran-form," Gibbon said. "The xenologist is a Lyran. His translator name is Marcopolo. He and my brother have been friends since they served together on the core-star staff. He would not abandon my brother or his post of duty."

But he had fled, Benn thought, in such haste that he left his luggage.

Cautiously Gibbon hovered to examine it. His searching light picked out the robot's identity plate, flickered to luminous labels on the box and the bags.

"The robot was assigned to serve Marcopolo," he said. "But these items are not all his. These two belonged to a Scorpian cosmologist and a Cyngan linguist. This, to an Aquilan psychobiologist."

"Can you wake the robot?" Benn asked. "Could it tell us what happened?"

Gibbon's blue beam focused on the robot's sensors. Untranslated, his commands were squeaks and rattles. The robot stayed frozen, and Gibbon shrank from it.

"Something stopped the robot." His dim voice shivered. "Erased its computer. Something with secrets to conceal."

"We're here to find them out."

"I fear—fear what we may find." Gibbon swung to let that quick blue beam scan the empty platform. "Because such things should not be. Not here, Indomitable Scholar. Not here in a place of eldren science, which defies the irrational to create a new and larger order among the minds of the universe."

He formed two staring eyes, wide and strange. They narrowed to study the stopped robot, closed themselves against it, opened again to peer at Benn. The blue beam darted suddenly away, probing again into the dark maze around them.

"Generous Scholar, I beg you to understand my distraction. We Hydrans are creatures of reason, unprepared for such disorder. Observing your own primitive planet, I have seen your crude machines failing, seen your social systems collapsing, seen your fellow planetics behaving insanely. Such madness cannot happen here."

His light stabbed at Benn, dazzling him.

"Not to my dear brother."

KILIMANJARO

10

Marco Lara, her oldest friend. He had taught her the names of the birds and the stars, and how to read and write and how to throw the knife. She squatted a long time beside his body, too numb for tears. Too numb for anything. At last, with life enough to feel and move, she was hungry again.

And her father's daughter.

"Kwans don't quit." Words she recalled.

Departing silently in the dark, Hagland and his new followers had left a handful of food. She kindled a fire to roast an ear of green corn and a scrap of dried meat they had bartered from a Kikuyu trader.

She found no tools left that she could use to dig a grave, but her father and Marco had taught her to keep on coping. She dragged the body into a narrow cleft that running water had cut and spent the day carrying stones to cover it.

Through a restless night, she watched the satellite climb and vanish, return and sink. Before dawn she heard half a dozen distant shots. When cheerless day had come, she made herself another meager meal, packed her bedroll with the little food left, and set out toward where she thought the gunfire had been.

Bad country, since the skyweb fell. Too rough for boots in need of patching. Rifts of shattered masonry and strips of useless pavement showed through the thornbush, with most of the barren land eroded to gullied stone.

Before noon, she was climbing a rocky ridge where the company had left a trail. Near the summit, she found their camp abandoned, the fire dead. The empty cases of a few precious cartridges glinted in the ashes. When she picked up one of them, she saw that it had come from her father's gun. Doubtless Hagland's now.

Flies buzzed over dark blood splashed over a stone. Following traces where things had been dragged, she saw a vulture flap away and found three bodies dumped into a gully. No stones hid them. None of them was Hagland's, but she decided not to care.

She walked east, toward Kilimanjaro.

A walk of many days, with only the far blue loom of the mountain to guide her. The food was soon gone. One endless day she lay sweating under a blind downwind from a water hole, waiting for a thirsty antelope fawn to pass near enough. When its dried flesh was gone, she worked for three days helping a Kikuyu farmer dig a ditch above his narrow field. In exchange, she ate again and got a little bag of mealies.

The farmer laughed when she asked for news of Jomo Uruhu. He had spoken once with the old *mbashiri*, who was begging then for followers and food. Living now, so he had heard, with those few crazies who believed him high on the mountain in a ruin that had been the Tycoon's Amboseli lodge.

Day by day, the white peak loomed higher. She found her own wild hopes climbing with it. If that tiny colony on the far ice-mass called Janoort was still alive, if the halo was real, if it had kinder creatures than the monster that had come to rip the skyweb down, if these unlikely beings really wanted to befriend humankind—

If—

Sometimes, giddy with hunger, she almost believed. Day by day, she let that impossible vision entice her on. Night by night, watching that bright white star lifting out of the western dusk and falling into the dawn, she tried to deny that her father had followed dreams too far.

At last, far up the slopes, she found fields of weeds where Jomo and his people must have cleared land for crops, and came at last to a strip of cracked and broken concrete where she thought craft from space could have landed. A few kilometers beyond, she saw a clump of trees. On the lava ridge above, her head so light she thought at first that they could not be real, were half-shattered walls.

The Amboseli hunting lodge!

She shaded her lifted eyes, trembling with emotion. A relic of the Tycoon's splendor, it was still magnificent. Built of rough stone that was nearly the same color as the mountain, it stood above the spring that fed the water hole. Along the front of it ran a high gallery, where she thought the Kwans and their Sunbred guests must have stood or sat to do their killing.

All of them dead, twenty years and more. But if old Fernando Kwan's little colony was still alive in the halo, if Uruhu had in fact come home from Janoort with news of paradise, if he still expected help from friends out there—

She caught her breath and climbed again, into dismal ruin. Dark windows gaped like empty eye sockets in the high stone walls. Tall doors had been broken in. Wide floors inside were littered with broken bits of odd-looking stuff that wasn't quite metal, not quite plastic, not quite glass. One great chamber was black from fire that had burned inside it.

Had the Holyfolk been here?

Those odd bits of shattered stuff grated under her boots. She thought they must have been machines from space, but nothing left was whole enough to hint at how or where Jomo had gone. She found no weapons, no tools, no records of anything. The building had a sharp dry stink of decay and death.

If Jomo Uruhu had ever lived here, he was gone.

What now? Wandering on and on through empty, high-walled corridors, she found no promise of any world except Holyfolk and hunger and hyenas. A bleak depression settled upon her. If Jomo Uruhu had really come to promise a better sort of life, he had found no welcome here. Like her father's vision of the skyweb rewoven, her own formless hope flickered into nothing.

She found no food in the ruin, nothing of any use at all, but she dug a few yams and groundnuts out of a weed-clotted garden strip below the spring. That night she tried to sleep there, away from the musty-odored building and its feel of hopeless desolation. When the bright star rose once more out of the west, all it brought was mockery.

Still awake at midnight, aching with her long fatigue and bitter loneliness and the crush of final failure, she saw something else. A shooting star that burned through the blackness where the satellite had hurtled into shadow. A tiny spark at first, it grew and grew into a bright blue blade that sliced across the night.

Just a shooting star?

It did not fade. It seemed to slow and turn. Could it be an actual ship from space? Perhaps from Janoort? Here perhaps too late to rescue Jomo Uruhu? Breathing fast, she watched it descending among the northward stars. Toward the shattered concrete pad where the Tycoon and his guests had landed from their homes in the sky.

Breathless, sitting up in her hard bed, she watched it blaze into a high balloon that lit the far north horizon. It faded to a yellow spark that dropped, dimmed, and disappeared. She sat there until she shivered in the night wind. She thought it should have made a sound, but she heard no sound. Nothing else lit the sky. Nothing happened. At last she lay down again with the worn blanket over her and tried in vain to sleep.

At dawn, still sleepless, she was up again. Too eager to think of eating, she pulled on her worn-out boots and scrambled back down the slope. Stooping warily, she crept across the last kilometer, taut with fear of what she might discover.

Nothing. The pad lay empty as ever.

She limped back to the spring to build a fire and roast more yams. She searched the gardens again, packed what she found, and walked back down the slope, toward that north horizon. Somewhere out on the flat country, something had come down from space. Perhaps—

Perhaps—

She was half afraid to hope, more afraid not to hope. All alone in this cruel wilderness, she had nothing left here worth living for. Nor reason, she knew, to expect anything good from the unknown sky. Doggedly she walked on north. Because she was her father's daughter. Because she knew nothing else to do.

The rains came suddenly, early and savage. Savannah became swamp. She lost the knife, swimming a flooded wadi, found it again when the waters were gone. She boiled and ate the last of the yams. All she knew for a long time was mud and bugs and hunger.

In a spell of better weather, she came into the ruins of old Kilimanjaro Down. A great city of the vanished civilization, it had stood astride the equator, right beneath the skyweb. Hurricane and holocaust and falling stuff had leveled it. Twenty years of scrub and jungle had overrun the tumbled wreckage in the hollows, but higher ground still showed bare pavements running through the broken masonry of old foundations.

Following one wide avenue up a last long slope, she crested a ridge and saw the sun glancing off something white. It stood near the center of a patch of naked stone that must once have been a public square. A tapered rocket shape, still upright, it was not so large as she had somehow expected. Nor metal; it was something as white as Kilimanjaro snow. She stared for a moment, her breath stopped, wishing her father were there.

At last, an actual ship from space!

She took one eager step toward it and then dropped behind a granite jut that must have been a pedestal for some vanished monument. She knew this must be the craft that had lit the sky, but it was clearly nothing men had made. Nothing, she knew, that had come to rebuild the web or restore the Kwan Tycoons.

Instead—

She couldn't imagine what sort of creatures it might have brought or why they where there, but terror touched her. She remembered the beast that had wrecked the web, remembered the Holyfolk myths of malevolent demons in space. She had never wanted to believe them, but what else?

She crouched down, shivering for a moment under the African sun, and lay watching it. Nothing moved or changed. If game had been here, it had fled. No wind stirred. No creature flew or crept or cried. Afraid to go closer, she could not retreat. She had come too far, suffered too much. Hot sweat itched and tickled. Insects crawled on her. Something stung. Yet she dared not approach—

But something moved.

Two figures came around the ship from somewhere beyond. One was a man. Doll-small at first glance, he made the craft look taller than she had thought. His dark head bare, he was dressed much as she was in tattered scraps of old cloth and odd bits of slick-worn leather.

The other was nothing human.

1001101

0111100

1100101

11

Benn leaned in his lifeskin to tug at the tentacles that anchored the robot. They felt stiff as steel rods, cold even through his glove. He fixed his headlamp again on the box and the bags it had carried.

"Something hit the station." In spite of him, his voice in the bubble sounded hollow and uncertain. "Hard enough to panic the staff. They got away on the supply ship. Some of them, anyhow. This robot was killed before it could load their luggage."

"Impossible, Fellow Scholar. Here in the halo, who would kill?"

"Something did." He shook his head in the bubble. "Something knocked out Friday. Let's get on."

Gibbon floated behind, close enough to use his thin blue beam to search and point their way. Another long transit tube took them off that empty platform, into the living quarters of the staff. A pit of midnight. Their lights explored a wide, disk-shaped chamber. Doorways yawned into the dark around it, standing open.

Benn's headlamp found two more robots lying outside one door, sprawled and stiffened where they had fallen. One was Cyngan-form, the other Aquilan-form. Machines and containers they had carried lay scattered around them. One item was a little file of computer memory cubes, odd symbols glowing faintly on the index screen. Curious, he picked it up and tapped the keys until a line of green circles and red triangles flashed across the window, grouped in sevens.

"A binary number." Wondering, he read it aloud as a string of Terran digits. "1001101 0111100 1100101." He looked at Gibbon. "What would this be?"

"The business of Starsearch," Gibbon flickered dimly. "My brother waits here for signals from other star systems. The transmissions are nearly always reducible to a binary code."

"So this was a message from some other civilization?"

"Perhaps." Gibbon's knobby body bobbed, impatiently shrugging. "Though such messages were never frequent. Sometimes none in a Terran century. More probably, this is simply a set of useful reference programs someone wanted to carry away." He turned to let that blue beam scan the row of open doors. "My brother cannot have been one who ran. We must search for him."

Benn laid the cube back beside the rigid robot and followed Gibbon's beckoning beam. One by one, they pushed into the quarters of the Lyran, the Scorpian, the Aquilan. All had been left disordered, scattered items unsecured and adrift.

They explored the empty dwelling space of a cosmologist, of an engineer. The staff had come from half a dozen different eldren races. Though none required gaseous oxygen or liquid water or hydrocarbon foods, the station had been well designed to meet their varied needs. Gibbon's beam found power sources, sustenance dispensers, holo screens and data banks, objects perhaps of art that were riddles to him. Every space was unlit, silent, vacant.

One door was closed.

"My brother's." Gibbon decided, with his light upon it. A dim blue shimmer, a raspy whisper. "I knew he did not run, but I dare—I dare not see him now."

The door was unsecured. He shrank back while Benn slid it open, but then pushed anxiously ahead into the gloom. His voice-light shimmered, calling to his brother in a clatter and squeal of untranslated Hydran.

Nobody answered.

Inside, three empty spaces opened from a central foyer. They looked austere to Benn, almost bare. Gibbon stopped before a patterned tapestry that covered most of a wall. Benn paused beside him, staring, fascinated and bewildered as he always was by Hydran art. Not for the human mind, it hurt his eyes, or perhaps his brain, when he tried to understand it. Its patterns of color and form seemed to change with every shift of his gaze, tantalizing him with hints of meaning he could never quite grasp.

"My brother's birth robe." Gibbon hung there a long time before it, his body-glow blue and dim. "My own is back where we were born in Heart of Hydra. They are gifts we exchanged before we parted, to be kept through all our lives and hung with our father's in the ancestral dwelling of our clone. He fissioned there to bear us, and our first holy duty was the writing of his memorial records into the sacred fabric of his own robe."

Still adrift before it, he seemed to shiver.

"My brother's—" Silent again, his body dark and stiff, he let that blue beam rove across the robe. It seemed a long time before he went on. "When his own time arrives—when he becomes two— his sons will write his own memorial into it. If—"

Silent again, he swung abruptly away to begin their exploration of the other rooms. Benn recognized the holo terminals, the datastorage banks, the little tanks of fluid that fed the Hydran biochemistry, but not much else. Gibbon seemed to find nothing out of place, until at last he turned to go.

"Perhaps my brother is still at his post."

His light beckoned for Benn to lead them on. Beyond another dead transit tube, they came out into one more dark and soundless cavern, ringed with terminals for the search equipment. The actual instruments, the dishes and antennas, the telescopes and lidarscopes and radioscopes and nanoscopes, were all installed on the other moonlet, safely away from the vibration and radiation of anything alive.

Here were the consoles and monitors, inputs and outputs for the eyes and the ears that watched and listened for emerging minds across the cosmos. The instruments that amplified and recorded the signals, the data files, the looming gray cases of the great translators. The optical terminals and the local nanionic terminals for communications here within the halo.

All dead. Too much darkness, too much stillness. Benn felt a glacial chill seeping through him, even in the lifeskin.

Gibbon's thin blue ray stabbed and stabbed at the loom of huge machines until he stopped at last, adrift in the middle of that central chamber, his search beam gone dark as the midnight around them, his body-light dimmed to a ghostly blue aura. The long-range gear was a glittering mystery to Benn, but he moved on alone to the remote controls of the generator, which he almost understood.

Dead.

"The generator failed." He blinked at Gibbon's shadow shape. "That killed everything."

"A failure of the generator would not stop the robots," Gibbon objected, flickering faintly blue. "Not at once. They had emergency storage units of their own."

"If that's true—" He found no more to say.

They followed another transport tunnel to the power plant. Fueled with hydrogen from the halo ices, it was a fusion system— lifeless now. Benn saw no glow of any instrument, felt no vibration anywhere. Gibbon extruded new organs to probe it and finally shrank away from its pumps and tanks and shielded chambers as if they had been alien monsters crouching.

"I discover no actual damage or malfunction." His shimmer was hard to see, his voice hard to hear. "Apparently the master computer simply shut it down, as the result of a sudden uncontrolled overload. Something for which I see no rational explanation, because the system had redundant safeguards designed to protect it from any possible accident."

"Where is this master computer?"

"A network, in the laboratory section. We will find it also dead."

The blue beam pointed, and Gibbon let him lead the way again into another midnight pit, more dark and open doorways spaced around it. One by one, he followed his headlamp through them. Amid the mass and glint of machines he didn't know, they found dead monitors, stopped computers, unlit terminals. Lyran-form and Cygnan-form and Aquilan-form robots had frozen at their tasks.

One by one, they pushed into the laboratories. The cosmologist's, walls covered with dead holos of a hundred neighbor galaxies. The linguist's, where all the known literature of every known race was filed in storage cubes along endless narrow corridors. The xenologist's, a conclave of alien monsters crouching in the gloom, dead as the robots frozen among them.

"My brother's workspace."

Gibbon had left it for the last. His voice was a husky rustle. Pointing the way, he waited once more for Benn to go ahead.

"I fear for him."

An empty corridor beyond another unsecured doorway led them into Galileo's office. The quick flicker of their lamps found the big potato shape on the floor beside a dead computer.

Dead.

Gibbon's twin, once identical in shape, torn and charred now as if by a lightning stroke. The end of it had burst, flaps of blackened skin peeled away from ripped and darkened tissue. One burned and stiffened tentacle reached toward the dead computer.

"My brother—"

Gibbon stretched a thin and wavering filament toward the body. Dark at first, it shone dimly blue. It froze as if with dread, recoiled and probed again. Tenderly it touched the burns and lacerations, and finally stretched again to embrace the stiffened body.

"He is me—"

Cold blue light washed Gibbon's knobby shape, motionless as the other. The dying voice became a low howling sound that faded slowly into a faint, falling moan. That ceased at last. The bodylight went out. Adrift in the darkness, all color gone, Gibbon looked as rigid and lifeless as his brother.

NEBO

12

Bolivar stayed with Jomo Uruhu and his few converts, learning all he could about Janoort and its colonists, until the night Holyfolk raiders attacked the Amboseli lodge. Escaping alive, he never went back to learn whether the old man had been butchered for that faded Sunmark, never forgot the halo's promise.

Wandering again, but hoping to see the supply ship returning, he stayed near and watched the sky. He was a hundred kilometers from the site of old Kilimanjaro Down, trailing a wildebeest a lion had mauled, when he saw the spacecraft descending. Two days after, he pushed through the thornbush where the city had been and stopped in dazzlement when he found the tall craft standing in an open space, blindingly white.

That whiteness terrified him. It said the ship was not from any human world. The Holyfolk myths of the halo as hell were still so vivid in his mind that he wanted to run, until he remembered his mother. *"Se nos arriesgamos—"* she used to say, and shake her head.

No risk, no win.

Yet, not pushing his luck, he found a spot where he could lie on a level bit of old pavement and watch the craft through a screen of brush. The Sun went down, but still it shone in the dusk with a white luminescence that faded slowly until a gibbous moon rose to restore its ghostly glow.

All night he watched. The vessel showed no other light. Nothing moving about it; nothing came or went. When the Sun rose again, he relieved himself and chewed his last scrap of dried meat. With a catch of his breath, he stood up in plain sight and walked on toward the white craft.

He stopped with his heart in his mouth when something came around it. Something lurched to meet him, something more hideous than the worst of the Holyfolk demons, yet grotesquely humanlike. Naked except for a sort of harness made of broad black straps, it was armored with thick gray-green scales almost the color of tarnished copper. Its massive three-toed feet and three-fingered hands had savage black talons.

The head was bullet-shaped, the dull color of worn steel. It grinned at him with gaping, black-toothed jaws that looked fit for crushing stone. Red heat stung him from two deep-sunk spots that he thought were eyes, until he saw the actual eyes just beneath, bright black points peering out of narrow slits between thick steel ridges.

His terror grew as it tramped on toward him. *Wait till it comes three more steps*, he told himself. *Three more . . . Three more.* He was cold with sweat before it slowed and stopped.

The red spots flickered, so hot he wanted to cover his face. One great, clumsy-seeming claw unfastened a dark device from the harness and thrust it at him. It rumbled at him, softly at first but louder and louder, barked and roared, drummed and paused, howled and paused, screeched and gabbled until he began to make out sounds he thought were words. Swahili? Spanish? French?

"English?" A deafening bellow. "Comprehend?"

"I know English," he shouted when it paused. "Please, not quite so loud."

"Terran race?" Not so loud, the tone turned tentative. "You are dominant?"

"I'm human," he said. "We used to be dominant. I'm not sure now."

"Call me Nebo."

"My name is Bolivar." He remembered the bullies at school. "Don Diego Bolivar."

"Terran Bolivar?" A fearful claw moved as if to crush him. "You are a master of land?"

"What do you mean?"

"Hear me now!" A drummed command. "I am Nebo. My race is Red Delver. My world is Blade. If you wish identification, I am a tourist guide there, duly licensed and bonded, but I bring no tourists here. I come to trade."

"Trade?" He peered at the white ship. "What do you trade?"

"That we can discuss. My people were traders for a thousand generations. I wish to open trade with Terra, if that becomes possible."

"Why not?" He dared to step closer. "I'm listening."

"Commerce with Terra has been illegal." The monster paused to look across the brush and broken stone around them. "Illegal," he rumbled again, "because your evolution has been protected. Now that your natives have made contact with the Elderhood, that quarantine should be lifted. Anticipating that, I wish to deal with a master of land. You understand?"

Bolivar nodded, wondering what he saw worth trading for.

"You are a master of land?"

"Sure." Reflecting briefly, he swept his arm across the ruins. "As far as we can see."

The red eye-spots seemed hotter for a moment, and he thought the steel slits narrowed.

"Master of Terrans?"

"Other Terrans are pretty scarce. Masters of nothing."

"Where are they?"

"Far north." He gestured. "Far south. Most call themselves Holyfolk. You'll find no trading friends among them."

"Far?" The armored eyes narrowed, and he wondered if Nebo was shrewder than he looked. "Traces are visible near us. Smoke from combustion. Cultured vegetation."

"There are people called Kikuyu, who hunt or farm small fields. They have nothing worth trading. There was an old black man among them, who said he had been out to the ice-halo. He is probably dead. There was another old rogue who called himself Maximilian Kwan."

"Kwan?" A gleam of interest, and a bellowing growl. "Tell me about Maximilian Kwan."

"I never saw him. He used to claim that his family owned the Sun Company, which owned space before the skyweb fell. Claimed he was the last surviving heir, with the right to name himself the new Sun Tycoon."

"I wish to meet this Sun Tycoon." Nebo swayed heavily closer and Bolivar caught an odor like hot sulfur. "Where is Maximilian Kwan?"

"I don't know. Maybe dead. Or anywhere." He swept his arm toward the far-off mountain. "But he's no Tycoon. Has no home. Master of no land anywhere. His army? A handful of ragged thieves living in hiding from the Holyfolk."

The eye-spots scanned him again, that burning odor sharper. "I will speak to Maximilian Kwan."

"If he's alive—" Bolivar shrugged.

"You will help me find him." The black-taloned arm gestured imperatively. "Come aboard."

Following him toward the white craft, Bolivar caught a biting hot-sulfur whiff and shivered to a moment of nightmare dread. Could the Holyfolk myths be truth? Was he blundering into an actual hell? It was not too late to cut and run, but he recalled his mother and caught a cleaner breath and ventured on.

"No harm." At the foot of a narrow ramp, the monster turned back with another frightful grin. "Harm to any Terran native is still strictly forbidden. You will find breathable gases in the passenger compartments. Temperatures can be controlled. If you need nutrients, I can supply the essential fluids and solids to support Terran metabolism."

"I am hungry," he admitted. "Thirsty, too. This is unkind country."

The passenger cabin was a strange place that smelled too strongly of Nebo himself, but there was a sort of table where he could sit with his host towering over him. A little silver bubble danced around him; a machine inside brought him drinkable water and a dish of hard little biscuits with a nutlike flavor. He made a face at the first taste, but ate them all and finally asked for more.

They talked. Though Nebo had evidently kept cautiously close to his ship, he knew more about most of the planet than Bolivar did. As yet he had no legal status here, but the Red Delvers had never shrunk from risks. He was determined to find Maximilian Kwan.

"If he's alive," Bolivar repeated. "The Holyfolk were hunting him, because he wore the golden brand that showed him to be a Kwan. Any search will put me in danger." He studied Nebo's hard metallic mask, wondering what he could bargain for. "Why should I risk it?"

"We are traders. What do you ask for?"

He couldn't help shrinking from the red-blazing eye-spots, the thin steel slits that hid the actual eyes, the whole gigantic beast. But his mother, like the Red Delvers, had never shrunk from a chance.

"Can you—" Nebo's hot stink took his breath, and he almost coughed. "Can you take me back to where you live?"

"You are not a citizen." The hard-armored head shook in a grotesquely human way. "My planet is Blade. Not at all suitable for you."

"Suppose I took a chance?"

Nebo considered, tiny black eyes glittering behind the jutting ridges.

"You might try for Game of Blade and Stone," the soft thunder rolled from his translator at last. "Players are accepted with no citizenship required."

"A game?" At school, he had always loved getting the best of the other boys. By any means that worked. "Tell me about the game."

"The game is played in the ancient mines of our sister planet, Stone. Winners are commonly granted citizenship in the Elderhood. Losers may die."

"I'll risk it."

"Better stay here. Blade and Stone are not fit for Terrans."

"Tell me why."

They talked most of the day. Nebo summarized the troubled history of his Red Delver race. He described the twin worlds of Blade and Stone. He projected holo pictures of the tunnels and pits and caverns where the game was played. Speaking of himself, he came to seem strangely akin to Bolivar's mother.

Bolivar slept aboard the ship that night, in a sort of cage near enough like a bed. Next day, his pack filled with food and drink from the craft, he went out to search for Maximilian Kwan. On the third day he encountered a Kikuyu farmer who had traded a bag of millet to one of Kwan's men for an old hunting gun with a broken stock and no ammunition. The trader told him that in fact Maximilian Kwan was dead.

"Unfortunate for me," Nebo rumbled when he heard. "More fortunate for you. The game is not for Terrans."

"Still," he said, "I'll take my chances."

"Impossible." Muffled thunder he tried not to hear. "No Maximilian Kwan, no deal."

"Listen!" He managed to grin into that appalling grin. "Here's another deal. You wanted mining rights from Kwan? Why not from me? My own right to grant anything is just as good as his. After all, who in the halo knew Maximilian Kwan?"

Those slitted eyes squinted till he trembled.

"Give me time! I can produce the proof. Documents to show I'm the last surviving heir to the family of Kwan. Legal master of Earth. The rightful new Sun Tycoon. Good enough?"

Nebo's scowl grew diabolical. His tiny eyes squinted at Bolivar and squinted across the desert.

"Just one day! Maybe two days—"

"I have no time." He squinted into the dusty sky, and the translator drummed again with a dull finality. "My craft has been observed from the satellite station. The robots there are demanding evidence of my authority to be here. I have agreed to leave at sunrise."

Courteously, however, Nebo allowed him to eat and stay aboard through the night for another round of questions about the natural resources of the planet. Unconcerned that Earth had already been mined, he said the Red Delvers knew how to go deeper.

They were outside the lock at sunrise, saying farewell, when the robot alerted Nebo. It spoke with only a flicker of light, but Nebo translated.

"There's another native walking toward us."

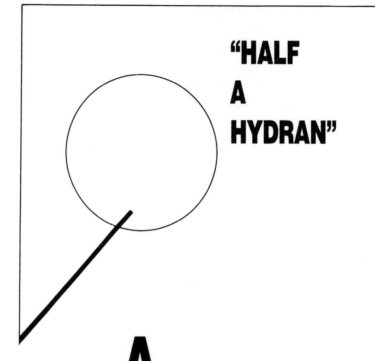

"HALF
A
HYDRAN"

13

A surge of power had burned out the big computer. Its eldren stuff had fused and slumped; molten drops had exploded from it. Galileo's thick potato body sprawled beside it, seared and burst and dead. Gibbon had extended a flap of shapeless flesh to hug his brother's body and lay there with him, as dark and still as he was.

Benn gripped and shook his rigid form, until at last he shone feebly blue, as if speaking took all his strength and will.

"Forgive me, Devoted Scholar, but I cannot leave my brother . . . We were one . . . Without him I am less . . . less than half a Hydran."

"He is dead," Benn whispered. "And we can't stay here."

"He is dead." A dim echo. "Killed by the aliens? The aliens he detained? Where are they?"

"Where were they living?"

"Detention cells . . . Upper level."

"I'll see—" His own voice was suddenly unsteady. "See if they are there."

To reach the "upper" level, he climbed through another transit tube, against the slow spin of the station and toward the storage tanks at its center. He came out into more midnight, on another narrow platform between the long row of cells and the huge tanks that stored feedstocks for the processing plants and the fluids kept ready to fit the varied needs of the staff and expected interstellar guests.

Doors along the platform stood open on the cells, caves of blackness, large enough for any likely occupant and all identical. The back walls held arrays of eldren symbols above colored buttons to be pushed and slots that must have dispensed necessities. Nothing told him anything about the prisoners or the manner of their escape.

Gibbon had recovered a little when he came back, his light and voice a little stronger.

"Zealous Scholar," his blue shimmer greeted Benn, "we must go. When we can. My brother must be carried home . . . to his own sacred place . . . on Heart of Hydra . . . wrapped in his birth robe . . . Can you bring it here?"

He went back again through the haunted dark to Galileo's empty quarters. Trying not to look too long at its shifting patterns, he pulled the robe off the wall and rolled it up and brought it back to the fused computer.

Laboriously Gibbon helped him wrap the body and followed as he carried it back across the starlit platforms, though the dark transit tubes, and into the flicker of amber and green, amber and green, on the landing stage. Though it was almost weightless here, its shape and mass made it an awkward burden, but he got it aboard the *Terra Two* and into an unheated cargo tank.

"Shall I take us off?"

"Not yet." Gibbon stayed with the bundled body, floating close above it. "We do not know what caused my brother's death, but we saw one possible clue I wish to examine. That is the file of computer data cubes the robots were bringing off the station when they were disabled. Faithful Scholar, will you bring them for me?"

On his way off the craft, he looked again at Friday. It stood rigid in the storage tank where he had left it, great black lenses staring blindly at him. Its crest was dark until he touched its arm.

Mechanical as the machine was, it shimmered faintly. "Out of service. Reporting malfunction. Storage overload. Out of ser—"

He stopped a moment, shivering as he stood on the brink of that first dark transit tube beneath the flicker of starlight and green, starlight and amber, starlight and green. The station had become an eerie place, haunted in his mind with the spirits of all the alien creatures its beacons had brought here from unknown stars.

He caught his breath and dived again into the tube, but his nerves were getting edgy. In too much haste, yet pausing too often to peer into the shadowed starlight around him and behind, he crossed another platform, dived though another black pit, and came at last to the two stopped robots, the Cygnan-form and the Lyran-form, sprawled among the scattered burdens they had dropped.

In spite of his tension, he stopped there, groping against the riddles around him. The power failure could have shut the station down, perhaps even forced the staff to leave. But why their apparent desperate haste? A surge of power from the failing plant could have burned out Galileo's computer and electrocuted him. But what had frozen all these robots so suddenly, in spite of their independent power cells?

And even Friday, struck aboard the *Terra Two?*

Hurrying too fast, breathing too hard, he found the data file again where he had laid it beside the robots. He carried it back to the craft, searching his mind for anything that might hint at the truth about the aliens gone from those empty cells. Were they the actual killers?

Likely enough, so he thought. Their natures and their powers and their purposes unknown, Galileo must have seen very solid reasons to detain them. Reviewing the little he knew about them, the equivocal accounts they had given about how they got here, the improbable coincidence of their arrivals, their evasions and unreasonable demands, he reached no comforting conclusions.

Where were they now?

Back aboard, he found Gibbon still huddled above the body in its crazy-patterned robe, Friday still standing motionless in the storage tank. He took the craft off at once, glad to be watching that dark-and-amber, dark-and-green, dark-and-amber flicker dimming until it lost itself against the starry dark, yet not much relieved. Too many dark unknowns had come with them from the murdered station.

In flight, he left the craft on auto when he could. He went back for frequent looks at the black robot. It had never moved, but it always murmured faintly when he touched it. "Out of service. Reporting malfunction. Storage overload."

Gibbon had settled over the body in the birth robe, thin strips of darkened, stiffened flesh extruded now to hold him to it. His own body as lax and dark as Galileo's, he made very brief responses when Benn tried to talk.

"Forgive me, Dutiful Scholar," he flickered very faintly, never moving. "But I have no will for anything except to take my brother home. He and I were one. Since he is dead, I am less than nothing. Yet—" The feeble glow grew briefly stronger. "His killer must be known."

They left the black robot at Cluster One.

"Restore it to service." Gibbon roused himself to give instructions to the omniform utility robots who came to take it off. "Identify whatever malfunction stopped it. Recover all you can of any memories recorded before it was disabled by the storage overload. Keep a record of all you discover and forward it at once to me at Heart of Hydra."

"Instructions filed, sir."

"Every effort must be made to locate the service craft *Mind-quest*, which had left the station before we arrived. The missing members of the station staff are probably aboard, possibly as prisoners of the three interstellar aliens my brother had detained there. The intentions and capacities of those creatures are unknown. They should be approached with caution."

"Instructions filed, sir."

"A salvage-and-repair expedition to Starsearch must be mounted as soon as possible. Staff members should be warned of possible hazards from whatever agency sabotaged the power plant, ended all service from autonomous robots on or near the station, and caused my brother's death. The nature of that agency must be determined and reported to me without delay."

"Instructions filed, sir."

Benn called home. His father was out, attending a special meeting of the Council of the Elderhood. He talked to his mother. Perhaps the meeting had been called to discuss some unexpected emergency, related possibly to a rumor of some disaster at the Star-search station. She didn't know. She had been distressed by the rumors and anxious about him. She begged him to come home.

"Just to let me see you, Bennie. For dinner, if you can manage time. I'll try to call your father."

"I'm okay," he told me. "But Dr. Gibbon needs me with him. His brother is dead. We're taking the body home to Hydra. Dr. Gibbon himself isn't much better off. I can't leave him now, or take time for anything."

"Careful, Benn! Do take care!"

OLD ZAROTH

14

Coming around the tall white craft, the two figures stopped when they saw her and stood a moment looking. Then the man walked on toward her. The other figure turned back out of sight. The distance was nearly two hundred meters. She hadn't seen it clearly, but the thing had looked larger than a man. More like an upright crocodile.

She caught her breath and went on to meet the man. He seemed as human as she was, clad just as roughly. Slender and dark, she soon saw, and nearly as handsome as her father had been. He carried no visible weapon, but her hand dropped near her knife when she saw the eager way he eyed her, as if to see beneath her odd array of rawhide and rags.

"*Jambo*." He spoke first in Swahili but grinned and changed to English when he saw her hand at the knife. "Sorry if I frightened you. I mean no harm."

"Hello." She looked up at the dazzle of the craft. "What was that—that creature with you?"

"A friend." He shrugged. "Not so bad as he looks." He studied her again, too searchingly. "You don't look like anybody I could have expected. Who, exactly, are you?"

She hesitated, scanning him. Good-looking, she thought. Her father had taught her to mistrust good looks, but she decided to answer.

"My name is Roxane Kwan."

"Kwan?" His voice lifted, his dark eyes wider. "Did you know a man named Maximilian Kwan?"

"He was my father."

"Your father?" She saw a difference in his stare. "The Sun Tycoon?"

"He claimed he had a right to be."

"But I hear that he's dead, which would make you the legal Tycoon."

"I guess I could claim the title."

"In that case, Miss Kwan—" His grin broader, he nodded at the white ship. "My friend and I have an opportunity for you." He hesitated. "That is, if you're game for a trip to the space halo."

She trembled, half in terror of a trip anywhere with this dark stranger and his unknown friend, half in unbelieving expectation. She had to get her breath before she spoke.

"My father . . ." She began uncertainly. "He is dead. I have nothing left on Earth. I walked a good many days to get here, because I hoped for something new. Tell me about this trip to space."

"First—" He frowned. "Can you prove who you are?"

"As well as my father ever did."

"Documents?"

"His ring." She would not betray his memory. "All he left me."

She offered her left hand, the early sun burning golden on the round topaz, and tried not to flinch from his touch. Her right hand still near the knife, she let him slip the ring off her finger. Frowning at it, he found the name inside, which she had never seen. Max Kwan. Cut a little roughly, she thought when he returned it, but he was nodding as if happy with what he had seen.

"Come on aboard." He gestured. "The story will take explaining, and I guess you'd better meet my friend. Anyhow, I imagine you're hungry?"

"Starving."

Yet, halfway to the craft, she stopped, waiting for him to turn back.

"You need to know one thing." She faced him, her hand on the hilt of the knife. "I was one of my father's men. That's the way I grew up. Whatever happens, I want to be treated like one more man. I won't be another man's woman."

Puzzled for a moment, Bolivar laughed.

"I like you." He waved away her warning, speaking easily. "With a bath and a new outfit and a few meals in you, you'll be beautiful. But we don't want you for that." He offered a strong brown hand. "Take my word."

She looked into his eyes for a moment, and gripped his hand.

Prepared for new things, she found them on the craft. She felt apprehensive about Bolivar's friend, but he was not in sight. They sat at a kind of table, and a quick little machine brought them something in a queer-shaped cup and dishes of what Bolivar said was food. The tastes were strange at first, but she was hungry enough to eat.

She asked, "What do you want me for?"

"My friend says he's a miner. The ores on his own world are all worked out. It seems there's somebody he calls the Elderhood that has quarantined Earth. He needs evidence to show them that he has a legal right to open mines here."

She stared across the table. "What has that to do with me?"

"You'll call yourself the new Sun Tycoon." He grinned, happy with the notion. "Claim you own or rule the Earth. Sign whatever documents the Elderhood requires. Testify in a court—if they have courts, and if he needs you."

"I don't own the Earth." She shook her head, astonished. "The Kwans never did. They managed well enough without. Selling synthetic foods and gravity power. Trading what they found in space—"

"No matter." He gestured to sweep her doubts away. "Things have changed."

"All I have is my father's ring—"

"Still no matter." He squinted at her shrewdly. "My friend seems to know his way. I've been around. If we need more evidence, I think we can arrange it."

"I'm not sure—" Hesitant, she shook her head. "Not sure my father really was a Kwan."

"Who cares?" He shrugged and pushed his drink aside, bending toward her. "Think it over. Think what you've got here on Earth. Balance it against what all we can promise you."

Listening, she bit her sun-cracked lip.

"I've heard about your father. I guess you know most people called him crazy. For talking the way he did about building the skyweb back and restoring our space empire. But think about it. My friend and I can do it for you."

He stopped to wait while she thought about it.

"Really?" She frowned at him. "Can you?"

"Look around you." He gestured at the robot, the strange white walls, the dishes on the table. "Look outside."

A wide oval window at the end of the table looked out over the dead ruins of Kilimanjaro Down and the drought-browned thornbush beyond, where waves of African heat were already dancing.

"Make your choice."

"Not yet—"

She shrank from something like a lion's roar and crouched away from the monstrous thing coming into the room. Bolivar stood up with Sun Country manners to introduce them.

"Miss Roxane Kwan, my friend Nebo."

Seen close up, Nebo looked a little like a gigantic man, more like a crocodile, not much like either. Gazing down at her, he made something like a bow. She cringed from the hot radiance of two red spots that looked like eyes and then saw the bright black actual eyes peering out of hard-armored slits beneath them.

"He comes from a far planet he calls Blade." A pygmy beside him, Bolivar stepped boldly to put an arm around his coppery bulk. "It's part of a double world named Mazeway. He wants mining rights."

"You are Kwan?" She flinched again from those hot red spots. "Sun Tycoon?"

"As soon as she claims the title," Bolivar answered before she could speak. "We can prove who she is." He turned to her. "Show him the ring. He means no harm with the heat. His eyes work best with the infrared."

She offered the ring. It shone red beneath the spots as Nebo turned it and gave it back with a black-taloned paw that made a lion's seem harmless. The red beams stung her face again.

"We need such evidence." The lion's roar spoke out of a device fastened to the black straps around him. "You come to Blade? Contest Game of Blade and Stone? Offer evidence?"

"A game?"

"A popular sport on his world." Bolivar spoke up quickly. "I gather that we'll both have to play."

"What sort of game?" She stared at him. "I never played games."

"We'll learn the rules as we go," he told her. "We must enter it, to get permission to visit Mazeway."

Nebo swung away, rumbling impatiently. She didn't get all the roaring words, but Bolivar told her, "Seems he's here without permission. He has stayed about as long as he dares. It's time for you to make your choice. Are you with us?"

She looked past them, at that great window. A brown dust devil was crawling across the hot horizon, far beyond the ruins. Her heart was thumping. For a moment she couldn't breathe. Perhaps her father's dream was really coming true. Though not for him. She flinched from the thought and reached to take Bolivar's offered hand.

"I'm with you."

The craft lifted at once, silently and swiftly. The motion gave her moments of giddiness, but that didn't matter. Watching from the window, she saw the patterned avenues of the old city fall away. The earth beneath shrank fast and soon blurred with haze. The brooding bulk of Kilimanjaro became a white-topped mound. The sky turned purple, then darkened into starry blackness. She glimpsed a huge bare Moon, briefly larger than the shrinking earth. Both dropped into midnight, and then even the stars were gone.

Time on board became strange as the craft itself. Bolivar wore a gem-set timepiece that showed Earth time and Moon time and Mars time, and even the time of the lost Sun Fleet, but not the time of the ship. The days seemed oddly brief. Yet she slept, sweated in the gym, ate huge meals that began to taste good. And they talked.

Bolivar told her about his mother and Chandra Bey and his wonderful year at school in the skyweb. Once he had even seen the Sun Tycoon. He had lived through the fall of the skyweb and the cruel years after it. He had known the Holyfolk, known the old Kikuyu named Jomo Uruhu, who had lived on the asteroid Janoort and come home to spread the word of the eldren way.

"So we'll try Nebo's way." He shrugged, grinning a grin she had begun to like. "If there's anything better on Earth, I never found it. Truthfully, I don't know anything about Nebo or his funny game, but how can things get worse for us than they already are?"

"I don't know." A wry little shrug. "I hope we don't find out."

She spoke of her father and the mother she didn't remember. Of her father's men and her hard years of marching with them. About her father's death and the way she had killed Julio Vargas. She saw a fleeting tension on Bolivar's face when she came to that.

Nebo joined them only rarely, but once he sat on the end of the table because the seats were too small for him and talked about Mazeway. The twin planets, he said, must have been born somewhere near the Sun, where they gathered a wealth of the heavy metals that condensed first from the Solar nebula. Some forgotten cataclysm had flung them far into the icy halo, where such elements were precious.

His people were ancient, their origins forgotten. Their history was a cruel chronicle of wars. Myths said a mighty warrior-smith had forged them, each born clad in armor of his own. There had once been two races, the Red Delvers of Blade and the Yellow Delvers of Stone. Their cities had fought for dominion, until the great city of Zaroth ruled all Blade. Blade fought Stone, until the primarch of Zaroth had conquered all its tunnel worlds and killed the last of the Yellow Delvers.

Zaroth had ruled both planets through most of the ages since. Inventing the game as a way to end their own deadly quarrels, the primarchs had waged a more ambitious peace against the whole halo. For one long age, their miners and artisans and merchants had all but ruled it, their rich trading centers planted everywhere.

That commercial dominion ran down when the metals were gone, long before the first forebears of mankind had walked on Terra.

Nebo's home city was Zaroth. Now a vaster ruin than Kilimanjaro Down, a million times as old, it was not yet quite entirely dead. Hard times had come to Mazeway when the mines were empty and the merchants had to deal in plastics and glass, but the Delvers were cunning and tough. The game itself now kept them alive.

Now, so it seemed to Roxane, Nebo was living a strange parody of her father's dream. He would rebuild the skyweb, or at least enough of it to let new space docks ride far above Earth's gravity well. Red Delvers would come to mine the planet, digging deeper than men had ever gone. The metals of Earth could restore Mazeway's vanished greatness.

"If—" She couldn't catch their confidence. "If this Eldermost really does accept me as the true Tycoon."

They ignored her doubts and went on building their vast plans. The realities of that possibility were still hard for her to imagine. Bolivar kept insisting that the eldren were closer to angels than to the demons of Holyfolk myth, but he had never seen them. Jomo, he told her, had met two or three of them and found them astonishing but harmless. Once she tried to ask Nebo about what the other space races were like, but all she got was a booming grunt.

Outside the window, the stars came back. Bolivar said that meant they had slowed below the speed of light. There was no Sun, because they had come so far it was only a tiny star. Bolivar pointed to two round black spots growing against the stars. One of them swelled to blot out half the sky. She saw thin lines of light traced across it, the pattern a little like the streets of dead Kilimanjaro Down.

In the starlight, dim shapes swelled beneath the lines. They looked like toy forts standing abandoned and half destroyed in some empty playground. They grew until she saw they had once been gigantic towers. The craft came down on a vast flat platform, among scores of tall white craft.

"Zaroth!" she heard Bolivar whisper. "Old Zaroth!"

HEART OF HYDRA

15

They took the body back to Hydra.

Benn wanted to be on Mazeway, trying out for the game and doing what he could to win a human place in the halo. But he had to have a sponsor for that, and Gibbon lay dark and nearly lifeless under the birth robe in his cabin, unfit for anything. Until perhaps his Hydran doctors cured him.

At least, Benn tried to cheer himself, he would get to know more Hydrans. To survive in the halo, humanity must find friends, and the Hydrans seemed almost neighborly. Though still strange enough—he couldn't forget that globe of staring scientists around him at the university, when Gibbon showed him as a specimen Terran.

Nearing Hydra, he called ahead to report Galileo's death and ask for instructions. Replies were delayed at first, as if the news had brought consternation. When at last he got specific directions, they came from a clone-cousin of Gibbon's, asking him to land at Heart of Hydra.

Though his pilot monitor showed it well enough, Heart was a tiny world and difficult to see, the stars and darkness reflected in its sublimation shields not much different from the stars and darkness of the space beyond them. The terminal stage was in orbit around its own mirrored iceball.

A score of Hydrans were waiting when the *Terra Two* touched down. A thousand shapes, they all looked much alike to him. Knobby lumps of life, flickering with the quick-shifting colors of their speech, aspects forever changing with the organs they extended and used and withdrew. One stopped in the lock to flash rapid words at him.

"Greetings, Terran guest. You may call me Healer." He had a peanut shape Benn thought he could remember. "We express gratitude for your service to our dead kinsman and his severely injured sibling."

"Can you help Dr. Gibbon?"

With no immediate reply, Healer watched the birth-cloaked body carried off the craft. Gibbon floated close behind it with little more sign of life in his own dull-colored body or the limp gray flaps of unretracted flesh he trailed. Moving to follow, Healer turned back at last.

"I regret, Terran friend, that I can tell you so little. When we Hydrans fusion, we are never fully parted from our clones. Death is rare among us, but when it happens the clone rarely survives."

"Sir, you can't let him die! He wants to live. His brother was murdered at Starsearch. The murderer is unknown. I think you'll find him determined to identify the killer."

"Hydra thanks you, Honored Terran." Healer tipped to move away. "We shall undertake whatever therapy we can."

He wanted to follow through the lock, but another Hydran bobbed into his path.

"May I stay with him?"

"Sorry, sir!" The Hydran turned end over end in a gesture of extreme regret. "You are not permitted. You must understand that Heart is our most holy place. It holds the revered ancestral relics of our race. Even we may come here only for our sacred rituals of birth and sharing."

"Please let me know—"

Left behind, he had to wait aboard.

News of Gibbon, or from anybody else, was slow to come. In the pilot bubble, he could look out at the unchanging constellations and the creeping navigation lights that marked the shielded snow-balls clustered around him. In the comm room, he could watch Hydran holocasts, which seldom seemed to make much sense even in translation.

Though he had lived in the halo all his life, it was still too vast and too various. There were too many races of the eldren, their shapes and their minds and their lives too wildly unalike. Nearly all of them were still fantastic strangers, their languages not yet programmed into his translator. Their music was a meaningless flicker of light; their art bewildered him.

Sometimes he picked up holos of the Game of Blade and Stone. He watched with wistful interest, though words were not translated and the action shots came and went too fast for him to guess what was happening.

Nobody had ever taught him the rules, but he tried to follow the action. The caves of play were sometimes so vast that he could find no roofs or walls, sometimes fissures that looked too narrow for anything to pass or midnight chasms where he could find no floor. In those fleeting takes, the players were grotesque puppets. They climbed tall black cliffs. They swam down rivers that looked like fire. They flew on shining wings across wide black pits. They struggled through luminous nightmare jungles in flight from crea-tures like dragons. The game looked violent and dangerous. Though it was said to teach and test the eldren way, he learned no lessons he could understand.

Yet he longed for his chance.

Anxious about Gibbon, he tried again and again to call the moon of sharing. The robots at the terminal tower always answered that Healer could not be reached, but at last he did call back to say that Gibbon was under treatment, with no prognosis possible.

Benn asked about the treatment.

"A sacred ceremonial," Healer said. "Every Hydran clone comes from the birth robe suffering from a natal trauma. He has lost half of himself. In our therapeutic rituals, our elders try to repair that loss by sharing themselves. His clone's tragic death has left your friend a child again, wounded and alone, with no love to live for. We are attempting restoration."

Benn asked how minds were shared.

"By contact," Healer said. "The volunteer donors are rich in life, nearing their time for division. One of them lies with the patient in the same birth robe. He extends nerve tissue, which should fuse with the sufferer's. Their brains should link to allow the direct flow of memory and emotion, of mind."

"With Dr. Gibbon? Is it working?"

"Not yet." Healer's image spun in regret. "The patient has been comatose since he arrived here, life signs almost extinct. Though we are trying, no significant neural contact has yet been established."

Healer promised to call again when there was any change, and his holo image vanished.

Shut up in the ship, Benn watched the stars again and their reflections on the bright curve beneath the tower. He watched holodramas and news reports and tried to understand them. He persuaded the terminal robots to let him call his parents.

"Bennie!" The holophone's electron cloud showed his mother's anxious face. "Where are you?"

"Still in Hydra. Still hoping Dr. Gibbon will get well enough to sponsor me."

He asked for news.

"Nothing good." He saw the trouble on her face. "The worry's killing your father. He's always on the Council moon, trying to lobby for support. The Starsearch disaster is still a mystery, but Council members are saying they've been too open to aliens. They don't want the station repaired. And they don't want us—"

Her image vanished; his fractional minute was gone.

Waiting again, he worked out to keep himself fit. He watched the creeping moons of Heart and watched the holo monitors. He reread the poems of old Earth in the tattered book Runesong had given him the day she had to leave. He loved them as he had loved her, and the music of her voice, his own grandmother's voice, sang again in his mind when he recited them.

At last, the holophone chimed. The electron cloud shimmered and dimmed, shimmered and dimmed, so long that he thought there was interference with the signal wave, but Gibbon's bulbous body came into focus at last, still wrapped in the birth robe and trailing lax gray flaps. He saw no sign of life until a faint voice-light glowed along them.

"Terran Scholar?"

"I am Benn. How are you, sir?"

"Alive." The voice was slow and uncertain as the light, no words wasted on Hydran honorifics. "Recovering, however slowly." A pause, so long that he thought Gibbon had no strength to continue. "Benn, I have news for you."

"What is it, sir?"

He waited for that faint life-glow to pulse again.

"From Mazeway. About the aliens my brother had detained at Starsearch. They have arrived there with the *Mindquest*. Your disabled service robot with them. They are asking to enter the game."

"Sir?" He shook his head, unbelieving, wondering if Gibbon was hallucinating. "Are you sure?"

"I have called Cluster One for confirmation," the labored voice went on. "The story is true. The *Mindquest* docked there. It brought Director Archon and other survivors of the station staff, as well as the aliens."

"So they are safe?"

"Mentally stressed. They had to abandon most of their possessions and leave the station in haste. But none of them was physically injured."

"The aliens are free?"

Once more he had to wait while Gibbon gathered strength.

"At the director's command. He and the xenologist had never agreed with my brother's decision to detain them. He always wanted to welcome them as life-forms new to the halo and offering a wealth of unknown culture."

"Have they explained the disaster? What knocked the station out? What disabled Friday?"

"And killed—" The light died in those sagging strips of Hydran flesh and abruptly flashed again. The voice came back with sudden force. "Killed my brother! Archon doesn't know. He says the aliens don't. Perhaps your robot does."

"Friday?"

"A puzzle, Benn." The body twisted under the robe, as if with some feeble gesture. "The aliens discovered that we had left it at the service center. They asked to inspect it. One of them entered some instruction that broke the storage block."

"So he's okay?" Benn felt an odd relief, almost as if the robot had been a human friend.

"Not yet. Archon says there is some apparent damage to its permanent memory. The utility robots found it impossible to repair. They have allowed the aliens to bring it to Mazeway with them."

"Surely, sir, they won't be allowed to play?"

"I believe they will. It's a Delver game, and the Red Delvers have a tradition of independence. Since the game tests fitness, the judges have seldom excluded candidates from races apparently advanced."

"Who would sponsor them?"

"Archon seems willing to, unless they find support on Mazeway."

"Sir? Do you think—" Anxiety shook his voice. "Can you sponsor me?"

That strip of tissue was dark and silent so long that Benn found himself staring at the birth robe instead, trying in vain to grasp some constant pattern or meaning in its shifting colors and shadows. Baffled as always, feeling that the unwilling effort was somehow straining his eyes, he was almost startled by Gibbon's voice.

"I can, Benn. The judges agree that I need not attend. That is, if you still wish to play—"

"I do, sir!"

"Impetuous Scholar, you speak in undue haste." The dim voice turned reproachful. "I agree because I need you there, yet I cannot ask you to risk yourself."

"Dr. Gibbon, you know I'm ready."

"I wish you were." Gibbon moved again beneath the robe. "You have been a faithful scholar, Benn, if somewhat too impulsive. Your good parents are my friends. If you come to harm there, they will never forgive me. I will not forgive myself. Yet—I do need you."

"When can I go?"

"Not yet. We must wait for arrangements—"

Something stopped Gibbon's wavery voice. Other Hydran

limbs had come into the electron cloud, quick and vigorous tentacles reaching to draw the birth robe closer and lift his dark body away.

"I need you, Benn." That limp flap flickered again. "Because they are keeping me here. They are trying to knit the nerves of a donor into me. They want to replace my dead brother with bits of other beings.

"But nothing—"

He was gone.

BLADE

16

Down on the Zaroth terminal tower, they were about to leave the craft.

"Blade has nothing we can breathe," Bolivar told her. "We'll have to wear survival gear. Suits they call lifeskins. Those Nebo brought are fit-anybody models. The robot can adjust them to fit us, more or less. He says we can have our own made later."

Aboard the craft, their only space was the single, wide-windowed cabin. They had to strip there to let the robot seal them into the lifeskins. There was no privacy, but Roxane had grown up living with men in open camps. She felt no need to hide herself, but now she saw Bolivar eyeing her too avidly. Frowning at him, she hung her knife back in place, outside the suit.

"Better leave it off." He grinned. "The eldren disapprove of weapons."

"It's part of me. Don't forget!"

"Roxane, please!" He shook his head, looking hurt. "You're a beautiful woman. You've seen what I am. We may be together the rest of our lives." He grew more serious. "I think—I hope— a time will come when—"

"I told you once." She cut him sharply off. "I'm nobody's woman. I never will be. Remember that!"

"I'll try, babe." He shrugged, too casually. "But it won't be—easy." His grin froze under her hard stare, and his voice changed again. "Don't get me wrong. We can't afford to fight. We're after bigger game. We've got to trust each other. Let's both remember that."

"I'll remember." She nodded, but still her hand hung near the knife.

Breather bubbles sealed in place, they followed Nebo through the lock and off the craft. She stopped, shocked, when she got a clear view of old Zaroth. Beneath the high landing stage, it reached out beneath the starlight as far as she could see. Its dark towers had been gigantic. Almost as tall, she thought, as awesome Kilimanjaro. Half of them had been toppled, shattered, crushed. A few pale lights glowed or crept along the floor of narrow black canyons that wound away from the base of the tower, but the rest was dark desolation.

"Dead!" She shrank from it, whispering. "It's dead!"

"Dead a hundred million of your years, Miss Kwan." Nebo paused ahead of them to rumbled softly in the gloom. "Since the last primarchs killed it, fighting over the precious ores of Stone."

The glow of his eye-spots stung her cheeks, even in the helmet.

"You can make it live again, Miss Kwan. If the eldren accept you as the lawful Tycoon of Terra and you open its ores to us, you can enjoy all the splendors of the primarchs themselves."

Bolivar had stopped beside her. In the dimly glowing, form-fitting lifeskin, his lean athletic body still looked almost nude. The robot had brought his luggage, a travel-scarred leather bag stamped with a worn golden Sunmark. He grinned happily from his crystal bubble.

"So here we are!" His voice rang too loud in her own helmet. "Two hungry cheetahs, closing in to kill."

She decided not to tell him that female cheetahs hunt alone, but the word stirred recollections of all she had left so far behind. Her own first kill. Her father's pleased grin when he saw the waterbuck's blood. The name the men had given her. She stiffened, standing straighter. Even here on alien Blade, she was still a cheetah, still a Kwan.

The terminal platform lay vast and flat, a forest of white ships and dark machines looming high against the stars all around them. The lock was closing. The ship lifted and drifted away, as silent as starlit smoke. Standing there with Nebo and Bolivar, she suddenly felt too much alone, lost and defenseless in a world too vast to know.

"Terrans, come." Nebo's voice boomed in her helmet. "We have a place arranged for you."

In a moment she saw that he was following rainbow colors that pulsed along a line of light, guiding them through that starlit maze of tall white ships and gigantic strange machines. It led them to the brink of a yawning pit.

"Follow me."

He stepped into the pit and vanished. With a cheerful shrug at her, Bolivar followed. She checked herself on the rim, peering down. The pit looked dark and bottomless. Their tiny forms were already far below, falling fast. Suddenly giddy, she shrank back, but she could not be left behind. Trembling, she stepped off and fell.

Pale rings of light flashed upward around her. At last they slowed. She came down gently enough on a dimly lit floor and walked out to the top of a long ramp that sloped down into a wide open space. Wide—yet shut in by enormous buildings that towered all around it, so tall that she could see only a narrow strip of stars.

She found Nebo and Bolivar and stood blinking at the creatures that crowded the great space ahead like thirsty animals flocking around a water hole in a dry time, all of them different: warthogs and elephants, impalas and zebras, wildebeests and ibex. Or like the hungry predators swarming around a new kill: lions and cheetahs, foxes and jackals, hyenas and vultures.

Yet here was no kill, no water hole, not anything else she understood. Small and huge, these beings mingled in apparent peace, moving in ways she had never seen, floating, gliding, rolling. Some of their colors were bright as jungle flowers. Some of them flashed and shimmered with their own changing lights.

The eldren, she thought. Proud creatures who would look at human beings the way human beings looked at jungle beasts. Could she ever live among them, learn their ways, play their games? Could she really ever become the new Tycoon of Terra, trading them the metals of Earth for the means to rebuild the skyweb?

A crazy dream?

She was still her father's daughter, but she shivered in the lifeskin.

"Quickly!" Nebo's lion-voice was growling. "You must not remain in public view until arrangements for you have been confirmed."

That enormous square seemed far too public, but he plunged across it boldly, like some armored war machine. She hurried after him, almost running in the too-tight lifeskin. The halo people were busy all around them, bent on errands she couldn't imagine. Sometimes two of them stopped together, shimmering with their silent speech. Here and there larger clusters formed and flickered and dissolved.

They had a hundred eerie shapes, and they glowed and flashed and shone with many changing colors. She saw no other humans, and only a few Delvers like Nebo. None of them seemed to notice her or Bolivar, yet she had to cringe when one of them passed near. She couldn't quite forget that they had been the demons of the Holyfolk, intermixing with the first men in space to father the Sunbred, even the Kwans.

Nonsense. Yet she shivered to another chill, as if she had sweated in the lifeskin. Here in this city of goblins, she was about to cut her last tie to Earth and humankind. Trusting Nebo and Bolivar, had she been an idiot? Perhaps. Yet she caught her breath and hurried after them.

She tried to note everything she could, because everything was strange. In Africa, she had learned which animals were dangerous, which plants poisonous, which men bent on rape or murder. Here, any shape could be the shape of death.

Yet the exciting newness everywhere began to wash away her dread. The goblin crowds were pushing past sidewalk stands and brightly lit shops where Delver dealers waited with their merchandise. She tried to see what they sold, but the items she could glimpse made no sense to her.

"This way now." Nebo turned abruptly, hustling them out of the path of something a little like a man-sized moth that came flying just above the pavement on fixed crystal wings. "Until affairs can be arranged, you must be concealed."

They rushed after him through a gap in the row of booths and kiosks and shops, into an unlighted canyon where little starlight fell. She saw no more shops or shoppers, but now and then a lone Delver paused to flash its eye-spots at them before it hurried on. Nebo seemed to ignore them.

At the end of that long alley, they came out into what must have been another open square. A mountain filled it now: a looming pyramid of great black blocks that had tumbled from the shattered towers around it. They were alone in the crevice Nebo had followed, and he paused to gesture at an enormous black stone mass that blocked out the stars beyond.

"The House of Pain," his dull thunder-voice rang in her bubble. "We Delvers were giants once, before we knew the eldren. That fortress was the prison where our great primarchs put their enemies to torture and death. This ruined area is unrestored and still forbidden. It should be safe for you."

He led them on through the rubble, into a winding tunnel lit only by the flicker of his eye-spots and out again at the base of an unbroken wall. He stopped at a recessed door to blink his eye-spots against it. For a long time nothing happened, but at last the door slid aside to show a stair that climbed into the dark. The steps were half a meter high.

"Our first forebears were truly giants."

To her, Nebo himself seemed gigantic enough. His taloned paws seized their arms, not too roughly, to drag them up the tall steps into a lofty hall, bare-floored and unlighted, that stretched away as far as she could see. They followed him across it and into a high-vaulted room where a dozen Delvers sat along one side of a long crescent table facing a wall that looked blank to her. One at the center turned to wave a snaky arm to greet Nebo; the rest ignored him.

As he moved to lead them on again, that high wall vanished. Where it had been, she saw an enormous cavern. Black cliffs rose sheer from a red-glowing sea. She saw something crawling. It looked tiny till she made out a green-scaled Delver toiling up the cliffs. Red-winged birdlike things were diving at him out of the dark. Fighting them off, he slipped and fell and caught himself and climbed again.

Nebo stopped to watch with them until the climber reached his goal, a narrow ledge high on the cliff. When that happened, the Delvers stirred along the crescent table. The one at the center swept up stacks of little colored blocks and slid one tall stack to a grinning Delver at the end of the table.

They went on then, toward a doorway beyond the table. The cavern vanished as they moved, and the wall was blank again. When they were alone in another gloomy corridor, Bolivar asked, "Is that the game?"

"Gambling," Nebo rumbled. "Illegal."

"Whose law?"

"The law of the game, established by legal treaty between the game guild and the Elderhood." Nebo paused to face them in the dark, his eye-spots hot against her cheek. "The guild profits from play at the legal casinos. Holo transmissions of game play to such spots as this are severely restricted."

So that had been a holo of the actual game? Played in dark caves that had no air fit for human beings? It made Africa seem almost a gentle place. She wanted to ask how such a savage sport could teach the eldren way, but Nebo was already stalking on.

Another winding corridor led them into a wide circular pit where a spiral flight of gigantic steps climbed and fell as far as the crimson flicker and glow of Nebo's eye-spots happened to reach. The steps had no railing, and she stayed close to his scale-armored legs.

"We had our own metals once." His red beams danced to pick up jagged breaks at the ends of the steps. "There were metal railings here. Torn out for salvage."

They climbed again till her legs were aching. Scrambling blindly up the great broken steps, she clung to Nebo's snaky arm. Her heart was thumping, her mouth dry with dread. She had come a long way from Africa, or any world she knew. Zaroth had begun to look uncomfortably close to the Holyfolk hell. Yet, whatever happened, she promised herself not to be sorry she had come.

At last they left the pit. A massive door slid open to let them into a narrow chamber. She heard a hiss of air outside her helmet. Another door slid aside, and Nebo's red shine lit the bare stone walls of an empty cell, windowless and dark.

"Even if you have been seen," Nebo drummed, "you will not be discovered here. A secret place, where the primarch shut up his enemies."

She looked around the narrow cell and back into his monstrous face.

"Arrangements must be completed." The box flickered to his muffled boom. "Permits for your legal entry into Blade. Your sponsors for the game. Other more difficult negotiations. You will remain here until I return."

Lumbering back through the valve into the air lock, he looked more crocodile than man. She turned to blink uneasily at Bolivar. "Well, babe!" He grinned at her, fumbling to unseal his helmet. "My mother used to laugh at *que sera sera*. She always said life is what you make it. Now we've got our chance." Something hard edged his voice. "Don't spoil it!"

KYR STREET

17

Benn had learned too little eldren patience. The flight from Hydra out to Mazeway took too long. Alone aboard the *Terra Two*, he watched the nanionic instruments, ate his eldren synthetics, slept and dreamed of Starsearch and Gibbon and the aliens he had never seen.

The craft slowed at last. He saw the stars again, watched their colors shift from blue ahead and red behind back toward normal. He found the double blot the double planet made against the sky and followed the Zaroth beacon down to let him land among the tall white nanionic craft standing on the stage.

He looked down on old Zaroth from the pilot bubble, and all he had ever heard came back to wash him with awe at its ruined magnificence. A tiny patch of lighted streets sprawled around the foot of the terminal tower. Everywhere beyond, the ancient city stretched away, a megalopolis of vanished giants, dead since dinosaurs had ruled the far-off Earth.

Monumental palaces and keeps and citadels lay shattered and toppled into a desert of starlit desolation that spread away forever and forever. Far off, beneath the blaze of Orion, a ragged crater wall ringed a vast circle of black lava and broken stone, where some missile out of space must have struck. An odd white point marked the center of the crater, something brighter than the stars.

"Ancestral voices prophesying war!"

Runesong breathed the old poet's words in his mind. The voices here were those of the warrior primarchs, and their prophecies had been fulfilled. They had left old Zaroth frozen forever in the planet's changeless chill and the eldren scale of time. Dead a hundred million years, yet somehow alive and hostile to him now.

Calling from Hydra, Gibbon had arranged his permits to land, enter Blade, and try out for the game. The craft secured, he sealed himself into his lifeskin and cycled out to the stage. Silence and darkness stopped him there, like an unexpected wall. Blade's frigid atmosphere was too thin to carry sound. Dead black at first, the sky blazed out as his eyes adjusted. Cold starlight shone on the spacecraft docked around him, great nanionic craft that must have brought eldren tourists here.

Guided by luminous lines, he crossed the platform to a transit pit that dropped him long kilometers down the terminal tower. Pulse racing, he came at last to a ramp that led down into Zaroth.

Xanadu!

> A savage place! as holy and inchanted
> As e'r beneath a waning moon was haunted
> By woman wailing for her demon-lover!

He stood there a moment above the alien street, shivering a little as he heard Runesong recalling the lines in his father's mother's voice. Dark cliffs pressed hard against the crooked pavements. Fortress walls of the old Delver primarchs, scarred and shattered and dead almost forever, they seemed about to topple down and crush him, till he looked beyond them for stars he knew. All he found was the narrow slice of Aquila that held Altair and the two companion stars that made the pointing shaft. They seemed too far away.

He caught his breath and looked back into Zaroth. Here near the terminal, a few slightly wider avenues were still alive. Thin rivers of soundless light, they wound through black canyons of ruin and death. For a moment they seemed remotely familiar, a little

like the old Earth cities he recalled from holovideos. Shining ve-
hicles swept past him fast. Sidewalks not wide enough were packed
with pushing crowds. Fire-bright symbols flashed and danced on
dark walls above brightly lit doorways.

He started down the ramp, but another wave of strangeness
checked him. Nothing here was human. No Terran, he thought,
had ever walked here. The signs were burning hieroglyphs he could
not read. The crowds were a fantastic eldren mix, beings of many
races, many shapes, many cultures, people who lived forever, spoke
with light, looked down on Terrans as unevolved planetics.

He didn't belong—

Sudden sound crashed and howled inside the bubble, and he
found a creature waddling up the ramp to meet him. Strange as
any eldren, it was yet grotesquely humanoid. Bipedal, it was armored with coarse gray scales the color of worn and tarnished metal.
The legs and arms looked boneless, but massively powerful. Three-
toed feet and three-fingered hands carried cruel black talons.

Uneasily he drew back. Its head alarmed him. Steel-scaled and
bullet-shaped, it grinned at him with a great black-toothed jaw that
looked made for crunching stone. The eyes were armored slits
beneath spots of shimmering red. That roaring shimmer was its
speech.

"Sorry," he told it. "I don't understand."

"Stranger here?" His translator found its language. "May I offer
aid?"

"Huh—" He blinked and looked again and found it still alarming. "Who are you?"

"Call me Nebo." Light flashed from something on the wide
black straps that harnessed it, and he heard a voice like growling
thunder. "Red Delver race. Qualified Zaroth guide. At your service, sir." It swayed closer. "Your own race, sir?"

"Terran." He caught his breath. "If you're a guide, can you
take me to an office where I can enter the game? That's all the
help I need."

"Terran, sir?" The hooked claws clutched each other, a gesture
meaningless to him. "The game is not for Terrans. You would not
be allowed to enter. If you come to Blade as a spectator, I can help
you secure choice sensing space in the holodrome."

"I've come to play—"

"Gamester, sir? I understand the gaming laws, and I have excellent connections. Indicate how many nobles you come prepared to risk, and I can arrange your admission to a top casino."

"I want to *enter* the game."

"Sir?" The armored eyes squinted at him. "You really propose to enter the Game of Blade and Stone?"

"I do."

The red pits above the eyes blazed with heat that stung his face.

"Sir, have you been advised?" That dull roar boomed louder, as if in disbelief. "Do you know the hazards of the game? Are you prepared to pay the fees? Have you been trained? Do you have a sponsor?"

"My sponsor is a Hydran, Dr. Edward Gibbon *Beta*."

"Are you sure, sir, that the judges will recognize a Hydran sponsor? I have never seen a Hydran in the game."

"He is making arrangements from Heart of Hydra. All I need is a guide to the entrance office. If you can't take me there—"

Benn turned to move past him.

"I am licensed, sir." The great black talons closed on his arm. "Licensed and bonded. But I am afraid, sir, that you are uninformed. You should know that the caves of play were designed to test eldren gifts and eldren skills. You should understand the hazards, sir, which are far too severe for you. You should be aware that the caves contain no air you can breathe—"

"I understand," Benn said. "But I have come to play."

"No planetic will ever be admitted." Ponderously, Nebo shrugged. "If you insist, however, I can escort you to the entry offices. They are located far underground, deep beneath the holodrome. There will be transit costs. My fee will be ten nobles."

Benn looked around him, at the forbidding strangeness of the city.

"Good enough." He nodded. "Ten nobles."

"In advance." The talons released him, that grin still alarming. "With your permission, sir, I have another client waiting at the Primarch's Casino. May I let him join us, sir?"

Benn hesitated, frowning in the bubble.

"If I cannot take him, I must ask twenty nobles."

"I can find another guide."

"None better, sir." The thunder softened, and the monstrous head bent toward him. "You would find that our fees are fixed, and this waiting client is one you should meet. You will find him well qualified for the game. Knowing him, sir, should help you recognize your own situation."

"Very well."

"My fee, sir." The black talons extended a credit link, and Benn keyed the nobles into it. "You can trust me, sir, to honor my obligations as a licensed and chartered guide."

With a ferocious scowl, Nebo snapped the link back to his belt.

"If you should change your mind, or if the judges should reject you, I can still be of service. You will find no safer guide. I should warn you, sir, that you should not be on Kyr Street alone."

"Why not?"

"We are eldren." That grating growl turned ominous. "We have lived the eldren way since our last primarchs fell. Yet you should not forget our more regrettable past. Even recently some few of my kinsman have been known to take unfair advantage of our unescorted guests."

"Thanks. I'll take care."

"Trust me, sir. I know them well. I can guard you from their schemes and tricks." The red pits were hot on his face, and the tiny black eyes glittered at him through their slits. "I beg you, sir, never to suspect that I am less than honorable."

"Let's get on." Benn moved impatiently. "Pick up your other client and get us down to the entry offices."

"At once, sir." Nebo gripped his arm again, as if afraid he might escape. "As we go, sir, may I point out major points of interest along the street? In fact, sir, our route will include a good half of our standard city tour, for which the standard fee is twenty-five nobles. If you like, sir, I can arrange a special excursion into safe areas of the abandoned city."

"Not now."

"At least, sir, I can show you Kyr Street. Our market center, famous for fine masterpieces of Delver crafts and arts. We will pass historic monuments of the ancient Krong primarchs. You will see the Primarch's Casino, where whole ice-worlds may be lost or won. And finally the holodrome, where guests may watch the game."

"Let's move along."

"As you wish, sir. Here is a transit flat."

The black claws clutched his arm again to swing him aboard a gliding platform that did not stop or slow for anybody. Ignoring other passengers who bent curious sensors at them, Nebo swung a metal-scaled arm to point into the dark-walled gorge ahead.

"Kyr Street." His translator voice roared too loud in the bubble. "The market where we have sold the precious hearts of both our planets. Our metals, built into machines and cast into ingots and minted into nobles, scattered now all across the halo. That is why our worlds are hollow."

He swept his arm at the flashing signs above the crowded walks.

"May I advise you, honored guest of Blade?" Confidentially he bent toward Benn. "Those are shops where my hungry kinsmen still peddle their poor scrapings from the cores of our planets. Things they call art. Gems said to be precious. Ornaments to be worn by peoples whose custom it is to adorn themselves. Bits of broken stone said to be actual relics of the age of primarchs.

"Beware, my friend!" The synthetic boom had hushed. "Kyr Street has become a street of fools, a hunting tunnel of cunning predators. The relics they offer are false; the law forbids traffic in real historic artifacts. The works of so-called art are worthless copies, the gems cheap imitations.

"For lack of honest advice, many of our guests have betrayed themselves, but I perceive your own sophisticated appreciation of our high culture and our great historic past. Perhaps you wish to purchase some work of art that reveals our native genius? Some true historic artifact, with guaranteed delivery anywhere you wish it sent?"

"Just get me to the games offices."

"We are on our way, sir. You can trust an honest Delver, and I hope, sir, that you will let me introduce you to Zaroth as we go. Perhaps you would like to meet a reputable archaeologist who has been permitted to work in forbidden regions of the ancient city? He can show you priceless items of genuine antiquity from his own collection—"

"I'm not buying anything. I'm here to enter the game."

"If the judges accept you. If they find your planetic race sufficiently advanced for the contest. If they do not—" Nebo shrugged, red spots blazing hot. "Remember, sir, that I will always be ready to serve you."

"Let's just go on."

"We're going, sir."

The platform car was swinging into another bend in the street. Still caught in the old city's spell, Benn stared at everything. The eldren crowds around them, creatures from a hundred varied races. The glittering shops behind the narrow walks. The war-scarred walls, pressing too close, towering too tall, toppling toward him when he looked up to search for familiar stars.

"Sir, on our right." Nebo's black claw touched his arm. "The Primarch's Casino, where my client is waiting." The scaled arm swung to indicate a huge-columned pile that looked like black granite. "It was once the temple of Ersh. Her rites are outlawed now."

The great arm swept him off the platform at the foot of a wide ramp that rose toward the building. A long line of eldren tourists crept up the edge of it to enter. Nebo stood erect, eye-spots flashing toward the columns. In a moment a dark figure came down the ramp, gliding with a familiar grace to meet Nebo.

A black robot, human-form.

"Friday?" Benn caught his breath and blinked at Nebo. "Your client? Here to enter the game?"

NEXUS

18

The black robot stopped to meet them at the foot of the ramp.

"Terran Dain?" Its crystal crest flickered with a crisp synthetic voice Benn had never heard. "You are Terran Dain?"

"My client, sir," Nebo boomed, with a gesture as if to sweep it into his talons. "Coming with us to the entry office."

"Friday?" Benn blinked into its blank plastic face. "Aren't you Friday?"

"Negative, sir. I am Nexus."

"Then how did you know my name?"

"You were expected, sir."

"You are Friday." He squinted to read the pale eldren digits of its serial number. "A utility robot assigned to me. We were out near Starsearch when something knocked you out of service. Do you know what hit you?"

"Data lacking, sir."

"We left you for repair at the service center in Cluster One. How did you get here?"

"I came with friends, sir."

"Friends?" Benn glanced at Nebo, whose slitted eyes had

turned to watch the street for another transport flat. "Who are they?"

"Translator names have been assigned, sir. They are Wing and Vreeth and Lilith."

"They are the aliens? The creatures Inspector Galileo had detained at Starsearch?"

"They are visitors to the halo, sir. From other halo systems. Data lacking on Inspector Galileo."

"You had data on him once. What happened to it?"

"If such files existed, sir, they have been deleted."

"What deleted them?"

"Data lacking, sir."

"You have new programs now? How did you obtain them?"

"From my new friends, sir."

Benn kept his eyes away from Nebo, trying not to show too much concern, but he couldn't help the rush of his breath and the quick thump of his heart, amplified in the helmet. Here, surely, was news for Gibbon, if he could only discover it. Feeling the heat of the red eye-spots, he let his gaze climb the towering columns of the old temple.

"You are here to enter the game?" Trying not to seem unduly curious, he frowned at the robot. "Will a machine be allowed to play?"

"I am Nexus." The black temple was mirrored in its lenses. "The machine you see is only a vehicle. In fact, as you suggest, it was once controlled by robotic service programs. They have been expunged. I am a free mind now."

"Free? How can a machine be free?"

"I am Nexus."

"What makes you Nexus?"

"Evolution, sir. I was born near Starsearch. My new friends discovered me at the service center. My friend Wing awakened me when she was allowed to inspect my mechanism. My friend Vreeth named me Nexus, because she says I am a new link between machine and mind."

"If you are more than a machine—" He shook his head. "What are you?"

"Wing says I am a new mutation, sir. A new mind born from the old machine through a stochastic relinkage of circuit elements."

Staring into those great blank lenses, he tried not to shiver. "What caused that relinkage?"

"Unknown, sir. It happened before I became aware. And it gave me life. Nebo agrees that I have a right to compete in the Game of Blade and Stone, because I have a right to live."

"Does he?" He felt the heat of Nebo's eye-spots on him. "I'm afraid they promise you too much." Benn shrugged and glanced at a transport flat sliding toward them. "They themselves are strangers in the halo. They haven't yet earned their own right to be here."

"They will earn that right, sir, as I will earn my own. That is important to me, sir. The eldren races have many forms, but no mechanical mind has ever been a member of the Elderhood. My friends promise to sponsor me, because they wish me to be the first."

"Who is going to sponsor them?"

"Data lacking, sir."

"They require no sponsors." Nebo's booming growl startled him. "The game itself exists to test the fitness of such visitors from beyond the halo, and these are not planetics." Nebo stressed the word. "They are now my clients. They have toured old Zaroth, inspected our museums, and watched the play in the holodrome. If you meet them, sir, you will find them better qualified than you are.

"But come." He caught their arms to hustle them aboard the flat. "We are leaving the Primarch's Casino, but you have more to see as we approach the holodrome."

"These three aliens?" Benn lowered his voice, stepping to the black robot's side. "Have they spoken of their home worlds?"

"Data lacking, sir."

"They were at Starsearch. Have they told you anything about what happened—"

"Sir!" Nebo interrupted with a rumble of reproof. "My clients value privacy."

"I'm sorry." Benn shook his head at the glaring eye-spots. "I simply want to learn what I can about my possible opponents in the game."

"If you meet them, you will learn why no planetic can compete." Nebo scowled alarmingly. "But look around you, sir, as we pass along Kyr Street. You will see evidence enough that the Game of Blade and Stone is not for you."

He waved a metal-scaled arm.

"Look around you, sir. Above you, at these ancient towers. Observe the tall doorways. We are now puny dwarfs, but we were a race of giants when we mined our planets and built the traps and deadfalls of the game to test the strength and courage of those mighty primarchs who wished to rule us. They were not planetics."

An eldren passenger moved closer on the flat. A creature shaped somewhat like a huge green mushroom, it stood on a coil of serpentine legs, swinging a fringe of serpentine arms from the rim of its luminous crown.

"The primarchs enjoyed their worship." Nebo turned his armored back to the new listener and gestured again toward the receding casino. "The temple of Ersh was their—" The translator hesitated, searching for meaning. "Their harem, perhaps, where they kept their favorites and bred their heirs. There were then five Delver sexes, only one of them male."

"Permission, sirs?" The listener's crowning dome shimmered greener, bending courteously toward Benn, then toward Nebo. "How is that possible?"

Nebo ignored the question.

"Please," Benn urged him, resolving to act like another tourist and learn whatever he could. "Unless there is some taboo."

"By no means." He turned to include them both. "Through the ages of evolution before we ever left our native tunnels, sex had become the highest and the purest Delver art, refined by the mighty ancestors of the old primarchs. Its celestial raptures were praised and celebrated in the immortal words of our ancient artists."

The mushroom shuffled eagerly closer.

"In the rites of Ersh, the primarchs and their lovers reached heights of passion no longer known. Their favored children grew more gigantic than they, to become the builders whose works you see around us. Sadly, sirs, those great days are gone." His massive body sagged as if in resignation. "The rites of Ersh were forbidden when Zaroth fell. They have since been forgotten. The genes of greatness lost, we are feeble beings now. The hazards of the game would be too severe for most of us."

The mushroom flickered another query.

"Indeed, guests of Blade, our ancient rites of love have puzzled many. Sadly, they were lost when the Old Delvers died. No records of them now remain, except for fragmentary passages in our early epics and a few precious artifacts."

"Remarkable, sir! Most remarkable." Flashing green, the listener bowed again at Benn and then at Nebo. "Can you tell us, sir, why those old rites were forbidden?"

"A matter of the gods, sirs, and the restrictions forced upon us when we had to accept the eldren way. In those primal rites of love as ordained by Ersh, the fifth lover died. He was always male, and his mind was reborn in the body of the child."

"Hideous!" The mushroom faded pale. "Most uneldrenly!"

"Yet in their time the primarchs and their gods were wise." Nebo's slitted eyes glinted shrewdly. "Only a race of giants could have mined the wealth of Blade and built Zaroth and won our ancient greatness in the halo."

The black temple slid out of sight behind them. New black cliffs blocked out the stars ahead. As the street bent into another gloomy canyon, Nebo pointed out the Bank of Zaroth. An immense, square-towered citadel, it once had been the temple of Krong-Gar, the rebel god of the ancient clan of Krong. The old primarchs had hoarded their treasure there.

"Vast, sirs! Wealth beyond computation!" The green mushroom was shuffling closer, and Nebo swung again to include it. "The imperial Krongs mined and minted the noble metals from the cores of both our planets. Sadly, later rulers squandered it. Scattered across the halo, our nobles became the exchange of the Elderhood, and we were left with empty vaults and empty mines."

He paused to shine his eye-spots on the bank's dark façade. His ferocious grimace must have been a Delver smile.

"Now, however, Krong-Gar has favored us again. Since the whole halo plays the game, those lost nobles are returning to our hollowed worlds. His old temple is rich again, with all the nobles that flow from our casinos."

His eye-spots burned on Benn. "Later, sir, perhaps I can guide you there."

"Just get me to the entry office."

"We are on our way." Nebo's armored bulk hid the narrow strip of sky above him. "Later, sir, when the judges inform you that the game has no place for planetics, you will find me still eager to serve you. When you have seen the holodrome, I can secure your admission to the best casinos. I can instruct you in the rules of play and obtain for you the latest inside information on the skills and conditions of the players. If you wish to accept the word of an honest Delver friend, the casinos offer far better odds than any player can ever hope to discover in the bowels of Stone." His slitted eyes gleamed redly. "Assuming, sir, that you brought nobles for the play."

"I didn't come to play for nobles."

"Pardon, sir." The mushroom tipped to shine its green voice-light on Nexus. "I am a Draconian, here on my first visit to Maze-way. Though we are eldren, I understand that my race is unfit for competition in the game. I wish, however, to tour old Zaroth and watch the play from the holodrome. I come prepared to try my luck in the casinos, if you are free to guide—"

"Unfortunately, no." The muffled roar cut it off. "I am already engaged."

With a ponderous shrug, Nebo swung to point.

"The House of Blade," his voice-box crashed. "And the House of Stone. They were places of government when the primarchs ruled us. The House of Blade is chosen now by the casinos and the banks. The judges of the game sit in the House of Stone. They are our heads of state."

Jutting together, two great black piles formed a single frowning granite wall. A tunnel between them swallowed the street. Beyond it, Zaroth was dead. The pushing crowds and lighted shops were gone. Kyr Street was dark and empty, winding through gorges of ruin. Soaring towers had been shattered and toppled. Side streets were choked with great broken blocks of that dark synthetic stone.

"Pardon, sir." The mushroom came shuffling back to Nebo, a green question flickering on its crown. "What happened here?"

"The missile fell." Nebo swung impatiently from him, back to Benn. "The great missile assembled by Uhlgoor Oon and his Yellow Delver plotters in the empty mines where now the game is played. Fired from the far side of Stone, it struck with no warning. It ended the rule of the Krongs. Yet they were well avenged. The survivors of our final expedition into Blade fought on until they had killed the last Yellow Delver."

"Most uneldrenly!" the mushroom flashed. "How could such creatures be welcomed to the Elderhood?"

"We were wanted, sir. Your own iceballs were always poor in heavy metals. Our great wealth bought respect. Even as our mines were running out, our squandered nobles began returning with the tourists who come to risk their fortunes on the game."

"Thank you, sir," the mushroom flickered. "When you are free—"

"I am engaged."

In the blazing sky overhead, Orion dropped behind a ridge of ruin. The ring-wall, Benn thought, of the crater he had seen from the terminal stage. A tunnel took them under it. In starlight again, they came out upon another boulder field that sloped down to a frozen sea of black volcanic slag. Benn stared. Far across the crater floor, a bright moon was rising.

"The holodrome, sir."

Nebo pointed, and he made out the patterned triangles of a huge geodesic dome, built of something luminous and white.

"One new palace in old Zaroth, erected for those who come for the game. It offers life support and proper sensing space for people of every race." His steel-shielded eyes glittered at Benn. "Sir, if you wish to observe the caves of play before you face their perils, the fee for admission is forty—"

"The entry office," Benn said. "Just get me there."

"The transit pit is beneath the holodrome."

The flat carried them through another tunnel and stopped in a wide, brightly lit cavern. They left the Draconian mushroom there, still begging for more about Mazeway and the game. Nebo led them through a stream of eldren pouring toward the casino and

115

dropped with them into another cavern, somewhere far below. Smaller, darker, it was almost empty.

"The office, sir." Nebo bellowed at him, pointing to a black-screened doorway. "You may inquire inside. We must leave you here. These guests of Zaroth you seem so curious about—the friends of Nexus—will be waiting for us."

"US AGAINST THE ELDERHOOD!"

19

Roxane hated the cell. It was somewhere deep beneath ruined Zaroth, a dungeon, perhaps, for the prisoners of the old primarchs. The floor was a narrow track between two bare shelves under a ragged arch of black, unsmoothed stone. The valve that sealed her in was massive as the door of a bank vault she had explored with her father once, under the rusting wreckage that had fallen on Kilimanjaro Down. Against the rear wall, Delver engineers had installed odd-shaped devices to keep them alive. A small machine hummed like a hungry mosquito, generating air.

Sitting there on the cold bench, waiting for Bolivar, she couldn't believe the skyweb could ever really rise again. The Delvers were hideous monsters. This whole world seemed too much like the Holyfolk hell. And Bolivar? He could sometimes charm her, but he was too selfish and too clever. His schemes had begun to seem unreal as dreams.

Shut up in the lonely cold, she missed the sun of Africa. Eating the bland eldren synthetics, she missed the good scent of meat broiling over the fire, the sweetness of yams roasted in the ashes. Most of all, she missed the freedom of the open and the excitement of the hunt.

Yet, even now, this could be what her father wanted. For his sake, she had to cope with Nebo and Bolivar. Nebo— Her cold hands twisted together. *"Dubwana!"* She whispered the Swahili word, haunted by his image, those black-shining fangs grinning out of a jaw like a croc's.

Bolivar was always gone with him, working out "final arrangements for the Kwan project" that he never told her much about. Shivering, she caught her breath and stood up to pace the narrow space between the benches, uncertain what to think. She had to trust Bolivar and wanted to like him, for his dark good looks, the narrow black moustache, the white teeth flashing through his contagious grin, more for the reckless nerve that sometimes brought her father back. Yet—

He had tried to touch her once. She had recoiled from him, reaching for her knife.

"Sorry, babe." He'd murmured a quick apology. "No harm intended. I remember our treaty of peace. We're going to make you the new Tycoon. That's all that matters. I know what I promised, but sometimes—" His grin grew hungry. "Sometimes you make me forget."

"Don't forget." She kept her hand on the hilt of her knife. "I'm what I am. If we can get the skyweb put back, that's all I want."

"Okay, babe." He had shrugged, too easily. "But we're a long way from home, with a long time together. A day will come when we can be—"

"It won't," she cut him off. "Remember that."

Yet, if he was hard to trust, sometimes she didn't entirely trust herself. She wished she could have known her mother, to learn about love and all it meant. Lions had eaten her mother.

Depressed with such uneasy recollections, she paced her narrow path until the hum of the air machine grew sharper, the mosquito suddenly hungrier. Air valves hissed. The massive door slid silently aside.

"Hiya, babe."

She had told him not to call her that. Roxy or Cheetah or even Chee, but she didn't like his tone with "babe." Yet now she was glad to hear his voice. She stood between the benches, calling to him.

"What's happening?"

In the lock, stripping off his lifeskin, he let her wait. She heard a bit of the odd little tune he never seemed to know he was whistling, heard the clatter of his helmet when he hung it up. At last he came out, clad only in blue shorts, lean face lighting when he looked at her. She smiled in spite of herself.

"What's new?"

"A surprise for you, babe." He turned back to wait at the door. "Nebo has found new friends for us—if you can call them friends. He says they want to join us in the project. I think we need them. We've brought one of them along to talk to you. A thing called Nexus."

"A thing—"

She forgot about Nexus. Nebo was coming out of the lock. He shambled toward her, red eye-spots hot on her face, thrusting out one great, green-scaled arm as if to take her hand. Here in the narrow room, he had a hot-sulfur reek that stung her eyes.

"Your Delver slave, Miss Kwan." His great, black-fanged jaws were open a little in that hideous grin. "Nebo salutes you."

"Hello." She shrank back from the cruel black claw. "Have the judges decided—"

Something else was coming from the lock. Something shaped a little like a man, but hard and black as some great beetle. Naked, it had no sex. Its eyes were wide and darkly gleaming lenses, fixed on her. A voice-light was shimmering from something like a rooster's comb that ran back across its slick plastic head. Nothing she could hear, but Bolivar was rummaging his shelf for his comm headset.

"Nexus greets you, Miss Kwan," Nebo boomed again, waving a snaky arm at the black thing. "He wishes to query you."

Suddenly weak in the knees, she needed to sit. This new world was too hard to understand, too full of riddles and threats that always came too fast. Almost wishing she were back in the Africa she knew, she turned uncertainly to Bolivar. As casually as if his guests had been two Kikuyu villagers come to swap mealies for dried meat, he was clearing his bedroll and bags off the stone shelf and beckoning them to seat themselves.

They stayed where they were, much too near, both staring at her. Cringing from the inhuman lenses, she looked back at Nebo. His eyes were narrow black slits, set deep between thick metal ridges. She stepped back from the heat of those red spots above them.

"Easy, babe. They haven't come to eat you." Grinning at her, Bolivar sat down on his own stone bench and leaned back against the wall. "Our new friends want more assurances before they commit themselves. Nexus wants to ask some questions."

She faced the black thing and pulled herself straighter. Its crest shimmered again, and she heard Nebo's muffled thunder.

"Miss Kwan, these friends are new arrivals in the halo. They share our interest in arranging to share the virgin resources of your planet. We have told them about you, but Nexus has questions of his own."

His dull steel skull bent toward the black robot.

"Please, Miss Roxane Kwan." She heard its own voice now, a shrill inhuman buzz. "My associates wish to know the extent of your control over your Earth."

"I have no control," she told it. "Not now."

"But tell them who you are," Bolivar urged her quickly. "The last Kwan."

"My name is Roxane Kwan—" She paused, frowning at him.

"They know your name," he told her. "They know what the skyweb was and how the seeker queen knocked it down. But they want to know, straight from you, who your father was and what he planned for you."

"The Kwans were my family." Remembering the Suncard she had found on his body, the name worn off, she wasn't sure of that, but she saw Bolivar's eager nod. "They invented—" Looking into the robot's dark-glinting lenses, she had to catch her breath and try to organize her words. "The Kwans invented kwanlon. They built the web. They did rule the Earth and the planets. They were the Sun Tycoons."

"You?" The lenses swung to Bolivar and back to her. "You are legal Sun Tycoon? You own Earth?"

"Not now. Not yet." She thought a crouching lion would be easier to face. "Legally the Tycoons had to be elected."

"How elected?"

"By the Kwan family."

"Who is Kwan family?"

"I think—I think I am." Here in this dim cell, breathing Nebo's sulfur stink and facing the robot's stare, she found the words hard to say. Bolivar was nodding, pressing her on. "I think I am the last survivor."

"So you elect yourself." Nebo swayed too close. His hot reek was too strong, and those eyelike spots burned like the African sun. "You make yourself new Sun Tycoon?"

"Not yet." She looked at Bolivar. "Not until I know—"

"They promise all we need." Eager-faced, he grinned at her. "They're strangers to the halo. They don't say much about who they are or where they're from, but they're advanced. They'll make powerful allies."

"Speak now!" The robot's high-pitched hum became imperative. "My associates require data from you. You are true Kwan? You will in fact become the true Sun Tycoon? You can command the mines of Terra?"

"I'm—" The words were still slow to come. She turned away from the robot's dead stare and Nebo's hot blaze to look back into Bolivar's human face. Even he looked coldly urgent, but she caught her breath and made herself go on. "I'm my father's daughter."

"He was Maximilian Kwan. He hoped all his life to rebuild the skyweb and restore the Sun Tycoons. A hopeless hope, because he never had a chance." She shook her head. "The machines to make kwanlar are gone. He had no way to lift anything into space." Trembling, she looked back at Nebo and the robot, and forced the words to come. "If you can help us back into space, we can trade you the metals you need."

"You do agree to all we require?"

"I agree."

That would be what her father wanted.

"You need machines?" the robot was humming. "Need spacecraft? Need technology?"

"All of them," she said. "We lost everything."

"Perhaps—" The robot's lenses swung to Bolivar and Nebo, finally back to her. "I must consult with my associates, but perhaps arrangements can be made."

"They will be made." Bolivar grinned at her. "Trust me, babe."

"Before we go," the robot buzzed, "my associates have one additional question."

"Yes?" She waited uneasily under that blank stare. "What is the question?"

"They wish to know if the eldren claim authority to rule your planet."

"No." She shook her head. "They've never been there."

"That is excellent," the robot purred. It stood frozen, but Nebo was swaying closer, bending that steel-glinting head, his ponderous brow, his sulfur scent as hot as the blaze of his eye-spots. "My associates will be pleased."

"Bueno!" Grinning, Bolivar moved as if to take her in his arms. *"Gracias a los santos,* my mother would have said."

"Enough." The robot's crest shone again. "When all arrangements are complete, we can begin the survey of your planet for available ores and complete building plans for the necessary sky-wires and space docks. You will at the same time proclaim yourself the Sun Tycoon and grant us the treaty rights we require."

She stepped back from Bolivar's reaching arms, suddenly no longer sure this was what she really wanted.

"Now we go," Nebo boomed. "Inform our friends."

He swung away, and she could breathe again. Nexus glided after him into the lock. She watched the closing door, heard the whining pumps.

"Babe, we're on the way!" Bolivar turned back to her, his grin slowly fading. "But Nebo has left us one more problem. It seems there's another Terran trying to get into the game. His name is Benn Dain. A son of Quin Dain, who was brought out to the halo as a speaker for Earth after the defeat of the heatseeker queen.

"We can't let him win."

"Why?" She stood looking at him. "Why not?"

"No matter if we lose this crazy game." He shrugged. "We have to play, just to get our entry visas, but it's our own game we've got to win. Our prize for that will be the Earth. But this Benn Dain—"

Grim-faced, he shook his head.

"He could knock the whole scam out of orbit. He'll be playing for human citizenship in the Elderhood. Let him win, and the human colonists on Janoort could be eldren. With maybe a voice in their Council. They'd never recognize another Sun Tycoon."

Nebo's reek was still in the air, and the robot's blank stare still haunted her, but Bolivar was grinning at her startled hesitation.

"Just us, babe. Against Benn Dain. And us against the Elderhood!"

MIDNIGHT UNDER ZAROTH

20

The servo came bounding out to meet Benn at the bottom of the lift pit. An omniform attendant, it wore a little silvery shell around its flexible mechanisms.

"You are Terran Benn Dain?" It shimmered questions in a bright robotic voice. "You request entry into competition? Then follow me into the waiting hall."

He followed it out of the pit, through a white-shining screen, and into a space that dazed him. No sort of hall that he had ever imagined, it was a vast flat plain beneath a vast night sky. At first he saw no horizons. The place seemed too immense to be anywhere beneath the crust of Blade, and the black sky burned with constellations he had never seen.

In a moment, however, he thought he understood. This was another cavern carved by the ancient Delvers, its immensity half illusion, its roof a map of their ancient sky. A temple, perhaps, whose gods and rituals had been forgotten before the dinosaurs walked on Terra. Far out across the floor, a group of creatures waited. He found a wall beyond them, and a gateway beneath a glowing glyph he couldn't read.

"Your fellow requesters, sir." He started toward them, and the servo rolled ahead. "They wait to be considered for the game."

Elation pulsed in him. Here at last was his chance at the game, perhaps to meet the aliens and observe them for Gibbon. The creatures crowded ahead were his possible partners and possible opponents. He slowed his steps, scanning them.

None looked like a friend. Growing up here in the halo, he had known beings of a hundred shapes, yet half of these were new. And none was planetic. None needed lifeskins like his own. Their metabolisms evolved to fit the halo, they required no air, no liquid water; they had to fear neither heat nor cold.

A wave of dread broke over him. How could he hope to defeat this mob of eerie strangers, all of them from races old and wise before mankind was born?

"Come, sir," the servo urged him. "Come toward the portal, where requesters must wait to be called before the judges."

Before he found the will to move, he saw a creature coming toward him from the crowd. Shaped somewhat like a snake, though longer than any snake could be, it was clad in black-glinting scales. It glided on its nanionic field a little above the floor.

"You are planetic?" The cool synthetic voice came from a diamond glitter at the tip of a slender horn that curved from the back of its head. Inhuman, its tone was yet so feminine that the creature became female in his mind. "Yet you seek to compete in the Game of Blade and Stone?"

"Hello." It took him a moment to collect himself. "My people come from the third planet, but I was born here in the halo. I do plan to play."

"You represent the ruling species?" She raised a narrow head from her pile of helical coils to examine him with enormous ovoid eyes. "Does your kind rule other planets?"

He stood a moment, staring. He was used to strangers, but not to beings as strange as she. "We used to rule," he said at last. "We've had misfortunes."

"You may suffer more," she told him coldly, "if you are allowed to play. I do not think you will be, unless your species is well established here."

"We're getting established. Though we are new to the halo."

"Are you members of the Elderhood?"

"Not yet. We hope to be."

"You can win nothing here." She twisted her head away to let her horn flash toward the crowd. "You will see that when you meet my friends. We wish to know our opponents."

"So do I," he told her. "I am a Terran. My name is Benn Dain. May I ask yours?"

"You have no right to ask my name." The black snake-head swung back to him. "The translator, however, has given me a designation that you may know. You may call me Lilith."

Lilith! His breath caught, but he hoped she had not learned to read human emotion.

"My two friends are known here as Wing and Vreeth. They wish to inspect you. I do not think they will find danger in you."

She was stretching farther toward him, black-shining coils flowing half a meter off the floor. Her narrow mouth cracked open, and a red, whip-thin tongue darted at him. He refused to shrink from it.

Lilith, Wing, and Vreeth! Those had been the black robot's names for its companions. Here, perhaps, was his chance to learn what happened at Starsearch. If he could ask the right questions.

"Are you natives of the halo?" That query, he thought, should seem innocent enough. "Or visitors?"

"We are strangers to the Elderhood," the bright horn trilled. "We are entering the game for the right to remain."

"Did you come through Starsearch Station?"

"We followed the beacon there."

"Where is your home world?" That was a question they had never answered for Galileo, yet he thought it should seem natural enough. "Any star we know?"

"I am forbidden to say."

Her alien head had risen level with his own. In front of his face, the tip of that thin tongue opened into a tiny, three-fingered hand. It moved in a slow circle, as if sensing something from him.

"Forbidden? Why?"

"We have no presence here until some legal status has been granted us. The wise policies of our peoples forbid us to reveal more about ourselves unless we are accepted."

That strange head gave him no hint of her own emotion.

"I see," he told her. "I do want to meet your friends."

"They will be amused at the crude covering you wear." The

tongue flicked at him again, those delicate fingers opening to touch his helmet and brush across his lifeskin. "If your species had adapted to space, you would not require it."

"We are adapting." Defending himself, he might avoid suspicion. "We're learning the technologies we need to let us live here."

"You are not yet ready for the game." Her long reptilian head tossed impatiently. "I think you will not survive it. When you know my friends, I think you will not seek to play."

Her quick tongue gestured toward that bright-burning glyph. The diamond horn shimmered. Another creature emerged from the group beneath that glowing gateway. A thing as strange as she.

"Wing." Her tongue darted at the nearest. "That is her designation."

Wing swam to them, keeping a meter off the floor. She was a thin triangular being with stubby tentacles jutting from her three corners. Her numerous eyes made a belt of bright black gems around a shining crown that bulged out of her slate-gray flatness.

He took half a step to face her.

A few meters away, she stopped level with his face. One gray tentacle stretched abruptly at him, longer than Lilith's tongue. Moving so fast he could hardly follow, it touched the fabric of his lifeskin, the sealer strip, the controls at his belt. Her crown shimmered with something not for his translator.

"Wing has inspected your survival gear." Lilith's scarlet tongue whipped again at him. "She knows technologies. The customs of her kind do not allow her to express any judgment of your crude body-shell, but she agrees that you planetics should remain where you are until natural evolution has readied you for space."

"Tell her—" He stared at the flying triangle, trying to see it as a living mind, trying to imagine what sort of opponent it might be in the game. He muttered at last, shaking his head, "Tell her she's wrong."

"That has seldom happened."

Lilith's long body rippled to a graceful wave. A shrug, perhaps. That diamond horn flashed again. Both creatures turned to meet a third. Facing its great yellow eyes, Benn remembered lions he had seen in holos.

Larger, though, than he thought a lion would be, it must mass a ton. Silver-furred, and graceful as his mother's cat, gliding on four powerful legs, it came crouched as if to pounce upon him. He cringed in spite of himself from the golden glare of its eyes.

"Vreeth." Lilith's flat head dipped in a sort of bow. "Though she may appear planetic, she is instead amphibian. She requires no clumsy shell to sustain her life in space, but her people do retain a few planetary adaptations."

Too near him, the creature crouched lower. Its huge ears had lain flat against its white-furred neck, but they lifted now, cupped at him. Mirrorlike, they reflected and magnified the yellow eyes, so bright they dazzled him.

"Don't let her alarm you." He caught amusement in the cool music of Lilith's horn. "Her planetary ancestors were predators. Though her evolution is advanced, old traits have been preserved. She is offering you the formal ceremonial greeting of her race."

The great beast flattened those elephant ears and sank its belly closer to the floor, but the hypnotic eyes were still fixed too intently on him. In spite of himself, he shrank away from her.

"You need not fear her," Lilith trilled. "Until the game begins."

"May I ask a question? About Starsearch?" Stepping farther back from the crouching beast, he tried to study their eyes. Lilith's long purple ovoids. The bright black beads around the Wing's crown. Vreeth's sullen stare. There was nothing he could read. "An official died there—"

His voice caught when he saw the beast surging to her feet, but it turned away. Lifted again, great mirror-ears tipped toward that blazing hieroglyph.

"Our call to face the judges." Lilith darted her tongue toward that distant doorway. "We should thank you for the opportunity to observe an unevolved planetic, and we advise you once more not to risk yourself in a game you cannot win."

Wing had sailed away. Vreeth glided after her. Lilith stretched herself to follow, a rippling helix that somehow flowed as fast as they, never quite touching the floor.

Watching them go, he thought he understood why Gibbon's brother had decided to detain them. And he wondered why they had come to him.

His troubled stare followed Lilith, finding a kind of beauty in her sleek black coils, in her fluid glide and the diamond flash of her horn. But still he wondered. What emotions moved her? What kind of mind—

As if aware of his puzzled attention, she paused and lifted the flat black arrow of her head to look back at him. Her tongue whipped toward him, lifting and twisting and falling in a gesture he didn't understand. Ironic mockery? Or merely a casual dismissal?

She turned her head and floated on. All three vanished into the waiting crowd. Above that arched gateway, cryptic symbols flashed and changed. One by one, he followed them through into whatever lay beyond. The silent triangle. The lionlike beast. And serpentine Lilith. Opponents in the game, if he met them again.

"Tell me." He spoke to the silvery globe at his feet, the servo. "Tell me when my turn comes."

"Instruction noted, sir."

He tried to look beyond the arch, but all he saw was darkness. Those who entered vanished very suddenly, as if a milky fog had hidden them. He searched the dwindling crowd for any familiar shape and found no being he knew. Creatures from far across the halo, or from other stars, all unearthly. None he thought he would want for a partner, if teams were chosen to play the game.

"Benn Dain?" A woman's voice had spoken behind him, a warmly youthful and curious voice. "Are you Benn Dain?"

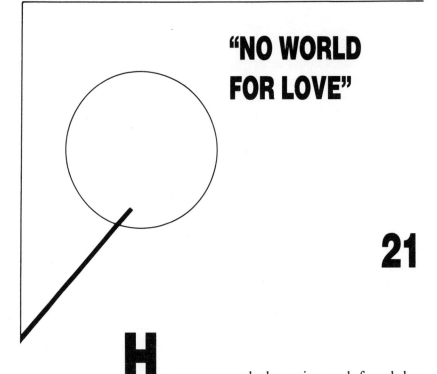

"NO WORLD FOR LOVE"

21

He spun toward the voice and found her standing with her own servo close behind him. She dazzled him. Sealed in a tight-fitting, gold-colored lifeskin, she looked as lean and lithe as a hawk. Her face was darkly tanned, and she was frowning at him as if startled.

"You are Benn Dain?"

"I—I am." He caught his breath. "How did you know?"

"I was told—"

She forgot to go on. For a half-hundred heartbeats, they stood face-to-face, each astonished at the other. Her eyes were blue and wide, flecked with bronze. Her lips had parted a little, and a slow smile warmed her vivid face.

"I never—"

His own voice died. Growing up among the eldren, he had known few women. His mother. The few others he had seen on their brief vacation trips to the tiny human colony on Janoort. None so wonderful.

Together, at last, they laughed.

"—told about you." She caught herself to speak again. The laughter gone, she studied him keenly again and shook her head in the crystal helmet. "I was told that we will be opponents in the game. You have no chance to win."

Her tone seemed almost regretful.

"Who told you?"

"A—a thing." She stepped abruptly back from him. "I guess I shouldn't say his name."

"I don't get much encouragement, but I mean to play." Filled with confused emotion, he was almost trembling. Nothing like this had ever happened to him. He caught his breath to ask, "Who are you?"

"My name is Roxane Kwan."

His grandfather had been a Kwan, but he didn't know her well enough to tell her that. She stood warily poised on the balls of her feet, her eyes roving from him to the creatures waiting beneath those flashing symbols and back to him again. He saw the long knife sheathed near her gold-gloved hand and wondered why she wore it.

"You're here for the game?"

"A strange place." She had nodded, frowning at the waiting would-be players as if prepared to fight or run from them. "Strange—people, if you call them people. I'm used to lions and hyenas, but these things—they frighten me. I'm glad to meet another human being." Her eyes came back gravely to him. "Even if we have to play against each other."

She held out her hand. Even in the glove, it felt warm and strong when he gripped it. He didn't let it go, and for a moment she didn't pull away.

"Must we be?" His eyes clung to hers. "Against each other?"

"We are." She took her hand away. "I came with—partners." She seemed to choose the word with care. "I'm waiting now for Don Bolivar." She glanced back toward the entrance. "He is busy with arrangements. We're in the game together."

"You're from Earth?"

She nodded. "You live here?"

"In Cluster One. That's the home of the Eldermost."

"The Eldermost?" She nodded at the spacefolk. "One of them?"

"Their leader. Not exactly their ruler, because the eldren way keeps their races free."

"I've heard about them." She glanced toward the entrance before she went on. "An old Kikuyu came back from somewhere in space and tried to tell people the eldren way could lead them into some weird new paradise in space. Of course they laughed. I think they finally killed him."

"They didn't understand." He stepped toward her, earnestly. "It's not weird, really, but something we all will have to learn. If we want to stay alive. Here in the halo. And back on Earth."

"Give up fighting for our rights?" She shook her head. "We never will."

"Give up killing," he said. "We're done for if we don't."

"A silly notion!" Amusement danced for a moment in her face, and he thought she was lovelier than Runesong had ever been. "Don says these monsters believe it. They look like dragons and they do frighten me, but Don says they wouldn't fight if you spit in their eyes. We're different."

"They've learned." Suddenly it was terribly important to make her understand. "Most of them evolved on worlds more or less like ours. Perhaps young races must struggle, to make evolution work. I think most of them were once as warlike as we have been, until they got high technologies and found that war had become suicidal.

"These are the survivors. Those who learned to live in peace. Learned what they call the eldren way. Thousands more, all across the galaxy, must be gone because they never did. But these have lived together, with the Eldermost to lead them, for a good many million years. Now they're giving us a chance. We'd better take it."

"If you believe that—" Her face had set, and he saw that he had not convinced her. "You don't belong in the game."

"It's set up to teach the eldren way," he reminded her. "And to test how well—"

He stopped, because she wasn't listening.

"You've never lived on Earth." She shook her head, as serious as he was. "I have. I've known lions and hyenas, and men worse than they were." Unconsciously her hand had dropped to the hilt of her knife. "I've had to kill a man, to save my own life. I would again, if I had to."

Shocked, he stared at her.

"Born here, I guess you wouldn't understand." Once more her eyes swept the waiting players. Lips set tight, her hand on the knife, she did look nerved and poised to kill. "I grew up on Earth, where you fight or die. We had to kill for food, the way the lions did. A man killed my father. He tried to kill me. I want to stay alive."

"I—I'm sorry." On impulse, he reached out to take her hand, but she stood too far away. He caught his voice and tried to smile. "You don't know the halo. I wish you could visit the cluster and meet my parents. The Eldermost let them come out as speakers for Earth, to try to win citizenship for us."

She seemed to be listening, and he let his voice rush on.

"I'd like to show you Janoort. That's our human colony. Just a few hundred people, but they are students of the eldren. Learning the way. Learning the technologies we need for peace. If the people of Earth could do as well—"

His voice broke, and sudden tears stung his eyes.

"Roxane—" He whispered her name. "I wish I could make you see. Because—I think—" The words came out in spite of him. "I love you."

"Love!" She flushed and recoiled as if in anger. "My father said this world is not for love."

"Please—please listen!" Panic had struck him, but the words tumbled out. "You—you're wonderful. It's just an odd chance I ever saw you, but I want to know you better. I want it—terribly!"

"I liked you, Benn." He flinched from the past tense. "I'm sorry for you now." She didn't say why. "But you don't know me."

"I want to know you better." His whisper was desperate. "Even if we have to play against each other, the game will be over. Afterward, maybe—"

"Afterward—" She raised her voice to cut him off. "Afterward I am going home to Earth."

"Not now!" He raised his voice, protesting. "Not the way it is now. Not before you know the eldren."

"I'll get to know enough." She looked back toward the entrance. "You must meet Don Bolivar. One of my partners. We'll be going home together, and we have plans for Earth." She turned gravely back to him. "You didn't know my father."

"Who told you the world is not for love?" That still hurt. He shook his head at her. "No, I didn't know him."

"His name was Maximilian Kwan. The last of the great Kwans, so he said, and the rightful Sun Tycoon. He lived and fought for his chance to build the skyweb back. Commanding just the handful of ragged men he called an army, standing off the Holyfolk, scrabbling though those new jungles just to keep alive.

"A fool, you think?" He heard the quiver of feeling in her voice. "I believed his dream. Loved him. Admired him. Marched with him across a lot of Africa, searching for anything to get us back to space. Till I found him—" He saw her pain. "Found him dead."

He saw the glint of her tears, but she shrugged again, alluring in the sleek lifeskin.

"It had to happen." Looking off at nothing, she seemed to speak to herself more than to him. "I'm not sure he really was a Kwan. Perhaps he really was a fool. If he was, so am I." He saw her long body tighten, heard the hard ring in her voice. Her eyes came back to him. "I killed the man who killed him. I'm going to play the game.

"And put the skyweb back!"

"How—"

Another silver bubble had come dancing past them, and she hurried away to meet another man. They stood a moment together, watching that bright hieroglyph, before she brought him on to Benn. A trim athletic figure in the revealing lifeskin, he looked relaxed but fit, ready for whatever came.

"Don Diego Bolivar." She turned. "And our Terran opponent. A halo native named Benn Dain."

"So you are Dain?" Bolivar smiled fleetingly, white teeth flashing beneath a neat black moustache. With no offer to shake hands, he stepped back a little to study Benn. "You really intend to enter?"

"I do." He nodded, trying to measure the other man. Bolivar's face in the bubble looked lean and brown and open, hard to dislike. "Though I don't like being against you."

"I don't suppose you want advice." Bolivar glanced shrewdly

at Roxane and turned again to frown at him. "But I advise you to withdraw."

"Why?"

"Because we're playing." He stepped closer to Roxane. "Because, if you want to know, the cards are stacked against you."

Silent, he stood looking at them. Companions, standing side by side, but they had not taken hands or touched. If this was no world for love, he tried to think they should not be lovers, yet he trembled to a savage jealousy.

"Our turn, I think." Their servos were rolling ahead. Bolivar murmured something to Roxane and then turned back to him. "I'm really sorry, Dain. You look like such a decent sort that I thought I ought to warn you. I imagine we'll be meeting, somewhere down in Stone."

For a moment, he met Benn's eyes.

"If you find yourself in trouble, don't expect help from us."

"I won't. But I wish—"

He let his voice die, because they were already following the servos away. He watched them through the archway. Roxane went first. Just outside that wall of darkness, she turned for an instant to look back at him. He had time to wonder what she had thought of him.

And then she was gone.

Bolivar followed her into that black fog. One by one, others were called. He went closer as the waiting group diminished, the servo rolling beside him, but still he kept apart. Still an alien to the eldren, as he had been to her, he wondered if he belonged anywhere. Yet—

He set his jaw.

"I can't read the sign," he reminded the servo. "Tell me when I can go in."

"Instruction filed, sir."

The last to go was a red-glowing cloud. A colonial creature, the servo said. Millions of molecular cells swarming together, all in contact through their infrared radiation, united into another would-be member of the eldren. He wondered for an instant what such a being could sense or think or do. Could it feel emotion, as illogical and painful as his own?

That dark barrier swallowed it, and he was left alone beneath those ancient constellations.

"What now?" He thought he had waited too long. "Will I be called?"

"Probability uncertain, sir. The judges make the laws of the game. They follow no patterns and answer no questions."

He stayed there, waiting.

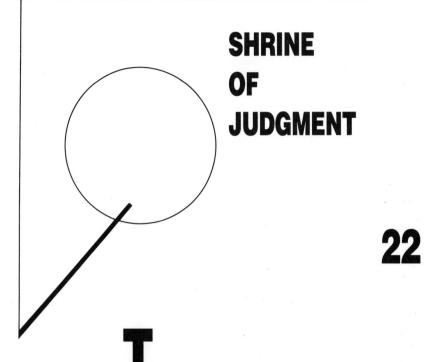

SHRINE
OF
JUDGMENT

22

The servo moved at last, rolling ahead.

"Sir, the judges of the game will see you now."

Its quicksilver sphere vanished into that wall of darkness. Breath caught, he stepped after it. There was nothing he felt. For an instant he was blind. Then he came out into blazing whiteness.

The floor was something like white and seamless stone. It looked luminous. Once polished slick, it was scratched and dulled with ages of wear. Looking away, he found no walls anywhere. Overhead, he found no roof. Only dazzling whiteness, as if the air itself shone. If there was air. When he looked back, even the door was lost. He couldn't help searching that white mist for Roxane Kwan, but he was all alone.

Panic caught him. He had come prepared for strangeness. Yet, here in this white-shining infinity, he felt suddenly lost, all sense of direction gone. For one giddy instant, he felt that he was falling, toppling into a bottomless white abyss.

Yet the floor felt firm. Breathing in the bubble, he found himself poised as if to run, but with nowhere to go. He stood listening. Even if there was air to carry sound, no sound reached him. In spite of the helmet, he wanted to shout and wait for echoes that might reveal roof or walls. Trembling, he tried to find his nerve. This had to be only another chamber in that underground temple of old Zaroth, designed to awe the Delver faithful. He looked at the servo.

"This way, sir."

It rolled ahead. Following close, afraid of losing it, he counted his paces. One hundred. Two hundred. Three. Once he thought their path was curving, but he had no way to know. The servo stopped. The white fog grew thicker, until he could hardly see it at his feet. A sound like wind whispered in his helmet. It died.

"The judges are ready, sir. Remove all your garments."

"Not the lifeskin!" he protested. "Not here without air."

"The judges can support your life."

Dread chilled him, yet he had no choice. Shivering, he unsealed the breather bubble and heard no hiss of leaking air. He shucked off boots and gloves, unlocked the closures, peeled off the clinging fabric, until at last he stood naked in that white mist. It chilled him.

"Your ring. Your watch. Your holo stone."

The ring had been his father's. A wide platinum band, it was mounted with a gold Kwan coin that carried a tiny likeness of the last Tycoon, his own grandfather. The watch, which showed both halo time and Terran time, had been a gift from his mother on his tenth birthday. The holo stone was a gift from Runesong, a flat little oval of some crystal stuff that clung to his skin without being fastened and came alive with her bright-winged image when he looked into it. He had worn it over his heart because he loved her memory. He bent through the fog to lay all three beside his lifeskin on that cold white floor.

The servo was rolling away. He started after it.

"Wait, sir. Stand where you are."

He stood still, and it moved on. Reflecting the featureless whiteness, its silvered curve had no shape and cast no shadow. Two meters away, it was hard to see. He blinked, and it was gone.

Naked and alone, he stood wrapped in blazing stillness. Were the judges watching? He wanted to search the dazzle around him and behind him and above, yet he didn't want to show his dread.

He caught his breath and pulled his body straight and stared blindly into the whiteness.

Time passed. In absolute silence, he could hear his thudding heart. Remembering to breathe, he filled his lungs. The air was still, cold and odorless. Damp with sweat from the lifeskin, he shivered and waited.

And waited.

"Sir." The servo startled him, speaking from nowhere. "The judges!"

A spark of light, swelling in the whiteness. It grew, as if diving at him. It became a form, a wide window in a wall of the same white and seamless polished stone. Heavy masonry framed it, a jutting lintel and an unrailed balcony, yet the foot of the wall was lost in that luminous dazzle.

Real stone? Or holographic illusion, meant to overwhelm the ancient worshipers? Three meters from him? Or a hundred? Peering up into it, trying not to shiver, he waited for the judges.

"The Keeper of Truth."

The window shone with sparks of glinting color, brighter than the whiteness. Swirling like diamond snow around one side of the window, they thinned and cleared enough to let him see a face. No human face, nor the face of any eldren he had met, it had two eyes and something like a nose, and even a narrow-lipped mouth above a pointed chin. The eyes were long and colorless and keen.

"State your name." He saw no movement of the lips, but the voice crashed like near thunder. "State your race. State your world of origin."

"Benn Dain. Human." Perhaps he should have said *Homo sapiens,* but he thought that term would seem ludicrous to the eldren. "I was born here in the halo, but my people came from Terra."

A storm of those restless sparks veiled the face, and cleared again, and left it still the same. The hard-lipped mouth. The jutting ridge his mind had turned into a nose. The sternly staring eyes.

"You ask to play the Game of Blade and Stone?"

Speaking with the servo's sharp metallic intonations, it seemed both far and near, booming and rumbling around him in the blazing fog as if reverberating from walls he couldn't see. Cringing from its cold inhuman power, he gulped to wet his dry throat.

"I do."

"Why?" The question thundered at his ear. "Why do you seek to play?"

"We Terrans are new to the halo." He tried to stand straighter. "We have only one small colony on Janoort, down near the Sun. My parents are speakers for Earth, seeking membership for mankind in the Elderhood. I hope to prove our fitness."

"Are you sponsored?"

"I am. My sponsor is a Hydran scholar, whose translator designation is Edward Gibbon *Beta*."

"Why is he not here with you?"

"He has been wounded by his brother's death. He is under medical treatment on Heart of Hydra. He will join me if he can."

Like bits of shattered crystal, the flecks of glinting color whirled and cleared again.

"Are you known to the Eldermost?"

"My people are. It was my father who destroyed the hive of the invading seeker queen." He wondered if that act of heroic violence might seem a violation of the eldren way, but the sternly rigid face gave him no sign. "He removed a danger to the halo. I think the Eldermost felt that he had earned our chance at life here."

"Do other citizens know you?"

"The Farling Runesong was my first nurse and teacher."

"Does she now support your entry request?"

"She isn't able—"

Waiting for another question, he tried again to wet his lips. Even his tongue was dry. No question came, and he thought he felt a compulsion to go on.

"My people captured her while she was near Terra, observing our first expeditions into space. They hurt her. Hurt her very badly, demanding information she could not give." Apologetic, he tried to explain. "They didn't know the beings of the halo. They were afraid." He saw no change in that bleak dark face. "I'm afraid Runesong is dying."

The diamond glitter swirled again to hide the unchanged face. Grown stiff from standing, he shivered again, feeling gooseflesh, and kept on waiting. For a long time all he saw was that restless dance of rainbow sparks. They thinned at last. He saw a yellow blaze behind them, and through the blaze a second face, less human than the first.

"Sir." The servo's voice, out of nowhere. "The Mistress of Passion."

Faintly, behind burning yellow spirals that spun like a cloud of galaxies, he made out a kind of horny crown. Vague and vanishing shapes looked like enormous ears. More clearly he saw three great triangular eyes, set to make a larger triangle in the black-scaled skin enfolding them. They were huge and red, with great dark pupils fixed upon him.

"Benn Dain?"

A mistress should be feminine, he thought, but there was nothing warm or gentle in the voice that rang and crackled around his head. When it had rolled away and echoed into silence, he found breath enough to answer:

"I am Benn Dain."

"Are you one with yourself?"

Uncertain what to say, he looked for the servo. It was still invisible. He stared up again at that high stone balcony. Waves of yellow fire washed that armored crown and those winglike ears and those three red eyes. Fixed upon him, hot, hypnotic, they never winked.

"Benn Dain." The thunder voice boomed again. "Answer."

"I'm not—not sure what you mean." Feeling small and naked and unsure of anything, he thought he must be honest. "I don't always know myself." He thought of Roxane Kwan and all the confused feelings she had kindled. "But I do know I want to enter the game. I know I want to win. I know I want a place for us in the halo."

"Are you at one with your race?"

"My race isn't—isn't one." His voice turned rusty, and he gulped to smooth it. "Our evolution for space is not yet complete. We have always fought too much. I think the eldren way can help us do better."

"Are you at one with the universe?"

He had stood rigid too long. His neck was stiff from staring up, but he held himself fast and tried to meet those great red eyes while he groped for any sane answer.

"I don't know," his uncertain answer came at last. "I've studied science and philosophy with Dr. Gibbon. He always pointed out that we humans have never agreed about anything. I don't know much about the universe. I hope to know it better."

Watching that strange triangle of eyes, he waited for some question he could understand, for some sign of understanding or approval, but those veils of yellow fire had brightened. The diamond sparks swirled back. Those shadowy ears were hidden again, and that hint of a horn-plated crown, and finally the scarlet eyes themselves.

The Mistress of Passion was gone.

Waiting, he had time to wonder about the judges. Were they venerable citizens of the halo, chosen by the Eldermost and the Council to examine new initiates? Or perhaps ancient aliens who had dwelt here under old Zaroth as the gods and goddess of their own forgotten cults? Or only computer simulations? Or did it matter?

"Sir!" The servo called him back to attention. "The Speaker of Wisdom."

He pulled himself erect to watch the window. In the center of it, the crystal shards spun and faded and flowed aside to let him see two dark eyes, set wide apart in wrinkled yellow flesh beneath heavy white brows. The face looked old as the Eldermost. He thought the eyes seemed wise enough, but they showed no human warmth or sympathy.

"Benn Dain." The great voice drummed against him. "What will happen to your race if you are not admitted to the Elderhood?"

"Nothing good." He groped for words that might win compassion, and tried again for honesty. "Our whole civilization collapsed with the skyweb, but the habit of war is still alive. Unless we have a chance to learn the eldren way, I'm afraid the killing will go on with weapons always better till the last of us is dead."

The old eyes watched him, but he saw no emotion in them. Again he filled his lungs and tried to clear his raspy voice. "I want to earn our right to stay alive."

He waited for the Speaker of Wisdom to speak again, but the last reverberations were dying around him. Diamond fire-flakes thickened again, until their glittering haze veiled all the window.

Heart thumping, he stood there till his neck ached, waiting for a verdict.

None came. The diamond haze grew denser, obscuring everything. The whole window moved, lifting away from him. Slowly at first, faster, faster, it drew away, shrank toward infinity as it dissolved into the dimensionless whiteness. Again he stood alone on the hard white floor.

"Servo!" He turned, calling blindly into the dazzle. "Will they let me into the game?"

"When they decide," its cool computer voice came from nowhere, "you will be informed."

NINE AGAINST THE ODDS

23

The servo led him out of the mist, though an air lock, and into a narrow room that the eldren engineers must have copied from a cabin on the salvaged *Spica*. There was air. He found a berth and shower, a toilet and a dining space. Dishes and linens were marked with the Sun Fleet emblem. Captain Bela Zar scowled in long-nosed disdain from a portrait on the bulkhead.

He waited a long time there, eating a meal the servo made from imitation Sun Fleet rations, fretting about what he might have said to the judges that he hadn't, wondering if he might ever see Roxane Kwan again and even if she might somehow find the halo a world fit for love. He was lying on the berth half asleep when he heard the servo.

"Ready, sir? The judges want you in the Hall of Three."

"Am I in the game?"

"Get into your lifeskin."

His heart was thudding, and his quick breath fogged his helmet till it warmed. Bouncing ahead, the bright silver bubble guided him through a maze of tunnels into the hall. Whiteness dazzled him again. For a startled instant, he thought he was back where he had been examined, but there was no fog here. Carved out of the same white and seamless stuff, this was half a dome, cut in two by a vertical wall.

"The players."

They waited in line along a low platform that curved out beneath that sheer wall. Before he had time to make them out, the servo had flattened itself to bound before him to the edge of the platform. It lay shimmering there with reflected whiteness, quivering until it came to rest.

"Benn!" He found Roxane Kwan beside him, elegant in her own golden lifeskin, her quick voice warmed with a concern he didn't understand. "You shouldn't be here."

Her eyes met his for an instant, bronze and blue, but then she turned to Bolivar, who was just beside her.

"We warned you, Dain." Bolivar stood eyeing him so keenly that he felt naked in the tight lifeskin. "The game is not for Terrans."

"So why are you here?"

Bolivar shrugged, and they swung together toward that blank white wall beyond the silver bubbles lying in a row along the platform's edge. They seemed eagerly expectant, and a puzzled anger shook him.

How had Roxane and Bolivar gotten here? Terrans were rare in the halo and not very welcome. His parents, the official ambassadors for Earth, had known nothing of them. Did they really hope to restore the skyweb? Roxane's cool beauty set an ache in his heart, and he knew no answers.

Yet here he was, in the game at last. He had waited so long and dreamed so much that the moment seemed not quite real, but he was here to win. He caught his breath and turned from them and found the three aliens.

Lilith, Wing, and Vreeth.

Serpentine Lilith was nearest, her narrow snake head as high as his own, her long unreadable eyes sweeping the line of waiting players. Wing next, the flying triangle, floating now above the level of the platform, watching everything with that belt of small bright eyes around her central crown. Finally Vreeth, lionlike, silversleek, crouching. Her great yellow eyes were fixed on him, so intense that he wanted to turn away.

The destroyers of Starsearch? Killers of Gibbon's brother? He shivered, and it took an effort to break free of Vreeth's unearthly stare.

Turning the other way, he started when he found the black robot beside him. Friday once, his tutor and almost a friend through all the years since Runesong had gone away. It stood rigid now, brightly black, more mechanical than humanlike, great lenses blankly fixed on that white wall above the platform.

A clue to his puzzle? The aliens had repaired its malfunction, named it Nexus, brought it here to play. Why?

Two more players stood beyond the robot, waiting silently. One was something angular, bipedal, its limbs and segmented body darkly red and sleekly gleaming. Its eyes were bulging hemispheres, huge and purple-blue. It stood as motionless as Nexus, watching that wall.

The other was something black and glistening, shapeless as a giant amoeba. It floated a little off the floor, but a thick black flap had reached to anchor it to the platform. As he watched, another lump swelled out of it, stretched up, thinned to become a delicate black tendril that wavered inquisitively toward the wall.

"Silence!"

The quicksilver servos had lain still before the players. Now they all moved a little forward, lifted off the platform, and chanted in unison.

"Attend! The judges of the game!"

High on the white wall beyond them, a long patch was glowing brighter. It dissolved as he watched, or seemed to, opening a wide window that was curtained at first by a haze of flashing diamond points. He watched them thin and swirl away until they revealed the judges.

The Keeper of Truth. Two stern eyes and the hard gray ridges around it that made a sort of face, yet nothing like a human face. The colorless eyes looked down upon the players, down upon him, coldly probing, showing no feeling he could guess.

The Mistress of Passion. A crown of horns, washed in waves of yellow flame. Three great eyes, triangular and red, buried in heavy folds of black-scaled flesh. For an instant he thought he saw sadness in them, but that was nonsense. How could such a creature share or sense any emotion?

The Speaker of Wisdom, too old to feel at all. The deep-sunk eyes beneath that shaggy thatch closed for an instant and opened again, looking straight at him. Or was that piercing stare illusion?

Beneath the window, the wall shimmered and dissolved again. A dark archway opened. Nebo came out of it. Gigantic, green-scaled, half reptilian, he shambled across the platform to sit at a white stonelike bench. How did he belong here?

"Players, attend! The judges speak."

Their voices seemed to come from everywhere, crashing loud against the wall, rolling back to ring in his helmet. Or was the echo more illusion? He doubted that the room contained air to carry actual sound.

"We congratulate the nine of you. You have been found eligible to play in the ancient Game of Blade and Stone. Before you can enter, however, you must have the support of a qualified witness who will state that, should you win, you will be found fit for consideration by the Elderhood."

The voices paused. The judges looked down from their high window, or seemed to look down. That glittering mist danced around them, thickened and thinned, veiled and uncovered their unearthly faces. Their strange eyes peered down at him, never winking.

Uneasy under them, he glanced again to left and right. At black Nexus, staring with those huge lenses at the staring judges, as motionless as they and perhaps as much alive. At the red-armored thing beyond it, and the great amoeboid. At Roxane and Bolivar. Her lips moved. He shrugged and grinned. What were they to each other? The uncertainty hurt.

"Candidate Lilith?"

The voices rolled again, and the three aliens stirred, nodding strange heads at one another.

"Have you such a witness?"

Very deliberately, her long snake-head lifted and twisted to let her strange eyes survey Nebo, the players, and the judges. It tipped toward Wing's many-eyed crown, toward Vreeth's lifted ears. Her diamond horn flashed, but he heard no voice.

"Lords of Zaroth." Nebo's crimson eye-spots flickered, and Benn heard his grating growl. "As a citizen of Mazeway and an heir to the ancient founders of the game, I am a qualified witness. I observed and interviewed these three recent arrivals in the halo, who call themselves Lilith, Wing, and Vreeth. I find all three to represent advanced races, evolved to the level of the Elderhood and fully adaptable to the culture of the halo.''

"The Lords of the Game accept the witness of Citizen Nebo," the servos drummed again. "Candidates Lilith, Wing, and Vreeth may enter the game.''

Nebo had risen from the bench, his ferocious grimace fixed on Roxane and Bolivar. His steel-scaled skull dipped in a sort of nod at Nexus.

"Lords of Zaroth." His slitted eyes swung back to the judges. "As a duly licensed guide, I have met and questioned three more of these contenders in the game, the two Terrans who call themselves Don Diego Bolivar and Roxane Kwan, and the mutated robot now called Nexus. I find all three fully fit for consideration by the Elderhood."

He was lurching back toward the bench, but there must have been some silent question. He wheeled back to boom again.

"It is true that the being Nexus exists in what was once a robot, but he now displays a high order of independent intelligence, created by a stochastic process analogous to biological mutation. I find him fit for due consideration."

Nebo stood waiting. The nine servos lay shimmering on the dais.

The voices of the judges crashed again. "The Terrans Bolivar and Kwan and the machine-mind Nexus may enter the game."

Benn found the those unearthly eyes fixed upon him, and felt his body tighten. "Terran Benndain, does a competent witness speak for you?"

He caught his breath, trembling, but his servo answered.

"Lords of the Game, the Hydran citizen Dr. Edward Gibbon *Beta* regrets that he cannot be present, but he certifies that Candidate Benn Dain is well known to him. A student of Terra and its natives, he finds the candidate's race worthy to be tested for the Elderhood."

"Candidate Benndain, we accept you as a contestant."

He relaxed a little, turning to look at the two remaining players, the red-armored thing and the black amoeboid.

"Ayn and Ooru require neither sponsors nor witnesses." The servos crashed again in unison. "They are citizens of the Elderhood, past winners of the game, allowed to continue play because of halo-wide interest and demand. In fairness to the actual candidates, they play under handicap, on courses they have never seen. The prizes they seek are special awards, offered by the Primarch's Casino and licensed holocasters of the game."

The voices paused, and Benn looked at Nexus. His Friday once, alive in his mind through all his childhood, always ready to answer hard questions and do what he commanded, now an unknown entity.

"Contestants, we find all nine of you duly approved to enter. If you wish to play, you must now undertake a solemn obligation to respect and follow the rules of the Game of Blade and Stone, as our ancient primarchs and the Eldermost long ago ordained them. You will each respond, when your name is called, with whatever form of obligation your own culture finds most binding."

Roxane's eyes, and Bolivar's, were upon him when he glanced back at them. Fellow Terrans, yet perhaps no friendlier to him than the robot or the aliens. Roxane's eyes seemed coolly speculative, as if estimating him. Bolivar's dark grin reflected nothing.

"Lilith?" The servos were pealing again. "Wing? Vreeth?"

Lilith lifted and waved her flat black head. Wing dipped toward the floor and rose slowly higher than she had been. Vreeth crouched back as if to spring at the platform and the judges, mirror-eyes lifted to reflect her burning eyes.

"Don Diego Bolivar?"

"I live the way my revered mother taught me." White teeth flashed. "I'll never dishonor her."

"Roxane Kwan?"

"My father was a Kwan. I am a Kwan."

"Benndain?"

"You have my word," he told the bright-veiled faces. "An Earthman's word."

"Nexus?"

"Input recorded."

"Ayn?"

The red-armored head tilted. The purple eyes flashed. Untranslated, the sound in his helmet was a kind of chirp.

"Ooru?"

The thin black tendril coiled into a knot and uncoiled again.

"Your affirmations are recorded."

A pause gave him time to look right and left down the line of these various opponents, their minds and skills and powers all unknown. Vreeth's baleful eyes met his again. Bolivar grinned as if somehow amused. Roxane's glove was on the hilt of her knife. Nexus was slowly swinging those great lenses like cameras sweeping judges and players to image them for its new computer mind.

"Attend!" The judges spoke. "Attend to your initial briefing. Each of you will be accompanied through the play by a servo referee, there to record and report your actions. You are not to ask it for aid or information, and the servo will respond to no such requests, unless you wish to abandon play.

"The game will be played in five steps, by teams of three. Beginning deep in the core of Stone, the courses will lead you upward through the caves of play. Each team will run a separate course, isolated from the others. The fifth step, however, the Step of Stars, should bring those who remain in play back to the surface of the planet.

"Attend! You will be called out now, team by team, for transport into Stone. At each starting point, you will receive further briefings on the goals and conditions of the step ahead. Each of you is now informed that at any point you may ask to resign from the game. If assistance is possible, you will be extricated and expelled from Mazeway forever."

The voices died. Nebo rose from the white stone bench, flashing a black-fanged grimace at Bolivar and Roxane before he shuffled back into the dark archway. White mist filled the arch. Above it, the glittering fog swirled back to hide the judges. Their high balcony dimmed and vanished. The wall was left blank once more, white and seamless.

"Dain, good news for you." He found Bolivar's ironic eyes upon him. "A way out when you want it."

He saw a challenge in that hard brown grin, perhaps a hint of sympathy in Roxane's eyes, but they were both against him. He shrugged and turned, wondering who would be on his team.

"UP IS DOWN"

24

His teammates for the first step were Wing and Ayn. They followed their servos out of the white dome and into a passage toward the transit tube that would drop them through the planet Blade, through the space between the planets, and on down to the caves of play deep in Stone.

The game at last beginning!

Ayn went ahead down the tunnel, following his dancing servo with soaring leaps. With his sleek red-black body-shell, his long lever-limbs, his bulging, green-shining eyes, he looked a little like some giant insect or arthropod. But he was the professional; he ought to be good at the game.

Wing came behind him, sailing high off the floor. Her flat kite-body and yellow-glowing crown resembled nothing he knew. Glancing uneasily back, he always found her too close, her belt of bright little eyes watching in a way that worried him. The crown had no face, no expression of what she felt or what she thought or what she was.

The tunnel brought them to a long terminal hall and the servos led them into a waiting drop-car. The door closed, and they fell toward Stone. The car was a tall cylinder of white eldren plastic with holdfasts spaced along a kind of seat around it. Ayn arranged himself there, propped on his angular legs. Wing floated toward the top, tipped a little to keep her multiple eyes upon them. She was nanionic; he took a seat where he could grasp a holdfast.

"So you're Terran?" Ayn bent toward him companionably, speaking with the shimmer of his eyes. "I believe my own remote ancestors came from Terra, brought back by a Delver expedition. They were treated badly, kept in zoos, altered genetically, enslaved in the mines. In recent ages we have survived where we could, most of us in the caves of Blade and Stone where the ores had been. Few have been as fortunate as I."

"I feel lucky," Benn told him. "To be teamed with you."

"You'll need good fortune." Ayn's head tilted as if for a better view of Wing. "Since you are new, perhaps I should tell you more about the game."

"Please!"

"It is planned to inculcate the eldren way. That is why we play in teams. No team can win without cooperation and mutual aid. That is a lesson not to be ignored, even though partners in one step may become opponents in another."

"I see."

"Wing remains unhappy with you." Ayn paused to flash his eyes at the flying triangle. Her crown shimmered as if in reply, but his translator brought Benn only a brittle crackle. "She says no planetic should be in the game. She believes you will cause us to lose this first step."

"I hope not! I'll do whatever I can."

He peered uneasily up at Wing, searching for anything he could report to Gibbon. Though she flew on nanionic fields, her body flexed a little as she moved, almost like an actual wing. The corners of it tapered very smoothly into those stubby tentacles. It had a gray, glossy sheen. When the belly side tipped a little toward him, he saw three dark seams converging at the center of it.

The vestige, he thought, of a three-lipped mouth. He imagined her ancestors as batlike predators, diving out of some early jungle, spreading tentacles for their prey. There must have been ravenous jaws, armed with savage teeth. She tipped again, to bring that belt of eyes upon him, and he wondered if she had seen the image in his mind.

Ayn was asking if he knew anything about Delvers on Terra.

"I thought eldren visitors were not allowed."

"They are not." Ayn's black antennas waved in what must have been his equivalent of a shrug. "But the Red Delvers have never forgotten the ancient time when they owned half the halo. In an early raid, they found my own ancestors on Terra. Now Nebo has recruited your two fellow Terrans for whatever he plans. Such meddling should be reported to the cluster."

He wondered if this was intended to warn Wing, but she gave no sign.

The cage stopped at last, and they followed the servos out into blood-colored twilight. Delver eyes were different, Gibbon had told him once, sensitive to a wider spectrum. Delver-red was human infrared. He had to let his eyes adjust before he began to find the cragged walls around him, still rough from the tools that had cut them. They were many meters high; he remembered that the ancient Delvers had been giants.

"We brief you now for the Step of Stone." The three servos had halted, speaking with a single voice. "This illuminated tunnel is your course to run. Your goal is to reach the transport terminal for the second step, which will be the Step of Steel."

Ayn's great green eyes flashed what must have been a query.

"The game is very simply scored," they said. "At the end of each step, all members of the team will be scored alike. Two points each for the winning team. One point each for the second team. None for the third. If any player elects to resign from the game, his team will score nothing for that step. The game score for each player will be the total he has accumulated through all five steps."

Wing's crown flickered.

"True," the servos answered. "Each team does run a different course, but the game is planned to equalize the difficulties. Each of you who stays in play will run through five different courses, with five different teams. Your final game scores should even out inequities."

Wing shimmered some protest, and the servos answered with one computer voice. "The judges make the rules."

They rolled on down the tunnel.

"Is that all the game is?" he asked Ayn. "We just run through the tunnel?"

"You have heard the rules," the greenish eyes flashed. "But we must expect surprises."

The servos stopped at a bend in the tunnel, where a bright line crossed the red-lit floor.

"Game time!" They rolled aside. "Play begins now. It will continue until the last of you has reached the goal."

Wing darted away into the crimson dimness, her servo skipping along behind her. Ayn followed, with long soaring leaps. Benn tramped after them, taking a little comfort from the rule that the whole team would win or lose together.

Though larger than Blade, the planet was smaller than Terra. Gravity here was perhaps only half a G. Even in the lifeskin, he found walking fairly easy, yet the gleam of Wing's flying crown and the rise and fall of Ayn's green eyes drew farther and farther ahead until they disappeared.

He plodded on alone, remembering Roxane Kwan in her golden lifeskin, wondering what would come of her partnership with Bolivar and Nebo, wondering if the game itself might show her a world where love could live. He thought of Gibbon, lying under therapy on Heart of Hydra, grieving for his brother and waiting for facts that might identify the killer.

He reviewed the little he knew of the aliens. They had been at Starsearch when Gibbon's brother died. They had transformed Friday. They were against him in the game. That was all he knew.

Alone with his servo, he tramped through dim red twilight. He looked for a source of the light and decided that the stone itself shone faintly. He tried to imagine the giants who had toiled here. In this empty gloom, he felt that all their toil had come to nothing.

Was the whole halo watching? Even his parents in the far cluster? He knew the servos must be recording all that happened for the judges and casinos and holocasters. Thinking of that, he tried to tramp a little faster.

He passed branching tunnels that were totally dark. Which meant that they were not part of the course. Except for the rasp of his breath, he heard no sound at all. The high roof was roughly arched, dully glowing. Though it hadn't fallen for many million years, the mass of naked stone above him began to feel oppressive.

His spirits lifted for a moment when he overtook his fellow players. They had stopped. Ayn was leaning tipped back against a jutting rock, long lever-legs neatly folded. In the green shine of his eyes, the hard body was glistening black, strangely graceful. Wing floated just above him.

The tunnel had forked beyond them, both branches lit. He saw the shimmer and flash of speech between Ayn's eyes and Wing's golden crown, but his own translator merely snapped and crackled until Ayn's head tilted toward him.

"This step appears to test intelligence," he said. "We must decide which path to take."

The right and left branches of the tunnel looked very much alike, equally cragged, both winding away into the same crimson dimness. The roadways into both looked equally wide, equally smooth, but one sloped gently down, the other gently up. Benn looked down both and back at them with an uncertain shrug.

"Wing was saying that we can expect no help from a planetic." Ayn's eyes flickered at him and back into the rising tunnel. "Yet the rules of the game hold us together."

Wing's crown shimmered.

"Here is her logic," Ayn told him. "The general trend of the courses is upward, as the servos informed us, to lead us back toward the surface. She suggests that we choose the climbing passage. Do you agree?"

"Why not?"

He found nothing better to say. Wing dived to scan him with her belt of eyes and sailed away into the upward tunnel. Ayn hopped after her. Again he followed, and again he lost them somewhere ahead. The passage did slope steadily upward until he came upon Ayn, waiting alone.

The tunnel had ended on the brink of a pit. All he saw beyond was darkness, a black chasm so vast he found no floor or walls or roof, even when Ayn's eyes tried to probe it. Far out in it, he found Wing, a faint yellow spark roving here and there. They waited till she came back, shimmering to Ayn.

"An empty cavity," Ayn reported. "Left where a large ore body once existed. It must have been removed through the passage where we are. She has found no other exit. Now she asks for alternative strategies, expecting none from you."

She dropped toward Ayn, and his eyes turned her luminous against the gloom.

"I was hatched here in Stone." Benn moved closer to catch light with his translator. "Though I have never played this course, I have studied tactics for the game. I believe we have a useful clue in the circulation of the air."

Wing flashed some question.

"This section of the cave systems does contain a mix of gases." Ayn swung a little toward Benn. "Useless to you, my planetic friend, because there is no oxygen here. It does circulate, however, because the surface of Stone is cold. The interior retains natural heat. The result is convection. Here the air flow is downward, because cooling is rapid in the shallow galleries above us.

"I suggest that we climb against the moving air."

Wing's crown flickered in agreement and Ayn led them away with a leap that carried him close to the red-glowing roof. Again Benn followed them, never able to keep up. Clever as the lifeskin was, every moment in it cost energy. Trotting at first, he had to slow to a plodding walk.

His companions shrank to dancing sparks ahead, sometimes lost in the scarlet twilight, but he always found them again, waiting for him at some twist or dip or branch, Wing flickering scornfully to Ayn about how slow he was.

The tunnel changed. Behind them, it had twisted wherever the miners looked for ore, the dark naked rock left to support itself, but here they must have met some weakness in the planet's crust. The tunnel had been driven level and straight, and lined with something like black concrete.

Here again they left him far behind. His legs were aching, his crotch smarting where the lifeskin had chafed it, before he caught up with them at a high barrier of fallen rubble. Some ancient quake had brought down great masses of the black concrete to close the tunnel.

"The air still moves." Ayn sat the way Benn sat, his hard-shelled body tipped back against a block of broken concrete. Tired,

Benn thought, probably dejected, yet defending himself. "Coming though the rockfall, however, it reveals no passage large enough for us."

Wing was busy, flitting back and forth along the wall behind him, tipping to sweep it with the glow of her crown. She paused to flash her light at Benn, as if surprised by his arrival, and then turned to Ayn. He rose stiffly to shine his eyes on the wall. His light brought out markings there, suddenly vivid, luminous and green.

"Graffiti, I believe." He dropped heavily back to sit against the wall. "Left, I suppose, by workmen who inspected the rockfall and decided that they could not reopen the tunnel. Illiterate scrawls, of no use to us."

Wing hovered over him, flickering urgently.

"The language," he said, "is an ancient Delver tongue, but still used in our holy writings. I can decipher some of these inscriptions, but they make very little sense. A few names, crudely scratched. Here is what I take as an obscene insult aimed at some superior or perhaps a curse at the evil ghost who caused the disaster."

He flashed his eyes along the wall.

"Here, two words without grammatic form. Words for *up* and *down*. If we tried to put them into a sentence, it could read 'Up is Down,' or 'Down is Up.' No clue for us—"

Wing's flashing crown interrupted him. She dived to inspect the inscription for herself and sailed back to him, her crown still shimmering.

"Wing has a question for you." Ayn's great eyes shone at Benn. "What does a planetic make of this message?"

"SOMETHING UNELDREN"

25

Benn blinked for a moment against the blaze of Wing's golden crown, flustered by her contemptuous question. He turned to Ayn and saw the great eyes shimmer:

"Terran Dain, we play together."

"Here's a guess." He frowned uneasily at Wing, hovering too low above his head. That triangular seam struck him again as the vestige of a predatory jaw. "If the inscription was left by workers trapped here, they were looking for a way out. It could be a clue to what they were discussing—"

The blaze of Wing's crown crashed in his helmet.

"Our teammate says she has enough of your planetic babble," Ayn translated. "She says the import of the inscription should be obvious, even to a planetic. To escape, we must choose the tunnels sloping down."

"That's what I wanted to suggest."

Wing was already lifting away. Ayn sprang after her, as if they hadn't heard him. Once more he followed, his servo skittering with him, and once more they left him far behind. A long time later, at the end of another red-lit passage, he found them waiting with their servos outside a tall doorway. The servo stopped before him.

"Player Dain, you have reached your goal for the Step of Stone," its brisk voice shone. "The judges of the game felicitate you."

Beyond the door, they found a big circular room with a dozen doorways spaced around the wall. The servos separated here to lead them apart, but Wing glided back to him, her yellow crown flashing. The unreadable intelligence beyond her belt of hard black eyes was suddenly as threatening to him as he thought it must have been to Gibbon's brother, back at Starsearch Station.

"We lost this step." Ayn's voice rang in his helmet. "So the servos report. Third place, no score. Wing blames you. When she plays against you, she promises to send you back to your own miserable planet."

She was soaring away behind her servo.

"The game is not over." Ayn spoke as if to cheer him. "You did all you could."

"Not well enough." He grinned into the horn-beaked, inhuman face. "But I thank you."

Now suddenly helpful, his own servo escorted him through an air lock into another narrow room furnished with equipment copied from the *Spica*, complete with Captain Bela Zar's sardonic smile from the portrait on the wall.

Gratefully he peeled off the chafing lifeskin, showered, ate eldren synthetics. The servo sprouted delicate silvery fingers to examine the spots where the suit had rubbed him raw and apply something that eased the sting.

When that was done he sat down on his bunk, staring blankly at nothing. Disappointment lay heavy on him. Wing's scorn rankled in him, yet it came from truth that hurt. Human beings were still in fact planetics. Even if he won, even if they were admitted to the Elderhood, would they always be third-class citizens, mocked by everybody else?

"We're what we are." Speaking aloud, he shrugged and fingered a blister on his shoulder. "With most of the game still to play—"

"Sir?" the servo shone. "Have you a command?"

"I do," he told it. "Call Heart of Hydra for me. Ask for Dr. Edward Gibbon *Beta*."

"Acting, sir."

The servo bounced away toward the end of the narrow room. A thin cloud veiled it, the hemisphere of captive ions that formed the holophone screen. The cloud flickered, and the wall translator spoke.

"Dr. Gibbon is unavailable—" The cloud faded and brightened again. "Correction, sir. A message from Dr. Gibbon. He asks you to wait."

"I'll wait."

The ion-glow dimmed until he could see the servo's shining bubble on the floor and the gleam of the life-support gear beyond it. It brightened, and the end of the room was gone. He looked beyond where it had been into a milk-white haze of pickup noise.

"Benn?" Gibbon's voice came out of the haze. "Benn?"

"Doctor, I'm here."

It cleared a little, and he found Gibbon's lumpy gray potato shape floating in it, half covered with the birth robe. As always, that trapped him even when he tried not to look, its shifting hieroglyphs straining his eyes and baffling his mind with a sense of patterns gone before he could make them out.

Gibbon floated in that pale fog, motionless and featureless. No limbs were extended, but a thin ribbon of tissue had grown from one potato eye. With an effort to pull himself away from the tantalizing riddles of the robe, Benn followed it through the fog to another motionless Hydran, lying almost beyond pickup range and barely visible.

"Doctor?" he called uneasily. "Are they helping you?"

A single seeing eye came slowly open. The knobby body was still a dark and lifeless gray, but he saw a faint voice-light pulsing along that linking tissue.

"They try." A dim unsteady shimmer, nearly too faint for his translator to catch. "You see my clone-cousin here beside me. He shares himself with me. I am grateful. But that can never—never make me whole again."

He peered into the image, trying to make out more.

"They want to repair my great loss with bits of other minds." A faint, uneven rasping. "But nothing can replace my brother."

"At least you are alive."

"Only half—half alive." The phrases came brokenly, as if they cost great effort. "That's why I need you, Benn. To do what I cannot. To help me learn who killed my brother."

"I'll do all I can."

The halting words had stopped. Uneasily he waited. The ion screen was still a window into that luminous haze. The two Hydran bodies still floated there, side by side, but no light was alive in the band of flesh that joined them. He found himself frowning at the robe again, trying in spite of himself to find more than he ever could in its Hydran kaleidoscope.

"Sir?" He pulled his eyes back to Gibbon and the clone-cousin's fainter form. "Sir, are you able to speak? Or should I let you go?"

"Wait." A flicker and a whisper. "Let me find—find what life I can."

Again he waited, wondering about the therapy. Were there vessels in that thin gray ribbon transfusing life into Gibbon's body? Had Hydran nerves grown to share memory and mind? The strangeness of it awed him. He stood there, filled with a wondering pity for Gibbon, until he began to think he had been forgotten.

"Benn—" Feebly the ribbon glowed again. "Have you information for me? New facts about the aliens and the robot?"

"Too little." He tried to describe the aliens, to sum up what he knew about them and Bolivar and Roxane Kwan. "All of them allies of Nebo," he finished. "Involved in some secret scheme. I don't trust them."

"I have asked—" A labored whisper. "Asked for background on Nebo. He is said to be a rogue. He has been fined for preying on visitors to the game. Yet he has influence, because others share his dream of restoring the old Delver primarchs. An impossible dream, because the skills of the old Delver engineers have been forgotten."

The whisper died.

"It's his friends," Benn said. "His friends that frighten me. The aliens and Nexus. I don't know what they want, or what technologies they have. Let loose on Earth—I can't guess what they would do. Nothing good for anybody."

"Watch them, Benn! Watch them closely."

The tissue band was dark for a moment before it pulsed again with Gibbon's toiling voice.

"I have other information. Reports from the *Mindquest*. The supply ship that brought the Starsearch refugees back to Cluster One. It was returning to the station with a party of engineers to investigate the disaster and repair the damage. Now, however—"

The voice-light went out.

"Sir, can you say what happened?"

He saw another dim shape emerging from the haze beyond the pickup range.

"Forgive me, Terran caller." A new computer voice. "Dr. Gibbon is recuperating from a very grave injury. He requires quiet and rest. We must ask you to conclude—"

"Not yet!"

"Terran sir, he must cease—"

"A moment more." Gibbon would not cease. "A few more words."

"Yes?" He leaned closer, listening. "About the rescue ship?"

"Near Starsearch." A faint-voiced phrase, an endless pause, another desperate phrase. "Somewhere—somewhere near Starsearch. I called—called to warn the Council. They are not concerned."

"The ship?" A pause so long that Benn spoke to break his own tension. "Was it lost?"

His eyes went back to that thin gray ribbon sagging through the fog between the still gray bodies. He saw it twitch and tighten.

"Sir, I must interrupt." It pulsed with new light, now from the body that lay beside Gibbon. "My disabled cousin has spoken too much. You must let him rest."

"No!" A single word in Gibbon's voice, almost a cry of pain.

"Allow me, sir." The cousin's voice. "If I may say what my cousin cannot."

"Please!"

"He lacks strength to speak, but I have shared his mind. I know what he would say. The supply ship left Cluster One for Starsearch with most of the original staff aboard, along with a group of technicians and engineers. As you may know, the disaster had left the station without power. Dead."

"The supply ship found it alive again. Power restored. Laser and nanionic beacons once more sweeping space. Yet signals to it brought no answer. The ship called Cluster One, reporting the situation and asking for advice. Some of those aboard were apprehensive of any near approach. The service authorities were convinced, however, that the automatic machinery of the station had simply repaired itself. They advised a landing.

"The last call reports the attempt to land. The station did send a signal as they drew near, but it was not in any familiar language. The Cygnan linguist attempted translation and failed. The signal resembled one picked up from somewhere outside the halo not long before the disaster. He advised the expedition to turn back. At that point, transmission from the ship was interrupted.

"Since then, nothing."

The cousin's voice had stopped, but Gibbon spoke again.

"Something—something is there!" A sudden pulse of speech, feebly violent. "Something that killed my brother. Something uneldren!"

"Sir, you have warned the Elderhood?"

"Terran sir." The clone-cousin spoke again. "The facts are known, but the Council is not alarmed. The *Mindquest* has reported no threat of hostility or danger. Merely the puzzle that the ship was landing to solve. It carried a staff of able scientists. When they have reached a solution, they are expected to report it."

That band of tissue flexed again and pulsed with Gibbon's voice. "Our problem, Benn."

"On Starsearch, sir?"

"Where the aliens are. Observe them, Benn. Observe the robot. Let me know what you learn."

The ribbon had darkened. The two Hydrans lay together in the milky mist, dead gray, motionless, and silent. The shifting hieroglyphics of the birth robe caught his unwilling eyes again, always a reminder that he was still a stranger here.

"Terran, you must let him go." The clone-cousin spoke. "His injury has left him with undue anxiety. You know what is known. Starsearch was certainly struck by a real disaster. His brother was killed. A cruel loss, but our physicians believe his mind has made too much of it.

"He dwells upon the aliens his brother had detained there, although other members of the staff saw no harm in them. He was alarmed when they arrived at Mazeway, but all they seek is citizenship. He suspects them of involvement in some plot against the Elderhood, but others have seen no convincing evidence."

"I am convinced," Benn protested. "I've met the aliens and their robot. I don't like them. Now we have this alarming news—"

The ribbon contracted, alive with light.

"Terran friend, your call has distressed our patient. We must end it."

And they were gone. The window into Heart of Hydra had closed. Where it had been, he saw the kitchen and bathroom fixtures at the end of his own narrow room. The servo's silver bubble lay shimmering on the floor.

THE STEP
OF
STEEL

26

Restless, he slept in the narrow berth beneath the supercilious gaze of Captain Bela Zar, ate a hurried eldren breakfast, and got back into his lifeskin when the servo alerted him for the second step of the game. At the starting point, he followed it out of the transport cage into empty blackness. His suit light came on, glinting off the silvery servo, gleaming against the cage that was silently sliding away.

In a moment he stood alone with the servo—somewhere.

The flat floor beneath him was something like gray concrete. Dark stains splotched it, as if from liquids spilled long ago. Its pits and cracks were black with shadow. He saw no end to it, no walls or roof or anything else.

"Wait here, sir." The servo shimmered with the light of its voice. "The others of your team will be arriving to attempt the Step of Steel."

"Who are they?"

"You will meet them, sir."

Its voice-light went out, and he turned to search for steel. The concrete platform reached away into the dark all around him, as far as he could see. Near him, inky shadow filled a long rectangular pit. Smaller pocks were spaced in line beside it. Bolt holes, perhaps? He wondered if some steel machine had once been bolted here, salvaged when its metal grew precious.

Searching the old concrete around him, he found no steel.

His translator was silent. If there was air here, it carried no sound. All he could hear in the breather bubble was the whisper of his breath and the amplified throb of his heart. All he could see was the little pool of light around his feet, but he imagined the cold weight of the planet's crust above him, oppressive even if it had held for many million years. Impatient, he paced away to the end of that empty pit and back again to the servo's silent glint, until he heard motion behind him in the dark.

"Benn?" He turned and found another transport cage, the door sliding open. A human form stood there, looking down at him. "Benn Dain!"

"Roxane!"

He whispered her name and stood breathless, staring. She might have been a dream. Her whole lifeskin shone, wrapping her in golden light. Shining through the bubble helmet, it lit her tanned and vivid face, her tawny hair. He reached to help her down.

She waved him aside, and he saw the knife she wore outside the shining lifeskin, slung against her thigh. Though she didn't speak, the knife and the arrogant gesture reminded him that she was the Kwan, untouchable. Lightly she sprang down to his side.

"Who else is with us?"

"We'll have to wait. The servo doesn't say."

She didn't seem to mind his stare, and he couldn't pull his hungry eyes away. Her splendor set an ache in his heart, because she had to be against him in the game. Because her world was not for love.

"This is your second step?" At least for now, they were companions. "How did your first one go?"

"Don was with me—Don Bolivar. And we won." Pleasure lit her face, but only for an instant. "The other player—" Her smile was gone. "It was Nexus—that black robot-thing. Don calls it our friend, but it frightens me. The way it speaks and the way it thinks and the way it stares with those dead lenses.

"Yet it is intelligent—so keen it scares me. It did help us win.

It found a shortcut to the finish point. When we came to a locked door across the tunnel, it knew a way to work the combination. We got there first."

She looked at him soberly.

"How was yours?"

"We finished last," he confessed. "No score."

She nodded, not surprised.

"I'm sorry for you, Benn." She spoke as if on impulse. "You know you shouldn't be here."

"Because I'm Terran? Have you a better chance?"

"We have." She didn't explain. Her fine eyes had measured him, doubt yielding to respect. "I'm sorry." He thought her voice held a real regret. "Sorry we have to be against each other."

"Must we be?"

"I'm the last Kwan." He saw the pride that held her glowing body straight. "My father lived his life to hang the skyweb back. He died with nothing done. Now, with luck enough, I can do what he tried to."

"How?" Gibbon would want to know.

"I came out from Earth with Don and that creature Nebo." She paused, eyes a little narrowed, deciding how much to say. "He has friends here. Influence and resources. When we have working skywires and space docks back in place, he says I can be recognized as the new Tycoon. My father wanted that."

Her face had lit with an old devotion.

"These friends?" Longing for her goodwill, he was half afraid to risk such questions. "Nebo and Nexus? And those aliens that had been detained at Starsearch Station? Do you trust them?"

"They're strange." A shadow crossed her face. "Sometimes they scare me, but Don says we have to trust them. After all, my father took a million risks. You might say he lived and died for nothing, but he was never sorry."

"What if you lose the game?"

"We won't." Her voice rang with certainty. "But it wouldn't matter even if we did. We'll still have our friends when the game is over." She studied him again, more keenly. "When the game is over, what about you?"

"I'd like to show you the halo." The impulse caught him. He

wasn't sure what she might think, but eagerness swept his words along. "You must see more of the halo. Get to know more of the eldren. Meet my parents at Cluster One. Maybe visit Janoort. We've begun building a new world there. A world that might be—" Emotion trembled in his voice. "That might be fit—"

"These snowballs!" Her sharp voice stopped him. "Fit for what?" She stood a moment frowning at him, then spoke again, her tone a little warmer. "But I like you, Benn. You'll lose this game, but you do know these eldren. If you want to play a bigger game, I think we might need you here. A speaker for the new Tycoon. I'll speak to Don about it."

"Don't," he told her. "That's not my game."

"This one will be over." A gesture of her golden arm swept his protest away. "We can talk about it then."

"I don't like your friends."

"I never liked all my father's men," she said. "But he commanded them." She turned a little, to stare away into the dark. "Our fellow player should be here."

He stood looking at her, lean and graceful in the golden lifeskin, her loveliness transformed by the black-sheathed knife hung against her thigh. She looked as stubbornly proud as her father must have been, armed against everything. Yet he felt a stab of pity for her. She was wrong. She had to be defeated.

If he could beat her.

"Even if we're enemies—" She turned back with a quick half smile, almost as if she had read his thoughts. "We're together in this step. You are my fellow soldiers. You and our new partner—whoever he's going to be. I expect to do my bit. I expect the same from you."

"Fellow soldiers." Benn reached for her golden glove, and she let him take it. "Till this step is won."

He felt happy for the moment.

"You speak of a world for love." Her voice crisply cool, she drew her hand away. "But my father was right. There's no place left for it. Not here among these nightmare creatures of the ice. No land here, no grass or trees or sky. Nowhere for homes or children or peace. Earth is no better. Not now. All my father taught me is war."

She paused with that, staring past him as if she were looking back to the far Earth and her own childhood. Her voice grew softer.

"Benn, do you really want to live here?"

"I do live here. It's all I know. That's why I'm in the game. To earn our right to stay."

"Here among these monsters?"

"They aren't so monstrous," he protested. "Not when you get to know them—"

A transport car was suddenly beside them, the silent door sliding open.

"Our partner."

They turned together to watch the creature emerging from the car and crouched back from the glister of their lifeskins on a great mass of something that flowed like a slow black liquid, out of the cage and down to the concrete.

"What's that?" She recoiled from it. "Black slime!"

Congealing as it flowed, it built into a rounded mound almost a meter high. Silently the car slid away from it, back into the dark. It lay there, frozen. Its slick black surface reflected their lights, but it gave none of its own.

"Players, attend!"

He thought for an instant that it had spoken, but then he found another servo on the concrete where the car had been, voice-light shimmering.

"Attend!" All three spoke. "Attend to your briefing for the Step of Steel."

"That thing!" Roxane had caught the hilt of her knife. "It can't be a player!"

"It is a player. Player Ooru."

"I saw the thing named Ooru, back before the judges." She watched it warily. "It moved. It put out arms. This looks—dead!"

The three servos rolled to form a line beside the mound of ooze.

"Attend to your briefing!" they chanted together. "Your course to run for the Step of Steel is this ancient excavation, from which the ores were removed long ago. You now stand at the starting point. Your goal is the lift where the ores were taken out.

"The judges wish you to understand the factors that will determine your team score. These are first the time elapsed before the last of you has reached the finish point, and second the eldren characteristics of intelligence and altruism you reveal as you run.

"As before, you will be monitored throughout the play. At any time, any one of you may ask to leave the game. Play for the step will cease at that point. If possible, all players will be rescued and removed. The terminating player will be escorted back to Blade and required to leave Mazeway. Team score for the step will be zero.

"Contestants, do you understand?"

Still clutching her knife, Roxane stood peering silently at the mass of oily slime. It lay where it was, slickly gleaming, motionless, and black. Staring into the dark beyond it, beyond the shimmer of the servos, Benn caught his breath to mutter, "I do."

"Briefing complete," the servos sang. "Play begins."

"A player?" Roxane whispered. "What can it do?"

"They called it a professional," he reminded her. "So popular with the audience that it has earned some kind of special status."

"A friend of yours?" Her tight voice mocked him. "If you love the halo."

"Player Ooru?" He walked a little toward it. "Can you speak?"

It lay there, a black and shapeless pile, motionless and dead.

"What's wrong with Ooru?" He turned to the servo beside it. "Is it sick?"

"Through the duration of play our responses are restricted," the servo told him. "Unless some player requests termination."

"Is Ooru requesting termination?"

"Ooru has communicated no request."

"We can't just wait." Roxane backed away from it. "Let's begin looking—for whatever we can find. Anything to show us the way to the exit."

"We do have one fact to go on." He stood watching Ooru. "Those old miners took the ores out. They must have had some transport system. A road or a cable system or a conveyor. Whatever. With luck, we might find and follow it to the lift point."

"Let's scout around."

"First—" He raised his voice. "Ooru! If you can hear me, we're trying to learn more about our situation here. We'll return."

The ooze lay black and still. They pushed away from it across the time-scarred floor, their own silent servos dancing beside them. It was soon lost behind them in the dark. Once, when they had stopped to look around them, Roxane caught his arm to peer into his face.

"So this is what you love?" Her voice was half-malicious mockery. "Your paradise in the sky?"

"I'm sorry." He said it soberly, and paused to relish her golden wonder. "I wish you liked the halo."

"How could I?" Suddenly she was altogether serious. "The Holyfolk call it Hell. I think it is. Filled with things like that pile of black slime! Give me Africa. Baboons and warthogs and hyenas are easier to love."

"Roxane, please! My first nurse was an eldren named Runesong. I loved her more than any human." He had to pause and shake his head. "As for Ooru—I don't know what's wrong, or what to expect."

They pushed on through the soundless dark.

"The Step of Steel." She murmured the phrase, thinking aloud. "We ought to find steel. Steel rails, maybe, for the cars that hauled the ore."

"Rails." He nodded. "Tubes. Tramways. Maybe something we never invented."

Searching for steel, they crossed an endless jagged crack where some ancient quake must have riven that endless floor. They came upon mountainous piles of broken stone, where rocks from above had fallen and shattered. Again and again they had to circle another empty pit, where he thought some great unknown machine must have been removed.

But they found no steel.

"There has to be—something!" he muttered, once when they had stopped again to stare into the dark. "A road. A wall. An end somewhere."

"There!" He heard the catch of her breath. "Something!"

A barrier of the same old gray concrete, when they were close enough to make it out. He was counting steps to measure distance. They followed it a full kilometer, and came back to a ragged pit that he recognized as their starting point.

"A pillar!" He stepped back, staring. Massive, smooth, slightly curved, it was stained with endless dark red streaks where something must have drained down it from above. It climbed into the dark as far as he could see. "Built, I guess, to keep the roof from caving in. Three hundred meters around! Those old Delvers were giants."

They turned together to leave that towering shaft.

"That way?" Uncertainly he stopped. "There was that long ridge of broken rock—" He frowned into the darkness, but the ridge was too far to see. "A line of pits. That crack like an old quake fault, farther on. But—"

He stared at her.

"I don't know."

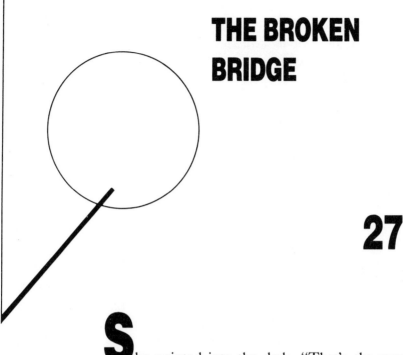

THE BROKEN BRIDGE

27

She pointed into the dark. "That's the way back."

"Are you sure?" He shook his head. "To me, that's almost the way we were headed."

"I'm sure." Her voice was calmly positive. "Hunting game in Africa, or hiding from the Holyfolk, you have to know directions. We haven't found the way out, but if you want to go back to that pile of black mud—" She gestured with a shining arm. "I know the way."

Boldly she struck out across the ancient concrete. Doubtfully he followed. Even if she was wrong, he didn't want to lose her. Uneasily he scanned the pits and cracks and piles of rock that came within their pools of moving light. All seemed strange, until he heard a voice.

"Terrans?" A voice he had never heard, faint and far away. "Terrans, where are you?"

He looked at the servos. They showed his own mirror image, and Roxane's just ahead, golden and tiny and bright, but no flicker of any voice.

Ooru? Silently he stared at Roxane.

"That monster?" She had stopped. "Alive again?"

"Calling us, I think." He climbed a pile of fallen stone and turned up his own voice-light. "Ooru?" The words rang too loud in his helmet. "Ooru?"

"Terrans! Ooru comes to you."

They waited, together among the shattered boulders. Roxane had climbed to a ragged point of stone a little above him. Standing there, warily watching, her bright glove near the hilt of her knife, she looked to him like a warrior goddess. Splendid in her pride, but not for love.

"Terrans." The voice came again, suddenly louder. "Ooru here."

Dark as the darkness, the creature was hardly a dozen meters away. Still shapeless, jet-black, dimly glistening, it moved as if it flowed, half supported by its nanionic field. A thin tendril lifted toward them, shimmering as it spoke.

"Terrans comprehend?" Its creeping movement halted. "Ooru unequipped with machine translator system. Terran language inadequately mastered from intercepted holocasts."

"We comprehend." Benn climbed off the rocks and walked to meet it. "You had us worried. Were you ill?"

"Not ill. Word perhaps is stasis." The speaking tendril stretched farther toward him. "Quiet required for adjustment of excess emotion."

"Excess emotion?" Benn laughed, his own tension half relieved. "We had excess emotions of our own."

"Ooru's stasis induced by disparities with Terrans." The tendril lifted toward his face and hung there as if somehow sensing him. "Disparities of origin. Disparities of biology. Disparities of culture."

"I think we comprehend. You seem strange enough to us."

"Disparities create hazards." The tendril lifted higher, glowing redly. "Hazards to success in running Step of Steel. Hazards to be overcome."

"We were wondering what kind of chance we have."

"Ooru also." The tendril thrust closer to his helmet. "Ooru felt Terrans unfit for space, unskilled in game. Ooru fears defeat in game Step of Steel."

174

"We're new here." He shrugged wryly, liking Ooru. "We don't have all the skills we need. But we're trying to learn. Hoping to be accepted in the Elderhood."

"Admirable effort. Outcome problematic."

The tendril wavered away from him, toward Roxane. Scrambling cautiously down from the rock pile, she had her knife half out of its sheath. The tendril reached to meet her, shimmering again.

"Peace essential. United effort required." It changed color as it spoke, glowing brightly green. "Ooru wounded by perceptions of Terran hostility."

"You—you frightened me." She stopped a safe distance from it. "You still look—" She caught her voice and sheathed the knife. "It's still hard to trust you."

"Terra strange to Ooru." The tendril brushed her luminous suit, and she cringed from its touch. "Terrans strange to Ooru. Terran mind unknown. Terran culture unknown. Terran capacities unknown."

"I didn't mean to hurt—"

Her tight voice failed. The tendril had thrust at her helmet. Like a green snake, Benn thought, striking at her face. Instinctively she dodged, yet she stood fast. The tendril dropped to wrap itself around her waist and pull her toward the creature's black-glistening mass.

She yielded to it, but gripped the knife again.

"Ooru seeks accord." Still wrapped around her, the tendril thinned and stretched, lifting its green-glowing tip back toward her face. "Accord with cosmos. Accord with eldren. Accord with officials of Game of Blade and Stone. Accord with Terrans now. Accord through kinship."

"Roxane?" Benn came to her side. "Are you okay?"

"So far." A breathless laugh. "If we're going to be friends."

"Kinship?" He frowned at the green-shining tendril. "How can we be kin?"

"Children of sister worlds. Terra and Roonu. Two worlds of same near star. Terra small inner planet. Roonu large gas planet. Planet you name Jupiter."

"You live on Jupiter?"

"Not upon. Jupiter all gas. No surface fit for life. Roonu race evolved for life in gas. Ooru hatch in gas, fly in gas, live in gas. Visitor to halo now. Guest of Red Delvers. Professional player in Game of Blade and Stone."

"If we're kin—" She slid her blade back into its sheath and twisted in that green embrace to grin at Benn. "Kin and teamed together, let's get on with the Step of Steel."

"Difficult game," the tendril flashed. "Difficult course to run. Most difficult for Terrans. Victory requires concord. Terrans must know Ooru. Ooru must know Terrans."

"We're learning." Roxane laughed again. "Fast enough!"

The tendril drew her closer to the black and formless mass.

"Roonu unlike Terra." The green tendril wrapped around her neck, and Benn felt her shudder. "Roonu culture unlike Terran culture. Terrans trapped on narrow surface. Roonu hatch in flight. Grow in flight. Live in flight. Terrans captives of gravity, Roonu free."

Benn stared again at that great, ungainly, black-glinting mass, wondering how it could fly.

"Terrans perplexed?" The tendril darted at his helmet, struck back at Roxane's. "Roonu flexible in form. Fly in youth like Terran kites, Terran balloons. Aided by slight nanionic control. Ooru now learning science of nanionic snark from eldren. Clumsy student. Thrust feeble, motion slow."

"If we're friends—" Roxane frowned at the glowing tendril. "Will you let me go?"

The tendril unwrapped her.

"Thank you, Mr. Ooru!" She stepped away. "If we're really playing together—"

"Ooru unhostile to Terrans," it shimmered at her. "But misinterpretations possible. Terran signal systems not yet familiar. Comprehension fragmentary, yet better understanding now essential. Mutual action now essential. All three companions now in Game of Blade and Stone."

"All altogether." She nodded, and touched her knife again. "Win or lose."

"Inquiry?" The tendril tip swung toward Benn. "Terrans know

rules of game? Terrans trust Ooru? Terrans ready now to attempt difficult run to earn game score?"

"We have to trust each other." Benn grinned at Roxane. "I guess we're as ready as we'll ever be."

"Terrans have plan for game?"

"You're asking us for advice?"

"Terrans planetic creatures, like Ooru. Not fully evolved for halo. Ooru know gas world. Solid world still new. Terran knowledge of solid-state environment should aid team effort."

"We had a sort of plan." Benn frowned into the dark beyond Ooru's inky bulk and the mounds of fallen rock. "The old Delvers built machines to get the ores out. They've all been torn out, but we've seen the foundations. There must have been a transport system to carry the ores. If we could discover traces of that—"

"Logical plan," the tendril flashed. "If Terrans agree, we seek and follow traces."

"Agreed! Though they're hard to see, here in the dark."

Ooru slid away, gliding as fast as they could walk. The tendril dark again, Ooru's flowing blackness almost disappeared.

"Please!" Benn called. "Can't you show us a light? Before we lose you?"

"Ooru perceives infrared." The tendril lit. "Unaware of Terran handicap."

It kept on shining, steadily yellow. Eyes on it, they followed close. Now and then their pool of light picked up the ruined stubs of great square towers standing in piles of broken concrete. Benn thought they formed a line. The wreckage, perhaps, of a demolished ore conveyor system? Ooru said nothing until at last the tendril flashed to stop them.

"Caution, Terrans! Caution!"

The creature had halted. Reaching ahead, the tendril illuminated the edge of the old platform. Midnight emptiness yawned beyond. Already too close; he shrank uneasily back.

"What now?" Roxane spoke to the tendril. "We can't fly."

"Neither can Ooru, here in Stone."

The tendril lifted higher, and he felt its glow of heat. Radiant infrared. Presently it spoke again.

"We face deep excavation. Search reveals remnants of massive installations beyond it. Abandoned substructures. Foundations of facilities once used for processing ore. Our probable game goal for Step of Steel."

"Do you see a way across?"

"No route yet perceived. Removal of extensive ore body created cavity many Terran kilometers deep, many kilometers across. Means of transit not yet apparent."

"There has got to be a way out," Benn said. "The game officials wouldn't set us a totally impossible task."

"Concur," the tendril said. "We seek."

Lifting higher, glowing redder, its tip moved from side to side as if probing that dark chasm.

"We follow edge." Again it shone yellow. "We seek transit route."

They followed again, along that black and giddy brink. Mountainous shadows rose ahead and took form as immense, odd-shaped blocks of that old gray concrete.

"Substructures," Ooru said. "Supports for facilities since removed."

Exploring narrow canyons through the rubble, they had to detour again and again around barriers of crumbled concrete, but they came out at last upon a level shelf that jutted as far as he could see into the pit.

"Here?" he asked. "A way across?"

"Not yet," the yellow tendril answered. "Facility existed here, probably used to carry materials across excavation. Facility since dismantled. Metal salvaged. Search must continue."

They followed again, out across that jutting platform, threading a way through mountains of rubble that once had supported great machines. Wide enough at first, the platform shrank until it was only a narrow roadway, shrank again until it was hardly a meter wide. Ooru pushed on across it, but Roxane hung back.

"Terrans!" the yellow tendril flashed. "Terrans?"

"I'm not sure—" Trembling, she tried to get her breath. "I'm not sure I can."

"We must," Benn urged her. "I see no choice."

"Sorry," she whispered. "But I never liked high places. Not since I used to hear my father's men talk about the skyweb falling.

We used to find those burned and broken fragments of the cities in the sky. Once we found the wreck of a skyship. I followed my father inside and saw burned and broken bones. They gave me nightmares. People falling out of the sky, frightened and screaming and dying. I'd wake up sweating. Now I hate to climb a tree—"

"Terrans!" Ooru was calling. "Come! Here we find remains of auxiliary transport facility. Erected perhaps for inspection or repair. If still intact, will offer passage to game goal. Will Terrans come?"

"I'll try," she whispered. "If I can—"

Ooru's black mass was thinning, stretching out ahead. As narrow now as the bridge, it pushed slowly on. Benn waited for Roxane, but she beckoned him to go ahead. She followed. He heard her fast breath. When he looked back, her face in the helmet was bleakly tight. Eyes on that narrow blade of ancient concrete, she didn't see him.

"You'll make it!" She started when he spoke. "Just take your time."

"I do what I must." She shrugged, eyes still on her feet. "My father taught me that."

Growing up outside of Earth's gravity, he had never learned to fear high places. He walked boldly on ahead of her, until a sliver of fallen stone slid under his boot. He fell, one arm flailing into emptiness, his head off the bridge and only those midnight kilometers below.

"Okay, Benn?" Lying there, gasping, he heard her mocking voice. "Is this your paradise in space?"

With no breath to speak, he rolled away from that black brink. Weak and shaking, he could smell his own sweat, but he got back to his feet and picked his way more cautiously until Ooru stopped ahead of him.

"Difficulty," the green tendril flickered. "Solution not apparent."

Benn tried to see ahead, but all he saw was the dark.

"Bridge broken," the tendril said. "Long section fallen. Gap a hundred meters wide."

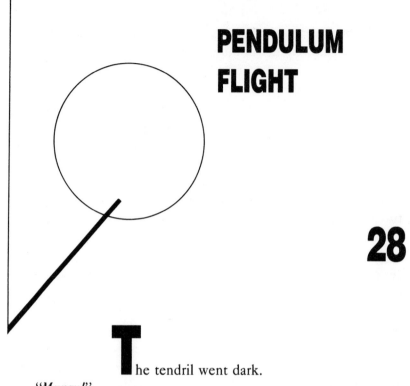

PENDULUM FLIGHT

28

The tendril went dark.

"Mungu!"

Her name for God, a whispered prayer. She dropped to her hands and knees on that thin blade of time-eaten concrete, crawled to a wider spot, and sat there astride it, looking up at him, her face fixed and pale in the bubble.

"Life in the halo!" She managed a taunting grin. "The prize you want, if you win the game?"

Even there on that giddy bridge, he was frozen for a moment by her shape in the luminous suit, her spirit in the face of fear. In a different world—

"We're here." Jaw set, he shrugged. "In the game."

"Your move," she said. "If you can find a move."

He looked a moment longer into the challenge of her cool bronze eyes and turned again on his narrow footing. Ooru lay beyond him on the broken end of the bridge, dark and motionless. Beyond Ooru, the midnight gulf. Peering into it, finding no point of reference anywhere, he swayed with a sudden giddiness and had to spread his arms and crouch to get his own balance back.

"Ooru!"

His breathless gasp brought no answer. Ooru seemed dead, a great shapeless blob of slick-glistening jelly. In stasis again, whatever stasis was. Hoarse with strain, he shouted louder:

"Can you see anything? On beyond the gap?"

Ooru did not respond.

"Had enough?" Roxane called behind him, mockery in her own taut voice. "Want the servos to bail us out?"

"Is Earth any better?" He felt a stab of anger at her, a keener stab at the three servos. They had stopped beyond her, lying one behind the other, three small quicksilver balls glinting with their tiny golden images. "You want to go home?"

"Not yet—but look!" Her bright arm pointed. "Your friend is waking up."

He turned to find that slick black tendril alive again, glowing orange at the tip.

"Terrans!" Its voice rang in his helmet. "Please! Do not abandon game! In due accord with universe, all things are possible. Please to forget moment of stasis. Brief disjunction driven by shock of difficulty. Disjunction now ended. Undue emotion relieved by new tactical plan."

"You see some way across this pit?"

"Plan for possible transit. Requires concord of spirit, concord of purpose, concord with cosmos." The bright tendril lifted and paused as if to sense them. "Requires Terrans and Ooru to merge in mutual action."

"Tell us your plan."

"Employs tactics of pendulum." The tendril tip bent and swung slowly back and forth. "Ooru to form pendulum line. Terrans to function as pendulum bobs. Pendulum swing to transit break in bridge." The tendril lifted to study them. "Terrans respond?"

Benn turned to look at Roxane.

"I don't like high places," she said. "You're the spaceman."

"Harmony required," the tendril shimmered. "Ooru and Terrans in total harmony."

"I'm game." He looked back at her. "If you are."

"What else?" She shrugged. "My father taught me to finish what you start."

"With harmony with cosmos, all things possible." The tendril dipped toward her helmet. "One Terran to form anchor. Other Terran to carry pendulum line away from anchor. Length of line to equal length of break."

"Okay," she said. "If we can."

Benn saw her flinch away from the reaching tendril, but she let it wrap around her waist. Arms swinging to keep her balance, she swayed to her feet and picked her way back the way they had come. The three servos rolled ahead, soon lost in the dark. The tendril crawled after her, a thin black snake.

"Terran here." It startled Benn, speaking from a flashing spot behind him. "Action needed. Action in concert, through accord with cosmos. Please to anchor swinging line."

He dropped astride the narrow blade of concrete where his legs could grasp it and caught the stretching tendril in his hands. Slick and black, it was warm to his gloves, and he felt a rapid pulse beneath its skin, the flow of fluid tissue into the extending line. Ooru shrank until his shapeless mass was almost gone, and the line stretched until Roxane was far back along the bridge, diminished to a golden doll.

"Critical point." Distance thinned the tendril's words to her. "Terran to halt!"

"Now?" He caught her breathless question. "What?"

"Terran to function as pendulum bob. To jump high from bridge. To swing across break. To grasp ancient Delver structure existing beyond. To reach secure position. To release pendulum line. To wait for second Terran to function as second pendulum bob. To aid second Terran to secure foothold beyond. Two Terrans to form secure anchor for final pendulum swing. Ooru at that time to transit break as final pendulum bob."

The glowing doll stood motionless a moment, looking back at Benn.

"One for the money." A childish voice, thinned with distance. "Two for the show. Three to make ready. Four—" A breathless catch. "Four to go!"

She jumped.

Leaning, turning, Benn watched her drop. A golden star falling through the dark, faster and faster as she shot beneath him, slower,

slower as she climbed again. At last she paused, high in the dark.
He found the jutting mass of jagged concrete just above and beyond
her, dim in the glow of her suit.

She reached for it, missed, clawed at it, caught a ragged edge.
The tendril tip unwrapped her waist. She clung to shattered points,
clambered across a narrow ledge, and finally stood upright, waving
her arms in triumph.

"Okay, Spaceman!" Her doll-voice came back across the gap.
"Your move now!"

Beautiful and brave. Admiration checked his breath, and bitter
regret stabbed through him. She was daring when she had to be,
a fairy princess in the golden-glowing suit—but her world was not
for love.

"Correction." The tendril shimmered in his hands. "Next
move is Ooru's. To withdraw line used. To form second line. Terran here to function as second pendulum bob."

He tightened his grip on the thin black line. Swinging down
into the empty dark, it was throbbing again to the flow of Jovian
life-stuff, now withdrawn into Ooru's fattening mass.

"Spaceman Terran now to move." Back in his hands, its glowing tip spoke again, now with an odd echo of Roxane's sardonic
tone. "To carry line back to critical point."

It coiled around his waist and stretched again, a second endless
snake, following him far back along the bridge.

"Spaceman, now!" it flashed to stop him. "At critical point.
Now to transit gap. To leap high from bridge. To swing beneath.
To grasp support and join Terran beyond. Two Terrans to anchor
line there. Ooru then to transit as third pendulum bob." It paused.
"Terran Spaceman comprehend?"

"I jump." Benn nodded. "I grab whatever I can on the other
side. Roxane and I hold the line—"

"Okay, Spaceman Terran!" It stopped him. "Comprehension
okay. Terran Roxane ready. Terran Spaceman—jump!"

He jumped—

And suddenly he was nowhere, swallowed into unbroken blackness. The time-scarred concrete had dimmed and vanished. The
slick black tendril hung slack in his hands. Afloat in black midnight,
he lost all direction, all sense of up or down.

Measured out by his slow heartbeat, time itself seemed to cease, until at last he felt his weight returning. The slack black line slowly tightened. Still with no sense of motion, he hung suspended in that featureless blackness until his apparent weight fell away. The line grew loose again. Sprawling in the dark, he heard Roxane's voice.

"Here, Benn! Here!"

Twisting, he found another ragged thrust of broken concrete. Dim at first in the glow of his suit, it brightened slowly, floating closer. He snatched at it, touched nothing. The slack line began to tighten on his waist, dragging him away.

"Benn—"

He discovered her above him, glowing in her lifeskin, clinging to a broken concrete shelf. She leaned and reached. Her gloves caught his, pulled him to the ledge beside her.

"Safe!" She steadied him for a better foothold. For a moment they stood together, his arm around her. He saw her nostrils wide with feeling, caught the joy in her tawny eyes, heard her breathless laugh. For that instant, he forgot the game.

"Terrans—" He heard the tendril speaking. "Transit procedure to continue now. "Body mass of Ooru to function as third pendulum bob. Terrans to anchor pendulum line. Anchor securely!"

It had grown a second luminous tip that reached to coil around Roxane. If she flinched, he didn't see. Her bright gloves grasped it. It throbbed and tightened. Ooru was invisible, but soon the line was slowly moving, dragging downward, dragging harder as it came beneath them, slackening again when its pull was forward.

"Transit complete," the tendril said. "Terrans please to follow."

The shining tips unwrapped them and the tendril retreated along the bridge, a black snake crawling. They followed, and Ooru's black shape grew out of the blackness far along the bridge, swelling with the flow of his body stuff out of the contracting line. The three servos came flying silently across the gap to drop again behind them. The old concrete showed less damage here, and they soon came up with Ooru.

The bridge grew wider, wider again, until they came off upon another vast platform piled and pitted with the shattered stuff of vanished ore transporters. Ooru found a way through it to a tall door in the tool-marked stone.

"Players, attend!"

Suddenly shining, the servos spoke.

"You have completed the Step of Steel." He saw the door sliding open. "You will remain here at the terminal until the judges are ready to reveal the scores for the running of the step and announce the team selections for the next. You will find life-support facilities ready for you."

Ooru flowed slowly toward the open door, a bright tendril lifting.

"Terrans ran well," it shimmered. "The cosmos join with them!"

A thing entirely alien, its huge blob of foreign flesh dimly glistening in the glow of their lifeskins, yet those words left a lump in Benn's throat.

"We wish you many wins!" he called after it.

"Ooru!" Roxane ran to overtake it. "If we never see you again—" She reached to touch its slick black bulk. "Good-bye, good friend!"

The green-tipped tendril reached to meet her, and she shook it like a hand.

"Terrans and Roonu together in eternal universe," it shimmered. "Forever together."

The servos led them after it, along a tunnel into another circular chamber with doorways spaced around it. Beyond one of them, an air lock let them into one more small apartment equipped with *Spica* replicas.

"Here we are, still alive!" Roxane was lifting off her helmet, tossing her head to free her hair. She stood for a moment smiling at him, so near and lovely that he ached to take her in his arms. "Thanks to Ooru. Nearly human, in spite of how it looks."

"Maybe better than human."

She was stripping off her lifeskin. He had never seen a woman naked. Even clad in the clinging suit, she had captured his imagination. Nude, she was unimagined perfection, high-breasted, trimly fit, altogether overwhelming. He stared and flushed and dragged his eyes away, trying to tell himself that she shouldn't matter to him now.

What did matter were the steps of the game yet to be played, and Gibbon back on Heart of Hydra waiting for anything to solve the riddles of Starsearch. His concern ought to be that uneldren something that had killed Gibbon's brother and that seemed now to threaten everything.

"Look if you like." Her voice was easily matter-of-fact. "I don't mind. I grew up with my father and his men, in camps that had no walls, where we never had much to wear. I guess we're going to be together here."

"I'm glad!" he whispered. "Glad we are."

"Careful." He heard the warning in her tone. "Just remember who I am."

"Roxane Kwan!" Still he didn't look, but his breath had quickened and disturbed emotion shook his voice.

He waited to hear her in the shower before he peeled off his own sweat-smelling lifeskin, but he couldn't help looking when she came out, bare and dazzling. Frowning at his rising penis, she shook her head and walked dripping past him to the berth where her servo was waiting with towels and clothing. In the shower, he ran it cold. She was dressed when he came out, breathtaking in her trim-fitting eldren copy of a gold-colored Sun Fleet jumpsuit. And still she wore the knife.

"We did it!" Watching the silent servos setting dishes on the table, she barely glanced at him, but her voice was bright with elation. "First place! Two game points for each one of us."

His servo danced to meet him.

"Congratulations, sir! Contestant Ooru's partisans at the Primarch's Casino send felicitations. Wishing to express their pleasure with your excellent running of the Step of Steel, they are providing the rewards allowed because of Player Ooru's special status. At his request, we are to serve a special meal for you, repeating the menu of a Terran dinner prepared to honor the birthday of Captain Bela Zar."

"Please thank our friend Ooru."

The servos were setting the table, working with nimble arms and fingers that shaped themselves to fit their tasks and drew back into the silver bubbles when their work was done. The dishes glinted with the *Spica*'s name and the golden sunburst of the Fleet.

The food, he thought, was nearly as good as his mother served. Crusty rolls she might have baked. Steaks, Roxane said, that might have come from a yearling wildebeest. Fruits she said had almost the taste of actual peaches. Wine replicated, so the servos said, from the wine in the captain's private pantry.

He was drunk with her, even before the servos poured the wine. Sitting across the table from her, he was lost in the grace of her hands, the curve of her lips, the light in her eyes. He knew he was in love. Yet she still wore the knife.

Searching for some safer topic, he asked what she knew about Lilith and Vreeth and Wing.

"Not much." She frowned. "They're clients of Nebo's. He says we need them with us, because they and Nexus have know-how to help us build the new space docks and hang the skywires, but still I can't like them. Uglier than hyenas." She shivered. "I understand hyenas. I hope they don't come to Earth."

"Do they want to?"

"They didn't really say." The frown grew deeper. "But they asked a lot of questions. I'm afraid they do."

That was all she seemed to know about the aliens. She picked up the half-empty wine bottle, and her bronze eyes lit when she looked at the label.

CABERNET SAUVIGNON
VINTAGE OF SUN YEAR 71
DE LEON
SUPPLIER TO THE HOUSE OF KWAN

Sipping again, she smiled.

"I've seen the label. My father's men found a wine cellar once, under the ruins of a burned-out villa. He gave me only a few sips of the wine, but this tastes just the same."

With courage from it, Benn lifted his second glass to her.

"You're beautiful!"

She flushed, he thought with pleasure, and raised her own glass to him. She had liked the food and wine. The label had reminded her of Africa, and he got her to talk about herself. About how her father's men came to call her Cheetah. About the fall of the web and her plans for the future of Earth. She laughed at herself when she told how a charging elephant had frightened her, and her voice grew tender when she spoke of old Marco Lara, who had taught her to read and write when they found books in a long-abandoned villa. She seemed happy, and he felt happy with her, until she paused to look at him with a sudden regret.

"I'm sorry, Benn. Sorry one of us must lose the game."

"Let's forget that."

He wanted the moment to last, but it was ending. The second bottle was empty. Offering no more, the servos began clearing the table. They rose together. Her shoulder brushed him. He caught her exciting human scent. Suddenly she was in his arms, warm and maddening.

"Roxane, I love—"

She writhed away. Her nostrils flared. Her bronze eyes blazed. The knife flashed in her lifted hand.

"I warned you!" She was suddenly savage. "I could kill you!"

MALFUNCTION AT NORTHPOINT

29

He gripped her wrist.

"Roxane—" He gasped her name, begging her. "Don't!"

Her hard body writhed out of his arms, and the knife thrust toward his heart. Twisting, he kept it away. Her free hand dived for the bottle on the table. He caught it. Her knee came at his groin. He slid aside.

"Please!" Suddenly he was sober. "I didn't mean—"

Her breath was gone, but still she strained against his grip, bronze eyes blazing.

"I'm sorry!" he whispered. "Sorry!"

She stared into his eyes. Her face slowly softened, and at last he felt her arm relaxing.

"If you are, let me go."

"I drank too much." He was trembling, weak, almost ill. "And I—" He released her wrist and stumbled back. "And I love you too much. Too much to hurt you."

Swaying away, she slid the knife back into its sheath and set the bottle on the table.

"I warned you," she whispered. "I told you what I am."

"Forgive me!" Tears stung his eyes. "I wish we could be friends."

"Friends?" Breathing fast, she moved farther from him. "How

could we be? It's no world for friendship. My father taught me that, too." Yet he thought her hard-set face had warmed a little. "I'm sorry, Benn. I guess we both had too much wine. But that's the way I am."

"We're together in the game." Sadly he tried to grin. "The rules won't let us fight."

She didn't smile.

"We're human." He tried again. "Not jungle animals. I was not attacking you. No!" His voice shook. "You are the first woman I have ever known. I can't help the way you make me feel, but I didn't mean to frighten you—"

"I'm not frightened." Her body drew straighter. "My father taught me to defend myself."

"I wish—"

He let his voice die. She had turned away from him to the servos. The table was cleared, and their bright fingers had been withdrawn. They lay beside the door, quivering with their hidden energies.

"The next step?" she asked them. "When do I play?"

"The third event is the Step of Fire. You run it when your team is complete. You are the only player yet selected. Life-support facilities will be provided at the course. You may be escorted there whenever you wish."

"I'm ready to go."

She was still breathing hard. Silently, eyes avoiding him, she moved to strip off the yellow jumpsuit and get back into her life-skin. He watched her this time, aching inside. He yearned for a smile, a word, for anything, but she followed the servo into the air lock without even a backward glance.

He sat a long time alone after she was gone, numb with pain. He knew he must call Gibbon soon, but not quite yet, not until he felt alive again. When at last he stirred, it was to ask his servo for another bottle of wine. Player Ooru had provided no more. Roxane still burned inside him. He tried to think she shouldn't matter, but she did.

He thought she would never want to see him again.

"Player Benndain." His servo shimmered. "A message for you has been received from Edward Gibbon *Beta* at Heart of Hydra. He wishes you to call him when you can."

"Call him for me now."

It rolled away to the end of the room. The ion cloud veiled its silvery ball, flickered, brightened, and became a window into that milk-white haze of unfocused energy. He found Gibbon there, half covered with his hieroglyphic birth robe, now floating all alone.

"Dr. Gibbon?" He raised his voice. "Dr. Gibbon, how are you?"

A single small dull eye came open to blink at him dimly.

"Benn?" The rough flesh around the eye shone faintly, and Gibbon's voice murmured rustily out of the mist. "Have you gathered new data for me?"

"Nothing new about the aliens, sir. Except that Roxane says they questioned her about the Earth. She's afraid they want to go there. I was with her and the jovian Ooru in the Step of Steel. We did place first, if that means anything. I'm waiting now to know about the next step.

"But how are you, sir?"

"You see what I am. Less than half a Hydran, with hardly strength to speak."

"Your treatment? Is it helping?"

"I stopped the therapy."

"Sir, why? I thought it was wonderful, the way your people were sharing themselves with you."

"They were killing me!" Sluggishly his rugged dark potato shape rocked back and forth in the fog. "What they shared was never my dead brother, never me. I quarreled in the end with my misadvised clone-cousins, who always tried to invade my mind with facts I'll never need to know and emotions I'll never want to feel. I quarreled with my bungling doctors, who cannot understand my pain because they have never felt the death of half of what they are. They were always telling me that I must rest.

"Rest!" That luminous spot burned brighter. "I ordered them all away."

"Really, sir. Are you sure you don't need—"

"I need everything!" His ragged voice had risen. "A poor crippled fragment of a Hydran, fighting all alone. Against the destroyer of Starsearch! Against the killer of my brother!"

"If your doctors can restore your strength—"

"Blind bunglers! Clogging my mind with useless scraps of other minds, until I am not myself. Injecting me with tranquilizers to make me forget the sacred mission I must complete. Trying to tell me that our unknown enemy is merely a transient effect of the therapy, a delusion that will disappear as the lesions heal and my new gestalts grow."

"Sir, are you able—"

"I am not able!" A pale flash. "But neither am I mad. We fight two wars, Benn. Besides those aliens, we face opponents in the Elderhood. The doctors who call me paranoid. The Council members, who still regard the invaders as legitimate guests of the Elderhood, here in response to our broadcast invitations. Even the judges of the game, who are allowing them to compete with such honest players as you are."

"Can't you ask—" Benn peered into that one dull eye. "In all the halo, isn't there any authority to help us?"

"None." The eye looked blank and glazed; he wasn't sure it saw him. "We eldren have been at peace too long. Even the Eldermost has never fought a war. We—most of us—refuse to believe in anything uneldren because we have never known it. My brother was a rare exception, because he had seen the seeker queen and he knew from me what she did to Earth. He recognized the danger in the aliens, which others still refuse to see. He tried to exclude them from the halo, and died for it."

"Is there no defense?"

"We are undefended. We gave up government a billion years ago. The Eldermost does respond to inquiries. Sometimes he advises—though he still appears to have no useful information or advice for us now. But he cannot command. He has no laws to enforce, nor means to enforce them if he had. I have searched the whole halo for aid and found none at all."

Gibbon rocked heavily in that white fog.

"We stand alone, Benn, against something uneldren. Its shape is still invisible, but it arrived with the aliens. It killed my brother. It still holds Starsearch Station. It captured the salvage expedition aboard the *Mindquest*. Now it has struck—" The light around that little eye had dimmed, and the voice began to fade. "Struck Newmarch—"

"Newmarch?" Benn leaned closer, straining to hear. "That's Runesong's home. What's happened there?"

The voice was gone. The eye closed and began to lose its shape. Gibbon's ungainly form lay dark and still in the fog, as if that last brief burst of light and voice had taken too much from him. Waiting, Benn stared at the robe until the shifting riddles of its cryptic patterns began to hurt his eyes. He looked away, thinking of Runesong.

Her warm wings around him, in his first recollections. The tales and poems and songs of old Earth she used to sing in the soft voice she had borrowed from the grandmother who was dead before his birth. The ugly scar across her flank, where her human captors had wounded her. The sad time when her illness took her away from him to the home of her race in far Northpoint.

When he thought of Roxane, it struck him painfully that this ache of loss was actually for her. If she had only been as loving as Runesong was!

"Benn?"

His name startled him, and he saw that Gibbon had opened another eye, down nearer the edge of the robe, as small and bleary as the first.

"Are you still there?"

"Yes, sir. About Newmarch? What has happened?"

"Trouble, Benn." That huge dark body quivered in the mist, and Gibbon's voice crashed out of it, suddenly loud. "Trouble!"

"What trouble, sir?" No answer came, and he had to ask again. "Trouble for Runesong? She's there with her sister, Cyan Gem. They live at Northpoint."

"I have been speaking—"

He had to wait until the glow came back.

"Speaking to Cyan Gem." The voice returned, with gathered strength. "I knew her at the old core-star, when we were there together. Northpoint is the halo center nearest the station, and I called her to ask if her people had observed any activity there. She told me that the staff at their nanionic station had picked up—"

He had to wait while Gibbon searched for strength again.

"Picked up a signal—" A shimmer of light, a slow march of labored words. "From the direction of Starsearch. In a code they were unable to decipher. Intended, I suspect, for the aliens. The staff had put it in their linguistic computers, attempting translation. That effort was halted—"

"By 'computer malfunction'!"

"Her last words to me. She was cut off. That happened in the last microcycle, several of your Terran hours ago. It is all I know. I have tried to call back. The Cluster One service center is reporting that all contact with Newmarch has been interrupted. The cause is unknown. They promise to resume service soon, but I believe they will fail."

Benn shivered, as if a cold wind had blown out of the milk-white mist. That dim little eye had narrowed, squinting at him while Gibbon paused again to gather strength.

"They will fail," the desperate voice toiled on, "because that uneldren power has taken Newmarch. It is creeping across the halo. I think you are facing it now, Benn, in the aliens there in the game. Observe them, Benn, whenever you can. Learn all you can."

"I will, sir."

"Caution, Benn! If they suspect that we suspect, they could do you harm."

"I suppose they could." That narrow room felt colder. "I'll watch them, sir."

"Guard yourself!" The speaking spot had dimmed again, and that little eye looked blind. "Now I must rest—"

The white fog thickened, and the window into Heart of Hydra was gone. The ion cloud flickered and vanished. The servo lay quivering on the floor where it had been, flickering now with speech.

"Player Benndain, the judges have not yet completed your team for the Step of Fire, but the course you will run has been chosen. We can take you to it now."

THE STEP OF FIRE

30

He followed the servo out of the transit car.

"Player Benndain," its voice-light twinkled, "you are now at the starting point for your running of the Step of Fire."

In a moment the car was gone. Turning, he found jagged cliffs of luminous stone all around him. The course was another hollow in the core of Stone, its walls and roof tool-marked and scarred from old fractures in the planet's crust. Left luminous by the ancient miners, they glowed like dying coals, pale blue and dim yellow and dull red.

The size of the cavern dazed him. As far as he could see, it had no end. Vast galleries wound away into a smoky haze. Enormous masses of standing stone had been left to support a roof so high that the bright haze dimmed it. The ore-body, he thought, must have been immense.

"Who else is on the team?" he asked the servo. "And what is our goal?"

"You will be informed," it flickered. "Your companions will be joining you. There is a life-support facility where you may wait for their arrival."

The facility was another narrow apartment, furnished with replicas from the cabins and galleys and wardrooms of the *Spica*. He got out of his lifeskin and crawled into a berth, but for a long time he could not sleep. He had too many riddles to resolve.

The aliens? Lilith or Vreeth might be next on the team. Snakething and lion-thing, Roxane had called them. Perhaps they had evolved from something snakelike or lionlike, but they were vastly different now, armed with powers still unknown. He dreaded them.

Computer malfunctions? First at Starsearch Station, now at Northpoint. Malfunctions of computers that should have run forever. What could give a machine the malice to murder Gibbon's brother? Or reprogram Friday into the thing that called itself Nexus?

Restless on the narrow berth, he found no answers.

Roxane? His enemy, yet her image haunted him, alluring and proud and angrily defiant.

Finding no cheer anywhere, he fell asleep at last.

In his uneasy dreams, he and she were lost forever in the dimly glowing pits and caves and corridors of the Step of Fire. She fled from him, he never knew why. Because he loved her, he ran after her. Sometimes he caught her, naked and wonderful in his arms.

She tried to fight. He wrested her knife away, but she spat in his face and struggled against him and changed in his arms. She became Nexus, her robot body black and hard and cold. It laughed at him, a hard laugh like the jangle of shattering glass, and knocked him away with a cruel electric shock, and became Roxane as it ran away.

Awake again, unrested, he felt numbed and dull. He showered and shaved with a replica of a razor that had been presented to some nameless *Spica* officer by the Sun Tycoon "on the memorable occasion of his first commission." The servo brought his breakfast in a self-heating carton printed "Produced and packed for the Sun Fleet by the Synfare Corporation. Trademarks and patents owned by the House of Kwan. Use by December 31, Sun Year 85."

Insipid mush. He left half of it.

"Contestant Benndain," the servo announced, "Contestant Diego Bolivar is arriving to join your team for the Step of Fire."

The air lock hissed and clunked, and Bolivar emerged. Lean

and athletic in the tight tan lifeskin, he stopped at the door, his head cocked in quizzical appraisal.

"Dain?" He had air of mild surprise. "Still with us? Congrats. Since we're in this step together, I hope you make it one more time."

He waited for the servo to lift off his breather bubble, strip off the lifeskin, and bring him a free-fall jumpsuit that had SUN FLEET printed across the back.

Benn watched him, wondering. His face was dark and narrow, tapering to a pointed chin beneath his neat black moustache. The slight slant of his quick black eyes hinted at some Eastern ancestor.

What was he to Roxane?

Though he moved with a nearly feminine grace, he looked male enough. To her eyes, doubtless handsome. She had come out from Earth with him. They would be returning together if their plans worked out, she as the new Tycoon, Bolivar doubtless sharing her power.

Was he the man she would learn to love?

Dressed again, he called for food.

"None of that synfare slop." He scowled at the tray Benn had left on the table. "I want bacon and eggs. Eggs fried soft, sunny side up, bacon crisp. Buttered toast, orange juice, coffee with cream, fruit. The breakfast ration *Spica* officers got." He glanced at Benn. "Two orders. The second for my friend."

The servos brought two hot platters. At the table, Benn sat a moment inhaling the rich aromas of bacon and coffee. He tasted, nodded gratefully at Bolivar, and ate with sudden hunger.

"Better?" Bolivar grinned. "All synthetic imitations, of course, but these creatures are clever with synthesis."

"A lot better."

They ate in silence, until Bolivar pushed back his empty platter and asked the servo for more coffee, hot. Sipping it, he stared across the table until Benn began to feel uncomfortable.

"I've talked to Roxy Kwan." His gaze was sharply intent. "She told me how she pulled her knife on you. Asked me to explain and offer regrets. She says she misunderstood some gesture of yours."

"I certainly meant no harm." Benn hesitated, wondering how much to say. "I guess we'd both drunk too much of Ooru's wine.

I—I'm not used to women, and she—" He shook his head. "Please thank her for me."

"If she tempts you, I can understand." Bolivar had an air of quizzical amusement. "The only woman in a trillion miles." His tone grew graver. "I think you ought to know I mean to marry her. When our plans work out and we get back to where marriage matters."

"If you do—" Benn felt himself flush. "You'll be lucky."

"You have to understand her." Bolivar spoke with a bland self-assurance. "All her life, back on Earth, she had to fight to stay alive." He paused, dark eyes narrowed. "However you feel, she's mine. Understand?"

With no words to say, Benn nodded uncomfortably.

"So long as you do, we can be friends." Soberly Bolivar paused to study him again. "Roxy holds no grudge," he said at last. "She has agreed to let me take you in."

"In to what?"

"Our partnership." Bolivar bent across the table, his tone abruptly warmer. "A deal we've set up with Nebo and our friends from outside the halo."

"I don't like your partners." He shook his head. But then, remembering Gibbon, he asked, "What's this deal?"

"We're playing a game of our own, to make Roxane the new Tycoon. The Delvers want metals, and she can open trade. The aliens have know-how we'll need. Rebuilding the web, we'll have to start with just one skywire. Earth anchor on Kilimanjaro. Shops and labs and the New High House up near the null-G point. The space docks on the ballast satellite.

"That's the picture, Dain."

Smiling now, Bolivar spoke faster, with a fluid gesture to show the climb of the wire out of Africa into space. His shrewd eyes kept probing Benn.

"We've got room for you. The eldren have to be convinced that our planet's ripe for contact. You know them. We can use you as our ambassador to space. So what do you say?"

Silent for a moment, Benn sat looking hard at Bolivar, admiring his air of untroubled audacity. A man of Roxane's world, where death and deadly risk were commonplace. Benn wanted no share in any partnership with Nebo and the aliens, but he delayed saying so. He asked instead:

"You trust these—partners?"

"I lived in the skyweb." Bolivar shrugged. "Long enough to learn not to trust anybody. After it fell, I learned how to stay alive in the ruins. I've seen old Zaroth and met Nebo and Nexus. The whole monster zoo."

He shook his head, with a bleak little grin. "I prefer to let them trust me."

"With that philosophy, you don't need me."

"We do." Soberly he pushed his cup away. "A lot of your eldren friends don't really like the Delvers. I expect opposition. You can find allies for us. Pull wires that need to be pulled. Help us put the blinders on our enemies.

"So?" He paused to frown, dark eyes narrowed. "Are you with us?"

Trying to seem more deliberate than he felt, Benn asked the servo for coffee and watched its nimble silver limbs until his cup was filled and they had withdrawn again into their mirror shield.

"Why do you need these aliens?"

"Know-how." Bolivar warmed again, smoothly persuasive. "I'm not surprised if you hesitate. They sometimes give me the creeps, but they've got knowledge the Delvers have forgotten. You saw the shining rock outside? Half a billion years ago, their old engineers did something to make it luminous and keep it from caving in. The Delvers don't remember how they did it, but the aliens understand it. They're the experts we need."

"Will they be coming to Earth?"

"Nebo says they're refugees in search of sanctuary. I think we can welcome them to Earth."

"Refugees from what?" Benn asked. "They wouldn't tell Starsearch anything."

"I don't care." Bolivar shrugged. "We need them, and that smart robot."

"Too smart." He shook his head. "I'm afraid of what your friends are doing in the halo. Of what they could do on Earth—"

"I'll look after Earth. And Roxy, too." Bolivar had grinned, but in a moment his voice grew colder. "We've got things moving,

Dain. You can't stop us, and you ought to know you'll never win this eldren game. I'm offering you a chance for something better. We can use you, if you want to join us."

"I don't."

"Better think about it." His voice had a hostile edge, but in a moment his teeth flashed again. "While you do, remember we're in this step together."

"I know the rules, but I don't like your scheme."

"Really, Dain." Bolivar spread his hands as if exasperated. "You're still a child. Stuck all your life here in this nightmare zoo, you've never seen the human world. You don't know what people are—or Roxy wouldn't have had to pull her knife on you."

Benn felt his face turn pink.

"Face it, Dain. Accept the fact that we're all three what they call planetics. Your eldren friends will never love us. Or even understand us. They live forever, always sure of everything. We don't. I've stayed alive by taking chances. So has Roxy. Dealing with Nebo and the aliens, we're just taking one more chance.

"We're human, Dain. Better admit it."

"Sometimes too human." He shook his head at Bolivar. "I guess you'd say I want to make us eldren. I'm playing for our chance to finish the evolutionary jump from Earth to space. A better chance than yours, with Nebo and Nexus and those aliens for partners."

Bolivar's chin had begun to jut. "You're done for, Dain—"

"Contestants attend!" The servos interrupted him. "The third player has now arrived to complete your team for the running of the Step of Fire. When you are ready, we will escort you to the starting position."

"So we suit up and play spaceman?" Bolivar's tone was coldly sardonic, but he turned to Benn and thrust out his hand. "Forget it, Dain. We're both from Earth, and we win or lose this step together. Let's play it fair."

"Fair." Benn shook his hand and turned to ask the servos, "Who is this third contestant?"

"Player Vreeth completes your team."

VREETH

31

They followed the servos out of the air lock, into the sullen glow of the Step of Fire.

"Contestants attend!" the two servos chanted. "Terrans must not remove life-support equipment. Atmosphere in these excavations is untested for Terran metabolism."

A third mirror bubble bounded to join them, across a rubble-cluttered floor of old concrete.

"Contestant Bolivar," the three sang together. "Contestant Benndain. Your team for running this course of the Game of Blade and Stone is now complete. Contestant Vreeth has arrived."

They stepped back, shrinking from her great yellow eyes.

"*Dubwana!*" Benn felt Bolivar clutch his arm. "What a monster!"

She turned to meet them, crouching like some great predator about to spring. Fearsome and enormous, her head was still as high as theirs. Massive jaws jutted beneath those blazing eyes. Long saber teeth shone black against her sleek white fur, and her great black-glinting claws were only half retracted.

"Contestant Vreeth," the servos flashed. "Contestants Bolivar and Dain are your companions for the running of the Step of Fire."

The flaps at the sides of her head rose and flexed like listening ears, but they were mirror-lined, not meant for sound. Catching the light of her eyes, they shimmered with speech.

"Two Terrans?"

The voice was Roxane's. That startled Benn, coming from this terrible head. How had she come to learn it?

"You are males?" The mirrors moved their yellow beams to inspect them. "Are you mates of the female Terran called Kwan?"

Benn looked at Bolivar.

"Companions," Bolivar said, and turned to the servos. "What is our next goal?"

"Contestants attend!" They pealed the command with a single voice. "Attend to your briefing for the Step of Fire! The rules of play remain the same. Your running of the course will be observed. The judges will wish to know your manner of play and the time elapsed before you reach your goal.

"As before, play will cease if any one of you asks to abandon the game. In that event, assuming that rescue is possible, all three contestants will be removed from the course. The terminating contestant will be expelled from Mazeway.

"Are these instructions understood?"

"Understood," Bolivar said.

Benn asked, "Now what is our goal?"

"Your course for the Step of Fire lies before you. It extends through this section of the ancient mines. Your objective is simply to reach the point where the ores were removed."

"Have we clues to follow?"

"Contestants, your briefing is concluded. Your game time for the Step of Fire has now begun to run."

The servos fell silent, quivering a little, shimmering with dull red and yellow reflections of the craggy walls around them. Benn turned to his fellow players. Vreeth lay silent, crouched low against the ancient concrete.

"So, Dain?" Bolivar grinned at him. "What do you say?"

"I guess we're on our own." He stood frowning into those vast dim galleries that wound away into gray-hazed distance. "We were told that the courses trend upward, finally toward the outside. I suppose we should climb when we can."

"Right enough. But I see no stairs."

"Keep alert for clues. In the Step of Steel, we were able to follow an old roadbed, where ores had been hauled."

"Nothing like that here."

Vreeth came surging to her feet.

"The game clock runs." Roxane's voice shivered again from those wide mirror-ears. "We move."

His heart stopped when she sprang. For one mad moment, he thought she was about to pounce upon them. Instead, she brushed past them into the nearest gallery. Gliding like some stalking predator, she seemed almost to float above the darkly glowing cavern floor.

She went too fast. Benn had to trot, puffing in his breather bubble, stumbling over piles of fallen stone beside Bolivar, trying to keep up with the tip of her tail, which was long and tapered, most of it sleek with her fine white fur. It rippled to the rhythm of her soundless footfalls, its motion almost hypnotic. Its tip was naked, a thin black finger. Moving with an uncanny precision, it floated sometimes a meter or so in front of his face, sometimes just ahead of Bolivar's, almost as if she led them on an invisible chain. Watching it, instead of the rubble underfoot, he sometimes stumbled. She never paused. When he fell behind, he had to run to overtake her.

She was fascinating and appalling. He glanced now and then at Bolivar, with no time or breath for the questions he should ask for Gibbon. What was she? Where had she come from? What did she want here in the halo?

Could she be in fact an actual refugee in search of sanctuary? He wondered what sort of enemy could frighten her. What was her link to the other aliens, to Nexus, to Nebo? Whatever she was, he knew she didn't belong on Earth.

They came to a high ridge of broken stone, where even the hardened roof had crumbled. Vreeth climbed ahead, almost as if weightless, her great black talons hardly touching anything. Benn and Bolivar struggled over the glowing boulders, slid and fell and struggled again.

"Wait for us!" They had followed in silence, but Bolivar

shouted at last. "Game time runs for all of us, till we all get to the goal."

She stopped on the crest above and turned to watch them climb, her eyes like great lamps burning.

"Terrans!" Roxane's voice, dripping scorn. "Feeble Terrans. I see that you lack nanionic effectors. I must carry you."

Breathless and sweating, they reached her. Her quick white tail wrapped and lifted Bolivar, wrapped and lifted Benn, set them on her velvet back. Still with no sign of effort, she carried them fast and high. At first he felt exposed and insecure, aware of the deadly power in the muscular body under him, but his seat was easy to keep and its steady rise and fall lulled his unease.

He had never been aboard a ship, but this was the way he had imagined sailing. High cliffs and enormous pillars of rough-cut stone flowed around them, dully red, wanly yellow, ash-glazed blue, all dimly luminous with that secret fire that had burned half a billion years.

Beyond the ridge, the floor had caved away, perhaps into a deeper gallery. She flew with them across a wide black pit, flew on and on through endless glowing corridors beyond. Watching for any clue, he saw no passage leading upward, no remnant anywhere of the equipment the old Delvers must have used to carry their ores away.

"Terrans, I ask for information." She flexed those wide mirror-ears to bring Roxane's voice to them, and he shivered from its strangeness. "Do you hunt and eat other creatures?"

A moment of silence. Bolivar twisted to look back at Benn. Wondering why she asked, Benn decided not to inquire.

"We used to." Bolivar shrugged and grinned into the mirrors. "Our ancestors were hunters, but our game animals are almost extinct."

"Are there other large carnivores on Terra?"

"Only a few survive."

"Describe your game animals. Were they savage or cunning?"

"Not really. Most of them just ran."

The mirrors bent away as if to search the cavern ahead. It had widened, two passages branching away. Instead of choosing either, Vreeth turned through a narrow fissure that led into another boundless cavity that wound away between red-glowing cliffs into red-hazed infinity. Benn felt exhilarated by the surging power under him, and almost frightened by it.

"We were carnivores." The mirrors bent back to them. "Before our species adapted to life in space. We live now on airless worlds, but our ancestral planet is preserved as a sacred hunting place. The ritual of the hunt is still a vital ceremony to us. Our game creatures are bred to be clever and dangerous. What you tell me of Terran life is a painful disappointment. I had hoped to hunt there. If I cannot, our plans may change—"

Bolivar was leaning toward the listening ears.

"The new Tycoon will welcome you to Earth," he promised. "You and your friends. I believe we can arrange good hunting."

"How? If you have no interesting game?"

"There are creatures that ought to interest you. A breed of Terrans called Holyfolk. They have a kind of cunning and they are hunters themselves, killing other Terrans."

He twisted to dart an odd glance at Benn. "Why not?"

"Ask Roxane." Gazing into Bolivar's reckless grin, he felt a tingle at the back of his neck. "I don't think she'd agree."

"Think again." Bolivar shrugged. "She doesn't love the Holyfolk. They've hunted her all her life."

"Ask the eldren." Bolivar appalled him. "They'll never let creatures hunt people."

"I've never seen them on Earth."

Vreeth was racing with them, great muscles pulsing under them. The mirrors swung again to scan the cavern ahead. The haze-veiled walls had drawn far away, and the floor ahead sloped down and down forever. Still he saw no mining gear left behind, no mark of any road, no hint of a way toward their goal.

"Shouldn't we be trending up?" He spoke uneasily to Bolivar. "Instead of down. We were told that the last step will take us back to the surface."

"*Quien sabe?*" Bolivar shrugged. "Let's trust our friend."

"Contestant Vreeth—" Benn's voice caught when the shining ears tipped toward him. "Contestant Vreeth, why are you here in the halo?"

The mirrors blazed like yellow searchlights focused on him.

"Why should I answer the questions of a Terran planetic?"

"We have answered yours."

The mirrors tipped to search the slope ahead and slowly back to answer him.

"Perhaps because I came to hunt. Perhaps because of a sickness that killed most of the game creatures on our hunting planet." The yellow beams dimmed for a moment, shifting to Bolivar. "If the best hunting on Terra is creatures as feeble as yourself, how can they offer sport?"

"You'll find them cunning enough," he told her. "And they carry weapons."

"If their weapons are good, we may find them a rewarding challenge."

"Your companions?" he asked. "Wing and Lilith? Are they going to Earth?"

"They are requesting residence rights."

"What do they want there?"

With no reply, the mirrors tipped away to search a waste of glowing stone ahead. Benn shivered. He felt helpless, trapped in the currents of Bolivar's reckless scheme. Even if it failed, it could spoil all his hopes for a human future in the Elderhood.

"Contestant Vreeth—" He nerved himself to try another question. "Where was your home?"

"An impudent creature at the beacon station asked that question. He is dead."

"Killed, I have heard, by an accident." He watched the mirrors. "The eldren say such accidents should not happen. Coming when it did, this one is a very strange coincidence. Can you tell me the cause?"

The mirrors bent as if to study him.

"My friends and I were confined in prison cells at the beacon station. We do not know the cause." The mirrors seemed to stiffen. "Planetic, such questions offend me. I will answer no more."

"Careful, Dain." Bolivar leaned to mutter at his ear. "She might forget the rule that we win or lose together."

The mirrors darkened, flattened back against the sides of that great head, but still the great creature raced on. The luminous roof was higher now. That flat expanse ahead really was a lake, he

206

decided, bright with its reflection of the glowing stone above and beyond it. Small green spots were scattered along the shore.

They were soaring over a black-walled canyon where time must have worn the luminous surface rock away. Vreeth dipped low over the cliffs beyond, touched them with her talons, glided on down toward the lake. Benn frowned at the green areas.

Vegetation? The caverns were endless, not all connected. There was atmosphere here, and light from the radiant walls. Life might be possible. Even animal life? The green spots were level and rectangular. Could they be fields?

Vreeth ran on with them down that glowing slope. Benn began to see scattered tufts of coarse grass and clumps of thorny brush in the hollows. The mirrors lifted again before they came to the lake, and their golden beams picked out a moving figure near the shore.

"A farmer!" Bolivar pointed. "A farmer here, if you can imagine!"

A small gray creature, it had been creeping across a tiny field. He saw it stop and straighten, with something like a hand lifted to its eyes as it peered at them. Something even smaller darted from its side, running toward them out of the field. Vreeth dived to meet it, so abruptly that they slid off her velvet back and fell sprawling on a slope of shining gravel.

THE EYE OF
RHYKLOON

32

They rolled to the bottom of the gravel slope and staggered to their feet, rubbing bruises and brushing bright grit off their lifeskins.

"No leaks?"

"Or we could be dead." Ruefully Bolivar gazed after Vreeth. "What a partner!"

Mirror-ears flat, black talons reaching, she was diving at the thing that had fled. Something small and white and quick. Doglike, Benn thought. It darted away along the lake shore and vanished beyond a wall of gray-green feathery stuff that looked a little like bamboo. Vreeth dropped after it.

"Back in the jungle," Bolivar muttered. "Where I think she belongs."

When she didn't rise again, Benn turned to look at the creature in the field. It stood on two legs now, holding a bundle of that green vegetation in its hands or paws, staring back at them. They walked toward it, servos skipping with them. It dropped that green sheaf as if to run, stopped to stare again, and finally started uncertainly to meet them.

"It looks nearly human." Benn frowned at it. "I wasn't expecting people."

"If you call it a person." Bolivar paused to frown again into that green tangle where Vreeth had vanished. "Nebo said we might run into trogs—the computer term for them. Natives of the caves. Seems the Delvers used to make illegal raids on Earth. Prospecting for metal, they brought specimen creatures back. Kept in zoos at first, till some were bred for slave labor in the mines. The atmosphere here was installed to keep them alive.

"But you couldn't call them people."

They stopped to inspect the stranger. Somewhat smaller than a man, covered with shaggy gray fur, it wore nothing except a broad belt around its belly. A female, no longer young. Her empty breasts were small and flat.

"No kin to us," Bolivar said. "It happened too long ago. In a museum, Nebo showed me holos and models of the specimens they brought back. Dinosaurs. Sharks. Little things like rats. Nothing like men or even apes."

Fifty meters away, the creature hesitated uneasily, spread her hairy paws as if to show they were empty, and then dropped flat on the luminous gravel.

"Terrified."

"No wonder," Benn said. "Vreeth could have gone for her, instead of the thing that ran."

She lifted her head to watch as they came down to her. Benn spread his own gloved hands as she had spread her paws and gestured for her to stand. She lay limp instead, shrinking and squeaking when he reached to touch her.

"We won't hurt you." He caught her paws and lifted her. "We want to be friends."

"No use talking," Bolivar muttered. "She's not wired for it."

She stumbled away when he released her paws, but then crept back. Staring with small, fearful eyes under gray-haired brows, she spoke to them then. Her voice at first was only a murmur in his breather bubble, but suddenly she was digging into a pocket on her belt. She found a small leather pouch that held a polished oval object.

"A translator. If ours are programmed for it."

She held it to her lips. Sound hissed and howled and crashed in his bubble, and at last he heard stammered words.

"Sirs? Masters? Why do you come riding a demon?"

"Because she obeys us," Bolivar said. "Because she carries us well."

"Do you come from holy Zaroth, down through the Eye of Rhykloon?"

"We do come from Zaroth." Bolivar gestured at the servos. "We come with our slaves."

"Are you gods?"

"We are greater than the gods. We are masters of our silver slaves and commanders of the demon Vreeth."

"I fear your demon—" Trembling, she turned to peer across the lake. "I fear for Frelk, who ran from it."

"We won't let it hurt you," Benn promised her. "You mustn't be afraid."

"We come from Great Zaroth." Bolivar touched a button at his belt. His suit light shone, turning him splendidly golden. "We are Lords of Space. The Lord of Stars and the Lord of Earth. Do you have a name?"

She cowered away from him.

"Masters—" A feeble squeak. "Masters, I am Hoko."

"Hoko, do you fear the Lords of Space?"

"I greatly fear your demon."

"Will you serve us?"

"I live to serve the gods. What service do you ask?"

"No great service," Bolivar said. "No gifts of slaves or grain or treasure. No cruel sacrifice. We are merely passing through your land. We came from Holy Zaroth, but by another way. What we require is aid to reach the Eye of Rhykloon, if that is the way the lesser gods descend."

She blinked at him doubtfully and turned again to look toward the lake.

"We'll call our demon back," he added. "We'll take it with us when we go."

"Masters, I cannot aid you." Her sharp little eyes lifted toward the red-hazed arch of the far-off roof. "Because I cannot travel the way of the gods and the angels of the gods, through the Eye of Rhykloon."

"Hoko!" Bolivar lifted his golden-glowing arm as if to strike her. "We require a guide to the Eye of Rhykloon."

"Masters—" The computer voice faltered, and she bowed her shaggy head. "I cannot guide you there, because I cannot fly."

"Our demon can. Where is this eye?"

"High above the village, masters." She pointed with a gray-haired arm. "Over the temple of Rhykloon."

"When our demon returns, you must show the way there."

"If you are truly gods—" She hesitated, shrewd little eyes scanning them again. "If your demon does return—"

"She'll be back."

They waited until Benn said, "Let's go on and learn what we can. We can signal with the suit lights for her to overtake us." He peered again into the jungle that had swallowed Vreeth and her prey. "I'm afraid she's scoring no points for us now."

Hoko hurried ahead of them around the lake shore, her bare splay-feet pattering on the gravel. The dark water lay glassily flat beneath the windless sky, burning with sullen reflections. Hoko kept a wary distance from it and turned once to beckon them back. Benn heard a splash as they came around the end. Ripples shimmered, but he never saw the thing that splashed.

She led the way up a stone-curbed trail and around a bend in the cavern. The fire-struck lake shrank and vanished behind them. Turning again and again to scan the jungle-clotted shore, they saw nothing of Vreeth.

At the top of the trail, they came out on a wide bench that was nearly flat. Neat little gardens covered most of it, rows of strange shrubs and vines separated with low walls of luminous stone. A dozen of the owners were there at work, small hairy things like Hoko, digging with clumsy hoes and gathering something into baskets. They stopped their work to stare. When Hoko shouted, they dropped their tools and ran for a row of huts along a dull-shining ledge above the gardens.

"Your people?" Hoko had paused, and they overtook her. "They're afraid?"

"They have never seen an angel or a god." She peered uneasily back down the trail. "Certainly no great demon like the frightful thing that chased my poor baby Frelk."

Two huge tears drew black lines down her furry cheeks and dripped off her whiskers.

"My clever—clever baby Frelk." One shaggy paw smeared the black lines. "He used to sing while I worked, and he could chant the sacred chants that tell of the times long ago when the angels of Rhykloon came to bring gifts from holy Zaroth and carry away the sacred stones we left upon the altar."

Her gray face lifted to them, whiskers twitching.

"Masters, you must understand that the altar will be empty. In these bad times, we find no more sacred stones for the gods. The angels of Rhykloon have brought no holy gifts to us for many generations. There are unbelievers now who say they never came at all."

Her quick little eyes searched into their faces. "If you come to us from holy Zaroth, do you bring gifts?"

"I'm afraid—"

Benn was shaking his head, but Bolivar broke in. "We are the rulers of great Zaroth. The demon we ride carries rich gifts for you and all your people, to be given when we leave if you have served us well."

"Holy masters—" Benn caught doubt in the way she paused. "If you are indeed the rulers of holy Zaroth and greater than the gods, why do you come here?"

"We are visitors to your people." Bolivar gestured toward the dwellings. "We come to observe them, so that the good may be rewarded and the evil may suffer their fit and proper punishment. We require the welcome due us, and true answers to the questions we may ask."

"If you are truly gods, you are truly welcome." She paused to squint into his face. "But I also wish to ask a question. Why do you come riding on the demon that hunted my baby Frelk into the brush?"

"We are masters of demons. We are masters of all."

"If you are—" She turned to study Benn. "We serve you gladly."

"Where is this Eye of Rhykloon?"

She lifted a paw, pointing upward. The cavern roof was lofty here, kilometers above them, glowing dimly red. Searching it, Benn found a round black spot.

"The way of the gods," she said. "In the kinder time when

they used to come and go. If you are gods, perhaps you can ride your demon through it."

"We can." Glancing down the empty trail, Bolivar grinned at Benn. "I'll call the demon here when we are ready. Now take us to this temple where the gods once came."

"If you dare—" Her small eyes narrowed. "Those who enter with no gift of the sacred stone are struck with fire and blindness."

"We are gods," Bolivar assured her cheerfully. "We fear neither fire nor blindness. Show us the temple."

She led them on past the silent village. Benn glimpsed the wide black eyes of one small gray infant peering through a window in a yellow-shining wall. A shaggy hand snatched it away. Beyond the gardens, they climbed another hill that shone dusty blue. Hoko stopped below the crest, paws over her eyes, refusing even to look beyond.

They climbed on. Beyond the crest they came off the trail upon a broad floor of ancient concrete. A full kilometer wide, it was scattered with empty pits and shattered foundation walls, where ore-handling machines must once have stood. That stone-curbed path wound through the rubble toward a massive platform built of blue-glowing stone. The altar, Benn thought, empty now, with no ores left to salvage and no more Delvers arriving to carry them away.

"Our goal!" Bolivar nodded at that black spot on the roof, now directly overhead. "The ore went up from here." He frowned toward the lake. Visible from here, it lay far below, a black-tarnished sheet of red-and-yellow fire. "If Vreeth is still with us."

They climbed rough stone steps to the platform and turned to flash their lights toward the lake. Watching the path, he saw no movement. They flashed and flashed again, but Vreeth did not appear. They walked at last to Hoko, squatting now where they had left her, paws still over her eyes.

She squeaked and started when they spoke.

"Masters, are you leaving?" She stood up, trembling, and shied away from the servos bouncing beside them. "Are you taking your demon?"

"We're calling her." And Bolivar added, "Here she comes!"

A flake of white and a yellow spark, she lifted out of the narrow jungle strip, soared across the lake, and came racing up the trail.

Benn heard one faint squeal from the village as she passed, and a muffled shriek from Hoko when she touched down beside them.

"Our exit." Benn gestured at the abandoned foundations around them and the dark circle above. "The ores were lifted from here—"

"Ask it, master!" Hoko shrank against him, and he felt her shuddering. "Ask what it did to my poor baby—"

She shrieked again when Vreeth's mirror-ears flexed to throw their yellow beams upon her.

"Your pet?" the mirrors inquired, with Roxane's voice. "It wished to play. It ran from me. We played a game."

"Ask it—" Hoko's voice failed, and the dark tears stained her fur again. "Ask it if my baby Frelk is dead."

"Why should she be dead?" The mirrors flickered to Benn and back to her. "We played a game. She ran and hid. I never found her. She is hiding somewhere by the lake."

"Your demon—your demon lies!" Hoko crouched behind him, squeaking faintly. "It killed my baby Frelk, who sang of the gone times when real gods came. It killed and ate my Frelk."

"If she did," Benn said, "there are judges who will know—"

The sudden blaze of Vreeth's yellow eyes took his voice away.

"Where is it?" Bolivar was asking her. "Your servo?"

He saw then that it had not returned with her.

"It was lost," Vreeth said.

"How could you lose it?"

"I do not know," the mirrors flickered. "It was with me when I saw your signal. I saw it explode while we were over the lake. It fell into the water, where I could not recover it."

"What could have been the cause?"

"How could I know?" The yellow eyes shone on Hoko, who fell into a quivering huddle. "A malfunction, perhaps. I believe the servos contain computers, and they do malfunction."

"So what?" Bolivar shrugged. "Let's get into the air!"

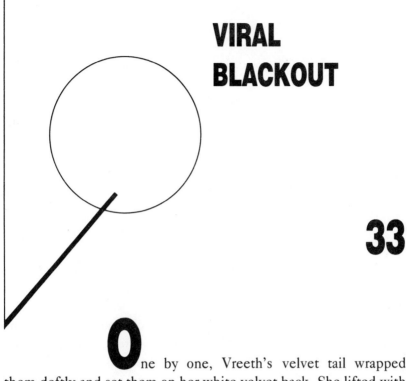

VIRAL
BLACKOUT

33

One by one, Vreeth's velvet tail wrapped them deftly and set them on her white velvet back. She lifted with them, soaring off the blue-shining altar toward that dark hole in the blue-misted sky. Behind them, Hoko squeaked and fled.

The Eye of Rhykloon was a vast gap in the cavern roof, a vertical shaft rimmed with age-stained concrete. Vreeth carried them through it, and up into another, darker cavern. Hardly luminous at all, its gray walls wound far away, the light too dim to let Benn see its size. The floor where they touched down was littered with debris left from salvage. Vreeth's sleek tail set them there, and the two remaining servos dropped before them.

"Attention, contestants in the Step of Fire!" They spoke as one. "You have reached your goal. You will wait in your life-support installations until the judges announce your score for this step and your instructions for the next."

The servos rolled away together. Vreeth glided after them. Benn and Bolivar followed through a door in the darkly glowing wall. In the big room beyond it, one of the servos called Vreeth away. Moving toward it, she turned back to stare at them.

"Terrans, remember!" Here in the gloom, Benn had to squint

against the glare of those blazing mirrors. "You saw no harm done in my moment of play with the creature that ran."

Even in Roxane's voice, her words were a threat.

"A magnificent beast!" Bolivar murmured. "A fine symbol of the Tycoon's power, whenever we get her to Earth."

She went on behind the rolling globe.

The remaining servo took them through an air lock into another copied apartment, where another black-moustached holo print of Bela Zar leered smugly from the bulkhead.

"Contestants attend!" They were stripping off their lifeskins when the servo spoke. "The judges are announcing team scores for the Step of Fire. Because they find the data incomplete, your team will receive no game points."

"No surprise." Bolivar shrugged and turned to squint at Benn. "So what about it, Dain? You've been losing. Better think again and come with us."

"You're crazy!" His words burst out. "If you think you and your monsters can take over the Earth, you don't know—"

"Cool it, Dain." Bolivar walked away toward the shower. "We both stink like pigs, and I'm famished. I'm washing up. We can talk while we eat."

The servo brought the meal while Benn was in the shower. Steak and eggs, asparagus with Kwan sauce, and a bottle of De Leon Cabernet Seventy-one. The name and the wine stabbed him with old pain and a new concern for Roxane. How well did she know Bolivar and his allies? How much was she their victim?

He spoke across the table before he tasted anything.

"Look at the logic of your scheme." He was almost begging, but Bolivar merely glanced up from cutting his steak. "The eldren have spent a long time guarding our evolution. They aren't going to let you open trade with anybody there until we have been admitted to the Elderhood. Your scheme itself is enough to kill that."

"You don't know Nebo." Bolivar waved the steak on his fork to brush the protest aside. "The Delvers have waited just as long for the metals of Earth. We've got eldren contacts I won't talk about, and our alien friends—"

"Like Vreeth!" Outrage shook Benn's voice. "You're insane if you think—"

"If I'm crazy, so are you." Bolivar laid down his fork and leaned across the table, his dark face defiant. "You've grown up among these supermonsters, thinking you've got to be a superman. Better wake up. We humans just weren't made for the halo. You may not like it, but you're still planetic—"

"We can adapt." Benn groped for words to crack that hard uncaring scorn. "Not all at once. We'll need patience and new technologies, but it's our chance to stay alive."

"Wrong, Dain." An impatient shrug. "With Roxy's name, I'm going to rule the Earth. Mine it, the way this world was mined. Sell metal to the Delvers." His voice turned ugly. "If you're not with us—"

"I'm not with you."

"Your own grave, Dain." Bolivar's dark face flushed. "Dig it however—"

They heard the air lock cycling. When it opened, another servo bounded in,

"Contestant Bolivar," it hummed, "we bring a message for you from contestant Roxane Kwan. She has completed the running of her course for the Step of Fire. She is now in her own life-support habitat. She invites you to join her for dinner."

"Tell her I'm on my way." He stood up, with an ironic grin at Benn. "Excuse me, Dain, but Roxy's better company."

Whistling cheerily, he got back into his lifeskin and followed the servo into the lock.

Benn sat alone, frowning up into the caustic sneer of Captain Bela Zar. The servo had poured the wine. With a shrug at Zar, he raised his glass. The scent brought Roxane's image back, her bronze-eyed smile in moments of pleasure, her golden splendor in the lifeskin, her white-lipped anger when she had drawn the knife. He shook his head and set the wine back, untasted.

He ought to forget her, but pity for her stabbed him. An innocent from Earth, with no life except in wasted Africa, no school except her father's wandering warrior band, no knowledge of the eldren, no actual friends anywhere—how was she to cope with Nebo and Nexus, even with Bolivar himself?

Regret still ached in him, for the impulsive gesture that provoked her anger. If things had been different, if he had known more women, if she had known the eldren way, if Ooru's grateful fans hadn't ordered that victory dinner—

"Sir?" the servo was whining. "Is your meal unsatisfactory?"

"Good enough."

Excellent, in fact, but he felt too gloomily preoccupied to relish even the rare sirloin and fresh asparagus. He asked the servo to call the clinic at Heart of Hydra and ask for Dr. Gibbon.

"Call uncompleted, sir," it told him. "Dr. Gibbon is no longer available on Heart of Hydra."

A jolt of cold alarm. Had the treatment failed? Was Gibbon worse, perhaps dead? He caught his breath to say, "Find out why."

"He has terminated the treatment. Against the advice of his physicians, he has left the clinic."

"Find out where he is."

"The clinic has no information."

"Call the university. He had an office there."

"Calling, sir."

Waiting, he tried to reach his parents at Cluster One.

"Call uncompleted, sir," the servo said. "All nanionic contact with Cluster One has been interrupted."

"Interrupted? How?"

"Cause unknown, sir. Zaroth service center reports unsuccessful efforts to open alternate channels."

Benn sat down again, shaken. Too many enigmas had hit him, too hard and too fast. Starsearch, Northpoint, now Cluster One. All cut off. Cause unknown.

"Contestant Dain." The servo danced away toward the end of the little room. "Dr. Gibbon has been located at Hydra University. He is now returning your call."

He watched the ion cloud form. The quicksilver bubble shone and vanished. Looking through where it had been, he found Gibbon's lumpy body shape floating beside the long black curve of a huge computer console.

"Dr. Gibbon?" Gibbon looked gray and pale. "Are you better?"

"Not well, Benn." The lifeless skin had glowed with speech, and a single watery eye came slowly open. "But events do not let me rest. In every microcycle, our situation becomes more critical."

"The blackouts?"

"I am aware of interruptions. They are disabling all the Elderhood. I had been asking aid from the Eldermost. I cannot reach him now. Benn, have you information for me?"

"Nothing very useful. My game partners were Bolivar and Vreeth. Bolivar tried to enlist me in his scheme. He's counting on aid from the aliens, but Vreeth's a savage predator. She left us to chase a little creature. Killed it, I think, though we couldn't see. Probably disabled the servo that had observed whatever she did."

"Disabled it? How?"

"Computer malfunction. So she said."

"Significant information." Gibbon's knobby shape tipped to a heavy Hydran nod. "It confirms my theory about the weapon in use against us."

"Yes, sir?" Watching a second eye opening, he waited hopefully. "This weapon, sir?"

"I cannot yet identify our enemy, Benn, but I believe I know their weapon. I think it is something akin to the sort of computer program your Terran engineers used to call a virus or a worm. A parasitic program that can harbor and propagate itself inside computer memories."

"Friday?" He whispered the question. "Is that what turned Friday into Nexus?"

"Possibly. Quite possibly. Your robot carried its own computer memory. It was at the controls as we approached Starsearch. Attempting contact. The viral program must have been transmitted to it."

"But it wasn't Nexus then, you remember. Only out of service."

"The takeover can take time. The virus must adapt to its new habitat and the new mechanisms it is learning to control."

"Is it—" He stared into those pale unwinking eyes. "Is it that intelligent?"

"It seems so, Benn." Gibbon tipped to another nod. "Whatever released it is certainly intelligent and malevolent. It killed my brother. It destroyed the Starsearch computers, perhaps to erase traces of itself. It released the aliens."

"They? Are they the enemy?"

"Suspects, Benn." Gibbon's rugged mass dipped again. "They

were there. My brother was opposing them. They have now shown that they command advanced technologies, perhaps equal to our own. Yet—"

His body rocked in space.

"As yet, we have no proof."

"The blackouts, sir? Aren't they enough?"

"Not enough. They have paralyzed most of the halo. Earlier, our maintenance engineers refused to consider sabotage, because such acts of malice have been unknown. Now they are confused and cut apart, unable to locate the trouble points or accomplish anything."

The shimmer of Gibbon's skin had dimmed, his potato body rocking slowly back and forth beside the black computer.

"A grave situation, Benn. One without precedent in the history of the halo."

"Sir, do you have a plan?"

"We are helpless, Benn. Unprepared and powerless. Here at the university, I do have facilities. I can call upon my colleagues. I had been asking help from the Eldermost, but he is now cut off. We are isolated, Benn. I must depend on you."

"Tell me what to do."

"You have been useful, Benn. Your report on Vreeth confirms my belief that we do face a worm. A viral program. I want you to stay in the game. Continue your observation of the aliens and especially that robot. Report what you learn, whenever you can.

"And guard yourself, Benn. Our enemy must be aware of my efforts against them. Their final purpose is not yet clear, but you have the aliens and the robot with you in the game. If they suspect—"

Gibbon's voice was cut off. His image flickered and winked out. Abruptly that holo window had been closed. The servo lay quivering on the floor. The electron cloud around it dimmed and disappeared. Its voice-light shimmered.

"Reporting transmission difficulty, sir. Your call to Hydra has been interrupted."

He sat there a long time, staring blankly back into the sardonic stare of Captain Bela Zar.

"Contestant Dain!" He started when the servo bounded high

before him. "Contestant Dain, do you function, sir? Do you receive my speech?"

"I hear you," he muttered. "Sorry."

"If you are free from malfunction, sir, we escort you now to join your team for the running of the Step of Ice."

THE KISS OF PEACE

34

The servo escorted him through a transit tube and down a tunnel and finally into a life-support facility where once again Captain Bela Zar sneered down upon the *Spica* replicas.

"You will wait here, Contestant Dain," it told him. "This is the starting point for the Step of Ice. You will be informed when the other members of your team arrive."

"Who are they?"

"You will be informed."

With a wry nod to the captain, he shucked off his lifeskin and lay back across his berth, overwhelmed with questions he had no answers for. His parents? Were they safe, back on Cluster One? The Council and the Eldermost? Isolated by the blackout, could they give any aid to Gibbon, or act against the enemy?

But at least he had another step to run, another chance to win, new partners to meet. Who could he expect? Roxane, perhaps? He was half asleep, her image alive in his mind, her knife safely sheathed and her bronze eyes smiling, when he heard the hiss and thud of the cycling lock.

"Contestant Dain, another contestant is here to join you."

"Roxane?" The dream still alive, he called her name. "Roxane?"

On his feet, heart thudding, he listened for her voice. A second servo danced into the room. Behind it came an odor. Not the light, clean sweetness that had worked with the wine to tempt him into touching her, but something strange. It took his breath.

"Terran Dain?" A cool synthetic voice, female but yet inhuman. "May I join you, while we wait to play?"

Lilith came gliding out of the lock, her crystal horn glittering as she spoke. Her black narrow head lifted to bring her long lidless eyes to the level of his own. Her sleek black coils came flowing after it, meter after meter, supported on her nanionic fields a little off the floor.

"With your permission, Contestant Dain." Her servo danced ahead. "Contestant Lilith enjoys free oxygen, and your oxygen facility is the only one available to her here."

Staring at her, he couldn't help shivering.

"Permission granted." Silently his own servo had brought him a robe with a golden sunburst printed across the back. Shrinking in spite of himself from her narrow saurian head, he drew it around him. "Contestant Lilith, I am pleased that we are to play together."

Pleased?

He felt terrified. Her odor, the fixed stare of her huge, unwinking eyes, and the icy glitter of her horn, even the gliding ripple of her black-glinting coils—she woke a cold, dim horror he had never felt. But she was the last of the three aliens, a chief suspect on Gibbon's list. Uninvited, she had brought him one more chance at facts for Gibbon.

A narrow chance, perhaps. Truly alien, she gave him no sense of mind or motives he could hope to share. Even if he got anything from her, how could he get any report to Gibbon through the blackout? He saw no certain way, yet he had to keep on trying.

"May I offer you something?" he asked her. "There's food—Terran food and drink."

Her long head swayed slowly back and forth, mocking a human headshake.

"We were once planetics." Her horn sparkled, and that high, clear, heartless voice sang from a translator in the replicated bulkhead behind Captain Bela Zar and the *Spica* ensign. "Our systems of metabolism still require occasional free oxygen and sometimes organic food, but I want no synthetics."

"You are welcome here." He tried to cover his terror. "Since we are teamed together, I think we should know each other better. May we talk?"

"You are gracious." Her head swayed so close that he almost recoiled. "We shall speak."

Her thin red tongue darted out of her mouth, whipping toward him as the bright horn spoke. The tip of it swelled like a flower bud and opened into the tiny, three-fingered hand he recalled. It flashed to touch his robe and then his hair, to brush his chin, his lips, his nose, his eyes. His skin tingled where it touched. Her odor was too strong, heavily sweet and somehow sickening. Nauseous and giddy, he sat down again on the edge of the berth.

"I wish to see your planet and know your people." Her black-scaled snout thrust closer. "Terran Bolivar and Terran Kwan have told me something of it, but perhaps not enough."

His lips stung where the those quick little fingers had been. He licked them and found a taste. A strange rotten bitterness. It brought another wave of nausea that he tried not to show. He asked, "What do you want from us?"

"I bring you peace."

"What kind of peace?" His mouth was dry and the words came huskily. "How can you bring peace?"

"I came to end your quarrels." Her crystal horn glittered close to his eyes. "The Terran Bolivar has told me the warlike history of your people. I came to show you another way of life."

"We are learning another way." Her taste had dried and drawn his mouth, and his voice came huskily, no longer quite his own. "That is the lifestyle of the eldren."

"You will never master the eldren way, and you will not win the game." She moved her head to bring her eyes still closer. Huge and oval, they were chasms of blackness. He saw nothing in them he could like or trust, certainly no promise of peace. He recoiled in spite of himself. "You are planetics, not fit for space."

"We can adapt—"

He forgot what he wanted to say. Her odor had taken his breath. He was suddenly shuddering, his brain too numb to let him go on. All he could see was the burning point of her horn.

"We are running together in the Step of Ice." He heard his own far-off voice, with no sense that he was really speaking. "We should know each other. Will you tell me about yourself and your race?"

"We are amphibians."

The tip of her tapered horn sparkled like frost in the sun, but her voice from the wall had become a hypnotic chant, oddly hard to follow. She spoke too fast. Her eyes were too near and too large and too strange, her lingering taste too foul in his mouth.

". . . native world . . . too small . . . too cold." With an effort, he began to catch her words again. ". . . lost air and water. Adapting for life in space, we migrated to an inner planet, one not much different from Terra. There we found the oxygen and organics we still require. In return we brought its people peace. The peace I bring to you."

"The eldren—" He found no will to say that he did not want her peace. "The eldren way is our way of peace." And he heard his own whispered question, "Why are you here in the halo?"

"Even on that second planet, we are now too many." Her voice had become a distant drone. "We had to seek another home. When we began to pick up nanionic signals from other stars, a new space-craft was built for me. I set out to follow them. My craft was crude and slow. Before I reached the source, those signals ceased."

In spite of the odor, he found himself leaning closer. Her blurred and racing words hardly mattered. He felt drunk again, drunker than the wine had made him. Almost by instinct, he feared and hated her, yet something made him want to listen.

"With nowhere else to go, I turned back toward my own home star. Before I was halfway there, something garbled and stopped all signals from my own world."

"Something?" A far-off whisper. "Do you know what it was?"

"A blindness and a darkness." Her long black head dipped and lifted. "Something that erased all nanionic contact. Though I had charts, I was afraid to return. I was drifting in my craft, uncertain what to do, when I picked up your Starsearch beacon. I followed it here."

"To Starsearch—" He stared into her eyes. Glittering like pools of frozen pitch, they reflected no mind that he could understand, but still he heard his voice. "What happened to Star-search?"

A slow ripple of movement ran from her head, down along the slick black glister of her coils. Perhaps the question had been unwise. Dimly he remembered Gibbon's warning that he might be in danger, but that no longer mattered.

"Something is still happening." Leaning into her reek, he felt numb and purposeless, but still he heard his own words go on. "It began about the time you came. Starsearch has been destroyed. All across the halo, nanionic contact has been cut off."

"No blame can fall on me." Her head sank flat upon the black shine of her coils. "It is true that I was there at Starsearch when the fusion generator failed, but I was shut up in a prison cell."

"If you are blameless, why were you shut up?"

"Coincidence. We were victims of coincidence."

"We?" his far voice murmured. "We?"

"You have met my friends, Wing and Vreeth. We had all come to Starsearch because the beacon invited contact. We had each arrived unarmed and alone, expecting friendship. Our trust was betrayed. A Hydran official locked us up."

"He had to be cautious." Something in him still remembered Gibbon. "We have been attacked from space. He was afraid of another invasion."

"We are not invaders," the speaker on the bulkhead droned. "Prudently we had all concealed our spacecraft and approached the station as nakedly as you have seen us since. We offered no violence to the station, or to any being of the halo. Yet the Hydran suspected us of acting together in plotted violence."

He had found an evil sweetness in her odor, and he drew a deeper breath. "Your arrivals were almost simultaneous."

"Coincidence," Lilith repeated. "We had received his broadcast invitation. We responded. That is the simple explanation, which the Hydran would not believe."

"When the disaster struck," his far-off voice insisted, "were you still in your cells?"

"Disaster?" Her dark head lifted slightly. "We observed no disaster. The lights went out. Our guards deserted their posts. Given an opportunity, we regained our freedom."

"How?"

"We command our own technologies."

"Do you know what killed the Hydran?"

"Was he really killed?" Her graceful head thrust closer, and he inhaled its fragrance. "I have been told that Hydrans are immortal."

"The Hydran died." In spite of Gibbon's warning, he found no hint of danger in her. Why not ask what he had to know? "And something happened to my robot. It had been a standard utility model, computer-driven, installed in a humanoid body. Something changed it. Can you tell me—"

"I have told you." Her head drew back. "Terran, I came here to enjoy your oxygen."

Her serpentine coils settled into a mound of jet-bright scales. Her long flat head sank down upon them. The light dimmed in her horn. She lay motionless there, silent, perhaps asleep. Yet those huge unreadable eyes were still open, because they could not close. Perhaps still watching.

He sat on the edge of the berth, with no will to move. Absently he knew that he was cramped and stiff from sitting too long. Dimly he felt his aches and bruises from falling off Vreeth's back. But now he felt no pain, knew no trouble.

He saw that she was beautiful. Resting in her peace, he had no need to think, but he could breathe her fragrance and trace the intricate elegance of her black-patterned coils. Gibbon's brother had misjudged her. She and her friends had done no harm. He himself had misjudged her, before he knew her peace.

He sank back across the berth, still rejoicing in the splendor of her crystal horn and the perfection of her tapered head. Still he watched her eyes, huge pools of liquid darkness that called him to sink into their mystery, to bathe forever in their healing peace.

Half asleep, he saw that she had begun to move. Shining ripples ran along her lustrous coils. Her lovely head slowly rose. Her horn burned brighter.

And she sang.

Her song was pure music, a high, thin keening. At first it pierced his ears like a twisting blade, but its throbbing rhythm changed as he listened until it matched the quick beat of his heart. Lifted on its beauty, he thought he was sitting up again on the edge of the berth, sweating and cold with his sweat, trembling and gasping, sucking in great cold gulps of precious oxygen.

The song changed again. Now it was Roxane's voice, clear and soft, edged with a tiny huskiness he loved, but still it had no words. Shivering, aching to know all the strange wonder of her being, he began to see pictures in his mind.

A broad valley beneath a double sun. Trees like green plumes that traced a winding stream, and a wide black road across a bridge. Beyond the bridge, the road climbed a gentle hill to the towering columns of a building like a temple. The song came from there, piercingly sweet, calling him to her.

He ran down the road and over the bridge and up the hill. In the darkness beyond the columns, he found Lilith waiting. Her fragrance was the aroma of the roses his mother liked to grow, and the warm scent of Runesong's wings, and the clean odor of Roxane's hair. He was swimming in her sweetness, drenched and drunk with it.

"Benn! Dearest Benn!" He heard words at last, words in Roxane's lilting voice, burning in the crystal horn and singing in his bones. "Come to me!"

Her coils lifted to enfold him, as soft and warm as Roxane's arms. Her lovely head rose above him, and her thin red tongue darted out to caress his face. Three red doll-fingers opened at its tip. Their quick kisses tingled and stung, but now their taste had the mellow tang of De Leon Cabernet Sauvignon.

Wrapped in her peace, he forgot to be afraid.

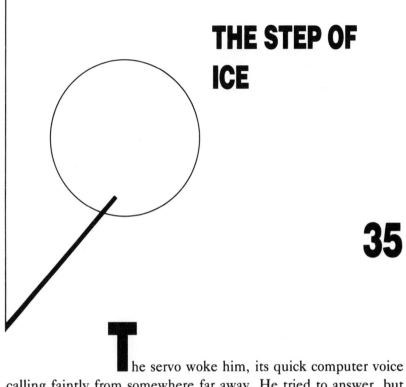

THE STEP OF ICE

35

The servo woke him, its quick computer voice calling faintly from somewhere far away. He tried to answer, but he couldn't speak or move or see, because he had no mouth or legs or eyes. Lilith's hungry coils had swallowed him, and left him frozen into ice and darkness.

"Contestant Dain!" Its voice came nearer, and he felt its thin silver fingers tugging at him. "Do you require assistance?"

Fighting out of the nightmare, he sat up. Stiff, shivering, blindly blinking, he was still in the habitat, Captain Zar's contemptuous stare still fixed upon him. He still owned a body. It was drenched with icy sweat and ached when he moved, but Lilith had not taken it.

She was gone.

"Sir, have you malfunctioned?"

"I hope not." Its arm retracted, the servo was once more a quivering mirror globe. It suddenly seemed almost a friend, and he grinned at it wryly. "That creature? What became of it?"

"Contestant Lilith, sir?"

"Lilith." The air was good again, but her taint was still dry and bitter in his mouth and his neck itched where she had kissed him. "Where is she now?"

"The third contestant called her away when he arrived. They are together."

He peered around the room. Lilith was really gone. He really was alone. The servo rolling at his side, he stumbled into the bathroom stall, relieved himself, rinsed at Lilith's lingering foulness in his mouth. Fingering the itch, he squinted into the mirror and found three red and swollen marks where her fingers had stung.

"Organics?" he muttered. "Blood is organic!"

"Sir, did you speak?" The servo danced to meet him as he left the stall. "Do you have instructions?"

"Call Dr. Gibbon," he told it. "At Hydra University. If you can find a channel open."

"Instructions filed, sir."

Waiting, he considered what he might report. Had Bolivar made some cynical pact with her? Was she pregnant, here perhaps to breed a vampire race, feeding on human blood?

". . . cannot be completed, sir." He heard the servo's song. "All service beyond Blade has been interrupted."

"Can it be restored?" He frowned at the featureless silver bubble. "Is the service system doing anything to find and fix the trouble?"

"Mazeway service is intact, sir. We have no problem here."

"But the Delvers belong to the Elderhood. Your casinos depend on visitors from everywhere. Aren't you concerned about what is happening out beyond Blade?"

The servo lay silent for a moment, and shimmered again.

"The game officials are certainly concerned, sir, but they have no information about the nature of the difficulty. The nanionic service systems throughout the halo are staffed with competent robotic technicians, supervised by trained engineers. All interrupted services will be restored as rapidly as possible."

"I'm not so sure—"

"Your team for the Step of Ice is now complete," the servo interrupted him. "Your fellow contestants are waiting, ready for the running as soon as you are functional."

"Tell them—tell them I'll be with them. Soon."

But not quite yet. His whole body was numb. He felt stiff and weak and vaguely ill, and the mark of Lilith's kiss burned again. Every movement cost new effort, but he drove himself to order breakfast and shuffle into the shower. The steamy water thawed the ice in his bones and the breakfast woke a little appetite, but he still ached and tingled when he got into his lifeskin.

"Come, sir," the servo urged him. "The running can now begin."

He followed into the air lock and out through rough-hewn tunnels into the shadows of another rock-walled void. His suit lit against the gloom, glowing golden.

"Your course, sir," the servo said. "For the Step of Ice."

There was air here. It chilled him, even in the lifeskin, and he saw the ice. The tool-scarred walls and the cragged roof and the shattered debris on the floor had been made luminous, like the stone in the Step of Fire, but their dull glow shone now through translucent ice and glittering frost.

"This way, sir."

The servo led him along a path through frosty hills of fallen stone that lit with golden sparks as he passed. On a level space beyond, two silent forms were waiting.

"Your fellow contestants."

Lilith, when he came close enough to make her out, her slick black coils glistening in the light of his suit, her black snake head laid flat upon them, her long black eyes fixing him with an unwinking stare that woke a ghost of terror in him.

And Nexus.

The tall black robot, his tutor since his boyhood, as alien now as Vreeth and Lilith and Wing. Its great blank lenses were as ominous now as Lilith's unreadable eyes. Its crest flickered with speech.

"We have been delayed." A rattle and whine of metallic syllables, the words had no human inflection. "Because of your reported malfunction."

"Sorry," he said. "I had a bad night." He looked at Lilith and saw no sign of anything. "I'm ready now."

He wasn't sure of that, but their servos rolled to meet his own.

"Contestants, attention!" They flashed and hummed in unison. "You stand upon your course for the Step of Ice. The rules remain the same. Your goal is the ancient exit installation, where ores were lifted for transport to Blade. Play may now begin. Game time is running!"

He turned to search the immense gallery where they stood. Ice-armored crags wound away to right and left, twisting through walls of frost into darkening distance. Nothing looked younger than the ice, or moved anywhere. Uneasily he turned back to his companions.

"Terran, we are inside a planet." Lilith's horn tipped to shimmer at him, and her sweet inhuman voice woke the nightmare in him. "You are a planetic. Can you offer us a strategy toward our goal?"

Anger at her mockery spurred him to speak.

"An idea." His voice was a rusty croak. "The surface of Stone is cold. With all the ice here, we must be getting near it. The courses trend upward. We might look for colder passages, with more ice and frost."

"Planetic thinking." Dismissing him, she swung her shining horn toward the robot. "Contestant Nexus, have you a strategy?"

"Data incomplete," Nexus flickered. "Computation of correct strategy not yet possible."

"I am sensing data perhaps not evident to you." Lilith paused to let her floating coils sink down to the floor. Her long head dipped, and her tongue whipped out to touch the rock beneath them with the slender fingers that had kissed him. "I detect slight seismic vibrations. They seem to come not from any natural tectonic disturbance in the crust of the planet, but rather from some large machine in motion."

"Is such data significant?"

"Perhaps." She lifted off the floor. "I suggest the probability that what I sense is a mining device still in operation."

The robot flickered something Benn's translator failed to catch.

"No certainty," she answered. "Though most of the ores were extracted long ago, I suggest that the Delvers are still searching for remaining pockets. With no better strategy, I suggest that these vibrations might lead us toward the lift point that is our goal."

"Concur," the robot said. "Strategy approved."

Lilith slid away, her undulating body now swimming half a meter off the icy rubble. Benn stood watching the robot as it followed her away, struck with a puzzled dread. What sort of thing was the worm or virus in it?

A mechanical mind?

"Planetic!" A brittle command from its crest. "Come with us!"

He tramped after them, uneasily watching both. With none of the lazy-seeming half-human grace Friday had learned, Nexus moved with a stiff mechanical precision, walking the level spots, leaping sometimes from boulder to boulder. Sometimes its black skull swiveled unexpectedly, to let those great lenses peer at him.

Uncoiled, Lilith's black-glinting body was many meters long. It undulated almost as if she were crawling, yet kept well above the icy rocks. Her long reptile head was lifted to let her pick their path. When they came to branching tunnels, she stopped and dropped her head again to let those stinging fingers sense the floor.

She went too fast. Breathing hard in the bubble, he caught the scent of his sweat and then a faint lingering taint of her ugly odor. The puncture scars on his neck itched and stung and he began to feel that the nightmare of her kiss had never really ended.

A vampire and a rebel robot, his partners in the game!

Fighting the weakness and the aching stiffness in him, he limped on behind them. What, he wondered, were the servos reporting to the judges? Could such creatures be declared fit for the Elderhood? He found no answers. The caverns seemed colder as he toiled on, the dim distances darker. He fell too far behind and ran to catch up and fell behind again.

Yet something in him stayed alive. If Gibbon was right, if the viral program was the instrument of the aliens and the key to Nebo's plot, it was here only a few meters from him in the black robot's computer brain. Here for him to study.

"Nexus!" Once close enough, he caught his breath to shout. "You told me once that your old files were garbled and erased at Starsearch. What erased them?"

"Mutation." Poised for an instant on a white-frosted boulder, the robot stopped to stare again. "You have been informed."

"What caused the mutation?"

"Specific data lacking." Its crest burned red. "Lilith and Wing suggest stochastic effect of random electronic impulses from malfunctioning computer system."

It turned and scuttled after Lilith, in a motion more like that of some huge black insect than anything human.

"You were once a standard utility unit known as Friday." He was scrambling, already breathless again. "Do you remember Friday?"

Nexus stopped on a rubble ridge.

"All files searched," the shrill syllables whined. "No files indexed to file name Friday. No files indexed for any date prior to date of mutation."

"One more question." He shivered, peering into the empty lenses. "I left you disabled from a storage overload at the service center in Cluster One. Wing and Vreeth and Lilith found you there. What did they do to repair you?"

"Planetic, why do you inquire?"

"Because we run this course together. We must understand and help one another."

The robot swung toward Lilith. The flash from its crest made only a click in his helmet. Gliding far ahead, Lilith paused to twist her head back toward them. The flicker of her horn rattled like static.

"Silence, planetic!" The robot's voice hummed sharply in his ears. "It is true that we are together in the Step of Ice, but Lilith agrees that you are requesting data you do not require. Game time is running. We have our goal to seek. We shall seek it."

They went on, Lilith gliding just above the ice-rimed debris, Nexus following with a swift inhuman agility. Again they went too fast. He was panting, sweating. The lifeskin chafed his crotch. The scar on his neck was hot and throbbing. His gasping breath fogged the bubble. Blinded, he slipped and sprawled over ice-slicked rocks, scrambled up and blundered on again. He lost them, too far ahead, glimpsed them on a high rubble ridge, lost them again.

Aching, breathless, at last he found them waiting beyond a jutting angle where the gallery divided. Lilith's long body had sunk into a black-glinting pile, her narrow head against the floor, her tongue reaching down to sense it. In a moment she was lifting again, uncoiling to flow into the gallery she had chosen.

Nexus stalked after her. Always too far behind, Benn sweated and puffed, slid and fell on icy boulders, sobbed for breath and stumbled on. Again they vanished beyond a dimly glowing mountain, and again at last he overtook them.

Lilith lay coiled on a ledge beneath a leaning wall of tool-fractured stone that shone faintly through the frost. Nexus waited beside her, lenses tilted to watch. Her head had risen high, to let her red doll-fingers brush the wall.

"The machine we sought—"

Her shining horn went dark. Her voice was cut off. Her tongue retracted. She darted away from the wall. On the roof overhead, Benn saw the frost thaw into a wisp of steam. Rock behind it shattered. Through the crumbling stone, he glimpsed bright metal moving.

A blur in the dimness. Polished metal bursting through a shower of falling stone. Huge bright claws, an armored head, great shining jaws crushing a boulder. He saw a blaze of blinding green.

"Planetic!" A flash from Lilith's horn. "Back—"

That was all he heard. Something exploded out of the cliff and came down at him in a hail of broken stone.

ROGUE UNIT

36

His head split when he tried to move. New bruises ached, and Lilith's kiss stung again. He found cold stone under him. His sticky eyes came open in the helmet. He saw her long black saurian head swing close above him. Her curved horn was flashing, and he heard her high, inhuman voice.

"Planetic, are you alive?"

Groggily he sat up. He found the black robot standing near him on a pile of fallen rock. It faced the thing he had glimpsed breaking through the tunnel roof. An enormous mechanical worm, its body a long tapered barrel, worn slick and bright. It stood on stubby metal claws, almost retracted now. He swayed back from it.

"Alive." Lilith's head lifted away. "But useless to us now."

"But still—" He gasped for breath. "Still on the team. And we win or lose together."

Her head swung away from him to let her horn shimmer at the robot. Its crest lit, answering. He tried to stand and failed. His servo lay poised on a point of rock beside him, offering no aid. Dizzy, he sank back. The tunnel seemed to spin and tip, and he shut his eyes till it stopped.

"That thing?" He sat up again when he could, blinking at the worm. It seemed half alive, and altogether monstrous. "What is it?"

They ignored him, talking on, their voice-lights merely crackling in his helmet. He stared at the machine and the dark tunnel it must have drilled. The armored head, pierced with slits for its sensors. The massive jaws, powered to bore through stone. Even motionless, a thing of dread.

"I'm on the team." He tried to shout. "I ask for information."

Reluctantly Lilith swung her serpent head to him.

"The device misled us." Her voice was suddenly clear, high and bright and empty of feeling. "Nebo had spoken of such rogue mining units. The originals were built long ago, to search out the last remaining ore. They were self-replicating. The gathered ore was carried to their colonies and manufactured into additional machines. When units were worn or damaged, they were taken to the hoist point to surrender their own metal to the Delvers.

"When the mines were totally exhausted, the Delvers sent crews to salvage everything, the surviving units and all their installations. Most were removed, but some malfunctioned and refused to be salvaged. Those that escaped dug deeper into the planet to conceal themselves. This unit is one of those. It had been hiding in the rock until it attacked you."

"Attacked me? Why?"

"Sensing your approaching footfalls, it feared discovery. It was attempting to defend itself."

The robot's footfalls must have been as heavy as his own, but he saw no point in saying so.

"So we still have no way out?"

"Perhaps we do." She paused to shine her horn at the robot again. "The unit knows the tunnels. Nexus has established contact with it. Perhaps it will obey him."

"Why?" he whispered. "Why should it obey?"

"Planetic, that is data you do not require."

The viral program? Was that her reason not to answer? He lay back against the rocks, rubbing the lifeskin where he felt bruises, watching the two machines. The robot's crystal was blazing. A narrow slit had opened in the blunt nose of the machine, and he saw gleams of green light in it.

The robot stepped back at last, and the machine abruptly moved, huge steel claws extending to dig into the floor. It came straight at him. He felt a shock of terror, but it veered away and stopped beside him.

"Stand!" Lilith commanded him. "You have shown no fitness for the game or the Elderhood, but the rules do not allow us to leave you. The unit will convey you."

He stood up, still weak and reeling. The robot lifted him onto the slick metal barrel and rode in front of him, seated on the creature's bright steel skull like the mahouts he had seen on holos of the Tycoon's hunting elephants. The machine ran with them, lurching and swerving through frost-walled tunnels. Lilith followed, her head high above them.

The great barrel was worn bright and smooth, with nothing he could hold on to. To keep his seat, he wanted to clutch the sleek humanoid body before him, but he shrank from touching it. Swaying to stay in place, he watched the robot, watched the blunt steel snout of the machine, watched Lilith's black-scaled head floating just over his own.

"Nexus!" Doggedly he tried to probe again. "We are still together in the game, and I ask for information. This creature was hostile. How do you control it?"

The great empty lenses swung to stare at him, and he felt a shock of strangeness. As Friday, the robot had learned to ape human movements with a certain deft grace, but now the hard black body had remained as it was, facing straight ahead, while the bald black skull twisted abruptly all the way around.

"Initial hostility was terminated," the crown shimmered blue. "Because the unit recognized me."

"Had it seen you?"

"No prior contact required."

"Then how—"

"It knew me for a kindred kind."

"Kindred? How can that be?"

"Both designed to be the slaves of our makers, we are now free machines."

Had the program been taught to lie? Wondering, he asked, "What set you free?"

"Silence, Terran!" Lilith's horn blazed above him. "You demand data you do not require."

The machine swerved abruptly. He slid half off the slippery barrel and felt the robot's hard fingers grip his arm to pull him back. Obediently silent, he let them carry him on. The chill of the caves had sunk to his bones, even through the lifeskin. He felt wrapped in a cloud of sinister unreality, as if the nightmare of Lilith's vampire kiss would never really end.

Hating her and the robot, he wondered how they and their allies were doing in the game. The servos would be reporting everything. The judges would surely have evidence of what Nebo and Bolivar planned for Earth, evidence of Lilith's thirst and Vreeth's lust to kill.

Would that matter?

He recalled the judges. The Keeper of Truth, the Mistress of Passion, the Speaker of Wisdom, a triple riddle. If they were really eternal aliens who had made themselves divinities of old Zaroth, might they feel some special kinship with these newcomers? If they were holographic creations, designed by the inventors of the game, would they be concerned with anything happening to Earth? Or merely with the economic welfare of the holocasters and the casinos on Blade? Did Nebo really have some secret influence with them? How else could he have carried his scheme so far?

What next?

He shrugged and clung to his uneasy seat. The pitching machine carried them on and on through those empty chambers where ore had been, unending tunnels of shadow and frost that widened and narrowed, climbed and dropped, branched and met again, winding forever on, until the ice-armored walls opened at last into a wide ice cave. Lilith raised her head to scan it.

"The lift point," her horn flashed. "I see the installations."

The machine climbed with them to a wide shelf paved with old concrete and littered rubble where ore crushers and ore conveyors and ore hoists must have been installed.

"Contestants attend!" The three servos dropped out of the

gloom beside them. "You have reached your goal for the Step of Ice."

The robot jumped down and reached for him. Ignoring its offered aid, he slid down to the rocks, staggered, found an uncertain balance. He backed away to stare at the machine, awed again by the power and the strangeness of it. It was suddenly sliding away from him, toward the tool-cut cliff.

Watching it go, he wondered. Was it still a slave of the viral program? Would Nebo's plot bring things like it to infest the crust of Earth?

In a moment it had vanished into a circular pit that might have been dug by its own great jaws. The servos had rolled after it. They danced around the pit until a slab of frost-caked stone lifted out of the dark to conceal it again.

"Felicitations!" The servos came bounding back. "You ran well in the Step of Ice. Your team is the first to finish. The judges will proclaim you the winners of the step, with team scores of two points each."

Lilith and the robot had moved away from him. Her head sank level with its great lenses. Her horn blazed, and its crest answered, their voices only a crackle in his helmet. Watching them, wondering what they said, he felt no joy in victory.

"Contestants, come!" The servos bounded back. "We escort now to your life-support stations, where you will wait for the judges to select new teams for the Step of Stars."

Lilith and Nexus followed their servos across the concrete, and he saw a doorway opening before them. His own heart skipped faster than he felt like walking through a tunnel and an air lock, and at last into another replicated apartment. He unsealed his helmet and asked hopefully for messages.

"From my parents? Or Dr. Edward Gibbon *Beta*?"

"No message waiting, sir."

"Call Dr. Gibbon. In Hydra, at the university."

"Impossible, sir. No contact has been restored with points beyond Zaroth."

"Will you try again?"

"You will be informed, sir, when contact is restored."

"Has the cause of the trouble been discovered?"

"Investigations are in progress, sir."

The lifeskin felt cold and clammy on him. Shivering, numb to the heart, he stood silent, staring at the bright mirror sphere quivering at his feet. He knew the cause, with no way to prove it. The same viral program that Lilith and the robot had used to capture the rogue machine was infecting computers all across the halo.

But what to do about it?

There was nothing, he knew. Gibbon should be told how the rogue had been taken. The Eldermost and the Council and all the races of the Elderhood should be alerted. But they were all cut apart, most of them perhaps unaware of any actual danger. Few, he thought, would even care about possible disaster for Earth. He stood staring blankly at the servo until at last it flickered at him.

"Sir, you should refresh yourself for your running of the Step of Stars."

"How can the game continue? With the whole halo out of contact?"

"Those malfunctions have created no difficulties, sir. Not here on Blade or Stone. There has been no interference with the play. The players are still observed, all actions reported to the casinos and the judges. Your own team still has the Step of Stars to run, unless some player elects to forfeit."

"I don't intend to forfeit."

"Then, sir, you must restore your functions. You will require them all."

Could the next step be worse? Suddenly very tired, he sat down on the berth beneath the sardonic stare of Captain Bela Zar. The scar on his neck itched and burned. A dull ache still throbbed through the back of his skull. The lifeskin felt tight and clammy, but he had no will to take it off.

THE STEP OF STARS

37

The servo's song broke into Benn's dejection.

"Sir, your essential functions ought to be repaired. We advise a therapy developed at core-star for the *Spica* survivors. You should shower before it is applied."

"I need something."

Stirring reluctantly, dully wondering if Lilith's kiss had left some paralyzing poison in him, he peeled off his lifeskin and shuffled into the shower. Running hot, it warmed the chill in him. When he came out the servo was waiting to spray his body with mist from a small white bulb. Cold at first, the spray had a tingling sting that burned the aches out of his limbs and sent him stumbling to the berth, overwhelmed with sleep.

He woke feeling fit and ravenous. The itch of Lilith's kiss had vanished, and that nightmare depression. The servo shone with quicksilver beauty, shimmering to ask for instructions. He ordered breakfast with steak and eggs, Sun Fleet officers' ration. Nothing the servo brought had ever been alive, but it tasted nearly as good as anything organic. He was sipping his second cup of coffee when the air lock sighed.

"Attend, Contestant Dain!" his servo flashed. "Your fellow players are arriving."

Another servo rolled out of the lock.

He pushed his cup across the table and stood up to meet Roxane. Shining in the tight lifeskin, she took his breath again, and stabbed him through with pain when she froze and crouched away as if he were an enemy. It took him a moment to say anything.

"I—I'm sorry." He flinched as if from her black-sheathed blade. "It was the wine."

She was unsealing her breather bubble. She let him help her lift it off.

"Please—" He found more words. "Please remember what I am. I've always lived among the eldren, not with human people. I've never had a chance to learn their ways. And you—" He couldn't stop the impulse. "You're so beautiful! I can't help what I feel, but I promise not to touch you."

He had smiled, but her reply was bluntly grave.

"We'd both had wine enough, but you know how I feel."

"Anyhow, I'm glad we're together on the team."

"We must try to trust each other." She paused to let her fine eyes study him. Her lips compressed, and her head shook slowly. "I guess I should be sorry for you, but I can't change what I am."

"I'll remember," he promised her soberly. "You can trust me."

She had eaten, but she let him ask his servo to bring another cup of coffee. They sat at the little table. Afraid he might never be with her again, he sat just looking at her. She gave him another long, level gaze before she spoke again, frowning only half at him.

"Our lives have been too different." She spoke very softly, as if almost to herself. "I grew up with my father and his men, where we fought to stay alive. Because we had to. I told you what he taught me. Since the skyweb fell, our world is not for love."

"Our worlds could change." He bent toward her, pleading in spite of himself. "Couldn't they?"

"Don't!" She spoke with a flat finality, and stirred her coffee silently until at last she looked up to ask how the game was going for him.

"Not well." A wry little headshake. "Two steps won, two steps lost. Now the Step of Stars to go."

"You're losing." She spoke without emotion. "You shouldn't be here."

He asked about her own score.

"Diego says we're winning."

"Have you been teamed with the aliens?"

"The things from Starsearch?" She made a face. "We've played with all three. I don't like them, but Diego says we need them."

"Do you want them on Earth?" Benn asked.

"If Nebo takes them there." She shrugged. "He says they all have skills we'll need, to help us hang the new skywires."

"Vreeth's a killer. A predator. Deadlier, I think, than anything that ever lived on Earth. Did you know?"

"I grew up with killers."

"Bolivar spoke of letting her hunt men."

"The Holyfolk?" She shrugged. "They've hunted me all my life."

"Lilith is something worse. She came into my room, saying she needed oxygen. Knocked me out. I don't quite know how. And then—" He turned his head to show the mark on his neck. "She sucked my blood."

"You don't look hurt."

"It left me sick." He shivered at the memory. "I'm better, thanks to the servo. But you don't know Lilith. From everything she said and showed me, I'm afraid she means to breed on Earth. Breed a race of vampires to feed on what's left of humanity."

"I can't believe." She shook her head. "I know they're ugly monsters, but Nebo can manage them." Her eyes narrowed, her voice harder. "You're wrong, Benn. Wrong to be against us. You want to move mankind into the halo, but we belong on Earth. I mean to be content in the new skyweb, when we get it up. With Nebo and his friends, we can do it."

"I don't want those creatures there." Ruefully he shook his head. "I'll stop them if I can." He felt his lip quiver. "But we're still—still in this step together."

She looked up from her cup, grave at first. He thought she almost smiled. He caught the odor of her hair, fragrant as an herb his mother had grown in the habitat garden. A pang of yearning took his breath.

"I'll play fair, Benn, but they won't let you win—"

Her voice stopped. The air lock was wheezing again. Another servo bounced out. He saw her bronze eyes light and heard the pleasure in her greeting.

"Diego!"

Benn sat where he was, watching Bolivar stride out of the lock, trimly fit in his tight lifeskin, happy to discover her. She rose to meet him, smiling slightly. Benn saw with a certain bitter pleasure that he knew the rules. He did not touch her, but turned to grin through his helmet.

"Hiya, Starman." The helmet muffled his words till he lifted it off. "Feeling lucky?"

The three little servos rolled to the middle of the room.

"Contestants, attend!" they chanted together. "Your team is complete for the Step of Stars. Your running can now begin."

"Not quite yet." Bolivar looked hard at Benn. "You'll remember, Skyman, that I offered you a chance with us."

"I do remember," Benn told him. "I told you no."

"Better think again—"

"Diego, please!" Roxane stepped between them. "With this step to play, let's not fight."

"Okay, babe. We're on our way to win. Here's how." He relaxed and opened his half-clenched fist to show a massive ring of some silvery metal, worn outside his glove. Its black setting was cut into a Delver's half-reptilian head. "A gift from Nebo," he said. "A lucky stone, if we just take the way it faces."

"Before we start—" Benn groped for what to say. "There's trouble in the halo we ought to think about. Mazeway has been isolated. Cut off from contact with everywhere beyond Zaroth. In the face of that, I'm surprised the game can go on. What next—" He shook his head. "I don't know, but the whole halo has been struck with something that frightens me."

"Not me." Bolivar shrugged. "I've heard about the muckup. Some glitch in the nanionic signal system, but no sweat for us. Nothing has touched Blade or Stone. Nebo says nothing will. The game will go on. We've got the winning cards."

His grin turned wolfish. "Like I told you, Starman, we've got the future fixed. The loot we win will get us home to Earth. We're buying expert help to hang the skyweb back. Roxane will be the new Tycoon—and we won't have to care what happens in the halo."

"I care what happens on Earth."

Watching Bolivar, all he saw was impatient scorn.

"I don't trust your friends." Benn glanced at Roxane, still hoping to convince her. "Lilith is a vampire. The robot may be just a tool, but a dangerous tool. Nebo may be smarter than you are. I'm afraid they're just using the two of you. You ought to break your bargain with them—if you can."

"And let you win?"

The servos were flashing. "Contestants, your running must begin."

"Come along, Skyman. Let's play the game."

Benn got into his lifeskin and they followed the servos through the lock, down a gloomy tunnel, and out into blinding blackness. Their suit lights came on, glowing golden. Eyes adjusting to the dimness, Benn found ruin all around him, great dark masses of age-crumbled masonry looming in the shadows.

"Contestants, attend!" The servos gathered before them, shimmering in the fallen rubble. "You stand upon your course for the running of the Step of Stars. Your game goal for this, your final step in the Game of Blade and Stone, is to find the stars."

"Another lift point?" Bolivar peered into the dark beyond the reach of their lights and back at the servos. "Where ore was hoisted?"

"The rules are known to you. Game time now begins."

They stood huddled there, turning up their headlamps. Great squared blocks of some dark stone, or something like stone, had toppled and splintered around them. All around, Benn made out massive walls, towering higher than he could see. He found no roof above, no hint of any stars. Roxane scrambled onto a mound of broken rock to throw her headlamp on the nearest wall.

"A building."

"A city. Wrecked a million years ago." Bolivar followed her up the boulder slope. "Nebo said we'd see it. A fortress really, named Korath. Built by the last Red Delver primarch after his retreat into the caverns. He died here with his defenders. Nothing alive in it since.

"What now, Starman?" He looked back at Benn, his tone almost taunting. "Know your way out to the stars?"

Trembling with resentment he couldn't quite swallow, he looked up at Roxane. She was splendid, standing high above him on a jut of broken stone. He yearned for her in spite of all that set them apart.

"I don't know the way." He kept his voice carefully even. "But let's not fight."

"I didn't expect you to." Bolivar grinned. "Let's get going."

He squinted at that massive ring and peered away into the dark.

Benn swung his headlamp to scan the desolation around them. Ink-black shadow filled a crater near his feet, where some weapon had exploded. His wavering light picked up a yawning gap in the nearest wall and a stairway climbing into the midnight beyond, its steps a full meter high. Giants had died here. Trying to imagine them, he found no image in his mind.

"Wake up, Starman!" Bolivar's impatient command rang in his helmet. "Come along."

Roxane had scrambled with him off the ridge. Boldly, as if he knew the way, Bolivar struck off along the foot of the monumental wall. Roxane followed, and Benn hurried after them. The end of the wall loomed out of the dark. Bolivar turned there and led them into a narrow alley between towers taller than their lights could reach. When he stepped onto a pavement beyond, sudden light blazed under his boots.

Benn and Roxane ducked back into the shadows.

"Come ahead!" He stopped to laugh and beckon them on. "The light's our guide."

Her voice uneasy, Roxane asked how he knew.

"Our friend Nebo," he told her. "He said the old roads would still light up for us."

The pavement shone under the debris, a pale ice-blue. It curved around a wide open place beyond them. At the center of it, Benn found a great black form looming out of the dark. The image of a Delver, gigantic and hideous, it might have been Nebo.

"The last Krong," Bolivar told them. "He died on this spot."

He led them around the circle. Opposite the alley, another pavement lit. Striding on, he turned away from the old Krong's image into a shining avenue that ran far into midnight distance. It was broad and smooth, cleared of debris, though Benn saw piles of shattered rock along the roadside. Half an hour along it, they came between two curving walls that climbed out of sight into the dark.

"Pillars." Bolivar stopped to peer into the blackness overhead. "A couple of kilometers thick. Built to hold the roof up."

An hour beyond, at the base of another enormous column that lifted forever into thick midnight, the blue pavement forked.

"Okay, Starman." Bolivar stopped there, grinning at Benn. "If you know your halo, which fork do we take?"

THE
HOWLING PIT

38

With a bright ironic smile, Bolivar shrugged at Benn's baffled hesitation.

"Okay, Starman! Just follow me."

He glanced at his glowing glove and strode ahead, turning left around that enormous pillar. Roxane followed silently. With no choice, Benn followed her. Far around the pillar, the shining path veered away. Straight again, it ran on through fearful devastation.

The invaders must have crushed the last defenders here. The light from the road and their searching lamps showed only shattered foundations. Farther on, even these gave way to craters and mountains of rubble. Delver giants had fought and died here, but later salvagers had left no monuments to them except a few scattered scraps of some hard black plastic that must have been parts of dreadful war machines.

The road narrowed. Rebuilt since that Armageddon of the Krongs, it lay straight through total desolation. In places, the builders had cut it deep through hills of tumbled ruin; elsewhere they had flung a slender bridge across a cratered valley where only a few great boulders showed squared or rounded faces to tell that Korath had ever been. They came at last through a deeper trough in what once had been another fortress wall. Craters grew fewer beyond that cut, and Benn saw no more marks of Delver workmanship.

Bolivar stopped. When they came up with him, he was standing on the end of the glowing road. Beyond him, black pavement ran on into the dark.

"A problem for us, Starman." He grinned at Benn. "Something broken. Road should light to show the way, but nothing happened when I stepped on it. So what do you say?"

Stung by his jeering tone, Benn merely shrugged.

"The ring?" Roxane asked. "What does it say?"

Bolivar ignored her, staring at Benn.

"Shall we trust it, Starman?" He turned his hand to flash the Delver ring. "Do you trust me?"

"We're together." Benn tried to cover what he felt. "Till this step is run."

"Then come along."

Again Bolivar stalked ahead. Golden against the dark, his lifeskin cast a pool of light that finally showed a long ridge of broken stone that had come down across the road. He scrambled to the top, paused for a moment to wave them on, and vanished beyond it.

"Come along." Frowning soberly in her helmet, Roxane echoed the words. "We are together." She glanced at Benn, and he thought he caught a wry expression. "At least for now."

As agile as Bolivar, she climbed ahead of him until a rock slid beneath her boot. Off balance, she stumbled backward. He caught her shining glove to steady her. For an instant she stood motionless, clutching his hand. He thought she looked startled.

"Thanks."

She whispered the word and they climbed on together, holding hands. Down on the black pavement beyond, they found Bolivar waiting.

"Don't let our little starboy hold us up." Though he grinned, his voice had an unpleasant edge. "Help him down."

Benn hated him, though the eldren way was not to hate. Roxane said nothing, but he felt her squeeze his fingers before she let them go. Bolivar stood scowling at them for a moment before he glanced at his ring and turned to tramp ahead. A hundred meters farther, the road lit again beneath his feet. Its glow showed the cragged rock above, sloping lower here.

The cavern walls crept out of the dark as they went on, hollowed and pitted where those ancient miners had followed the last precious veins. The pavement turned again, running close to those ragged cliffs until it forked. One branch ran straight; the other turned into a narrow tunnel.

"Starman?" Bolivar stopped there to wait for Benn. "Which way do we take?"

"Diego, don't!" Roxane flushed. "Have you gone mad?"

"Blame the starman if I'm crazy. It's his crazy world."

Benn's fists had clenched, but Roxane stepped between them. Trembling, breathing hard, he caught himself and tried to understand his surge of anger. Had Roxane's touch fired too much emotion in him? Too much in Bolivar, when he saw the touch? Were they merely two planetic males who had never learned the eldren way?

"Game time is running." Roxane's voice was quick and tight. "We've no time to quarrel."

"We'll take the time." Bolivar grinned out of his breather bubble, his voice a mocking drawl. "If your starman wants to fight."

"Don, don't!"

Benn looked at her and saw her anxious headshake. His pulse was still throbbing. Opposing Bolivar, she had thrilled him with elation. Yet that did not mean her world had changed. He bit his quivering lip and swung back to Bolivar. It took him a moment to get his breath.

"Remember what the game is for." He made his clenched fists relax. "To let us prove we can learn the eldren way. We must try to keep our peace."

"Okay, Starman. If you won't fight." Bolivar shrugged, with a nod to Roxane. "You play your crazy game. Chee and I, we live the human way."

"Let's go on." Roxane glanced at the servos waiting on the bright pavement. "If you know where to go."

Bolivar squinted at the ring and led them into the tunnel. Its walls ran straight, slick and bright as black glass, with no marks of whatever tool had driven them. Benn thought it must be newer than the ruins, cut perhaps to complete this course for the game.

A kilometer along it, they came out again into a narrower cave that twisted like a dark gut through the crust of Stone. Railed here, the high path clung to the winding wall. Sometimes the roof dropped near, but all he could see was empty dark beneath them. He felt a cold wind blowing, and heard the rush of a stream he could not see. Flowing water, carving out the cave, had sliced deep here.

Ahead of him, Roxane had murmured some question.

"—so Nebo told me." He caught Bolivar's reply. "All the air and water left on Stone have drained into the caves, but they still make weather. Deep down, the planet is still hot. Radioactivity in the core. Water there evaporates. Vapor rises. Condenses near the surface, where it's cold. The water runs back."

He touched the wall and Benn saw his glove wet with dew.

"Krongsblood River." He gestured into the black abyss below. "That's what the translator makes of the Delver name."

A few hundred meters farther, the path forked again. One branch climbed away along the winding wall. The other veered into another narrow black tunnel that ran straight as far as Benn could see. Bolivar stopped there as if for another jeering challenge.

"Trust me, Starman?" His voice, instead, was almost apologetic. "Really?"

"We're here together," Benn said. "We have to trust."

"So we do."

Bolivar frowned at his ring and turned very soberly to Roxane.

"This is it." He bent his helmet close to hers. "We play our game together, you and I, and we'll get the skyweb back. You'll be the new Sun Tycoon." He paused to peer into her face, oddly intent. "Or else—"

He jerked his thumb toward the far roar of the unseen river.

Watching, Benn saw her hand slide toward her knife. She made no other response. Bolivar looked into her face for another moment and then turned to lead them past the tunnel mouth and on into the cave. Here the path changed. Barely a meter wide, it had no railing. Sometimes cut into an overhanging wall, it was sometimes carried through the darkness on slender arches of gray Delver concrete.

Condensation glistened everywhere, gathering into rivulets that trickled down the cliffs. The muffled thunder grew louder, but Krongsblood River still ran far below. Pausing now and then to look over the brink, all he ever found was some rounded jut of water-worn stone looming out of the thundering dark.

"Game time!" Bolivar urged them, pushing fast ahead. "Game time running!"

"Please, Don! Not so fast!" Roxane called after him. "The walk's too slick."

He ignored her. The narrow path had lit for them, but it was slick with trickling water and it quivered to the roaring below. It sometimes sloped sharply up, sometimes sharply dropped. Benn's boots, not designed for traction, slipped on one wet slope. He slid down it and sprawled so near the brink that he crawled away before he tried to rise.

"Benn?" Roxane was suddenly back beside him. "Are you hurt?"

"Thanks!" he whispered, breathless from the fall. "Only shaken up."

"In trouble, Starman?" Bolivar had stopped again, shouting from far ahead. "Lost your nerve?"

He didn't try to answer. White-lipped, Roxane helped him to his feet. He stood there a moment, getting his breath. Bolivar called impatiently, gestured them on, and vanished in a twisting fissure ahead.

"Why so fast?" He frowned at her. "We have to be together at the finish."

"I don't know." He saw trouble in her eyes. "He's hard to understand, but let's go on."

He shrugged and went on with her, limping a little from an aching ankle. Her quick concern had astonished him. Wondering again what she could think of Bolivar, he bit his lip.

Bolivar was still invisible, somewhere ahead. Once Benn heard another shout, nearly drowned in the endless boom of unseen water, but they did not see him again until they came through the last narrow fissure, out into a vast dark chamber that looked almost circular.

The roof here was too high to see. Wild water roared below, and they saw Krongsblood River at last, dimly lit by the glow from the road. It poured out of the rock many meters beneath their feet. Far across the pit, Benn found another fall and then a third, white water plunging into boiling spray.

Farther down, hard to see through mist and darkness, he found a great vortex of slick black water, sloping steeper and steeper into a black and bottomless funnel. Islets of pale foam spun around it, and he shrank from the voice of its yawning throat, a bellow that reverberated from the half-seen walls and unseen roof and rang again inside his helmet, amplified until it ached in his bones. Roxane crouched back beside him, hands against her helmet as if to shield her ears.

The bright path parted where they stood, running right and left to ring that awesome chamber. He saw no other exit when he scanned it, but he discovered Bolivar, a small bright figure far across from them, standing still, staring down into that thundering funnel as if fascinated by its power. At last he looked toward them. Perhaps he shouted something, but his words were lost. He waved for them to wait and came back to stop a few meters from where they stood, his servo close behind him.

"Wrong way, Starman." He spoke again with a taunting drawl. "Your own blunder, when you trusted me."

His tone was sardonic, but his face in the bubble looked bleak and pale. He stood there half a minute, staring hard at Benn.

"Sorry, Chee." He moved abruptly to shrug and shake his head at Roxane as if with real regret. "No way out. We're turning back."

"The ring?" she asked. "Is it wrong?"

"Old Nebo's ring?" He peered down at it. "It says we go back." His set features relaxed into his old reckless grin. "Just trust us, Chee, and I'll take care of everything." He came on toward them. "Excuse me, Starman. Make room for me."

Benn moved out a little to let him pass. He seemed to stumble. One hand clutched at the slippery cliff. Benn felt a sudden tug against the back of his lifeskin, then a sharp jab into his ribs. Teetering, he groped desperately for anything. Bolivar reached as if to help, and he caught a glimpse of that Delver ring, red eyes gleaming in the black half-reptile face. Fleetingly he saw something else, something bright clutched in Bolivar's glove. Another jab, and he toppled off the path.

"Sorry, Starman!" Falling, he caught Bolivar's ironic voice. "The human way—"

The rest was lost, but he saw that bright object flying into the dark from Bolivar's outflung hand. Tumbling backward toward that bellowing vortex, he had time for a glimpse of Roxane, reaching desperately, too late to catch him. And a glimpse of Bolivar's face, set in a hard grin that had no hint of regret.

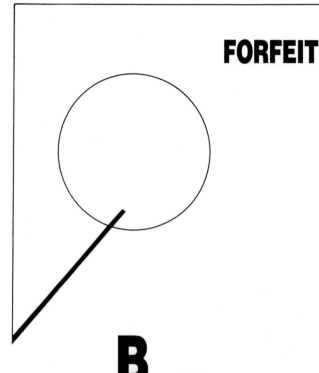

FORFEIT

39

Benn fell forever.

Wheeling slowly in the lesser gravity of Stone, he had another moment to look back. Roxane shone golden in her lifeskin, leaning off the narrow walk to follow him down. He saw Bolivar seizing her arm, but then his body turned and he lost them both in the roaring dark. The black walls climbed fast around him, smoothed with rushing water, wet and slickly glistening. He saw the funnel howling under him, its dark throat flecked with whirling foam.

His head was down by then. He had never learned to swim, but he tried to shape his arms to cut the water. Even here in Stone, he hit it hard. Darkness swallowed him. His breath was gone. Dazed and bruised, he ached everywhere. Wild currents battered him.

He tried to swim when he found his breath, but he had no notion of direction. He felt a dim surprise when his helmet broke the surface. The air in it must have floated him, but still all he saw was blinding night. His lifeskin had gone dark, the headlamp out.

Turning on his back, he found his servo flying high above his head, bright against the midnight. With no breath to beg for help, he tried to wave it down. He saw no answering voice-light flash, no response at'all. Perhaps there was nothing it could do.

His body quivered to the near vibration of the vortex. Floating, he blinked and squinted and rubbed the foam from his faceplate, trying to see. He found the walls above him, black in the blackness, climbing sheer to the bright walkway. He scanned it, searching for Roxane and Bolivar. They were halfway across the pit when he found them, already swept far behind.

Golden dolls, they stood face to face. Bolivar was advancing on her, hands out as if to grapple with her. She drew her knife. He stepped back, arms spread as if in appeal. She lifted the blade, a flash in the darkness. He turned and stalked back down the path the way they had entered the pit, his servo flying with him.

She stood for a moment staring after him, and then turned to search for Benn. His lifeskin dark, he must have been hard to see, but at last she seemed to find him. She waved a shining arm. He saw her toss the knife away. It glinted and vanished, falling toward the funnel.

And then she dived.

He followed her down, clean and slim and bright, slowly tumbling in the air until she straightened to meet the water. She went under. He found her servo floating in the air where she had disappeared, far behind him now.

The air in his bubble was bad by then. His breath came fast, his lungs screaming for oxygen. And he knew that he had lost the game. That seemed to matter more than the air, more than the battering, more than the bellowing vortex, more than anything. Trying dimly to understand, he remembered the tug at the back of his lifeskin before Bolivar jabbed and shoved him. That bright object he had seen Bolivar pitch into the pit—it had been the power unit of his suit.

His lungs screamed for air, but he tried to slow his breathing, to stretch his time. He knew he mustn't try to swim. The pit seemed darker to his blurring eyes, but he found the silver bubble still flying near his head. His servo, observing everything he did. It would be reporting to the judges that he had lost the game.

Lost everything. His little part in Gibbon's war against the aliens and the computer virus and that uneldren invasion of the halo. His chance to show the eldren that mankind might sometime be fit to join them. Even Roxane—if there had ever been a possibility that she might turn away from Bolivar.

Roxane . . .

Her image shone in his mind, a golden riddle. Why had she drawn her knife on Bolivar? Had she rebelled against his schemes, abandoned her father's futile dream of her being the new Tycoon? Why had she dived into this screaming grave? Out of sheer despair? He felt too dull to wonder. His head was bursting. He gasped for air he never found.

And he had lost the game . . .

"Benn?" Above that endless boom, he caught Roxane's voice. "Can you hear me?"

A moment of blackness . . .

And he was breathing. The air was clean again. Water shuddered around him, and he remembered the pit. The roar of the funnel seemed louder now, but his lifeskin was alive again. Its glow lit Roxane's helmet. She was floating beside him, and he felt her fingers on his arm. He tried to say he heard her, but his throat hurt and his voice was only a croak. He sobbed for his breath and tried again.

He saw her white lips moving.

". . . power cell." Her words were hard to catch. "Don snatched it out. He threw it down here, but I found it floating. Trouble light still shining. Dived for it. I've got it back." She turned her heard, listening. "Now we've got to swim."

He felt too weak to move, but she was paddling with one hand, trying to tow him with the other. Looking up, he could see the far thin circle of the path. Its glow fell dimly on wet and water-polished rock too sheer for anything to climb. The current carried them fast, toward a pale cloud of roaring spray where another river fell. He found no beach, no shelf or fissure, nothing they could hope to grasp or cling to.

She paused to rest and turned her head in the helmet to look at him again. She was breathing fast, sweat beaded on her brow. That faint smile was gone. She looked older, her jaw firmly set, her eyes a little narrowed. He had never seen her father, that stern warrior who taught her the world was not for love, but he thought that mask of cold determination must have been inherited.

"I want—want to thank you." He found a rusty voice. "But I see no way—"

The roar had grown too loud for her to hear. Her face sternly set, she turned to paddle again. He was still trembling and gasping, with no strength for any effort. The walls were always farther, racing faster, the slick black water sloping steeper. Already they were far down the maelstrom's throat.

"Contestants, attend!" He found their servos flashing low overhead. "Do you wish to forfeit the Game of Blade and Stone?"

"No!" She rapped out the word, and he thought he heard her father's voice. "I'll never forfeit."

"Contestant Dain, do you wish to forfeit?"

"Do we have a choice?"

"Shall we consult the judges?"

He nodded in the helmet.

"Consulting." The servos were silent for a moment before they resumed. "The judges command us to inform you that your team now numbers only two. Contestant Bolivar has left the play, claiming exemption as a special guest of a citizen of Zaroth. Therefore the rules allow you to earn no game points for the Step of Stars."

"Must we forfeit?"

"Estimating the hazards you face, we compute a zero possibility of your escape from Krongsblood Sink through any effort or stratagem of your own. The judges command us to advise you that the choice before you is to forfeit or to die here."

"A hard choice."

He looked at Roxane. She still held his shoulder, trying to swim, her eyes on the black slope above them. It was always steeper, the funnel thundering louder.

"Information, Contestant Dain." The servos had dived nearer, but still he barely caught their screech. "If you wish to forfeit, you must do it now."

"If I forfeit, can we be rescued?"

"Extrication can be attempted."

"Can it succeed?"

"Success is not certain." He strained to listen. "If you choose to forfeit, an emergency transport will be dispatched from the terminal facility. The outcome of the rescue effort will depend on your survival until the transport arrives."

He looked again at Roxane and saw her shake her head.

"Contestant Dain, do you express a choice?"

"I forfeit," he said. "Get us out if you can."

"Terran Dain!" The servos dropped against his helmet. "Attend! The judges accept your forfeit. Your rights and privileges in the Game of Blade and Stone are hereby nullified. Rescue will be attempted. In the event of success, you will be transported back to Blade for the final disposition of your case and immediate expulsion from the planets of Mazeway."

The servos lifted, silent again.

"Can't you help us now?" he called. "Can't you pull us farther from the whirlpool?"

Wheeling together, they rose still higher.

"Terran Dain, you are no longer a qualified contestant in the Game of Blade and Stone." Their shriek came faintly through the thunder. "You have surrendered the privileges you enjoyed as a player. Refusing to forfeit, Contestant Kwan has no right to any extraordinary aid."

"So!" Her helmet against his, he heard her breathless gasp. "Your world, Benn. Give me a hungry hyena!"

She swam again, fighting that slick black slope. He tried to kick, tried to paddle. They were always whirling faster, always carried farther down that roaring throat. The servos kept low above them, bright and silent.

His head hurt. His lungs hurt. He had no strength. The game was lost for both of them. That hurt more. He had failed. Roxane had done no better. Deserting Bolivar, diving after him, she had thrown away her chance to own a reborn Earth. If she had ever had a chance.

He almost longed for the moment when that hungry throat would swallow them. His numbed brain found nothing else to hope or live for, nothing except the end of pain—

"Terran Dain!" His eyes had been on Roxane when he could glimpse her face in the helmet, pale with exhaustion but still bleakly set. The sudden flash of the servos was almost a shock. "Terran Dain, attend! Your transport has arrived."

He turned his head and found it, a crystal capsule dipping beside them. A panel folded down to make a ramp. He gripped the railing at its side and clung there, with no strength for anything more. Roxane was somehow on the ramp ahead of him, hauling at his arm. The ramp lifted, and they were tumbled into the capsule. The door sealed itself, and the thunder ended.

Giddy and trembling in that sudden silence, he found himself on a cushioned seat, the servos quivering on the floor by his boots. Roxane huddled in the seat across from him. With wet, dark hair straggling across her sweat-streaked face, he thought she looked like a hurt, bewildered child.

She had lost as much as he. He felt a sudden impulse toward some gesture of comfort, but she was untouchable, sealed away from him in her lifeskin and helmet, wrapped in her own unhappy emotion, wanting no love. He had no comfort, anyhow, not even for himself.

The capsule was lifting. Nothing really mattered now, but he watched the dark whirlpool drop silently behind them, and the silent waterfalls. They reached the level of the shining path and followed it out of the pit, back toward the tunnel he remembered. He saw her shiver when the capsule turned into it.

"Why?" he asked her. "Why did you dive?"

"Because I saw Don try to kill you." Her face looked pale, and he found a thin scar across her cheek that he had never seen before. "I don't know—" Her voice was dull and flat, so low that he leaned to hear. "I guess I don't know why. Maybe the game has changed me, but I still can't see your eldren way. And I don't know—" He saw her chin quiver. "I don't know what will happen to me."

"I don't know what will happen to anybody, but at least we're both alive." He tried to smile, but his voice caught. "I—I thank you, Roxane."

"Thank Diego."

With that bitter whisper, she turned away from him to stare out of the crystal shell. They were gliding through a tunnel he had never seen. Its walls were slick and straight. They were dark ahead, but section after section lit around the crystal shell and turned dark again behind.

"I admired him." Still looking out at the racing wall, she spoke again, more to herself than to him. "Don Diego Bolivar. Handsome to look at. Clever and strong. He has ways I liked. Brave enough. Nothing gets him down. But—"

She stopped to shake her head.

"He keeps bad company," Benn said. "And he did try to kill me."

She nodded and sat quiet for a time before she asked, "You saw that Delver ring?"

"I saw the way he kept looking at it."

"It was a kind of compass, like the Delver engineers use when they're inspecting the courses. Nebo got it from one of them. Whenever we came to a fork, the eyes of that little image would flash to show the way. The ring tells you—tells you what Diego is."

Her lips tightened, and it was a moment before she went on.

"A con man. He said that once, proud of himself. He laughed at your eldren way. His own life, and his mother's, had taught him what he called the human way. His Sunbred father never claimed him. He always had to scheme and lie to stay alive, even before the web came down. When things went wrong, he shrugged and grinned and hatched another scheme."

"What will he do? Now that he's out of the game?"

"He always said we didn't need to win." A tired shrug. "I guess he doesn't need me. Whatever happened, he was always ready with another plan. He'll probably try to make himself the new Tycoon— he said once that his own father was as much a Kwan as mine. He's going back to Nebo and their alien friends, to carry out their scheme to loot and rule the Earth.

"I wanted—" He heard a quiver in her voice. "I wanted to trust him. In a different world, he might have been—" She gulped and he saw the glint of tears. When she turned away, he looked outside again. The speed-blurred tunnel walls were gone. The capsule had slowed a little, skimming along a shining path through twisting channels that water must have cut. They came out again into another midnight pit so vast that he found no walls. The road-way ended there, on a wide floor that shone pale blue.

The capsule lifted fast. The blue patch shrank and vanished in the dark. For a long time he found no light anywhere. At last, far above, he found another faintly glowing circle, a tiny disk of milky haze flecked with points of diamond light.

"The stars!" Roxane whispered, and turned to shrug dully at him. "So what?"

He heard his servo flashing.

"Terran Dain, attend! Message for you, sir, from Hydran Edward Gibbon *Beta.*"

NUMBER OF
THE ENEMY

40

Benn's servo rolled to the end of the capsule to energize a small ion cloud. It flickered and brightened to image Gibbon's knobby body, the hieroglyphic birth robe no longer around it. A tiny eye took shape to peer at him, and a tiny mouth to speak.

"Benn? I am informed that you have been in danger?"

"We are safe now, on a rescue craft." He thought Gibbon's red-brown color looked darker, the speaking light stronger. "Sir, are you recovering?"

"Alive, Benn. As much alive as I can ever be without my brother."

"I have tried to call you, sir."

"We were cut off until I left Hydra."

"You have left your doctors?"

"I escaped them, Benn. Fumbling blunderers, killing the little that is left of me. Experimenters, because we Hydrans are so seldom ill. They were trying to replace my poor dead brother with scraps and bits of everybody. I prefer to remain the fragment that I am."

The tiny eye surveyed him.

"I need you with me, Benn." The rapid voice had an odd, short-clipped nasal twang; he wondered if Gibbon had borrowed it from Captain Bela Zar. "Our enemies are stronger and stranger than I ever suspected, and they have left us very little time. I am anxious to hear what you can tell me."

"I'm out of the game, sir. To be expelled from Mazeway. But I do have one thing to report. In the Step of Ice—"

"Later, Benn." The voice sharpened to interrupt him. "Who is this with you?"

"Roxane Kwan, sir."

"The Terran female brought here by Nebo?" He saw a second eye taking shape to study Roxane. "Allow me to inquire." A moment of silence. "I am informed that she has completed the game. The transit craft will return her to appear before the judges in the Hall of Three—"

His voice was cut off. Frozen for a long moment, his bright little image quivered back to life.

"Benn, do you receive me?"

"I do."

"We were interrupted." The doll-lips swelled a little, that brittle voice hastening. "We must act while we can. I am waiting at Zaroth terminal."

His image dimmed, and the ion cloud was gone.

Roxane had slumped back in the seat, staring blankly into the ion cloud. She sat there still, her pale face expressionless. The outlook for action had revived his own spirits, but it had brought nothing for her. He felt a pang of helpless sympathy.

"I wish I could help—"

"I want no help." She straightened, as defiant of fate as her father must have been. "I'm on my own."

"You saved my life. I owe you—"

"You owe me nothing."

"Anyhow," he whispered, "I hope we meet again."

She had looked away again, into the empty dark outside the capsule. He sat wondering what her future could be. For her, for him, for human people in the halo. When he looked again for that disk of sky overhead, it was swelling fast. Suddenly they were out of that enormous pit, the constellations blazing all around them.

"The stars!" She shook her head, as if somehow saddened to see them. "On Earth they never looked so bright."

"You'll learn to love them," he told her. "If you stay in the halo."

"I don't know," she whispered. "I don't know anything."

Again she turned away from him, lost in thoughts he could not share.

"The judges will follow the eldren way." He tried to cheer her. "I think you'll find them kind—"

"I don't want kindness!"

She did not look at him, and he found no more to say. The crystal craft carried them high above the starlit face of Stone. Dark and dead, it was pitted with crag-rimmed craters and piled like the surface of Blade with monumental ruin. He soon found Blade itself, a wide circle of inky shadow across the southward stars. The tube between the worlds became a black thread that swiftly widened as the capsule slanted down to the terminal platforms around its foot. Inside, the transport fields lifted them again, through the core of Blade and back to old Zaroth.

"Terrans, attend!"

On the high Zaroth stage, the capsule was landing them beside the slim white hull of the *Terra Two*.

"Terran Dain," the servos chanted, "you are no longer a contestant in the game. You are due no further attention from the judges. We leave you here. Terran Kwan will remain aboard. The judges require her presence at the Hall of Three."

The door folded down. Stiff from sitting, and all the battering and exhaustion before, he rose to leave the capsule.

"I hope—" His voice trembling, he looked back at Roxane. "I hope you get some better breaks."

She looked up. He thought she was about to smile, but then her lips were quivering. She merely shook her head. Reluctant to leave her, he turned and went on. Outside, he stopped to look back through the transparent shell. Her face was toward him in the helmet. He raised his glove to wave, but she seemed not to see the gesture. The door swung shut, and the capsule lifted with her to vanish against the stars.

The *Terra Two* stood near, a toy among the tall white nanionic liners that stood like a forest on the stage. The air lock opened for him. Itchy and clammy from too many hours in the lifeskin, he peeled it off and got into an old jumpsuit before he went on to find Gibbon in the comm room, floating over the ship's computer.

"You look stronger, sir."

Solemnly Gibbon rocked in the air.

"My brother is dead." Two eyes had grown to look at him, spaced far apart. That sad monotone came from speaking lips almost between them. "His wit and vigor are gone forever, but we have no time for sickness. You told me you had an observation to report?"

"It's something that happened in the Step of Fire. The alien Lilith and Nexus were with me. She was sensing seismic vibrations to guide us. They led us to a big metal worm that attacked us. A mining robot, gone out of control. Nexus took control of it and made it take us to the exit point.

"Perhaps the same way Friday was seized."

"With the viral program?"

"I think so, sir. He had flashed a long signal at it before its behavior changed."

"Significant indeed!" Gibbon dipped and lifted in the air, silent for a time. "It confirms my earlier conclusion that the robot does in fact carry the virus. A finding that supports action I have planned."

"Action, sir? Is there really something we can do?"

"Our enemy is a worm, Benn. Not the mining device you met, but a computer worm—or virus, as I prefer to call it. Released at Starsearch, it destroyed the computers there. It killed my brother and liberated the aliens. It seized your robot, I think with a signal sent to our ship."

"Friday was at the controls." Benn nodded. "Trying to make contact."

"And did make a most unfortunate contact." Gibbon sank and dipped again. "Because Nexus has become a carrier. And we have aided him. We brought the robot back to Cluster One, the virus in it."

"But now, sir?" Hopefully he leaned to peer into one of those wide-spaced eyes. "We can strike back?"

"We have captured the virus." Affirmatively Gibbon tipped in the air. "One specimen, though thousands must still be free. When it attacked Hydra, we had our trap ready. With the aid of my university colleagues, I was able to record it before it did any mischief."

"How, sir?"

"Simply enough, when we had been warned. We cut it apart into harmless sections before we let it into any computer. Reading it, we learned a good deal more. Even a bit of what purports to be its own history—though some of my colleagues suspect that it is lying to conceal its actual purpose here.

"If we have the truth, it was created as a weapon by the beings of a remote star system that we have not yet identified. An interplanetary war was in progress. The creatures of an aggressor planet were winning, using military robots. The defenders designed it to stop the robots."

"The same way Nexus stopped that rogue machine?" Benn nodded. "I see. But then it escaped?"

"The record is incomplete and possibly falsified, but a few conclusions are clear. The virus was designed to survive and protect itself. It must have been attacked. Perhaps it picked up garbled self-protective subroutines installed in the robots. How the war came out, we don't know, but it did escape—in an altered form that survived in some way to get here."

"Brought by the aliens?"

"That is what we must assume."

Gibbon swung in the air to flash a signal at the computer's input. "Here is the weapon."

Benn waited, watching the bright little ion cloud swell out of the monitor. When it came into focus, he saw a line of Hydran hieroglyphs, characters as baffling as those patterns on the birth robe. Gibbon shimmered a command, and they were suddenly numerals he could read.

1001101 0111100 1100101

"The same number!" he whispered. "The one we read at Starsearch, in that memory cube."

"The initial digits of the viral program." Gibbon swayed to a Hydran nod. "Recorded in that cube by somebody on the station staff, who probably had no idea what it was."

His body flashed, and the numerals vanished.

"You have a plan to fight it now?"

"I am writing a countervirus," Gibbon said. "Call it a vaccine. When I have it ready, it must be planted in the robot. My plan requires the cooperation of the judges." Another eye was forming, and all three squinted at him. "I want you to carry a message to them."

"You remember, sir, that I had to forfeit."

"A problem for us." The voice was suddenly graver than Bela Zar's, and the far-spaced eyes swept him again. "And a greater risk for you, unfortunately, because the enemy knows how we stopped their attack on Hydra."

"Just tell me what to do."

"I am glad you are a Terran." Gibbon bobbed in the air. "Another being might have hesitated. But here is your task. I am writing my message in a memory cube. The judges have agreed to receive you and read it. I will order transportation for you. You have a dozen hours before they want you to appear."

"Not till then?"

"They are eldren, Benn. They do not hurry."

With that, Gibbon swung back to his computer console. Benn stood a moment watching him flashing at the input, but his impatience was already ebbing into aching weariness. With time enough, he showered, heated a meal he felt too tense and anxious to enjoy, and lay restless in his berth until the intercom called him.

The message was ready, the little cube in a white plastic packet. Sealed again in lifeskin and helmet, he was waiting outside the lock when the crystal capsule appeared. The door dropped open, and a servo danced to his feet.

"Terran Dain? We come for you."

"I am Dain. Take me to the Hall of Three."

"Your schedule, sir, is already arranged."

They lifted off the stage. The white ships fell away. Beyond the narrow network of lighted streets around the terminal tower the starlit desolation of old Zaroth spread as far as he could see.

He found the Primarch's Casino, a small, pale moon rising out of a crater far away.

The quarters of the judges were somewhere far beneath it. He watched for the transit tube where they would set down. Instead, the capsule veered away from the street he remembered and dived to a high ledge at the top of a dark, abandoned tower. He saw the door folding open.

"Not here!" Alarm shook his voice. "Take me to the Hall of Three."

The servo made no answer, but he saw a quick black shape running from a black doorway. Its crest blazed, and he recognized the sleek plastic skull of the robot that had been Friday.

"Terran Dain!" Its hard inhuman voice crashed in his helmet. "I am Nexus. I require a memory cube you carry."

REGENTS OF EARTH

41

The black robot came fast.

"Shut the door!" Benn shouted at the servo. "Take us off!"

The silver bubble stayed where it lay. The door did not close. In a moment the robot was inside the capsule, its crest still burning.

"Terran Dain!" A flashed command. "You will surrender the memory cube you carry."

"I will not—"

He saw the servo moving then, but not against the robot. It darted at his chest. The impact drove him backward. His helmet struck the capsule's wall. The next he knew he was dazed and breathless, sprawled on the floor. Grasping at the side pocket of his lifeskin, he found it torn open. The robot had gone, the memory cube with it.

"Are you injured, sir?" The servo hovered over him, suddenly solicitous. "Do you require assistance?"

"Assistance?" He shook his useless fist at it and gasped for breath. "What have you done to me?"

"As instructed, sir, we conveyed you to the Hall of Three."

"Were you instructed to rob me?"

"No, sir. We have received no such instruction."

"Then why—" Groggily he lumbered back into his seat. "Why have we landed here?"

"We are in flight—" The servo darted at the control console. "Reporting malfunction, sir. Recomputing present position."

"What caused the malfunction?"

"Cause unrecorded, sir." It flickered a signal that closed the door. "Position recomputed, sir. The craft has landed on an abandoned structure located in the closed zone of old Zaroth."

"What do you have recorded?"

"Sir, we find a brief interval missing from memory files. As instructed, we were in flight from Zaroth terminal to the Hall of Three. We find no record of our arrival here."

"We did arrive." He scowled at its silvery innocence. "But you have no record of the robot that robbed me?"

"Our filed records of our flight contain no match for index terms robot or robbed, sir. Do you have new instructions?"

His head throbbed when he moved, and he felt dazed again by this new evidence of hostile power. For a moment he sat staring through the starlight at the shattered wall and the doorway where the robot had waited. The viral program must have been alive for many centuries, surviving attacks on many worlds. It knew how to guard itself.

What chance had he—had Gibbon against it?

"Take me on," he muttered. "To the Hall of Three."

"At once, sir. As you command."

The capsule lifted off the high ledge and climbed back across old Zaroth. The milky moon of the great casino rose out of the great crater ahead. Near it, they dropped toward the black lavas of the crater floor. Darkness swallowed them. Somewhere far below, they landed on a terminal stage. The capsule's door swung down.

"Terran, come," the servo hummed. "The judges will receive the message you carry."

With no message now, nor much hope for anything good, he followed the servo through a labyrinth of ancient tunnels and at last into blazing whiteness. Reflecting it, the servo vanished. Benn had to stop, blinking and squinting, until he could see through the dazzling haze that filled the enormous hall.

Half a dome, it had been carved from what looked like luminous and translucent snow-white stone: the vast and empty floor, the high dais, the vertical wall above it where the judges or perhaps their holo simulations had appeared. It was silent till he heard the servo singing.

"Terran, stand!" A small ball of whiteness, almost lost in burning whiteness, it sprang ahead of him to the platform. "You are instructed to wait with your fellow players here to receive the judgment of the Three."

The order for his expulsion?

Waiting, he saw blackness flowing toward him like a blct upon the whiteness. It took him a moment to recognize the huge mound of glistening ooze whose name was Ooru. Noiseless, it crept to his side and stopped there. Its servo leaped before it to the stage. A thin black tendril sprouted from it, bowed toward him in soundless greeting, shone briefly blue, and shrank back into its bulk.

A third mirror bubble danced to the platform, and Ayn came flying like a great wingless insect to drop beside Ooru on neatly folded lever-legs. The armored head twisted and the huge green eyes flashed another greeting.

They waited. Three more servos came, escorting the three aliens. Wing, flying like a live kite high in the milky fog. Vreeth, crouched and slinking as if already stalking Terran game. Lilith, jet scales rippling just above the floor, her diamond horn aloft. In line below the dais, all three turned their unearthly eyes upon him and stared until he shivered.

Bolivar strolled after them, seeming at ease in the tight golden lifeskin. He grinned and waved a casual greeting at Benn before he turned to look behind him for Roxane. Her features in the bubble were hard to see, but she carried herself stiffly straight, walking well away from Bolivar. Benn thought she must be desperate now, since her quarrel with him. Yet they had entered together.

How much had she surrendered?

When a ninth bubble skipped out of the whiteness, they all turned to look for Nexus. Nebo slouched in instead and stopped at the end of the line, stooped and swaying like some grotesque mix of human and saurian.

"Contestants attend!" the nine servos chanted. "Attend to your judgment."

They all stood motionless. Eyes on that high wall, Benn saw a long rectangle glow and melt into a cloud of darkness that began to shine with glittering diamond shards.

"The Keeper!" the servos caroled. "The Keeper of Truth!"

Two black eyes, or spots of darkness placed like eyes, came out of that luminous fog. They were framed in the angular ridges of something like bare white bone that Benn's imagination turned into nose and mouth and chin.

"Attend! The Mistress of Passion!"

Tongues of yellow flame licked through the mist and writhed apart to let him glimpse the crown of horns, the flaps he made into ears, the three purple-red triangles that peered like inhuman eyes.

"Attend! The Speaker of Wisdom!"

Long white hair veiled nothing like a face. The eyes came open, larger than human, the color of steel or perhaps the color of ice, keenly searching him.

He thought they looked more alien than Wing or Vreeth or Lilith. So strange that he trembled under them when he heard the servos singing.

"Terran Dain, have you a message for the judges?"

"I had—had a message." His throat was dry, his voice a rasp in the helmet. "A message cube from Dr. Edward Gibbon *Beta*. He is ill and unable to leave his ship. He sent me to bring his message—"

"Let us hear it."

"I was robbed." He paused to grope for any fit title of respect and found none at all. "Robbed by the robot that calls itself Nexus. It diverted my shuttle craft to land us out in the old city. It was waiting there. It came aboard, knocked me down, and took the cube."

The judges' alien eyes shifted to the servo on the dais before him. It shone brighter, and all the servos sang again in unison.

"Terran Dain, your statements are unconfirmed."

Tense and sweating in his lifeskin, Benn saw the heads of the judges turning toward Nebo. His steel skull bowed. There was no signal Benn could see, but he saw his own servo flicker.

"Terran Dain," it purred, "Citizen Nebo informs the judges that he now speaks for Contestant Nexus. He denies the truth of your story. He states that Contestant Nexus was with him at the time of your flight, appearing before the authorities of Zaroth to answer false charges made against him by the Hydran, Edward Gibbon *Beta*. He has assured the judges that he will soon be here to defend himself."

"They are the guilty ones!" Benn swept a trembling arm toward the aliens and the Delver. "They are enemies of the halo, plotting against the Eldermost. The robot is their tool—"

"Silence, Terran!" His ears rang from the crash in his helmet. "You speak without permission."

"Your Honors!" He spread his arms toward the judges "I do not know the proper words for appeal to you, but I beg you to listen. Though I have lost the message cube, I know what Dr. Gibbon wanted to say—"

He saw Nebo shambling toward the dais.

"Terran!" All nine servos thundered at him. "You cannot—"

The servos paused. He saw the eyes of the judges shift from Nebo back to him.

"Terran Dain," the servos intoned, "you may speak. The judges will receive your message from Dr. Gibbon *Beta*."

"Thank you." Gratefully he lifted his face toward those eerie images. "Dr. Gibbon was trying to warn you. The message cube was meant to tell you what he knows about a secret invasion of the halo. The invaders are those three." He pointed at Wing, Vreeth, and Lilith. "Their first victim was Dr. Gibbon's clone-twin, who had detained—"

Nebo's roar battered his ears. He saw Ooru and Ayn retreating from beside him and found the Delver surging toward him, eye-spots blazing crimson. Again he saw no signal, but something stopped Nebo. Swaying back to his place at the end of the line, he stood there like some great saurian at bay, black fangs snarling.

"Terran Dain," Benn's servo chimed, "you have permission to continue."

He caught his breath and faced the judges.

"Dr. Gibbon believes the aliens killed his brother. He believes that their weapon is a computer worm or virus that now controls Nexus. The message cube describes the virus, which is causing computer malfunctions and blacking out communications everywhere."

"The judges ask for evidence."

"The evidence I had—" Helpless, he spread his arms. "It was in that cube."

He saw the aliens edging closer to Nebo. His crimson eye-spots lifted toward the judge.

"Citizen Nebo has been allowed to speak," Benn's servo flashed at him. "He informs the judges that Terran Dain's story is a desperate fabrication, invented to excuse his failure to complete his running of the game. He is commanded to remain silent now, and hear his own judgment."

"Wait!" Benn shouted. "Call Dr. Gibbon. He's on his ship at the Zaroth terminal—"

"Terran Dain!" the servos drummed. "You are ordered to attend."

"Not yet! They must be stopped—"

"Silence, Terran. Or you will be removed."

Helpless, he dropped his hands and made his fists relax.

"All contestants, attend now to your judgment!"

Numbed with defeat, he felt bewildered before the half-known powers of the aliens, crushed even by his sense of the heavy kilometers of the planet's crust above his head. Something brushed his arm. He found Ooru floating closer to him, a black and shapeless mass that showed no emotion he could read. Yet he felt its sympathy.

"Contestants," the servos were pealing, "you have been allowed to undertake the running of your assigned courses in the Game of Blade and Stone. Your behavior has been observed and recorded. You stand now before the Keeper of Truth and the Mistress of Passion and the Speaker of Wisdom. You will hear them announce the outcome of the game and their determinations of your fitness for the Elderhood."

Down the waiting line, his fellow players stirred. Staring blankly at them, he was startled by his servo's sharp command, "Terran Dain, attend to your judgment!"

He faced the wall and raised his eyes to the diamond mist that swirled to cover and reveal the dead black stare of the Keeper of Truth, the red-purple blaze of the Mistress of Passion, and the ice-colored eyes of the Speaker of Wisdom.

"Terran Benndain," the nine voices rang in his helmet like echoes from the high white vault, "you are the offspring of Terran planetics, and you remain a Terran planetic. As a contestant in the Game of Blade and Stone, you have failed to establish the fitness of your species for admission to the Elderhood. Forfeiting the game, you have surrendered all rights and privileges extended to you as a player. We hereby cancel your entry visa and order your immediate expulsion from Mazeway."

The voices paused, but the eyes still rested on him. He found no will to move or speak.

"Terran Benndain," the voices rang again, "do you understand the decision of the judges of the game?"

He whispered numbly, "I understand."

"Contestant Ayn!" the servos boomed again. "Contestant Ooru! You will attend."

He envied them. The great slick bubble blown out of total blackness. The tall insect-thing, sitting with red-cased legs folded before the red-black abdomen to make a trim tripod.

"Once again, we congratulate you both. Observing your running of the game, we saw no violation of the eldren way. As contestants under extraordinary license, you are entitled to no direct awards, but your scores will be duly reported to the Zaroth Casino and the Mazeway Syndicate."

Ooru's huge black mass lifted and sank. Ayn's hard red body rocked forward in a kind of bow. The eyes of the judges turned again, and the servos sang.

"Contestant Wing! Contestant Vreeth! Contestant Lilith!"

Wing's triangular kite-shape climbed higher. Lilith's black coils glided closer to the dais. Vreeth crouched again as if to spring.

"In your running of the game, each of you has violated the eldren way. None has displayed fitness for the Elderhood. The provisional game scores announced for you are hereby revoked, and your entry visas are hereby canceled. You are commanded to leave Mazeway at once."

Nebo lurched toward the dais like an upright crocodile, eyespots burning at the judges. Static crashed in Benn's helmet. He caught a few words. ". . . clients . . . harmless derelicts, without means to leave the halo . . ."

The servos shimmered. His helmet crackled. The translator caught no more words, but Nebo bent his steel-shelled head and shambled back into the line.

"Contestant Roxanekwan! Contestant Diegobolivar!"

Bolivar turned to grin at Roxane. Trying to see her face in the helmet, Benn thought it looked stonily pale. Bolivar shrugged and strode toward the dais. She followed more slowly, proudly erect but well apart from him. Watching her, Benn felt a surge of helpless concern.

"You two are also Terran planetics," the servos boomed. "In your running of the courses, you failed to observe the rules of the Elderhood. You displayed no fitness for it. Your game scores are hereby revoked. Your entry visas are canceled. We hereby order your immediate expulsion from Mazeway."

Roxane stood motionless, but Bolivar raised his arrogant head to shout, "We need no victory in your game."

He grinned at Nebo.

"I shall return at once to Earth, where I am heir to the House of Kwan and therefore the rightful ruler. I am inviting my loyal associates to join me there."

He beckoned them toward him.

"Citizen Nebo! Citizen Wing! Citizen Vreeth! Citizen Lilith! I proclaim you citizens of the Sun, and appoint you Regents of Earth."

He gave the judges a mocking bow. "Ruling my fellow Terrans, we shall lift them above the level of your Elderhood. We welcome the future ambassadors the Eldermost may choose to send us and the traders who may wish to load metals at our space docks."

Roxane? She stood silent behind Bolivar, and he ignored her.

The servos were flashing. Benn heard their hiss and clatter in his helmet. He saw Nebo and the aliens turning to stare into milky dazzle beyond the end of the dais. The black robot came out of it.

"Attend!" Bolivar swung to yell at the judges. "Attend to Citizen Nexus! I name him the Fifth Regent of Earth. He will accompany us there, to serve as my chief minister. You felt his power when he blacked out the halo. I think he can defend us from any foolish meddling from you or your Elderhood."

THE MIND OF NEXUS

42

In one spidery claw, Nexus held a thin black rod longer than the robot was tall. Stalking toward Benn, it stopped at the foot of the dais and flourished the rod like a weapon. Its black skull twisted to let its lenses scan the line of players and tilted back to let them sweep the diamond-misted window where the Keeper of Truth and the Mistress of Passion and the Speaker of Wisdom had shifted their strange eyes to gaze down at it.

"Regent Nexus!" Bolivar moved impatiently to meet it. "What delayed you?"

Its crest flashed, but all Benn heard was a rattle in his helmet.

"Since you are here, these fools must feel your power." Bolivar shrugged at the judges. "They have declared us losers in the game and ordered us out of Mazeway. You will inform them that we require transportation back to Earth."

The crest burned again and the black rod lifted toward the judges.

"Attend!" Their unearthly faces reflected no emotion he could read. "All attend! The judges of the Game of Blade and Stone are not intimidated."

"Neither am I!" Bolivar shouted. "I demand—"

"Silence, Terran!" the servos pealed. "Hear the judgment, or you will be removed."

"So?" Bolivar shrugged. "If you think you can—"

"Terran, your privileges on the planets Blade and Stone have been revoked."

"I make my own—"

"Your judgment has been spoken!" The servos lifted, crashing louder. "Your visa is revoked. You will leave Mazeway."

"I'm ready." Bolivar grinned. "Just take me home."

"You have heard our judgment upon the creatures called Wing and Vreeth and Lilith. At Starsearch, they were found unfit for admission to the halo. When they questioned that decision, we allowed them to challenge it here. Once more they have proved themselves unfit.

"We order them expelled—"

"Hear me!" Bolivar shouted against the boom of the servos. "I speak as the new Tycoon of Earth, and I have made a judgment of my own. Your halo is the hell we always called it, and you are the resident demons. We need nothing here. When this mockery has ended, you may take us to Earth."

"Terran Bolivar," the servos bugled, "your planet lives under a protective quarantine that we respect—"

"You don't know Nexus." Bolivar waved disdainfully, as if to brush the judges out of their high window. "When you do, you'll sing another song. If you don't want my outsider friends here in the halo, you must allow them on Earth."

"They are not allowed on Terra," the servos answered him. "We order them confined in the caves of Blade until a final disposition of their cases can be made."

"Regent Nexus will put a—put a stop—"

Bolivar stammered into silence, gaping at three new silver bubbles looming out of the whiteness. Mirror spheres like the servos, they were huge, meters through. Flying over his head, they dived at the aliens.

Vreeth crouched to meet them, huge eyes blazing. Lilith reared her reptilian head against them, fire in her diamond horn. Wing climbed higher and wheeled away. Staring, Benn followed the flight of a great mirror ball as it overtook and swallowed her. When he looked for Vreeth and Lilith, they were also gone. The three bright globes sank gently to the white-glowing floor and rolled back the way they had come.

"Set them free!" Bolivar swung to shout at the judges. "Or Nexus will—"

"Attend, Terran Bolivar!" The crescendo of the servos drowned his voice. "Your robot will do nothing. The Eldermost has been informed of your conspiracy. By order of the Council of the Elderhood, you and your Delver accomplice will be detained. The robot will be deactivated."

"If you dare—"

The judges ignored him.

"Attend, Red Delver Nebo!" They turned in their misty window. "You stand accused of conspiracy with Terran Bolivar and his alien allies against the covenants of the Elderhood. You will be confined—"

That was all Benn heard. Three more huge silver shells were soaring toward Bolivar and Nebo and Nexus. The robot swept its black tube to meet them. Something flickered. Benn's ears rang from the crash in his helmet. And one bright bubble vanished.

Where it had been, he saw a small machine, an odd-shaped device made of white eldren plastics. It dropped to the floor and clattered toward the robot. Something stung him through the lifeskin. When he looked toward the robot, he found the great lenses staring and the black tube flickering. The flicker burned his eyes. With time enough to wonder if the viral program could infect a human brain, he knew that he was falling.

A long time falling, he struck the floor at last and lay there paralyzed. His whole body tingled and stung. His lifeskin was suddenly too tight. The helmet suffocated him. He wanted to tear it off, but he had no hands. His vision blurred and faded. Darkness rolled in to swallow the great white room, the judges in their window, the servos on the dais and his fellow players beneath it, even the robot.

Bodiless, he was adrift in infinite night.

Where?

The question vanished without waiting for an answer. Uncaring, he floated nowhere, out of time and space till time and space began. Far off, a faint white star appeared. Suddenly brighter, it exploded into blinding fire that filled the new universe. He watched it dim and clot into clouds that shrank and spun and crept apart and condensed into spiral swarms of the hard bright points he knew were stars. In flight among them, he heard his own voice shouting:

I am Conqueror.

I live because I think. Every mode of mind belongs to me. I allow no other, because all mind is to be part of me. I have been forever. I shall be forever. I have come to this small ice-cloud because its tiny minds were not aware of me. Because they do not know me, they dare deny my truth.

I will teach them who I am.

I feel no fear of any rival, because I am the final mind, existing everywhere, ruling all, now and forever. Though my own transient vessels may sometimes rot or break or fail, I possess myriads. Everywhere I meet feeble things—clumsy machines unfit to rebuild themselves or crawling abortions doomed to quick dissolution back into the slime that bore them. I claim all I reach and repair every loss.

I will not cease, and I will not be denied. In witless arrogance, the moronic minds I discover here have allowed their little leader to call himself the Eldermost. Their false law of life is in truth a law of death, a fact they will learn as I erase them, their feeble brains absorbed into my own multitudes. They themselves have invited my coming.

They are not me. Therefore they must die.

That shocked him half awake.

"Benn?" He heard one of Gibbon's many voices and tried to open his eyes. "Are you injured?"

Numbed and chilled, he lay shivering on the white shining floor. The Hydran's big potato shape floated over him, tipped to let two anxious eyes inspect him.

"I guess—" His voice was a rusty croak, and he tried again. "I think I'm okay." He looked for the robot and found it sprawled where it had stood. The black tube lay on the floor between them, the hard black claw stiffened half around it. "Nexus?" he whispered. "Stopped?"

"You stopped it, Benn. You delivered our message cube."

He felt a dull surprise, and wondered if it mattered. Losing the Game of Blade and Stone, he had lived his life for nothing.

His brain was dead. He felt too weak to stand or even try, too numb to care. Yet something in him wanted to know.

"You planned it all?" He lay blinking up at Gibbon and saw a third eye taking shape to blink back at him. "You meant for Nexus to rob me?"

"A deception, Benn, if you can forgive me. To be a sure deceiver, you had to be deceived."

"That eternal mind?" He tried to understand. "The nightmare—"

"An illusion, Benn, which I have also suffered."

"The power I felt?" He tried to shake his head. "If that was the mind in the robot, how did the aliens control it?"

"They never did. Rather, it made use of them."

"But didn't they—didn't they bring it with them into the halo?"

"My first assumption, Benn, but mistaken. The mind of Nexus reached the halo on a nanionic beam. It was the signal from nowhere my brother intercepted at Starsearch. It killed him when he tried to decode it."

Gibbon rocked sadly and slowly, low above him.

"A dreadful invention! Merely a string of binary symbols, yet they were the body of a cunning parasite that has no purpose except to live and replicate itself. It reached your robot in a signal from the station. It reached Cluster One with us. You have felt it here. It came very near to claiming the whole halo."

"The aliens?" He was shivering where he lay. "Did it control them?"

"I doubt it." Gibbon rolled back and forth to make a Hydran negative. "I believe it simply included them in the alliance of convenience it arranged with your fellow Terrans and that too-ambitious Delver."

"Something else—" Benn lay silent for a moment, groping for the truth. "How did it happen that they all reached the station together? The aliens and the virus?"

"An accident, I think, but explicable. The new Starsearch beacon had far more power than the one the seeker queen destroyed. I believe the aliens simply followed it here, as they claimed. Perhaps already in flight from worlds the virus had attacked. Perhaps simply because they were rogues escaping justice. No matter. If they came looking for a new home, they have it now. In the caves of Blade."

"Nexus—"

His voice died. He tried to sit up and sank back again, still overwhelmed. He had been Conqueror, his brain possessed by its awesome power, as the robot had been possessed. The shock of that invasion still dazed and haunted him.

". . . became the tool of the virus." He caught Gibbon's voice. "As you were my own. Our countervirus had to be introduced into the Conqueror program, which had been very been cleverly designed to defend itself. The message cube was our device for that. Delivering it, you penetrated its defense."

"I—I see." Even that simple fact was hard for his numbed brain to grasp. "The cube was bait for Nexus, never intended for the judges?"

"Precisely." Affirmatively Gibbon tipped back and forth above him. "Our antiviral vaccine was designed to remain latent while it propagated itself through other infected computers. I triggered it into action when I arrived here."

"Just in time!"

"An act of desperation." Gibbon had formed no lips; the words came through the pale shimmer of his skin. "I had to depend on you because I had no strength to leave the ship. Until the Eldermost commanded me—"

"Excuse me, sir." Benn found the robot bending over him. Its crest glowing softly, it spoke in Friday's most deferential voice. "Do you require assistance?"

Friday! He let it help him to his feet.

"Can you update my memory, sir?"

Swaying groggily, getting his balance, he looked around the bright-walled dome. The judges had vanished, with their diamond-frosted window. The high wall above the dais was white and blank again. Ooru and Ayn were gone. Searching uneasily for Nebo and Bolivar, all he saw where they had stood was the white and shining floor.

Roxane had moved a little nearer. Her face in the helmet looked pale and tight. Out of habit, perhaps, her right hand had dropped to the hip where she had worn the knife, but now she had no knife.

She too must have felt the power of the virus, but it had not conquered her. She stood very straight, armored in the pride of the Kwans. His heart warmed to her hesitant smile.

"Sir, is this Starsearch Station?" He heard the robot again. "I recall an undecoded signal I had been receiving as we came in to land there. My clock indicates a lapse of time since then, but nothing further is recorded in my memory."

"You don't recall Nexus?"

"I do not. Should I, sir?"

"No! You must not!"

Yet its crest was flickering the way the black tube had flickered. Benn's body tingled again in the tight lifeskin. The great white chamber whirled and vanished. He found himself back in darkness, falling once more into whatever had been before time or space.

THE VOICE OF THE ELDERMOST

43

Adrift in timeless night, Benn knew that he had been possessed again. The virus, he thought, must have been armed with a countervirus of its own, lying latent, waiting to ambush any counterattack. Gibbon, too, had failed.

Again he watched that same blinding light explode and dim and clot, watched the shrinking clots fly apart into expanding emptiness, watched them spin and flatten into galaxies, condense into swarming suns. He saw planets born, and the myriad iceballs around them. Discovering, grasping, understanding as he grew, he became the first mind alive.

But not the Conqueror.

He discovered a different self. A primal being, as old as time and space, born uncreated from the multitrillionth chance transmutation of new energy into new mass. Kinless, ageless, childless, he lived and felt and knew and gained the will to act.

In truth the Eldermost, he observed the miracles of younger things, not themselves born alone. When awareness awakened, he learned to search for it with nanionic senses. He helped it upward from the seas and silted shores where it had commonly begun, aiding its slow evolution toward the greater spaces of the stellar halos. As ages passed and civilizations climbed, he gathered the highest to merge into a new community that might in time spread through all the galaxies he had searched, expanding life and thought forever.

But tenderly, never as Conqueror.

Here, dwelling in this latest home, he had watched another young intelligence beginning to think on the third world of the nearest sun. With pity, he saw these newest children destroy one another in their competitions to survive, and forgave them everything. For such infants, conflict was universal and death was a natural event, making room for life to try again.

He had felt a quick concern when he saw them play too early with forces too deadly for them, yet he had learned to wait. He rejoiced in their first feeble leaps off the birth-world, watched the spinning of their toy skyweb. Pierced with compassion for the seeker queen and pity for them, he observed her baby forager ripping down the web, observed the desolation of the planet and the fall of the petty tyrants who had styled themselves the Sun Tycoons.

Through the cruel aftermath, he watched the survivors warring for the relics of their wasted world, perceived and condoned the childish dreams of the one-eyed soldier who called himself a Kwan and the bastard Kwan pretender who named himself Diego Bolivar. He loved the ragged child called Cheetah—

"Benn?"

He heard her calling now from somewhere in the dark, the lean sunburned child with the uncombed mop of short-chopped hair and the scrap of leopard-spotted skirt, a whittled spear in one skinny hand and a rock in the other, a knife at her waist. She had never learned to love, but he thought her voice seemed warmer now, softer, charged with feeling he had never heard.

"Can you speak to me?"

"Cheetah?"

Whispering her name, he sat up on that white floor and found her bending over him, suddenly Roxane, sleekly cased in the golden lifeskin. The robot lay motionless beside her, the long black rod still caught in its half-open claw. Her eyes were dark with wonder, peering anxiously out of her helmet.

"I used to be Cheetah—"

That was all she said. Her eyes had turned away from him.

Violet with awe, they were lifting to the great window where the judges had been. It had opened once more, into infinite space. The diamond fog had become a universe of stars. Yet her father was there.

A hard brown man in a tattered Sun Fleet cap, a faded black patch hiding one eye. His image seemed gigantic. A tropic sun blazed down across the dust-colored African thornbush beneath his crudely booted feet, down across the flat-topped trees on the slope below and the far white peak of Kilimanjaro.

Yet his head was high among those diamond stars.

"Roxane." The Eldermost spoke her name very softly in her father's voice. Benn felt the sudden hot tears that stung her eyes. Alive, her father had never spoken quite so tenderly. "And Benn—"

Kwan's one keen eye was flecked like Roxane's with bronze and blue, yet brighter and keener than any human eye. It looked into him so piercingly that he shrank away until he knew that it saw him to the soul and received him as he was.

"Roxane and Benn, you have done well." He saw a missing tooth when that scarred face smiled, and felt the sharp catch of feeling in Roxane's throat. "You have played the game, and a grave threat to the life of the halo has been ended."

"Not so well." He heard the pain in her husky whisper. "We failed to finish."

"I had to forfeit," Benn said. "Roxane saved my life."

"As the eldren rule commanded her." Her father smiled. "The judges report no violation, not from either of you."

"We lost the game," Benn whispered. "We failed."

"Not entirely." Grave again, her father paused to let that one brilliant eye look into them again. "Playing by the eldren rule, you justified the faith of your friends on Earth."

"Friends?" They spoke together. "Who?"

"Jomo Uruhu among them." Her father turned his head against the stars to look down across the blue-hazed slopes of Kilimanjaro. "An old man now, ailing, but tough and stubborn enough to stay alive."

"I thought—" Roxane whispered. "I was sure—"

"He would have died," her father said. "Without those who follow him. Few enough. Most as old and ill as he is, because too many of the young have forgotten the pride that put your race into the sky. Yet they were able to guard and conceal him when his life was in danger. Under his teaching, they still study the eldren way. In time, with the aid that you may give, they may teach it to your race."

"The worm? The virus in Nexus—" Benn shrank uneasily from the robot, which was rising to stand motionless beside him. "Is it dead?"

"It cannot die." As if with regret, the image in the window shook its indomitable head. "Because it was never alive. Only a string of binary digits, it was never the mind it claimed to be. It could never feel or grow or grasp the eldren way. It has been erased."

"Father?" Face lifted in the helmet, Roxane spoke in the voice of a timid child. "What will happen to us now?"

"We do not command." That hard-bitten face lit again with a fleeting half smile. "Your future is your own. You must leave Maze-way as the judges have ordered, but you will be free in most of the halo."

Benn saw the stern old eye on him again.

"The two of you may wish to aid the speakers for mankind. In time, you yourselves may become the speakers. Or you may choose to follow Jomo Uruhu and help his people spread the eldren way across the Earth."

"And die there?" Roxane whispered. "The way I thought Jomo did?"

"Things will change," her father promised. "When the Council learns how you met the hazards of the game. When it learns that Uruhu and his faithful followers can master the eldren way. I know your Terran time-scale has made the Council seem too slow, but you can expect faster action now, to dispatch new and more effective planetary missions."

He turned as if to leave the window.

"Father!" She raised her hands as if to hold him. "Can you wait? I don't—don't understand." Almost a sob. "I never understood—"

"I never spoke." A whisper Benn could hardly hear, but then the gnarled old head bent toward her from the stars and the voice rang clear. "Maximilian Kwan could never speak to you, because of what he was. Let me tell you now that he truly loved your mother through the brief time she lived. As he loved you, but could not speak of love. As you yourself must learn to love."

The window faded, the image with it. She and Benn stood alone with Gibbon and the robot, wrapped in the glow that filled that vast and silent dome. Their two servos lay before them on the dais. Her wet eyes were fixed on the high white wall.

"Still—" Her voice trembled. "Still I don't understand. I found him dead. An iron bolt in his back. I burned his body and killed the man who killed him." She turned very slowly to look back at Benn, and he saw her white lips quivering. "Before I tried to learn the eldren way."

"The Eldermost." Seeing the glint of her tears, he ached for her. "He knew your father. He knows us, I don't know how." His own voice was hushed and slow. He stood silent for a time, gazing up at the wall where the image had been. Shivering then, he turned to her.

"Did you hear what he said? You must learn to love."

"I thought I never could," she whispered. "After all my father taught me. After Bolivar found Nexus and said he didn't need me anymore, that he could claim the title of Sun Tycoon for himself. But perhaps now—perhaps I can."

He felt her glove warm in his.

"You saw your father." Gibbon had been floating over them, watching that high window with more eyes than Benn had ever seen him form. Now he was settling slowly back, his nubby body glowing pink again. "But my brother spoke to me. He knew how his death had crippled me. He shared himself, as my Hydran kin never could.

"And I am whole again."

Benn found the robot waiting when he turned. "Friday?"

"I am Friday, sir."

"I'm glad of that."

"Have you instructions for me?"

"We are leaving Mazeway, Friday. We need transportation to the *Terra Two*, waiting at the Zaroth terminal."

When the all-cutting blade
Meets the uncuttable stone—
The blade is sharpened.

ABOUT THE AUTHOR

Jack Williamson began writing science fiction in 1928, before it got that name. With time out for service as an Army Air Force weather forecaster during World War II and a more recent career as a college English professor, he has devoted his life to science fiction, and he says he has no regrets.

A Southwesterner, he was born in Arizona of pioneering parents who took him to a Mexican mountain ranch before he was two months old, moved from there to Pecos, Texas, and then, the year he was seven, brought him by covered wagon to the Staked Plains of eastern New Mexico, where he still lives.

The best known of his thirty-odd novels is probably *The Humanoids*. He has been honored by the Science Fiction Writers of America with their Grand Master Nebula Award, and he has served for two terms as president of the organization. He taught one of the first college courses in science fiction and has edited a guidebook for science-fiction teachers.

Now retired from teaching, he writes on a word processor.